"Why did you marry me?"
Mary Kate asked abruptly.

Douglas's answer was swift, filled with his usual bold impudence. "I doubt not 'twas because you are the most beautiful wench ever to dare deny me access to her charms." His smile was sweet, but that unnerving gleam lurked in his eyes.

"Insufferable ape!" she snapped. "At least you married me before you tried again."

He stood up. "Temper, lassie, temper. You had too many protectors before, and I decided marriage was not so bad a penalty to pay for such a grand reward." Advancing, he pulled her to her feet, shaking his head in mock reproof. "You've far too many clothes on."

QUANTITY SALES

Amanda Scott

Border Bride

A DELL BOOK

Published by
Dell Publishing
a division of
Bantam Doubleday Dell
Publishing Group, Inc.
666 Fifth Avenue
New York, New York 10103

ISBN: 0-440-20724-X

Printed in the United States of America

Published simultaneously in Canada

November 1990

10 9 8 7 6 5 4 3 2 1

OPM

To Cindy Kaye
for her faith and her long memory
Thank you!

I

>>> <<<

Harsh, snow-laden winds whipped and roared through the late-October night, wreaking a chilling vengeance upon the southern Scottish landscape and piling huge drifts against the great gray stone manor house at Critchfield. The upper floors of the house were dark, for behind each decorative stone balcony the unglazed window opening was shuttered tightly against the cold. On the ground floor, however, the warm glow of welcome shone brightly through tall, leaded-glass windows, laying golden paths upon new fallen snow and setting snowflakes aglitter where they whirled and danced through the beams of light.

Inside the house, the great hall was warm and cheerful, the bagpipes loud, and the dancing merry. Mary Kate MacPherson laughed aloud when her partner, fair-haired young Kenneth Gillespie, nearly overset himself by attempting a double back kick directly in front of her immediately after completing a high, twisting leap in the air.

"Do you mock my skills, mistress?" Gillespie demanded, grinning down at her as they changed places.

"Nay, sir, truly," she replied without missing her own cross step. "Such graceful jumps and slidings must surely be the envy of all the other gentlemen."

"Are they, indeed?" The pattern of the dance separated them again before he could say more, but he was still smiling.

Mary Kate was enjoying herself hugely. She wore her favorite gown, a delicious confection of Florentine silk, its saffron color accentuating her smooth, red-gold curls and wide-set hazel eyes. Black Naples lace edged the gown's tight bodice and undersleeves as well as the simple ruff encircling her slender white throat, its color enhancing the perfection of her roses-and-cream complexion; and her skirts, instead of billowing stiffly over a farthingale, draped in fluid folds that swirled gracefully about her tiny satin-slippered feet when she danced.

Mary Kate always enjoyed a party, but Critchfield provided novelty as well as pleasure. Highland-bred, she had not been allowed to enjoy social life away from her home near the river Spey until recently when her father had at last given in to the persistent badgering of his sister Sarah, Lady Aberfoyle of Edinburgh, and had begun to allow visits to other relatives when social gatherings were in the offing.

Throughout the first few of these affairs Mary Kate had felt shy and unsure of herself among relatives who kept a close watch over her, allowing her to associate only with those young gentlemen, often stiffly uncertain themselves, who could be trusted to hold their behavior within acceptable bounds. However, here at Critchfield, not only was she farther from home than she had been before—for the manor was

well south of Edinburgh, nearly in border country—
but her aunt and uncle, though certainly as affectionate toward her as any of her other relatives, had ex-
hibited not the least desire during her week's visit to
play the strict chaperon. Consequently, with her confidence increasing steadily, even before this evening,
Mary Kate had begun to feel the heady power of her
own beauty and to realize that she was attracting a
veritable court of fascinated cavaliers, not least
among whom was her current partner.

Not only was Kenneth Gillespie tall, handsomely
fair, and debonair, but his father was an advisor to
King James, which fact provided the young man with
an impressive veneer of arcane wisdom whenever he
chose to affect familiarity with the goings-on at court.
Moreover, he possessed a sufficient amount of practiced charm to turn the head of any young woman.

Mary Kate had met him several times before coming to Critchfield, at functions such as this one, but
although he had always displayed polite interest in
her, his previous attentions had not been particularly
marked, and the possibility that he might have been
deterred by her more watchful relations had not occurred to her. Although she had already danced with
him twice that evening before he had asked her to
join him in the galliard, the fact that she found his
attitude delightfully flattering had seemed sufficient
reason to accept a third invitation without so much as
a moment's hesitation.

The galliard, as Mary Kate's short social experience had quickly taught her, was more of an acrobatic
display than a dance, especially on the part of the
gentlemen, and Gillespie, like the other young men
in their set, took every opportunity to show off his
skill. When he swung her high in the air, setting her
skirts awhirl and causing her breath to catch in her

throat, she thought fleetingly of stories she had heard of people who had broken their legs as a result of the wild skipping, leaping, and turning required by the dance, but then her feet touched the floor again, forcing her to concentrate upon her steps. The next part of the pattern included a difficult back-to-back turn while her partner retained both her hands in his, but no sooner had they reached that point in the dance than a thunderous clamor at the massive front door interrupted the festivities, bringing the music to a discordant halt.

The great oaken portals were swung wide at once to admit four men who stamped their booted, spurred feet and brushed snow from their heavy fur cloaks amid shouts of welcome and laughing shrieks at the sudden icy blast of air from outside. Servants were sent scurrying to tend the newcomers' horses and to provide food and drink, while pipers and dancers alike continued to gaze curiously at the snow-dusted men.

"Do you know them, sir?"

"Aye, mistress," Gillespie responded without taking his eyes off the four men, now being surrounded by an increasing crowd of the merrymakers. His casual tone was belied by an alertness in his wintry gray eyes as he added, "That is to say, I know two of them. The tall man with the dark hair and heavy eyebrows is the borderer, Sir Adam Douglas of Tornary, a close friend of the king. The stout gentleman who rushed to greet him, and who is even now clasping his hand so fervently, is Sir William MacGaurie. I did not realize he was here at Critchfield. Indeed, I had thought him to be still in England."

"England?"

"Aye. He supports the cause of the Queen o' Scots and has been actively seeking that unfortunate lady's release from the English clutches these many years past."

"Godamercy, then mayhap his presence here tonight means Elizabeth intends to set her free at last." The thought was an awesome one, for Mary of Scotland's captivity at the English queen's hands had taken place nearly a full year before Mary Kate's own birth, and it seemed to her therefore that for their queen to be a prisoner was simply a fact of Scottish life. She regarded Gillespie with wide, questioning eyes. "Do you imagine such a thing to be likely, sir?"

His only reply was a doubtful smile and a shrug of his shoulders before he suggested that since the pipers seemed to have regained their wits they might finish their dance.

Mary Kate consented willingly, though not before noting that Sir Adam Douglas, with a quick, curiously frowning glance around the great hall, had spoken briefly to Sir William MacGaurie, then signed to his own men to retire with him from the company. She soon forgot the incident in the gaiety of the party, however, so it was with no little astonishment half an hour later that, hearing her name, she turned to find her uncle standing just behind her with the tall borderer at his side.

Lord Critchfield made the introductions with a twinkle of delight and then, clearly believing that he had served his purpose, swung on his heel and departed before Mary Kate had risen from her curtsy.

She glanced up from beneath her lashes to encounter an impudent grin and dancing dark brown eyes. Douglas had changed to evening dress of emerald velvet, his hose puffed and slashed with white satin. Despite the prevailing fashion for tiny pointed beards, he was clean-shaven, and she thought him rather more civilized-looking than one might have expected a borderer to be, and handsome into the bargain.

"Shall we dance, mistress?" His voice was deep and resonant, and he had the poise and confidence of a man who knew his own power, an attitude that set him well apart from any of her previous partners.

Though she accepted his invitation warily, the dance was a simple, much more stately one than the galliard, giving him the opportunity to draw her into light conversation, which he did with the ease of long practice. She soon discovered that, although he was indeed border-bred, a branch of his mother's family had land on the river Spey just above her father's estates. When she looked surprised to hear it, he grinned at her, his eyes twinkling more than ever.

"Did you mistake me for just another border ruffian, mistress, albeit better dressed than most?"

"Not a ruffian, no," she replied carefully, feeling the betraying warmth creep into her cheeks at the thought of how nearly he had echoed her first opinion of him. Rallying quickly, she added with more spirit, "But I'd not have mistaken you for a highlander either."

He chuckled. "I'd be well enough satisfied, I think, if you could but believe I possess some good qualities of both."

She smiled up at him, then found it hard to look away, for the warmth in his gaze caught and held hers, and she suddenly felt as though she had known him for years rather than minutes. The feeling passed quickly, but added to the fact of his having relatives on the Spey, it was enough to allay her natural highlander's mistrust of anyone from the borders. Mary Kate soon fell victim, to an intoxicating degree, to Douglas's engaging manner and easy confidence, responding to his gallantry in a way that would ordinarily have been completely alien to her nature.

When their dance ended, he relinquished her hand to another admirer with a flattering air of reluctance, and as he moved away through the crowd of guests, bowing to one and shaking hands or laughing with another, her gaze followed his progress. She even experienced a twinge of jealousy later when he led first one then another damsel into the dance, and if she conversed with her own partners, she was unaware of the fact. When Kenneth Gillespie daringly sought to engage her hand for a fourth dance, she snubbed him so unconsciously that she failed to note the bewildered, ego-bitten air with which he turned away. Beside the fascinating borderer, Gillespie cast but a pale shadow.

Douglas caught her eye upon him several times, and she made no attempt to avoid his glances, even going so far as to return his impudent smile. Though she knew she was flirting outrageously, she found it impossible to stop.

When he came to claim her hand for a second time, she accepted with alacrity, too inexperienced to notice that his attitude toward her had altered, that his voice was a whisper warmer, his touch now a flickering caress. And if, when he swung her through a complicated step, he did so with a hint more energy than was entirely proper, Mary Kate was unaware, mesmerized by his extraordinary charm. Just the flash of his even, white teeth when he smiled was exhilarating. Indeed, the warmth of his hands when he touched her waist, her shoulder, or merely her fingertips was enough to send tremors of excitement racing through her body.

The music stopped at last, and he guided her toward the huge open fireplace where gillies were ladling out mugs of steaming mulled claret. Douglas procured one for each of them.

"Will you be too warm here by the fire?" he asked.

"Oh, no, sir. The hall is chilly if one is not dancing." She sipped cautiously. "Ah, it warms me all the way down!"

He laughed. "But you ought not to be chilled, mistress. You have danced often."

"I have," she agreed with pleasure. "Is it not remarkable? I have scarce missed a single turn."

"Not so remarkable as that," he said. "Not when you are by far the bonniest lass in the hall."

Her eyes twinkled as she regarded him from beneath her thick lashes. "There are others more beautiful than I, Sir Adam."

"Are there? I have not seen them."

"Blinded by their beauty, in fact, whilst you danced with them," she replied, chuckling. "I saw you."

"Art jealous, lassie?" He tweaked a curl that had escaped her coif. " 'Twas not their beauty but the spell cast by a red-headed witch that blinded me."

"My hair is not red! 'Tis copper-gold."

"If you prefer to call it so, though I am partial to red hair." He grinned at her over his mug as he took a long sip of the potent brew, but Mary Kate only wrinkled her nose in reply. Douglas used his sleeve to good purpose, then spoke again. "How is it that you speak English so well, lass? And with a most delightful accent, I might add. When your uncle said you were a hielan' wench, I confess I thought I'd have an opportunity to practice my Gaelic."

"Most highland girls of my class have some education, sir." She spoke proudly, knowing he would think it an unusual accomplishment, because she had often heard that border women, like Englishwomen, were rarely educated. "I took my lessons in the *clachan* near my father's estate, from Parson MacDole," she continued, grimacing at a sudden mental vision of that dour worthy with his beetling gray brows and the slender little ferule he carried as a reminder to those not sufficiently diligent in their studies. "And I do not have an accent, sir."

He chuckled. "You do, but 'tis an uncommonly beguiling one. However," he went on hastily, "you continue to evade answering my question. To hear you confess to even the smallest twinge of jealousy would content me well."

She reddened but was spared the difficulty of forming an acceptable reply when his attention was suddenly diverted to a point beyond her shoulder. Turning, she saw one of the men who had arrived with him beckoning from the doorway into the west gallery.

Douglas set his mug on a nearby trestle table. " 'Tis my secretary, Johnny Graham. I must leave, mistress, but I shall not tarry."

"It is of no import to me if you do, sir, for I intend to retire soon. The hour grows late, and my uncle's parties are like to last till dawn." She hesitated, looking around. Her aunt, who enjoyed all the advantages of self-declared and unsubstantiated ill health, had retired much earlier, and her uncle, having overindulged himself in his excellent whiskey, sprawled near the great fire, languidly casting dice with a group of his cronies, all in a like condition. Mary Kate laughed doubtfully. "Mayhap my uncle will leave his dicing long enough to escort me to my chamber."

Douglas shook his head. "No need to trouble him, lass, or to summon a servant. Escorting you will be my pleasure." Taking her mug from her, he placed it next to his own and gallantly offered his arm.

Although she knew it to be highly improper for her to accept escort from an unmarried gentleman, Mary Kate made not the slightest protest before giving him directions to her bedchamber. It was not even necessary for them to request a candle from one of the servants, because candles and torches had been lit in every public room and gallery in honor of the party.

They had reached the door to her bedchamber on the second floor of the west wing when the same young man who had signaled Douglas before approached them from the other end of the long gallery. "Sir," he said respectfully, "the others await you in your chamber, and Sir William grows impatient lest someone note the absence of so many at one time."

"Hold your tongue, lad!" Douglas snapped. "It clacks like a beggar's claptrap. Go and tell them I am just coming."

Graham turned away, his face crimson from the rebuke, and Mary Kate reached toward her door latch.

"One moment, mistress." Douglas pulled her around to face him. "I'll be rid of them soon," he murmured, folding her into his arms and lowering his mouth to hers.

Astonished though she was, the unexpected heat of his passion transmitted itself to her at once, flooding through her body, electrifying every nerve end. Mary Kate had never been kissed in such a way in all her eighteen years, and shock held her rigid for several seconds before she collected her senses sufficiently to shove her small hands against his broad chest in an attempt to free herself.

He released her with a sigh. "If you insist, lassie, but I enjoyed the experience very much and look forward to repeating it as soon as may be." Bowing deeply, he turned on his heel and strode off down the gallery.

Mary Kate stood for a moment, breathless, her cheeks flushed, her emotions on end. Surely, she thought, only a man bred in the borders would dare to use her so. The odd thing was that she was not as angry as, by rights, she ought to have been. Instead, she was strangely excited by the fact that he had wished to take such liberties with her. Reaching distractedly for the door latch, she had begun to lift it before young Graham's words echoed tantalizingly through her mind.

Kenneth Gillespie's reaction to the new arrivals had given her a fleeting notion of intrigue afoot, and that notion had later been reinforced by Douglas's wary attitude when he signed to the others to leave the hall. Were borderers, she mused now, not noted for their constant plotting and devilry? Suddenly convinced that Douglas had come to Critchfield to meet Sir William MacGaurie for some secret purpose, she allowed curiosity to overcome good sense without putting up so much as a token battle. With a darting glance in either direction to assure herself that the gallery was empty, she hastened after Douglas.

As she approached the room that she had seen him enter at the far end of the gallery, she could hear the low murmur of masculine voices, but she had to put her ear right against the door before she could make out any words.

"That Babington business," one man was saying, "has convinced Elizabeth at last that her own life is in jeopardy so long as Mary lives. I doubt there be any practicable course left to us now, MacGaurie."

"Sir Anthony Babington," replied a second, more gravelly voice, "though his heart was true, was a young fool, but more important than that is the fact that he was no more than a pawn for that devil Walsingham."

A murmur of protest greeted the remark, and Mary Kate searched her memory. The name Babington was unknown to her, but Francis Walsingham she knew to be Queen Elizabeth's Secretary of State, a man renowned for his devious nature.

The gravelly voice was speaking again in reply to the protests. "Nay, lads, 'tis true enough. My sources are infallible. 'Twas a wicked plot devised by Walsingham himself to entrap our unfortunate queen, and Babington walked into it just as tidily as you please. In point of fact, Mary's own courier was Walsingham's man, and Elizabeth was never in danger from anyone, least of all Babington. Walsingham intercepted all his letters to Mary and hers to him from the outset."

Outraged voices demanded to know whether Douglas thought the king would act upon such information, and after he had replied somewhat vaguely, Mary Kate soon learned from the lively conversation that followed that a commission had recently been formed in England to try the Scottish queen for treason as a result of her part in Sir Anthony Babington's assassination plot against Queen Elizabeth.

"They meet in the Star Chamber almost as we speak," said the gravelly voice, "and 'tis certain I am that they will demand her death."

Mary Kate froze. Rather than bringing news of the Scottish queen's imminent release, as she had so naively suggested to Kenneth Gillespie, she realized with horror that Sir William MacGaurie had brought warning of Mary's imminent danger of execution instead.

A new voice, louder than the others, demanded just then to know whether perhaps James VI liked being King of Scotland too well to intercede on his mother's behalf.

Douglas's tone was grave. "I do not know what Jamie will do. He treasures his throne but will not want to anger the Scottish people, many of whom, as you all know, are still pressing him to demand Mary's release. However, you must also recognize the difficulties encountered whenever one attempts to make him comprehend the power he holds against Elizabeth. As we all know, he could create a deal of trouble for her should he decide to cast his lot with France or Spain against her, but he sets great store by the alliance he signed only months ago and fears to annoy her lest she leave her precious crown elsewhere and not to him. Nonetheless, I agree that MacGaurie's news is ominous. Jamie must be told at once so that whatever can be done may be done quickly. I warn you, however, that I doubt even this news will convince him that Elizabeth is capable of signing Mary's death warrant or that of any other monarch. For her to do so would be to set a most undesirable precedent."

The gravelly voice said bleakly, "It is impossible now that both Mary and Elizabeth shall continue to live."

The tangle of voices rose again as Mary Kate leaned weakly against the door, amazed by what she had heard and trembling to think that she had listened in upon such a conversation—or upon any conversation, for that matter, for she had been strictly taught to regard eavesdropping as an unthinkably

disreputable action. A highland servant caught with
an ear to his master's door was assumed to be a traitor
attempting to gain information to be used against the
clan. For such an act, she had heard of people being
summarily executed without question or trial.
Though she had reason to believe that listening at
doors was not everywhere so violently disapproved,
such behavior was, according to her Aunt Aberfoyle,
consistently regarded as an unforgivable social sole-
cism. Surely, she thought, she must have greatly overindulged herself in her uncle's mulled claret to have
been guilty of such a contemptible act.

Her thoughts were interrupted by Douglas's voice.
"There is little else we can accomplish tonight,
though my own lads would do well to forgo the festivities below in favor of sleep, for we leave for Edinburgh at dawn." When someone suggested that more
haste than that was in order, he laughed. "We will
make greater speed by waiting for this storm to lift.
Besides, there is a wee, winsome armful waiting to
offer me the comforts of her bed and 'twould be un-
gentlemanly to disappoint her."

Furious to realize that he must be speaking of her,
Mary Kate snapped upright and nearly pushed open
the door to contradict him on the spot. But then,
cheeks burning, she came to her senses, flipped her
skirts around, and hurried back to her own chamber,
sped along the length of the gallery by mortifying
echoes of appreciative male laughter.

"How dare he!" she demanded of the ambient air as
she snapped the door shut behind her and slammed
the stout iron bolt into place. Pacing wrathfully, she
kicked off her satin shoes, letting them fall where
they would, and told herself bitterly that she ought to
have expected nothing less from such a man. Boast
how he might of maternal relations in the highlands,

Douglas himself was naught but a lowly, uncivilized borderer.

Had she not heard all her life that such men held women cheap? Had it not been recommended on more than one occasion that she ought to thank the good Lord for having granted her the privilege of being born in the highlands, where women were properly respected, where they could own property in their own names, where they might even become clan chieftains? Border women, like Englishwomen, were said to be regarded by their men as inferior beings, as mere chattel, in fact. Even among the upper classes the women were expected to bow before their men or to follow several paces after them, to obey them unquestioningly, and to have no intelligent thoughts or opinions of their own. Was it any wonder then that Douglas, clearly a power among borderers, should arrogantly assume that he might command any woman to his bed merely because he wanted her? She had been foolish to be swayed by his charm, to think he might be different. Clearly, he was just the sort of man she ought to have expected him to be. But he would learn a lesson tonight. He would not trifle successfully with Mary Kate MacPherson.

A fire crackled in the stone fireplace set into the north wall of her high-ceilinged bedchamber, and candles in pewter holders stood ready to be lit upon a table by the door as well as on the candle table near the cupboardlike bed opposite the fire. No chambermaid awaited her pleasure, for the young maidservant who had accompanied her from home had succumbed to a feverish cold and Mary Kate had sent her to sleep in the servants' hall so as not to contract it from her. She had intended to send for one of her aunt's maids, but now, with Douglas on his way at any moment, she had no wish to do so.

Beside the candle on the table near the door, there was also a ewer of water, a basin, and a flagon of wine, but Mary Kate had use for none of these items at present. Lighting the candles, then hastily pulling off her gown and flinging it onto a back stool in a black-edged, saffron-colored heap, she snatched the pins from her hair and let the red-gold tresses fall in a cloud of ringlets over her bare shoulders to her waist. Next she removed her petticoats and underbodice and reached for her night rail. Slipping the flimsy lawn garment over her head and flipping her hair free, she strode to the court cupboard and took out her fur-lined cloak, sheepskin mules, and her hair-brush, muttering unflattering descriptions of the Douglas character to herself as she wrapped the cloak about her slender body, shoved her bare feet into the mules, and sat down at the dressing table to yank the brush in hasty, rhythmic strokes through her curls.

Moments later she stepped to the tall, oak-shuttered window near the northwest corner of the room and, using the nearby latchpole, unhooked the shutters' high, upper latches. Leaning the unwieldy pole against the wall again, she dealt manually with the bottom hooks and pulled the heavy shutters wide, letting in the night's chill but also revealing the spectacular scene beyond the stone balcony's snow-frosted parapet.

Large, puffy black clouds still raced across the night sky, but the snow had stopped, and whenever the moon appeared through a break in the clouds, it bathed the white landscape below with a magical, silvery light. The temperature remained extremely cold, however, and with the brief thought that her relatives' money might better have been spent on thick, leaded glass than on balconies for every window, Mary Kate blew out her candles, flung off her cloak, and dived beneath the thick quilts piled atop the high, curtained, cupboardlike bed. Wriggling to get warm, she listened carefully for sounds of approach from the long gallery.

Several persons passed, but nearly ten full minutes elapsed before the door latch rattled and Douglas called to her in a low, seductive voice. She held her breath, a tiny smile playing upon her lips. He called again, more loudly, and rapped upon the door. Silently, she waited until, with an oath and a hefty blow of his fist upon the offending portal, he moved away down the gallery. Then, with a final wriggle, she turned onto her stomach and prepared to sleep the sleep of the innocent.

Fifteen minutes later she had reached that drowsy state which is neither sleep nor wakefulness when a muffled scraping sound and a heavy thump from the balcony brought her fully alert. Surely, she thought without moving a muscle, that had been a human sound, perhaps even a step; and, as fear raced through her body, the light in the chamber dimmed. Something or someone standing in the tall, arched window had blocked the moonlight.

Though her eyes were open, she dared not move her head to look directly at the intruder lest her movement startle him, for her first conjecture was that a thief had decided to take advantage of her slumber to search for booty among her belongings. But even as the thought stirred, she wondered what thief would dare attempt to enter a window fully thirty feet and more above the ground by way of a snow-crusted balcony.

Just then the intruder moved past the bed, and through quickly lowered lashes she saw his outline clearly against the glow of the dying fire. She could not mistake that tall figure, those broad, muscular shoulders, that easy stride. Indeed, he moved toward her now as though he were in his own chamber rather than hers. When he paused beside her, she shut her eyes more tightly, then had all she could do to keep from holding her breath. She breathed slowly and deeply, hoping that if he thought she was asleep he would go away again.

She sensed that he had moved nearer, then heard a rattling sound from the candle table near the head of the bed. He moved away again, and opening her eyes to slits, she saw him kneel before the dying fire. He gave it a stir with a kindling stick from the basket on the hearth, then tossed the stick onto the leaping flames and lit the candle he had taken from the table. Standing again, he turned more quickly than she had anticipated, and when she saw that he was grinning at her, she turned onto her back and sat up, clutching the bedclothes to her chin.

"Get out," she said, pleased that the words came clearly, even calmly, from her tightening throat.

His grin widened. "Ah, lassie, you mustn't be angry. You ought to have had more faith in me. I'll grant I was a long time coming, but you knew my business was urgent. 'Twas right cruel to lock your door against me."

"I don't want you here," she said carefully. "I never did. You merely thought to take advantage of my innocence."

He chuckled. "There was no mistaking your invitation, sweetheart. And as for believing you had really gone to sleep, I am not such a fool. I'd have been angrier had I not chanced to recall both your uncle's fancy for underscoring his windows with balconies and the highlander's unnatural love of night air. To leave one's shutters ajar is a dangerous and unhealthy practice, as all civilized persons are aware, but I was right glad to recall that misguided highland habit this night."

"There is nothing misguided about it," she informed him tartly. " 'Tis merely that men who learn to make do with naught but a plaid betwixt themselves and the elements are a hardier lot than you weak-kneed borderers." Nevertheless, she told herself, the habit could indeed prove dangerous, as she had just discovered. When Douglas moved nearer the bed, she wriggled back away from him. "What are you doing?"

"What I came to do," he said. When she squirmed to the back of the bed, he set the candlestick on the candle table, placed both hands on his slim hips, and looked down at her with a frown. "This game becomes wearisome, lass. I've proved my desire for you by risking my hide in a leap of at least a dozen feet from one damned balcony to another—"

"They are not so far apart as that," she said, in a voice that was beginning to fail her at last. "Not more than four feet, maybe six at the most."

"I am persuaded they are twelve feet apart at the very least," he said firmly. "And the parapets are blanketed with icy snow. Therefore, I have risked life and limb. Moreover, I have apologized for tarrying, though it was not my fault and it is not my habit to apologize. So, come now, sweetheart, comfort me." With these words, he put one knee upon the bed and leaned toward her, his right hand outstretched.

"No!" Shrinking away from him, she bumped hard against the wall. He paused then, his hand still held out toward her, and in the light from the fire, she saw his eyes narrow and experienced a sinking sensation in the pit of her stomach. Since she knew she dared not make him angry while he loomed over her like that and since he didn't seem open to reason, she blurted the first thought that came into her head. "Would you not like something to warm your insides first, sir? There is a flagon of my uncle's excellent wine on that table next to the door."

"But I don't—" He hesitated, watching her closely for a long moment. Then he smiled and, to her great relief, moved off the bed. "I see," he said. "You are not quite so experienced as you have led me to believe. Well, that is no bad thing, lassie. Mayhap a taste of the wine will do us both good."

Picking up the candlestick again, Douglas turned toward the door, and with the merest rustle of rushes from beneath the feather bed, Mary Kate scrambled out at the far end the moment his back was turned. It was but a few steps from there to the wall by the open window. Snatching up the latchpole without a sound, she flew across the cold floor on silent bare feet, coming up behind him just as he set down the candlestick and reached for the flagon. Without thought for consequence and with a strength she would not have believed possible, she whipped the cumbersome five-foot pole through the air as though it had been no longer or heavier than a riding whip.

Douglas sensed movement behind him at last, but too late. As he turned, the metal end of the pole caught him solidly on the side of his head, and with a look of blank astonishment, he collapsed like a tower of bairns' blocks at her feet.

Mary Kate stared at him for a long moment before the horrible thought that she might have killed him intruded upon her triumph. But once she had ascertained that he still breathed, she was conscious only of vexation that he had fallen across the doorway. Moving him proved to be no easy task, and by the time she had managed to drag him into the empty long gallery, he had begun to grumble and stir in a way that frightened her witless.

Whisking herself back into her bedchamber, she bolted the door, flew to relatch and bolt the shutters, and then leaped back into bed. Not until she had yanked the covers over her head did she realize how violently she was shivering, and whether that was from cold or from reaction to her own daring, she had not the faintest idea. Moments later, feeling stifled, she lowered the quilt to her chin just as the stout door to the bedchamber shook to a thunderous kick. The measured sound of retreating footsteps followed. Then came blessed silence. Douglas had recovered sufficiently to take himself off to bed.

2

❧❧❧ ❦❦❦

*M*ary Kate awoke the next morning to the extremely welcome news that Sir Adam Douglas and his party had left Critchfield Manor soon after sunrise. She departed for home herself that day, expecting, indeed hoping fervently, never to set eyes upon the handsome borderer again. The thought that she might likewise never again see Kenneth Gillespie did not so much as cross her mind, nor would it have troubled her had it done so.

In the months that followed, she stayed near Speyside House, although for a time there were still parties and other amusements to be enjoyed. Christmas came and went, followed by January and February with the worst of the heavy winter's weather. Then, some weeks after the dreadful event itself, news of Queen Mary's execution reached the highlands, reminding Mary Kate briefly of her last night at Critchfield Manor. The story was enhanced by such lurid details as that Mary had worn a scarlet petticoat, that she had been as beautiful as ever despite the surprising discovery that she had been completely bald beneath her wig, and that she had shown no fear when she knelt at the block. Although such minutiae fascinated her, Mary Kate spoke not one word of the matter to her father or to anyone else. Douglas and the others having obviously failed in their efforts to save the Scottish queen, the incidents at Critchfield now seemed remote and her knowledge, in view of the manner by which it had been obtained, somehow a thing better left unmentioned.

Her social life dimmed during the fierce winter months and was slow to improve even when it began to look as though spring had not forgotten the highlands, because her father continued to insist that the roads were too treacherous for travel. Though Mary Kate found many pastimes to amuse her at home, she longed for the gaiety and excitement of the house parties; however, such treats were denied her until the latter end of April when a misunderstanding involving herself and the son of one of her father's tenants finally caused big, gray-bearded Duncan MacPherson to change his mind about keeping his daughter close to home. Angrily he packed her off to visit her Murdoch cousins ten miles to the north, and since he sent her on her way with the ominous warning that she was not only to behave herself but also to put the thought of marrying *anyone* straight out of her head for the present time, it came as a profound shock to Mary Kate to be greeted upon her return with the news that Duncan himself had found her a husband.

Being neither a tactful nor a diplomatic man, he blurted out his announcement less than half an hour after she entered the house. Though Mary Kate had changed from her traveling dress into a simple light-green woolen gown before joining him in the little parlor that had been her mother's favorite room, she had not yet taken a seat, and upon hearing his words she went perfectly still, staring blankly at him, her hands tightly gripping each other at her waist. Although the room was lit by only two branches of candles and the dancing orange-gold flames in the small hooded fireplace, her pallor would have been noted by a more observant man.

"I say I've found ye a husband, lass," Duncan repeated more belligerently when she remained silent.

"I heard you, Father."

"Is that all ye can say tae the purpose?"

"I know not what to say," she replied in a calm tone that surprised them both. "Not a fortnight since, in this very room, you declared that I was too young to be contemplating bridals, and now I find myself on the brink of betrothal. 'Tis enough to rob Demosthenes himself of speech."

"Aye," he growled. "Trust ye tae fling me own words in my teeth. God's wounds, daughter, surely ye niver believed I'd marry ye wi' a farmer's son! I thought a visit wi' yon Murdochs would cure ye o' such foolishness."

She lifted her chin. "Since I'd never had the least notion that Robin MacLeod wished to wed with me, I never thought about it at all. I do not love Robbie as I would wish to love my husband."

"Love's got naught tae do wi' marriage. Such thinkin's nobbut rubbish. And, by the rood, ye'll no find a finer match than this one I've made ye, look ye how hard."

"You speak as though I am already a spinster, Father, although I am not yet a hopeless case by any means. I shall no doubt meet a host of good and proper gentlemen in June when my Aunt Aberfoyle takes me to Edinburgh."

"Weel, ye'll no be going tae Edinburgh," he stated on a note of triumph. She understood his tone if not his reasoning, for his sister Sarah, Lady Aberfoyle, had ever been a thorn in Duncan's side when it came to his daughter's upbringing. But Mary Kate had no time to reflect upon the matter, for Duncan went on at once. "Have I no said I've accepted the mon's offer? I've given Sir Adam me word, lass."

She had a sudden, swift vision of herself looking up into a pair of impudent brown eyes, a vision that was followed by a kaleidoscope of even more vivid, albeit less welcome mental pictures that caused her to regard her parent with no little dismay. He could not mean what she began to fear he meant. "Sir Adam, Father?"

"Aye," Duncan declared proudly, "Sir Adam Douglas, one o' the wealthiest men in all Scotland, though he do be border-bred. In troth, he's like tae become an earl one day, sae unco pack and thick do he be wi' young Jamie. And he wishes tae be wed in a twink, lassie."

"Sir Adam Douglas?" Even to her own ears the strained repetition sounded half-witted. But memories she had thought long buried were forcing themselves to the surface of her mind in a veritable eruption of outraged, confused thought. She shivered as though the chill winds from that stormy October night gusted now through the cozy parlor.

The strange chill was quickly replaced by an even odder tingling sensation that began at her toes and spread swiftly upward. Her hands trembled. It was as if, suddenly, she were watching this scene in her mother's parlor from somewhere outside her own body. Perhaps, she told herself, if her father hadn't fired the news at her so unexpectedly, she might be able to think more clearly. As it was, she found it

difficult to remember anything beyond the Douglas
arrogance, that cocksure manner in which he had described her to his friends, and more horrifyingly, the
astonished look on his face just before he had collapsed at her feet. What, oh what, she wondered
wildly, had possessed the blasted borderer that he
must needs offer her marriage? And what had possessed her otherwise sensible father to accept such an
offer?

" 'Tis no wonder you're betwattled, lass," Duncan
said then. " 'Tis amazed I am m'self the mon's no wed
afore this, he's that suitable. But he said he ne'er gave
it a thought ere his family began hounding him tae
beget hisself an heir. His father, Lord Strachan, is a
baron, ye ken, though that willna be sae much gin the
lad gets hisself belted."

Scarcely hearing his last words, Mary Kate turned
away toward the window. Duncan's initial announcement about finding her a husband had surprised her,
but for the few moments they had been discussing
her betrothal to an unknown suitor, it had been easy
to remain calm, to behave as she was expected to behave. She had even felt a tremor of excitement. But
the discovery that Douglas was the suitor came as an
unwelcome shock, and she struggled without much
success to keep a rein on her quick temper. "You cannot truly mean to marry me to Sir Adam Douglas,
Father," she said stiffly. "I have no wish to marry a
borderer, and I do not even like the man."

"What manner of ill-fared deaving be this, forby?"
demanded Duncan. "I've accepted the mon's offer
and ye'll marry him wi' nae more yaffing." Frustrated, he shoved a hand through his rough gray
curls. "Such talk disna become ye, lassie. I'd nae notion ye'd even remember the mon, for he said he met
ye only the once and decided tae make yon offer

when he found ye tae his liking and learned that
Parlan Drysdale's land, which will one day be his,
adjoins me own."

Though her cheeks flushed now with anger, Mary
Kate hesitated to speak, not knowing what she might
safely say. Duncan had bristled at her one brief display of temper, and the storm warnings were clear.
She was certain Douglas's offer had nothing to do
with land, unless he expected thus to acquire control
of Duncan's estate when Duncan died. But by Scottish law Speyside would be hers, and to a man of
Douglas's wealth and power it would be but a paltry
acquisition. She had no doubt he wanted her simply
because she had bested him, because he knew he
could have her by no other means.

For one brief moment she felt a near hysterical
urge to laugh, thinking the borderer had certainly
picked an effective way to be revenged upon her for a
clout on the head. But since Duncan took the matter
seriously, it was no laughing matter to her, either.
Her father's highland pride clearly stopped short of
whistling a border fortune down the wind.

She tried another tack, infusing a note of pleading
into her voice. "Please, Father, I remember Sir Adam
well. He is naught but an arrogant, disrespectful lout,
a man who holds women of low account. I disliked
him more than I can say." But her plea had no better
effect than to inflame his frustration to anger, and as
the storm broke over her head, she realized that he
had made up his mind irrevocably to the match.

She had always known, for custom decreed it, that
her father would one day provide a husband for her.
Whatever other rights young highland women had,
they were rarely allowed much say in such an important matter as marriage. And despite the fact that by
Scottish law a young woman could refuse any suitor,

a Scottish father within the confines of his home was
a law unto himself. For any offspring of his, male or
female, to act against his wishes would be scandalous.
Indeed, in many parts of Scotland—mostly lowland
areas where the Calvinists prevailed—such behavior
was illegal and was severely punished.

Mary Kate knew she could never openly defy
Duncan, who loved her dearly and who, she had no
doubt, was puffed up with pride that a man of
Douglas's stamp, borderer or not, had made an offer
for her. Moreover, Duncan's honor was at stake now
that his word had been given, and he obviously believed her distaste after but a single encounter with
her suitor to be no more than natural feminine con-
trariness.

She couldn't even tell him about her last night at
Critchfield, for with the clarity of hindsight, she was
too honest not to admit that her own behavior had
contributed more than a little to the borderer's assumption that she would be an easy conquest. That a
true gentleman ought, in her opinion, never to make
such an assumption would be deemed a mere quibble
by her father, who would, in his own masculine way,
condemn her loose behavior and declare the insult
well merited.

It occurred to her that she might edit the tale, ac-
centing Douglas's behavior while limiting reference
to her own, but she rejected the idea as soon as it
entered her head. Duncan would ask too many pertinent questions, and she was a poor liar. Even the fact
that she had successfully defended her honor would
avail her little with her father, for she was certain he
would, in view of his recent acquaintance with and
liking for Douglas, roundly disapprove of the rough
and ragged tactics she had employed. Impulse was
second nature to her, but she often came to grief

through not having thought out the consequences of her schemes ahead of time. She would not make that mistake now, she told herself. She would keep her own counsel. For once, she would behave prudently.

Duncan moved forward just then to lay one big hand on her shoulder. He was a barrel-chested, broad-shouldered man of above average height, and she automatically braced herself at his approach, thinking he was still angry, but when he spoke his voice was gentle. "Come, come, lassie. 'Tis a wondrous match, forby. Douglas has a mort o' gelt, and he's putting a bit by in your ain name for the privilege o' claiming your hand. He's got land of his ain, too, and he's agreed he'll no interfere wi' your claim tae me estates when I've gone."

"And you would take his word for that? A border's word? When you've told me yourself that a sensible highlander trusts none but his own?"

Duncan shrugged. "In troth, I like the mon." He gave her shoulder a squeeze. "I ken weel that ye fear leaving your home, lassie, but though ye may be a wee bit lonesome at first in border country, ye'll find your feet soon enow. I'll warrant ye'll have more gelt in your pocket and more servants at your beck and bay than ye'll ken what tae do wi'. 'Tis a great honor, lass, and one day ye'll be thanking me."

"Never," she said, gritting her teeth. Annoyed that he could believe Douglas's wealth might sway her as it had swayed him, she stiffened under his hand, although an instinct for self-preservation still kept her temper under some control. "I cannot marry a borderer, Father. He does *me* no honor!"

Duncan glowered. "What is this willna and canna? By Christ's holy rood, lass, ye overstep yourself, and I'll no brook such damned impertinence. Would ye shame me, forby, asking that I gae back on me word?

By God, ye'll accept the mon and be fidging fain of it into the bargain!" He was shouting now, and she freed her temper at last, wrenching away from him and turning, arms akimbo, to reply in kind.

"I will never be glad, Father, nor eager. Indeed, if you want this match so much, you may marry the man yourself, for I will not! Why should I consider *your* honor when you would force me to submit mine to the will of that . . . that prick-eared, border-bred Jack-sauce!"

When Duncan went rigid with fury, Mary Kate gasped in dismay, realizing at once that despite all her good intentions, she had allowed her temper to carry her beyond the limit of what he would tolerate. It was too late for remorse, however, for her father's immediate intent was only too clear. She stepped back, involuntarily putting up her hands to fend him off, though she knew such a gesture to be weak as well as useless, and despised herself for making it. In an attempt to recover her dignity, she said carefully, "I beg your pardon, Father. I ought never to have spoken so to you."

"Nae doot. Fetch a switch, Mary Katharine."

"Father, I—"

"Whist now, and do as you're bid." His gray beard bristled. "Ye'll no speak such nash-gab tae me, daughter. Not wi'out ye suffer the consequence, as ye ken full weel. Ye've met the mon but once in your life, so this blathering canna be but a bairn's wicked tantrum, which is a thing I didna tolerate when ye were a week lassock and willna tolerate from ye the noo. A swingeing's what ye've asked for, and by the rood, a swingeing's what ye'll get." He pointed toward the door. "Fetch me a switch."

Sighing, Mary Kate did as she was told, and when Duncan had exerted his paternal authority to his complete satisfaction, he threw the switch onto the fire and released her. "A bargain's been struck," he said sternly, "and a proper good bargain it be, sae ye'll submit wi' a good face on it. Sir Adam returns on the morrow tae speak wi' ye himself, as is proper. Ye'll don a decent gown, conduct yourself wi' propriety, and we'll be having nae more o' this defiance, gin ye please. D'ye take my meaning, lass?"

"Aye," Mary Kate replied, her manner grim but subdued. His meaning was clear, and she knew now that he would not hesitate to force her submission by whatever means he deemed necessary. Though Duncan was not by nature a harsh man, he could be an obstinate one, and she knew her own stubbornness was no match for his, particularly when, as now, she could not believe herself to be altogether in the right.

She wiped dampness from her eyes with the back of her hand, but the gesture brought her no sympathy. Duncan merely ordered her off to bed without her supper as he had done when she had misbehaved as a child. In general an indulgent parent, he had shown little tolerance then for her "damned insolence" and had never allowed her to be rude or impertinent to him or to any other adult, so she couldn't be altogether surprised that he had lost his temper with her tonight. Her behavior, she readily admitted —if only to herself—had been inexcusable. She had known the moment the offending words crossed her lips what the consequences would be, but she didn't mind the punishment as much as the knowledge that her father had made up his mind to the marriage.

She knew Duncan had been disappointed, even shocked, by her negative reaction to the match. He had clearly expected her to be delighted. For that matter, any girl in her senses probably would be delighted, she decided, because any girl in her senses would care more about Douglas's status and wealth than she would about being forced to live in border country under the arrogant man's thumb. But Mary Kate was not just any girl, and she was convinced that she would hate being married to a man who would insist upon treating her as his chattel.

Once she had reached her bedchamber, she flung herself down upon her bed and began racking her brain for a way out of the betrothal. However, by the time she finally fell asleep, none had occurred to her, except the slight possibility of appealing to Douglas's better nature if, indeed, he actually possessed a better nature.

When she joined her father to break their fast the following morning, though her demeanor was not cheerful and her greeting was subdued, there was nothing else that he could condemn in her appearance. Her hair had been brushed smoothly off her brow and confined in a delicate lace caul, and her indigo gown was cut in the latest style, sporting wide cuffs and a belled skirt, all lavishly embroidered with crimson and yellow roses on twining, leafy green stems.

"Good morrow tae ye, lassie," Duncan said heartily. " 'Tis a muckle fine day, and gin me nose tells me true, we've an excellent repast a-coming. I'll wager you're even more ravenous than what I am m'self."

Her reply was noncommittal, and she made no effort to further the conversation. Duncan allowed the silence to continue while the housemaid served their meal but regarded his daughter thoughtfully when, her expression still glum, she only picked at her oatmeal and ignored altogether the baconned herring he served to her with his own hands.

"Eat, lass. Ye mun keep up your strength. I've nae wish tae see ye swoon wi' hunger at Sir Adam's feet."

His words brought an unwelcome memory, and she bit her lip, avoiding his eye. "I'll not faint," she said at last, smearing marmalade on her muffin and nibbling it to please him.

"Mary Kate," he said then, warily, "I trow ye'll no shame me by behaving in an unseemly fashion."

"No, sir." She smiled at him, a glint of irony in her eyes. "I doubt it would serve any good purpose."

"Ha' ye come tae your senses, forby?"

"If you like to call it that. I doubt Sir Adam will agree to withdraw his suit, and so—"

"Och, ye'll niver ask such a thing o' the mon! 'Tis an honor he does ye, an honor tae the whole o' Clan Chattan. Would ye then disgrace the name o' Mac-Pherson wi' your foolish maundering?" He glared at her fiercely. "Ye'll obey me, lass, or by the rood, I'll make ye wish ye'd niver been born. D'ye mark me, Mary Kate?"

"Aye." She sighed. "But I cannot like the idea of marrying a man who will expect me to submit to his every decree in the manner I've been given to understand a borderer expects his wife to submit. It is not in my nature to behave even as meekly as my Aunt Critchfield behaves."

Duncan's brown eyes twinkled suddenly. "In troth, ye've little o' your Aunt Critchfield in ye, lassie. But consider, gin ye will, what Critchfield's life would be like had he married my sister instead o' your dear mother's."

The vision leapt to Mary Kate's eye of her uncle as she had seen him that last night at Critchfield, sprawled drunkenly in front of his giant fireplace throwing dice with his cronies. Into that same vision stormed the slim, wiry figure of her father's indomi-

table sister. Aunt Aberfoyle bowed before no man.
Indeed, she would have had Critchfield on his feet
and sober before the cat could lick its ear. Mary
Kate's spirits lightened considerably, and she looked
across the table at her father with a smile twitching
upon her lips. "You put the matter into perspective,
sir," she said, adding thoughtfully, "My future is still
in my own hands, is it not? If I must wed the man,
then by heaven, I promise you I will teach him that a
highland lady is chattel to no man. He must learn to
coat his commands with honey if he expects me to
obey them."

Relieved by her change of mood if not necessarily
by her words, Duncan grinned at her. "What ye do
after you're wed's nae concern tae me, lassie, but I
trow that even Sarah'd think twice afore misbehaving
herself wi' such a husband as young Douglas tae answer tae. And dinna be thinking tae run home the
first time he loses his temper wi' ye. I'd only send ye
back tae him."

Remembering the oaths she had heard and the savage kicks at her bedchamber door, Mary Kate was
conscious of an uncomfortable feeling that Duncan
might be right. Douglas already had a score to settle
with her. Nonetheless, she told herself firmly, before
she was done with the man, he would rue his latest
impudence. Drawing a long, steadying breath, she
smiled more cheerfully and asked her father when he
expected Douglas to arrive.

"He said he'd be along at half after ten. He's been
wi' friends, forby. Och, and there is one other sma'
matter." Duncan looked uneasy. "Ye mun understand
that Douglas hasna much time tae call his ain, what
wi' being at the royal beck and bay, as he be. He
wishes tae be wed as quick as may be."

"How soon?" Now that she had picked up the

gauntlet, so to speak, the details were relatively unimportant.

"I dinna ken. He said we should discuss it today."

"Well, it cannot be for at least a month," she stated calmly. "There are banns to be read, after all."

"Aye," Duncan agreed, but he looked doubtful. They finished their meal in silence, and then he suggested that she occupy herself in some ladylike pastime, preferably in the front parlor, so that he would know where to find her when Douglas arrived.

Mary Kate agreed unenthusiastically, since ladylike pastimes did not rank high on her list of favorite occupations. She was a skilled needlewoman, however, having in fact done the delicate embroidery on her gown herself. She enjoyed fancy work, but Morag MacBain, their housekeeper, had done the piecing, cutting, and hemming of nearly every item in her wardrobe. Several unfinished projects occupied her workbasket, because she often grew bored before her work was completed; however, despite that unenviable characteristic and although the work had been done in spurts as the mood struck her, Speyside House was strewn with colorful cushions, hangings, and quilts of her own design.

Repairing now to the parlor, Mary Kate disentangled from the litter in her workbasket an unfinished tapestry bellpull, its design of green wool worked around a series of silk-embroidered snow scenes only half-done. With a sigh, she straightened her tangled wools and silks and began to stitch.

By half-past ten she was bored with both the work and her own company, so ten minutes later it was with relief rather than any other emotion that she greeted the sound of approaching hoofbeats. Laying the tapestry aside, she hurried to the window where, screened from view by the green velvet curtains, she was able to observe Sir Adam as he dismounted and relinquished his magnificent chestnut stallion to a grinning stableboy.

Her first thought was that he was even taller than she remembered and more elegant. Well over six feet and as broad-shouldered as Duncan, Douglas was dressed in a white-clocked lavender doublet, his trunk hose puffed and slashed with darker purple. A lustrous, fur-trimmed cloak of rich purple velvet, pinned with an amethyst brooch to his right shoulder, had been tossed back in graceful folds over his left. He sported a falling lace collar instead of a ruff, and wore a velvet cap perched rakishly atop his neatly cropped dark curls.

Flipping a coin to the lad, Douglas adjusted his cap with a jaunty gesture of his right thumb and turned toward the house. The spring in his step as he approached the door told her plainly how eagerly he looked forward to the interview.

"Insufferable oaf," she muttered.

3

Mary Kate scurried back to her chair and picked up her needlework, forcing herself to relax and breathe deeply. For Douglas to see that she was agitated would not suit her at all. She would be calm, serene. Unfortunately, a good ten minutes elapsed, stretching her nerves to the breaking point, before at last the door opened. When it did, Douglas entered first, laughing. Behind him, Duncan avoided Mary Kate's gaze as she arose to make her curtsy, but she was not left long to ponder his behavior or to wonder at Sir Adam's merriment.

With a glint of devilry in his eyes, the borderer grinned and wished her good day, adding gently, "Your father tells me you want wooing, lassie." His grin broadened at her look of instant fury. "You need not look dismayed. I asked a blunt question and received a more telling response than I should have done with a tactful one. 'Tis always the best way. I have assured him that I have no intention of withdrawing my suit. A little courting is like to amuse me, I think."

" 'Tis more like to frustrate you, sir." She shot a speaking look at her father, and her eyes were still flashing when she turned back to Douglas. So much for his better nature, she decided.

Douglas indulged himself in an injured sigh. "Godamercy, lass, I know you've got a generous nature, but don't say you have already bestowed your affections upon another man."

"She has not!" Duncan snapped. "Och, there was a wee bit of pliskie nonsense wi' yon MacLeod a fortnight past, but I put an end to that soon enow."

"You were horrid to poor Robin," Mary Kate said tartly. "He offered for me only because you were so out-of-reason-cross with him that he thought he must have compromised my honor."

"And had he?" Douglas inquired, looking directly at her as he added with a touch of mockery, "You will, I trust, forgive my ill-mannered curiosity under the circumstances."

Mary Kate glared at him, but Duncan hastened to offer reassurance. "She misleads you, lad. What father would no ha' been angry tae discover clandestine meetings betwixt the daughter he presumed tae be safe snug in her cot and a tenant's son wi' scarce two wits or pence tae rub together? Naught tae fret over, o' course," he added swiftly when Douglas's heavy brows flew upward and Mary Kate flushed scarlet. "Nobbut innocent bairns, the pair o' them, but I sent him off wi' his ears fair scorched, I can tell ye, when he had the impudence tae offer marriage wi' m' lass."

"So I should hope," Douglas said. "I trust you set your daughter right as well, MacPherson. I cannot approve the habit of clandestine meetings."

"Och, I packed her off tae her Murdoch cousins tae

get over her sulks. Skelped her, too, o' course, not
that that ever has much effect on the impertinent lassie. Up tae another prank five minutes later, like as
not."

"Petticoats, I expect," Douglas murmured wickedly.

"What's that ye say?"

"Petticoats," he repeated, grinning now. "My father decided long since that females design their
clothing with an eye toward protecting themselves
from the just wrath of their fathers and husbands.
My sister's behavior improved remarkably after he
made that discovery."

"By the rood," Duncan said, casting a speculative
glance at his daughter's wide skirts. "I'll warrant he's
got the right of it, too."

Appalled by the direction the conversation had
taken and seething with indignation, Mary Kate
could hold her tongue no longer. "How dare you, the
pair of you," she cried, "to stand there discussing me
as though I were naught but a wayward bairn!"

"Very true," Douglas said gently. "We should be a
great deal more comfortable if we were sitting down,
but gentlemen may not sit, you know, whilst a lady
continues to stand."

"Oh!" So infuriated that she could not speak, Mary
Kate glowered at him, longing for the courage to slap
the grin off his impudent face.

Unfortunately, the wish showed itself in her expression, and her father said sharply, "That will do,
Mary Kate. Ye forget yourself. Sit ye doon at once
and mind your manners."

As she sank speechless into her chair, feeling as
though she tottered on the brink of hysteria, the bit
of tapestry that she had been working earlier slipped

to the floor. Douglas retrieved it, pausing in the act of restoring it to her to give it an appraising look.

"A Christmas theme and very well done, too," he said, handing it to her with a nod of approval. "I admire efficiency in a woman."

"Well, you do not find it in me, sir," she retorted. "That piece was intended to be done for last Christmas."

Encountering a glance from Duncan that boded ill for her future, she could only be grateful when Douglas suddenly dropped his teasing attitude, took a seat, and deftly turned the conversation to more general topics. Under his adroit management, Duncan relaxed and soon rang for ale. The men discussed the weather, hunting, horses, and other such harmless subjects, while Mary Kate remained silent, offering comment only when directly addressed. Finally, Douglas set his mug aside and rose from his chair.

"I must take my leave now, mistress, but I shall return upon the morrow to begin a proper courtship."

She did not deign to reply, but when Duncan would have expostulated, Douglas cut in smoothly, saying, "Pray do not take her to task, sir. I shall soon bring her to heel."

"I hope ye may, lad. She's a wild slip yet, wi'oot mense or discretion and wi' little moderation o' mouth, so 'twill be a muckle great task, but I surely hope ye may." He shook his gray head and sounded so doubtful that, despite herself, Mary Kate nearly grinned.

"Never doubt my capabilities, sir," Douglas replied confidently, watching her rather than her father. "I've got almost an entire fortnight in which to accomplish the deed, after all. The good Lord created the whole world in less than half that time."

"Aye, lad, that He did, but He didna have a female tae reckon wi' till it was done. Gin ye ken your Bible, ye will remember that He left her till the last and when He'd done wi' the lass, the poor mon required a full day's rest."

Douglas roared with laughter, and Mary Kate, sitting stiffly, ignored them both until he made his bow a moment later. Duncan walked out with him, leaving her to think over what had been said and to wonder what her father would have to say to her when he returned.

Douglas's comment about the Creation made it appear that he intended to devote an entire fortnight of his valuable time to her wooing. No doubt, she decided, he would then have to return to the king until it was time for the wedding. They had not discussed an actual date yet, but that would come in good time. It didn't really matter now.

She heard Duncan shout for his horse and, having expected a scold at the very least for her lack of conduct, she was relieved to discover that he meant to leave matters in Douglas's hands as he had been asked to do. Her temper had been her undoing yet again, and she realized with chagrin that although she had emerged victorious from their first confrontation, the honors for their second had undeniably gone to the borderer. She told herself sternly that the next time they met she would be calm and polite if it killed her.

Accordingly, she was all smiles and serenity the following morning when he arrived at Speyside House, but if she had hoped thus to confound him, she had underestimated her opponent. The ubiquitous twinkle lurked in his eyes when he greeted her.

"Is this the other side of the shrew, lassie?"

She lowered her lashes, a demure gesture that delighted him. Chuckling, he added, "You have many moods, sweetheart," and turned to Duncan, standing beside her. "At least my wife will never bore me, sir. I begin to believe I made an even wiser choice than I knew."

Duncan shook his head as though he knew not what to make of the pair of them and asked if Douglas would take some ale. But Sir Adam, who was dressed in breeks and boots, said he had a fancy to take his lady riding this fine, brisk morning.

The lady demurred. It was too cold. He would not wish her to risk her health in such uncertain weather, nor did she desire to keep him awaiting her pleasure while she changed her gown for more appropriate attire. And as a clincher, she informed him with wide-eyed innocence that she was by no means certain it was proper for her to ride out alone with him.

Douglas seemed perfectly willing to continue this exceedingly polite conversation, but Duncan soon had had enough of it. "Dinna be daft, lass," he said crossly. "The mon's bound tae marry wi' ye, and I trust him weel tae look after ye. As tae the uncertainty o' the weather, there's nobbut one wee cloud in the sky, which is nae great thing tae make a song about. 'Tis a fine spring day, forby, and the exercise will do ye good."

"If it be *your* wish, Father." She swept a curtsy, casting Douglas a mocking look, but the twinkle in his brown eyes only deepened. *Damn the man,* she thought. Even her father's trust, which heaven knew Douglas did not deserve, did not serve to curb his impudence.

Changing into her riding dress and jerkin took little time, and she soon rejoined the gentlemen. The horses had been brought around to the front and, outside, Duncan moved swiftly to examine the borderer's stallion with a close and expert eye.

"Forby, lad, he's a big 'un, but he looks sound enow."

"Aye, just under seventeen hands and the devil to go."

"Staying power?"

"I've had him nigh onto an hour at the gallop, and he's made some long journeys in his time." As Duncan ran a hand over the powerful, rippling haunches, Douglas added, "I've not tried him hunting, but he easily clears most hedges and dikes even under my weight."

"It was today that you wished to ride, was it not?" Mary Kate inquired sweetly as she adjusted the fastening of the safeguard that protected her skirts when she rode.

Masculine eyes met over her head in that look of combined regret, amusement, and helplessness that men have perfected in the face of feminine impatience over the passage of time, and Douglas apologized. "Sorry, lass. Given the slightest encouragement, I could discuss Valiant's points all day."

"I pray you will not do so today."

"Nay, we will go." Tossing her effortlessly onto her saddle, he gathered his reins and mounted the stallion, then said to Duncan, "We'll ride along the river toward Braelairig."

"Will ye be taking the lass up tae Ardcarach, then?" Duncan referred to the great castle on the Braelairig estates, owned by Parlan Drysdale, Laird of Ardcarach.

"No, sir, not today. My uncle is in Edinburgh. I doubt there is a safe, direct route from here anyway, only that long, circuitous road to the south of us. I've no wish to spend the day searching for a way up the glen, so we'll follow the river to the boundary between the two estates, then cut back through your fields. Be away three, maybe four hours, I should say."

Duncan nodded and waved them off. Riding down to the patchy trail along the riverbank, they turned southwest toward the source of the Spey, and Mary Kate drew a long, appreciative breath of the clean, crisp air. She loved to ride and had often followed this particular path, so when they came to an open space, though the trail disappeared into thick brown grass still bent from the weight of the winter's snow, she didn't hesitate to urge her horse to a gallop. Exhilarated by the cold air blowing against her cheeks, she failed to note that her impulsive action had caught Douglas by surprise until the thunder of hoofbeats from behind pierced her consciousness.

Looking back to see that he was gaining on her, his grin a clear-cut challenge, she bent low and urged her mount with a flick of her whip to a faster pace. It was no use though, for a few seconds later Valiant flashed past, and she saw with amazement that his rider was not making use of the light whip he carried. Duncan MacPherson, sportsman that he was, allowed none but the finest horseflesh in his stables, so when she finally reined in beside Douglas to see that the stallion was not even blowing, Mary Kate was filled with admiration.

"By heaven, sir, that is a magnificent beast." Breathless from her wild ride, she had no notion of how magnificent she looked herself with her flushed cheeks and her eyes brilliant with excitement. Her hat was askew, and red-gold curls had tumbled out from under it, giving a tousled, little-girl look to her face, but there was nothing childlike in the erectness of her carriage or in the fullness of her soft bosom as it heaved beneath her riding dress.

Douglas's grin broadened. "Aye, he is magnificent,

sweetheart, and you ride like a borderer, as though you were born in that saddle. 'Tis glad I am to see that you ride safely astride and have not been daft enough to attempt the sidesaddle. 'Tis a loathsome, dangerous contraption at best, I'm thinking."

Deep pleasure surged through her at his unexpected compliment. Until that moment her indignation at the unwelcome turn of events had armored her against his charm, but she was suddenly reminded of how quickly he had managed to stir her senses at Critchfield. His flashing smile and the twinkle in his dark eyes warmed her now, and since she heartily agreed with his condemnation of the sidesaddle, an invention beloved by the Calvinists since it was designed to force ladies to keep their legs decorously together while they rode, she silently resolved to observe a truce—for the moment, at least.

They rode on side by side, maintaining light conversation until hearing each other over the increasing roar of the river became too difficult. Soon afterward, they reached the wide, rushing brook and steep, granite cliff wall that formed the boundary between the MacPherson and Drysdale estates.

Mary Kate had met Parlan Drysdale, Laird of Ardcarach, only once and remembered him as a tall, thin, dour man, not at all the sort one would expect to rule an estate that seemed from her present position to be a lofty, inaccessible mountain fortress. Towering, rugged crags separated Braelairig from Speyside at that point where the fierce, roaring river swept from the rocky, steep-sided glen before proceeding northward through a slightly less rugged portion of the Cairngorm Mountains until its waters spilled at last into the Moray Firth. The sight at the opening to the glen, where brook met river, was wild, fearsome, and breathtaking. One would expect the laird of the aerie above to be plaided, full-bearded, and burly, with piercing eyes, a bellowing voice, and a claymore at the ready. Mary Kate shouted as much to Douglas above the din.

He laughed and shouted back, "You draw a fine portrait, lass, but isn't it proper for a scholar like my uncle to dwell upon the heights, too?"

She agreed but insisted that her fierce Gaelic warrior was a more romantic figure, and they turned back toward Speyside House, following the brook for a short time and then heading across rolling, open fields. When they came to a small, green, wildflower-strewn meadow with a sparkling burn tumbling merrily through its center, Douglas reined in.

"How about some refreshment, lassie?"

"An excellent notion, sir, for the water looks most inviting. Have you a cup, or must we make do with our hands? I can do so, you know. Have done since I was a child."

"My name is Adam, Mary Kate, and I can do better than a mere cup." He dismounted and unstrapped a leather bag from his saddle before helping her to alight. "I bullied the fellow at the alehouse where I'm staying into providing a proper meal for us. I ought to warn you at once, I've a prodigious appetite." He selected a broad, flat rock near the burn, and Mary Kate's eyes widened as she watched him methodically lay out two pewter mugs, a cottage loaf, a brick of white cheese, a cold whole chicken, four apples, a tin of biscuits, and a plugged crockery jug of malmsey wine.

"You'll need such an appetite if you mean for us to dispose of all that," she said. Removing her safeguard, she spread it out upon the ground and sat down, watching to see what else he would take from the leather bag. "Have you brought fine linen and silver knives as well, Sir Adam?"

"Just Adam," he said.

"Yes, sir. Have you?"

He grinned, shaking his head and handing her a neatly folded linen towel. "Faith, but you're a stubborn wench."

"Aye." She watched as he hacked the chicken to pieces with his knife, then helped herself to a leg, tearing at it with her teeth. Speaking around a mouthful of chicken, she said, "I thought Father told me you were staying with friends."

"I was, but they live beyond Braelairig, too far away for easy courting, so I plumped for the alehouse in the *clachan*."

"Oh." Having no wish to pursue the subject of courting, she asked him to tell her about his family instead, and the conversation drifted along amicably until they had finished their meal.

Douglas cleared away the remains, stuffing everything haphazardly into the leather saddlebag, but when Mary Kate arose and began to shake out her safeguard, he took it from her, dropped it on the ground again, and taking her gently by the shoulders, turned her to face him.

Suddenly aware as she had not been all day of how vulnerable she was, she looked up at him shyly, and Douglas kissed her. The moment his lips touched hers, she was transported back in time and space, and it was as though she stood before her chamber door at Critchfield once again. His hands were firm now upon her shoulders, and his lips claimed hers even more possessively than they had that night, but she had no wish this time to push him away. Instead, she found herself responding to him with a fervor that would have surprised her had she stopped to contemplate it. She did not think about her feelings, however. She knew only, with blinding clarity, that she had been wanting him to kiss her this past hour and longer.

She felt the muscles of his back rippling under her exploring fingers before she realized that her hands had moved away from her sides, and the warmth that spread through her body surprised and elated her. A small moan of protest escaped her when Douglas set her back upon her heels.

"Enough, lassie," he said, amused. "I dare not trust myself whilst you encourage me, for your method of quelling my ardor is not one that I choose to experience again."

She closed her eyes, willing her traitorous body to calm itself. Then, looking at him, she said steadily, "You provoked me that night, sir, but I do apologize if I hurt you."

"I've a hard enough head, sweetheart, though you needn't have been so rough. I had already deduced that your lack of experience was greater than I had thought it to be."

"I thought you were growing angry," she said. "I was afraid of what you might do if I persisted in refusing you."

He shrugged. "I was angry, but more with myself than with you. I realized that much just about the time you clouted me."

She bit her lower lip then gazed up at him limpidly. "You are well revenged upon me now, are you not?"

" 'Twas not out of revenge that I sought your hand, sweetheart, but out of desire." Looking directly into her clear hazel eyes, he said quietly, "I wrote my father to come to Speyside a week from Friday."

"Friday week! But why so soon?"

"We will be married on the Saturday," he replied. "I know, for Duncan told me so, that you thought to have more time, but the king cannot be trusted to spare me indefinitely."

"But the banns! They must be read from the pulpit upon three separate Sundays. And Friday is the proper day for weddings, not Saturday."

"I've a certain influence, even here, lassie. The banns have been waived. There was a price to be paid, of course, but one reading will suffice. And borderers do not wed on Friday."

"Good God, sir, but you take a deal upon yourself." Though she had been in a fair way these past hours to forgetting her quarrel with him, his high-handedness now was too much. "The women in *this* part of Scotland," she said in carefully measured tones, "expect to be consulted *before* the course of their lives is determined upon. You have already contrived to make my father forget that fact, but you must yet reckon with me." Muttering wrathfully, she turned away and began to pace back and forth, casting furious glances at him each time she turned. Her color was high, her eyes sparkled with wrath, and her fists clenched tightly as she beat them against her skirts in angry punctuation of her words. "I should have thought you would know better by now than to challenge me, sir. I thought I had taught you to have a care. But you are by far the most despicable, presumptuous, arrogant, domineering, self-centered, egotistical man I have ever known. Oh, even those words are not sufficient to describe you." She paused, glaring at him, then said through her teeth, "How I wish I knew the proper ones to tell you exactly how I feel."

He had been watching her stormy progress with suppressed amusement, but at her final words the amusement faded. "Be thankful you do not know such words, sweetheart. I dislike profanity in my women."

"Damn you!" she cried, defiance ringing in her voice.

But he only grinned. "You will have to do better than that, lassie. I shall teach you the words that will make me beat you if you like."

She gasped. "You wouldn't dare!"

"What? Teach you or beat you?" When a withering glare was her only response, he shrugged. "You tempt me, lass. Indeed, I suppose there are many who would insist that I owe you a right good skelping for the lump you raised on my head at Critchfield, but since I am not by nature a man of violence, I probably shan't beat you until after we are wed."

"I do not wish to marry you!" she snapped.

"After what happened here moments ago, I don't believe that," he said quietly, "but if you believe it, why have you not told Duncan about our first meeting? I'll warrant he'd not approve of my behavior that night."

"No, nor of mine." She looked up at him speculatively from beneath her lashes. When he remained silent, she said, "I am a poor liar when people ask pointed questions, and my father would want to know precisely *why* you behaved as you did."

His eyes narrowed. "Do you often tell lies?"

"Not often," she replied, looking away, then forcing herself to look directly at him again.

"It will be as well for you if you tell none to me, Mary Kate." His tone was still light, but there was an inflexibility in his expression that she had never seen before, and the hardness of steel appeared in his eyes as he continued, "I do not tolerate liars well. In fact, when I discover that a servant has lied to me, I punish him severely."

"So now I am to be ranked with your servants, am I?" she said, indignant again. "Well, 'tis no more than I expected, but you'll soon discover that I am not so meek as you would like, sir. You may have my father under your thumb, but I promise you, I am no such easy conquest. Before I have done with you, you will rue the day you contrived this marriage."

"Faith, what a vixen!" To her surprise, he chuckled. "To think that I began this marriage business on little more than a whim because your daring attracted me. But now I begin to look forward to many long years of companionship, sweetheart. Taming you will be a rare challenge and right good sport."

"Christ's blood, sir, do you dare to laugh at me?"

"I think it only fair to warn you," he said with gentle emphasis, "that 'Christ's blood' is one of the epithets I least desire to hear upon a lady's lips."

" 'Christ's blood,' " she retorted with relish, "is one of my favorite expressions."

"Nevertheless, it would behoove you to deny yourself the pleasure of its use." His tone was still gentle, but the dark eyes glittered. "Don't persist in this defiance, lass. I am a tolerant man by most standards— more than tolerant by those of the Calvinists—so you may lead me as merry a dance as you choose in private. But you might as well know from the start that there are three things I will not tolerate. Profanity from the women in my family is one such. Another is lying, and the third is having my personal concerns blazoned before the public eye. If I should chance to displease you, as I doubt not I shall from time to time, do not make your displeasure a gift to the rest of the world unless you wish to make me very angry indeed. Do you take my meaning?"

"Aye," she shot back, stirred to further rebellion by the simple fact that she had failed so far to arouse his temper. A voice at the back of her mind suggested that she was testing him and that it was perhaps an unwise thing to do, but she ignored the warning. Her voice fairly crackled. "I understand you well enough, Douglas, but I make you no promises. If I have a thing to say, I say it, and I have no greater care for your wishes than for those of your wretched Calvinists. Here in the highlands, we go our own road as ever we have."

She paused, but his lips were pressed tightly together and he said nothing. Goaded by his silence, she went on angrily, "You displease me now, Douglas, and since there be none to hear me save yourself and yon horses, I promise you this by Christ's blood, by the rood, by God's wounds, or His nails, or whatever else you like or do not like. Since I will not defy my father, I have no choice other than to marry you, but I will see myself damned to the fires of Hell before I will allow you to set yourself up as dictator over me, now or ever in the future."

"I had not planned to dictate," he declared grimly, "but if I do give you an order, lass, you will have no choice but to obey me, as you had best learn before you grow any older." Turning sharply, he strode to her horse, gathered its reins, and tied them deftly to the saddlebow. Then before she had the least notion of his intent, he gave the animal a sharp smack on the rump, startling it into a lumbering trot. Shocked and appalled, Mary Kate watched as her erstwhile means of transport loped off in the general direction of the MacPherson stables.

"What have you done?" she demanded, hurrying toward him. "Surely, you don't expect me to ride pillion behind you."

He swung into his saddle. "The question will not arise, sweetheart. You need a sharp lesson, and I mean to provide it as painlessly as possible, much though you tempt me to other methods. You would be well advised during your walk back to your father's house to contemplate your lack of conduct."

"Walk?" She stared up at him in consternation. "You cannot mean it. Why, 'tis all of five miles from here!"

"Your father said you need exercise, and the walk will do you nearly as much good as the aching backside you so richly deserve. No harm, barring sore feet, will come to you here on MacPherson land, and I'll give you an hour and a half before I come to fetch you." When a look of hopeful calculation sprang to her eyes, his lips twitched, but he flicked his whip lightly against his muscular thigh and his tone when he continued was uncompromising. "I'd advise you to avoid putting me to such trouble, Mary Kate, if you take my meaning."

Biting her lip in frustrated wrath, she watched as Douglas wheeled the stallion toward Speyside House and quickly urged him to a gallop. Moments later, horse and rider were out of sight over the nearest hill.

4

❧❧❧ ❧❧❧

$\mathcal{M}$ary Kate felt every pebble and clod along the way, for her boots were thinsoled and unsuitable for walking. However, despite aching feet, her anger and frustration spurred her on. Though she did not wish to suffer the humiliation of having Douglas ride out in search of her, she told herself firmly that she did not fear him. Not for a minute did she believe he would dare to make good his thinly veiled threat—not when they were not yet wed. Still, she mused, it was no doubt wiser just now not to test his patience further. At the least, he would tease her, mock her feminine weakness in not being able to cover such a distance as quickly as a man. At the worst, she would learn something more about the man's temper.

By the time she entered the front hall of the house, she had thrown away her hat, her hair was in a tangle, her face was streaked with dirt, her riding dress was dusty, and her train, freed of the safeguard and several times along the way having been wrenched free of grasping shrubs and thistles, was ripped and full of twigs and stickers. The door from the hall into the parlor stood ajar, so her arrival was observed by both men, seated at their ease, indulging in mugs of whiskey. Both politely got to their feet upon her entrance into the room, but Duncan, after one astonished look at her bedraggled appearance, burst into laughter.

"God's wounds, lass," he chortled, "but I trow ye've met your match and ken weel who will be master in your new home." Tears streamed down his face. Douglas, too, was grinning.

With a small cry of fury, Mary Kate snatched up her shabby train and left the room, slamming the door behind her with wrathful energy. Seconds later, it opened again, and Douglas caught up with her halfway up the narrow stairs.

" 'Tis unmannerly to walk out when you've a visitor, lassie," he said with a teasing grin. "Such a display of temper is most unseemly."

"Oh, you're hateful, the pair of you." She would have turned away, but he held her arm, his grip light but undeniable. Oddly, she noticed even through the thick cloth of her sleeve that his hand felt warm. There was warmth in his eyes, too, but his tone was firm.

"Mary Kate, since you have already made it clear to me if to no one else that you are not so opposed to our marriage as you have pretended to be and since your father and I have signed all the necessary papers, any continued display of reluctance on your part will serve no purpose other than to distress him. He loves you, you know, and has done only what he believes to be best for your future happiness." Giving her no chance to reply, he went on quickly, "I know you want to tidy yourself, so I will not keep you standing

here. I shall tell Duncan that you will return in
twenty minutes' time, and I trust that you will be
generous enough then to tell him you have accepted
my suit."

Mary Kate opened her mouth to tell him she would
do no such thing, but the look in his eyes and the
implacable set of his jaw dissuaded her. To discover
that border men were brutal to their women, particularly when provoked, would be entirely in keeping
with what she had already learned about them, and
his stern expression reminded her forcibly that he
might yet decide he owed her something for what she
had done to him at Critchfield. That last thought
brought another, that she could place no dependence
upon her father to protect her. Duncan had already
turned her over to Douglas, since he had let her—no,
encouraged her—to ride out alone with the man. As
a result of these hasty reflections, she agreed to
Douglas's suggestion with unaccustomed, albeit reluctant, meekness, and twenty minutes later, much to
her father's vociferous delight, she reentered the parlor, freshly gowned in pale blue wool, her hair
smoothly brushed and confined in a handsome lace
caul.

Douglas remained only a few moments after she
had formally accepted his suit, and Duncan stated
then that he intended to visit some of his tenants to
invite them to the wedding. "For there be little time
tae arrange a proper affair, lass, though ye'll no care
about that. There be neighbor folk aplenty tae see ye
proper wed, and yon Murdochs will come quick
enow. Would ye . . ." He paused to clear his throat.
"That is, shall I be sending for Sarah tae come?"

The hesitant query brought a twinkle to her eyes,
for she knew how much he would dislike having his
elder sister descend upon them. "No, Father. Aunt

Aberfoyle would not wish to make the long journey from Edinburgh with so little time to prepare. Perhaps, however, you will write to her and explain the need for such haste."

"Aye, perhaps," he agreed doubtfully. "But will ye no be wanting a woman tae stand up wi' ye, lassie?"

"Sir Adam has said that although his mother has been ill and will not undertake the journey, his sister, Margaret, may well be allowed to accompany his father. She can serve as my attendant if she will agree to do so."

He nodded. A few moments later, he was happily engaged in making plans when Mary Kate left him to retire to her bedchamber, where she sprawled upon her bed in what Morag would call a most undignified position, to think things out. Before she realized that she was tired, she had fallen asleep, and it was nearly four o'clock when she awoke. Feeling hungry, she wandered down to the kitchen and begged an apple, which she carried out to her favorite nook in the still barren garden.

She had finished the apple and was leaning back against the gnarled old tree that had borne it, thinking that thanks to her long walk she would be stiff on the morrow, when the sharp crack of a snapping twig startled her from her reverie. Peeping around the trunk of her tree, she saw Robin MacLeod striding toward her through the leafless shrubbery.

He was a slim young country lad with tousled brown hair and a long, narrow face, the most prominent feature of which was a pair of widely spaced, serious gray eyes. Of medium height and wiry build, he was only a year older than Mary Kate, and they had been friends since early childhood, when the two of them had spent their time happily tagging after Robin's older brothers and sisters. He came from a large and boisterous family, and Mary Kate had always been as much at home in their cozy cottage as in her own home.

"Och, Robin," she cried, "how you startled me!"

He flung himself down on the grass beside her. "I hoped I'd find ye here. Is your father still peeved wi' us?"

"No, he has other matters on his mind."

"Then we can be friends again," he said with satisfaction. "I dinna suppose we dare go night-fishing again soon, however."

"Oh, Robin, don't even think it."

"Dinna fash yerself, lass. I wasna asking ye tae go."

"No, I know, but everything is upside down. You probably ought not to be here at all."

"What's this, then? Ye've only just said—"

"I am to be married," she said bluntly.

"Married!" He sat up, gaping in disbelief. "But your father said ye was too young. Amang other things, he said that," he added with a grimace.

"I knew he must have been horrid to you after he sent me into the house that night."

"Och, weel, he was that, but it could ha' been a deal worse. He didna say anything tae m' father."

Mary Kate nodded, understanding his relief. "I feared he would say rather too much to him for comfort."

"Aye, but he did tell me ye was too young for marrying."

"Well, he changed his mind," she said grimly. "The wedding is to take place in a fortnight's time."

"A fortnight!"

"Aye, a fortnight. To Sir Adam Douglas of Tornary."

"Sir Adam Douglas!"

"Aye!" she snapped. "Do for goodness' sake, stop

repeating everything I say, Robbie. You'll drive me daft."

But he was following his own train of thought. "Then ye'll be Lady Douglas."

"I suppose I shall," she answered dismally, "but I do not want to be Lady Douglas. Indeed, I hate the notion, for Douglas is a borderer, and I do not wish to marry him, though in his impudence, he chooses to believe otherwise." Her voice began to rise as she recounted her ills. "He's truly the most arrogant, loathsome, dictatorial man I have ever met. He began by insulting me, then he laughed at me, and today he made me walk home from Braelairig in my boots. He's not a proper husband for me at all, Robbie. Like any borderer, he will expect me to curtsy and smile and kiss his feet."

"Kiss his feet! Why would he want ye tae do sae daft a thing as that?"

"Oh, you don't understand. I meant that he has no respect for what I want or what I think. He has not been bred to it, and he seems to have a Calvinist streak in him into the bargain, for he thinks I ought to submit to all his wishes, whatever they are, merely because he is a man and I am a woman. And my father, though usually a sensible man, thinks the sun rises and sets by him just because Douglas is a friend of the king and has lots of money and may be an earl one day."

"But then ye'd be a countess. Would ye no like tae be a rich countess, Mary Kate?"

She gritted her teeth. "You are just like them both. Men are so stupid. I tell you, I don't concern myself with such stuff. I hate him and I must marry him anyway and . . . oh, Robbie, I am so unhappy." The confusion and stress of the past twenty-four hours suddenly overwhelmed her, and to the young man's consternation, Mary Kate burst into tears.

"Dinna greet, lassie," he pleaded awkwardly. "I canna bear it gin ye weep." He knelt beside her and put a clumsy arm around her shoulders, at which encouragement she cast herself upon his thin chest, sobbing gustily. However dumbfounded, Robin kept his head to a sufficient degree to hold her and to make soothing noises in Gaelic, and her sobs finally began to abate. He was no doubt on the brink of congratulating himself for deft management of a distressing situation when a powerful hand clamped down upon his shoulder and thrust him aside to sprawl all aheap on the hard ground.

At the same moment, Mary Kate was jerked rudely to her feet by a grip of iron. When she looked up in dismay to see the furious face of her betrothed looming over her, her tears ceased as though a tap had been turned.

"Sir Adam!"

"Aye, Sir Adam, indeed. And what the devil is this?"

"I was only telling Robbie about our betrothal."

"I see." His expression remained grim, but a glimmer of amusement replaced the cold fury in his eyes. "So you are young MacLeod," he said, adding in Gaelic as fluent as their own that the boy might as well pick himself up off the ground.

Robbie nodded and got to his feet, keeping a wary eye on Douglas while he brushed himself off.

"It was not like you think!" Mary Kate cried indignantly.

"Hold your tongue, lass. We will speak of this later." Ignoring her outrage, he directed his piercing gaze at the hapless Robin. "Do you speak English, lad?" When Robin nodded, he added brusquely in that language, "Then, if you have the details of her betrothal clearly, I'll thank you to keep your hands off her."

"Aye, sir, ye've the right," Robin acknowledged gruffly, "but like she says, 'twas no like ye think. I didna ken what else tae do when the poor lassie begun tae weep."

Douglas chuckled, his customary good humor completely restored. "I believe you, lad. You don't look as though you've had much experience with distraught females." When Robin shook his head, he added in a confiding murmur, "You box their ears."

"Nay!" The boy's eyes rounded in disbelief.

"Aye, you will find that it answers the purpose admirably well. Try it. You'll see."

"I couldna strike Mary Kate."

"Then it is well that you are not going to marry her. She'd rule the roast for certain. You get on home now," he added kindly. "We look to see you and yours at the wedding."

Mary Kate followed Robin's rapid progress through the gray shrubbery, wondering what Douglas would say to her. He had leaped a trifle more quickly to anger just now than he had earlier, she decided. No doubt that was due to the borderer's natural inclination to protect his chattel. She could think of no other reason for the difference, especially since this time his anger had dissipated so quickly. However, she couldn't be certain that it had dissolved altogether, so she decided that it would be foolish to annoy him further by venting the remains of her indignation. When she realized that he still had not said anything, she wiped a lingering dampness from her cheek with the back of her hand and turned to face him.

He was regarding her thoughtfully, as though wondering where to begin.

"It truly was not what you thought," she insisted.

"I know that, lass." His voice was gentle. "But you should have taken him into the house as soon as he arrived. For all you may say, this place is too private."

She hadn't thought about that. She shot him a slanting look from under her lashes. "No one condemned private meetings between us when Robbie and I were eleven and ten. That such meetings must now be considered improper only because eight years have passed seems hardly fair."

He chuckled, as she had intended, and she began to relax. There was one more item, however.

"Will you speak of this incident to my father?"

"Should I not?"

"If you please. If you thought our meeting clandestine—by heaven, what a dreadful word that is! But if you thought it, then so will he, and if he thinks such a thing has happened again, he will speak to Ian MacLeod."

"The lad's father?"

"Aye."

"A harsh man?"

"Fearsome when he's crossed."

"And you feel sympathy for Robin?" When she nodded, he grinned. "Will you sympathize with me if I tell you my father is cut from the same bolt as yon MacLeod?"

"I wouldn't believe you," she retorted flatly.

"Well, he is. Mind you, most people think him no more dangerous than any jovial sporting man, though he was known in his youth to be one of the finest swordsmen to come out of the borders. In a good temper, he is the sort of man who cracks a jest and claps one heartily on the back. But when he is angry, he can still make me tremble in my boots, just as he did when I was twelve years old and had managed to enrage him."

"You tremble? Never."

"Scoff if you must, but bless you, lassie, I was like any other active lad." A reminiscent gleam lit his eyes. "Once I dabbled in just such a relationship as that betwixt you and yon MacLeod, though mayhap not quite so innocent as that. After my father discovered us, I was sore for days."

With a twinkle, Mary Kate said, "I begin to think I will like your father wondrous well, sir."

Douglas laughed. "A fine thing to say!"

"Well, I will like him. And I hope he beat you often."

"Not often, perhaps, but thoroughly. Aye, I thought that would please you. What a little fiend you are. That time I just mentioned it wasn't even my fault. The lady—a young cousin of mine—instigated the whole affair."

"I don't believe you. I know well how you border men take advantage of your women, and you should be ashamed to malign your poor cousin like that."

He grimaced. "Duncan warned me that you'd acquired some highland prejudices, and I'll warrant our first meeting did naught to allay them, but you might at least meet Megan and ask her about it before you say I've maligned her. She was young then, of course, and not yet married. Indeed, 'tis hard now to imagine her up to such mischief, so sweet as she is, but the tale is a true one." When Mary Kate only looked skeptical, he shook his head at her, but he was smiling again when they turned back toward the house.

A brief silence followed. "Adam?"

"Aye?"

"I thought you had gone."

He did not pretend to misunderstand her. "I did, but only to collect my gear and Lucas Trotter, my manservant. Duncan invited me to stay here until the wedding."

"Oh." More silence. "Adam?"

"Aye, lassie."

"You have not said yet about speaking to Father."

"I have no wish to stir coals." He grinned at her sigh of relief, and they entered the house to discover Duncan impatiently awaiting his supper. Conversation over the light meal soon turned to politics and the king, and Duncan asked whether it was true that there had been disturbances throughout the country since the execution of Mary of Scotland.

"True enough," Douglas told him, "though I am told you've seen little of that kind of activity here in the highlands."

"None tae speak about. 'Twas a muckle hard winter, and men have had aught else tae fill their time. In troth, though highlanders fight amongst themselves as oft as not, political strife is niver sae troublesome here as it be in the borders."

Douglas glanced at Mary Kate, but when she merely returned his gaze without comment, he said, " 'Tis true enough to say the borders are rarely peaceful and fair to say they are in a worse state now than usual. The king ordered peace, but so far his edict has had little effect, for Queen Elizabeth has most unfortunately failed to issue a similar edict. One cannot expect our lads to refuse to defend themselves against English raiders. People are angry, and not just with the English but with Jamie. They don't seem to understand how little power he actually had to stop the English from executing his mother."

"And was it sae little then?" Duncan asked.

Mary Kate held her breath.

"If you would believe Elizabeth," Douglas said slowly, "the execution was carried out without her approval. If she could not stop it, what could Jamie possibly have done?"

"Aye," Duncan muttered, "but what fool believes Elizabeth? They say the warrant carried both her signature and her seal."

Douglas smiled. Fortunately neither man was looking at Mary Kate, who could scarcely believe what she was hearing. How, she wondered, could Douglas pretend that the king had had no knowledge of Mary's danger when he must have carried the news to the royal ear himself? She had her mouth open to demand an answer to that question before she realized that she could not do so without betraying herself. Admitting that she had overheard the conversation at Critchfield would do no more than to arouse both Douglas and her father to anger, for she could prove nothing if the borderer denied his part in the business. Having arrived at this depressing conclusion, she could only be grateful when they changed the subject and Douglas began to relate amusing anecdotes of life at court.

The following afternoon a group of his friends arrived unexpectedly and, adhering to highland tradition, carried Douglas and Duncan off to Parish Hill, near the *clachan*, to celebrate the betrothal over mugs of whiskey. When they all returned a little the worse for drink, Mary Kate wisely decided to let them enjoy their supper without her.

Other than that one afternoon and evening, Douglas devoted his time to pleasing her. They rode together often and held long conversations on a wide variety of subjects. She discovered that besides being gifted in the art of telling an amusing tale, he could also be an attentive listener, and the interest he displayed in her thoughts and opinions surprised her, although she suspected that he was only attempting to charm her out of her so-called highland prejudices. No doubt, she told herself, once he had her safely under his thumb in the borders, he would expect her to put her mind to nothing more stimulating than obeying his wishes and running his household. It pleased her immeasurably, therefore, when his discovery of her prowess as a chess player clearly astonished him.

Chess was nearly the only indoor pastime to interest Duncan, so having discovered when Mary Kate was seven that she possessed innate skill at the game, he had taught her the finer points and encouraged her to play. Douglas readily admitted that she was an opponent worthy of his better efforts, and they played often. On one such occasion, a rather dismal and rainy afternoon, she once again nearly betrayed her knowledge of the meeting at Critchfield. They were discussing pawns.

"I used to think them but minor pieces," she said.

"Aye," he agreed. "Most players ignore them. But the end game is nothing without them, so a skillful player protects his. 'Tis much the same in real life. A king needs the support of his subjects, his pawns if you will. In wars they make up his armies. Remember that in Gaelic the pawn is called *fiann*, the soldier. Like soldiers, pawns are expendable in small numbers, but if the king loses them all, he will lose the war. In the more complicated business of statecraft, the same holds true. Look at Jamie now. He scurries from castle to castle trying to avoid public condemnation of his lack of action on Mary's behalf. He is afraid of losing his pawns—their loyalty at least—over the matter of her execution."

"Well, the people are right to be angry." Mary Kate

paused to consider her next move and, in light of
their conversation, decided to remove a pawn from
mortal danger. "She was his own mother, after all."

"Not really a relevant point, since he scarcely
knew her," Douglas observed dryly. "He was but ten
months old the last time he laid eyes upon her. Then,
too, an extra monarch running around Scotland, and
a Catholic monarch at that, might have proved as
much of an embarrassment to the Scottish people as
to their king. No one objected very strenuously to
her long imprisonment, after all. Thank you for moving that pawn, by the by." The bishop that had
threatened her piece now swooped across its erstwhile position to a place behind Douglas's king.
Mary Kate thought she could detect a weakness in his
defenses, however, and with her mind on the board
did not choose her words carefully.

"But the king couldn't have wanted her to be murdered, and he just let it happen. Why, as soon as he
heard—" Good God, she thought, what was she saying? In a flustered attempt to cover the slip, she
pushed her queen forward, attacking the weakness.
"Your king is in check, sir."

He chuckled gleefully. "I was afraid you wouldn't
succumb to that gambit. Guard your own, lass, for
the tables are turned." With that he interposed a
pawn in the space between her queen and his king,
thus opening a threatening pathway from his bishop
to her king. Mary Kate was left with two choices. She
could move her king or interpose her queen. The latter move would sacrifice the queen merely to delay
the inevitable.

"Damn your eyes, sir, I believe I must resign. If
you cannot achieve *mortshainn* within three moves after this villainy, you are not the player I judge you to
be."

"Aye," he agreed, smiling, "and I have always thought the Gaelic term far more colorful than its English counterpart. Your king finds himself not just checkmated but in a 'fatal predicament.' You were too impulsive, lassie. I have noted the tendency a time or two before. You play a remarkably fine game for a woman, but your strategy is instinctive, and you tend to forget while you concentrate upon your devious schemes that your opponent has plans of his own. But don't look so glum. Some of the best players fall victim to that fault from time to time, putting you in excellent company."

"Thank you, but I wanted to win, and it makes me feel stupid not to have guarded my queen more wisely."

"Like Jamie? What did you mean a moment ago when you said he let it happen?" His gaze was singularly penetrating, and she had the feeling, in her guilt, that he would read her mind. He had been gentle and kind for the past few days, and she knew he meant to please her. Still, there had been a time or two—like the previous evening when she had let a hint of sauciness color a reply to her father—when Douglas had surprised her with a reproving glance, reminding her uncomfortably of that overbearing manner she so disliked and, if she had to be honest, even feared a little. All too soon now, he would be responsible, legally, for her behavior, and she had not yet determined how she would manage to hold her own against him. She knew she had been unwise to challenge him so defiantly that day near Braelairig, and she had no wish to arouse his temper now. Nor could she doubt that a confession of her ill-gained knowledge would arouse it.

"Do you not mean to tell me, mistress?"

Her face reddened, but she answered steadily

enough, "I lost the thread of our conversation along
with my queen, sir. I was but trying to remember. I
think only that the king ought to have been able to
intercede to stop the execution. He is the king, after
all, and must have known of the death sentence
against her."

"As to that," he answered quietly, "you are entitled
to your opinion, of course. I can only repeat what I
said at supper the other evening. Jamie did send a
delegation to London, you know, to plead against the
sentence of the commission that tried Mary, but Elizabeth herself disclaims prior knowledge of the execution. She insists that she signed the warrant unwit-
tingly amidst a pile of other papers and that the deed
was done before she could order it stopped. If she
refuses to accept responsibility, how can anyone
blame Jamie?"

"Oh!" She caught her tongue between her teeth
and hoped the exclamation would pass as anything
but the expression of scorn that it was. How could
the man sit there, she asked herself, glibly talking of
knowledge and lack of knowledge as though he were
ignorant of the facts? Delegation indeed. James ought
to have dispatched an army. And he could have raised
one, too, if he had begun the task in October when he
first learned of Mary's danger. She dared a glance at
Douglas. The expression on his face was quizzical,
and she feared he would press her for further explanation. Instead, he changed the subject and began to
help her put the chess pieces away.

Not until later, when she lay in her own bed, did
she realize that Douglas could not accuse her of
knowing more than she ought to know without revealing his own arcane possession of the facts. She
was safe enough unless she betrayed herself com-

pletely, and she hoped she had better sense than to do such a daft thing as that.

The weather improved the next day, and by Friday the first crocus buds appeared in the garden. Douglas's father and sister arrived shortly before noon, having passed the night with the same friends Douglas had visited ten miles to the south. They came with an entourage, for Lord Strachan had brought his own servants, of course, and was accompanied by a number of friends who had traveled with him or joined his party along the way.

Mary Kate nearly laughed aloud when she met his lordship, for he matched his son's description exactly. He was very much the hearty sporting gentleman, and when he greeted them, he actually clapped Sir Adam on the back, causing that impudent young man to cast her a look brimful of merriment. With an effort she controlled her own amusement, allowing Lord Strachan to embrace her in a generous hug. But she did laugh when he remarked that his gay dog of a son sometimes presented the family with the most delightful surprises. In answer to an anxious question from Douglas, he replied that although Lady Strachan had not been thought strong enough yet to undertake the long journey to the highlands, she was nearly recovered from her recent indisposition.

"She sent a message to you, my little beauty," his lordship said to Mary Kate as he searched diligently through capacious pockets in his cloak. "Made her write it down, so I wouldn't forget what she said. I know it's here somewhere."

"I have it, Father," said the dark-haired young woman who had been standing silently behind him. "Only wait, I'll find it." Margaret Douglas jammed her hand into her overstuffed saddlebag, withdrawing it a moment later with the crumpled note. A vivacious young lady, taller and built along more generous lines than her hostess, Margaret had the look of her handsome brother about her, particularly in her hair and eyes. She laughed when she held out the note. "I hope you will not take offense, Mary Kate, but I have read it. 'Tis all polite nonsense, of course, and does not begin to express my lady mother's true feelings."

"Margaret!" two masculine voices protested in chorus.

"Oh, hush, both of you," she retorted with a chuckle. "Mary Kate will hear the whole from Mother herself the minute she meets her. Besides, you have made her think now that Mother does not approve."

Indeed, though Mary Kate had first been astonished to discover that neither Margaret nor Lady Strachan seemed to fit the mold for border women as she knew it, she was thinking precisely what Margaret expected. She said a little shyly, "I hope she does not disapprove."

"Of course not," Margaret said. "She is delighted. She practically cheered when Father read her Adam's letter."

Her brother interrupted this discourse, saying wryly, "Do you think you might fold your tongue behind your teeth long enough to follow the others inside. Mary Kate is shivering with the cold."

Margaret only laughed again, but she allowed herself to be bundled into the house nonetheless. Mary Kate was delighted with her. She had expected Douglas's sister to be a timid creature, especially since she was also the daughter of a man who could supposedly make Sir Adam tremble in his boots. She chose to disbelieve that particular tale, however, for Lord Strachan's gruff kindliness put her too much in mind of Duncan. Though Strachan was a border lord and therefore no doubt possessed many of the same faults as his son, there was nothing the least bit frightening about him.

5

❯❯❯ ❮❮❮

Mary Kate took Margaret upstairs to tidy herself after her journey, and they soon found themselves happily laughing and chatting together. Mistress Douglas confided that she, too, was soon to be wed.

"He is Sir Patrick Ferguson of Craigdarroch, and we have known each other since I was a child. He's older, of course, but I like him well enough, and our families are pleased."

"When do you marry?"

"In late August, I believe. My father means to take me to my aunt and uncle at Ardcarach House in Edinburgh in July, and the rest of the family will join us soon thereafter. You must come, too, of course. But, tell me, Mary Kate," she added abruptly, "do you *really* wish to marry Adam?"

Caught off guard, Mary Kate barely stopped herself from answering with an automatic negative. Though such a reply was clearly ineligible, she did not wish to commit herself with an unqualified affirmative, so she merely smiled in what she hoped was an enigmatic manner.

"Well, I should not wish to be his wife," declared Margaret frankly.

"And a good thing that is, too," Mary Kate told her with a laugh, "but why not?"

"He is too domineering. I am far more comfortable with Patrick, for over the years he has got into the nicest habit of letting me have my own way about things."

Perversely, Mary Kate could not help thinking that being married to a man who always let one have one's own way might become boring. Pushing this disturbing reflection out of her mind, she said, "You do not seem to me to be particularly daunted by your brother."

"Not as a general custom," Margaret agreed, "but I take good care not to anger him, I can tell you, for he inherited his devilish temper from our father. Neither one is easily aroused to anger, thank heaven, but when their tempers are stirred, I prefer to be elsewhere. Both of them have the most annoying notions regarding proper female conduct." Since Mary Kate had no good reason to doubt that statement and every reason to believe it, she held her tongue, allowing her guest to continue. "That," Margaret said, "is why my lady mother sent you that proper little message. She knew Father and Adam would both think it unseemly if she were to set her true feelings to paper. She had nearly despaired of Adam's ever getting married, you know. After all, he will be thirty in just two years."

"Deplorably ancient, in fact."

Margaret grinned. "You take my meaning well enough. Most men marry earlier than that. In any case, my lady mother is well pleased and will be better satisfied yet when she meets you."

Mary Kate replied absently that she looked forward with pleasure to that event. For a brief moment, while Margaret had been describing Sir Patrick Ferguson, she had thought perhaps there were men in the borders who would not expect their women to be always subservient. But Margaret's comments about her mother's hesitation to describe her true feelings put that thought to flight and reaffirmed Mary Kate's earlier convictions. Several moments passed before she was able to return her attention to her companion's cheerful conversation.

With guests to entertain, there was no time for rest before supper, and later that evening there was the highland foot-washing ceremony to be endured, when friends and houseguests gathered to watch the bride and groom wash each other's feet. This was no staid ritual but an uproarious one, filled with revelry and merrymaking, and most of the participants ended the evening in damp clothes. At last, however, Mary Kate could fall into bed with her own thoughts for company. She was not yet reconciled to the notion of marriage to a border knight, but she was beginning to feel a strong yearning to pit her mettle against his. She liked his father, had found a friend in his sister, and looked forward to meeting his mother, whom she was certain to admire. How could one feel otherwise toward a woman who thought, sight unseen, that one was wonderful?

Though she still assumed that Douglas expected to teach her to be properly submissive once they reached the borders, she no longer feared that he might succeed. Indeed, she welcomed the challenge of proving herself a power with whom he must reckon. Perhaps, she thought, as she drifted off, if she were clever enough, Douglas would soon shed the arrogant, domineering manner that surfaced so uncomfortably from time to time, and marriage to him would not be as dreadful as she had feared.

Shortly before sunrise the next day Morag MacBain woke her with a shake. "Coom, lassie," she urged, " 'tis no day for slugabeds. 'Twill be a glorious morn, and ye've flowers tae fetch, so up wi' ye the noo."

Mary Kate stretched languorously, then slipped out of bed, feeling an unexpected surge of exhilaration. Today was the day. She threw on an old brown tamsin gown and, a few minutes later, hurried downstairs and out into the crisp, gray, dew-ridden dawn, a straw basket hung over her arm. By the time she had climbed the steep hill behind Speyside House, the rising sun had begun to shoot fingers of golden light through the branches of the trees and shrubbery and across the new, emerald-green grass on the hillside. She gazed with delight upon a sea of early wildflowers nodding their cheerful heads in the light, chilly breeze wafting up from the river.

It took no time at all to fill her basket with flowers that would be arranged by the maids with dried broom, rosemary, and myrtle for her wreath and her nosegay, and when she returned to her bedchamber, two housemaids were filling the huge canopied tub with steaming, rose-scented hot water for her bath. Half an hour later, glowing and refreshed, she sat wrapped in a voluminous robe, brushing her hair dry before the crackling fire. The maids were gone. Only the housekeeper remained.

Mary Kate looked up at her through a curtain of hair. "Have our guests been aroused, Morag?"

"Aye, lassie. Mistress Douglas was let tae sleep longer than the others but will join ye here tae break her fast." She reached out to feel Mary Kate's hair. "That will be a wee while a-drying. Shall I brush it the noo?" Mary Kate handed her the silver-backed brush and luxuriated in the familiar sensation of the practiced strokes through her hair. When it was nearly dry, Morag announced that she would go downstairs to oversee service of the gentlemen's morning meal.

Before the buxom, gray-haired woman could do more than set down the hairbrush, Mary Kate jumped up from her place by the fire and gathered as much of her as she could hold into a tight hug. "Oh, Morag, you are so dear to me! I shall miss you."

"Och, not ye, lassie." But the hug was returned with interest. "Ye'll be sae thrang wi' yer ain home, ye'll soon forget the auld woman who loves ye like a daughter."

"I won't. You are the only mother I have known, Morag, and if Margaret Douglas had not agreed to stand up with me, I meant to ask you to do so. So there, now."

"Well, I niver heard o' such a thing!" exclaimed the old woman. "And me nobbut yer father's servant. Of all the unseemly notions, I niver heard the like. Nobbut what I'd be right proud, lassie," she added with the hint of a tear in her eye. "Ever sae proud, I'd be."

"No one hereabouts would have thought it improper," Mary Kate told her staunchly. "More likely they would have said I was showing sense for the first time in my life."

"Gae along wi' ye." Morag laid a wrinkled hand upon her hair. " 'Tis dry enow. I best be seeing tae yon porridge. Och, but that'll be Polly the noo, nae doot." She opened the door to a grinning housemaid laden with Mary Kate's breakfast tray.

Moments later the door flew back on its hinges with a bang and Margaret Douglas erupted into the room, a merry laugh upon her rosy lips. "Pray tell me

I have not missed my breakfast!" she exclaimed. "I am pleased that you have the good sense to eat before the wedding, Mary Kate, for you will be too excited afterward. Moreover, I am hungry now. The maid who fetched me said I needn't dress yet, so I've come to you in my night robe."

Morag stared, but Mary Kate waved her exuberant guest to a stool and invited her to examine the tray to see what might catch her fancy. She thought privately that if she had a night robe as magnificent as the one Margaret wore, she would wear it all day, every day, and not merely when she had dispensed with her farthingale.

Made of bright red wool, its bodice embroidered with roses in gold thread, the robe was trimmed with white lace, had sleeves trailing nearly to the floor in the medieval style, and was fastened around Margaret's narrow waist with a long gold cord. Since the garment was designed to be worn in comfort at the end of a day spent in corsets and hoops, it had no framework of its own but clung becomingly to her voluptuous figure. Her cheeks reflected the gown's bright color, her eyes sparkled, and her unbound raven hair fell in loose curls to her hips.

"You look beautiful," Mary Kate told her sincerely.

"Certes, ye cheer a room, Mistress Douglas," Morag said with a wry smile, adding, "I'll just gae doonstairs, lassie, tae see that all's weel wi' the menfolk. I mun make certain o' the food for the feasting, as weel, but I'll return when ye've done tae help ye mak ready."

Mary Kate poured herself a cup of ale, then poured out another for her guest. "Will you take porridge, Margaret?"

"Oh, Mary Kate, do not take ceremony with me.

We are family now, so I shall help myself. Did I hear Adam say last night that you will be leaving today?"

"Aye, after the feasting has well begun."

"What, no proper highland bedding?"

"Margaret!" Mary Kate blushed, but when Margaret only grinned at her and spread marmalade on a scone with lavish abandon, she added, "Adam wants to put as much road behind us as possible before dark. You know he is taking me to Tornary. 'Tis a journey that will take us at least five days, I believe."

"Well, it won't, and I do not believe he ought to deny you the fun of your own wedding festivities. You have never traveled with Adam, but I have, and believe me, though he may say five days, you'll do it in three. It is not as though you will travel with a cavalcade, after all, and the distance is less than a hundred and fifty miles."

"But tomorrow is Sunday, and moreover, that is a great many miles, for my father says the roads are in a dreadful state."

"The roads are dry," Margaret said, twinkling, "and that is all that will matter to my brother, Sunday or no. He says you are an excellent horsewoman, so although you might briefly honor some small kirk along the way with your presence, I'll wager you'll spend your third night at Tornary. You might as well spend tonight right here."

Mary Kate shook her head. Though she did not say so, she was grateful that Douglas's high-handed methods would prove useful for once in that they would spare her the embarrassment of the rowdy highland bedding ceremony with guests standing around the bed drinking to their health and their potential fruitfulness till none was left standing. She was grateful, too, to learn that Douglas would not expect her to spend her future Sundays attending day-long religious services. "Adam has already made the decision to leave as soon as we can manage to do so," she said quietly. "Tell me about Tornary."

"Tornary?" Margaret was instantly diverted, as Mary Kate had hoped she would be. "Hasn't he told you?" When Mary Kate shook her head, she narrowed her eyes thoughtfully. "Men are so stupid. Let me see, I have not been there for a long time. Adam said he brought back a great many furnishings from his trip to the continent last year when he visited France on the king's behalf, but men have no notion of what is suitable, so I put little faith in his assurance that everything is of the finest quality. You will not have rushes underfoot, however, except in the great hall, for he bought beautiful carpets. My lady mother has several of them at Strachan Court. He brought lace from Brussels, too, for my wedding gown, and it is exquisite, so he does have *some* taste."

"Yes, but I want to know what the house looks like, and what the nearest town is, and . . . well, all that sort of thing. The house must be fair-sized if it boasts a great hall."

"House?" Margaret stared at her. "My dear, Tornary is no house. It is a castle. Didn't you know?"

"A castle?"

"Aye, in Teviotdale atop the edge of a steep, bracken-grown slope on the north bank of the river Teviot. The proper name for the original pile, which overlooked a Roman road some five or six miles west of the present location, was *Torr na Righe*, castle of the king, and was no more than a motte and bailey on a hilltop overlooking Borthwick Water in the midst of a forest. Though I am no great hand at history, I do know that Tornary existed in the thirteenth century."

"So old?" Mary Kate was wide-eyed.

"Aye, it was English then, but later the castle was captured by Sir William Douglas, and by the early fifteenth century the property had passed to the Black Douglas earls, who built a courtyard castle where Tornary is now, on the river. The original is naught now but a pile of rubble crowning the hill above Tornary village. The Black Douglases displeased James the Second somehow, and the king himself stabbed the eighth earl, William, in Stirling Castle. Then, he defeated William's brother at the battle of Arkinholm and the Douglas lands were confiscated by the crown. My grandfather retrieved possession of Tornary partly because he was a bitter enemy of his own cousin, the Earl of Angus, whom James the Fifth detested, but even more, it is said, because he shared with the king a passion for bedding simple country girls. My grandfather could not boast, like the king often did, of having fathered eight children by his various mistresses, but I believe there were a number of them. In any event, he was not a man of violence, and whenever the political situation became heated, he very sensibly contracted gout and retired to Tornary. My father is likewise no fiery warrior, so he attracted no attention during the difficulties twenty years ago, and now the castle belongs to Adam." Pausing for breath, Margaret reached for another scone.

"I cannot believe I did not know," Mary Kate murmured.

" 'Tis true, though. You will be a proper chatelaine with keys clinking at your kirtle's belt. I am surprised that Adam said naught of it to you. Father deeded Tornary to him when he came of age, having by then built Strachan Court in Annandale for us instead. I have not been next or nigh Tornary since, but I loved it as a child. We swam in the river, played ghost in the

south tower, and rode our ponies 'round the pasture
betwixt the gatehouse-keep and the outer wall. That
is no more than a six-foot drystone dike now, but the
entry gates are impressive. They stand at the bottom
of the hill, away from the river, half a mile or so from
the castle. Adam loves Tornary," she added, smiling.

Mary Kate suddenly wondered if he had failed to
tell her out of fear that she would scorn his love for
the place. She was silent. For the first time she considered his feelings, how her attitude must be affecting him. If he truly wanted her for his wife, whatever
his reasons, it must be particularly frustrating to him
always to encounter her disfavor. Not that he had
seen much of that during the past week, she reflected.
She had been polite, even cheerful, in his company.
But she had also maintained a distance, mocking him
with her eyes whenever he exerted himself to please
her.

She rallied at the last thought. Had he not confessed that he had wanted her merely to satisfy a
whim? Did he not look upon taming her as a challenge? No matter how charming he could be, no matter how disarming his roguish smile, he was still an
impudent border knave who thought he had only to
crook his finger to bring her to heel like a well-
trained bitch. Let him learn his error. He had certainly never claimed to love her. If he feared her
scorn, so much the better. She let Margaret chatter
on, enthusing over improvements she would make at
Tornary if she were but granted the opportunity.

They were still discussing the castle when Morag
returned. That kindly dame shooed Mistress Douglas
off to her own chamber to dress, promising that if she
were quick in her preparations, she might return to
help put the finishing touches to the bride. With Margaret safely out of the way, she turned her attention

to Mary Kate, working with such efficient speed that that young lady was soon dressed.

Though it was customary for a bride to have a new gown in the first style of elegance, there had been too little time to have one made, so Mary Kate wore her mother's wedding dress, its ivory lace fitting snugly at the waist and then belling out over a cloth-of-silver underdress. Full sleeves trailed lace to her fingertips. Her hair was unbound, and the wreath of wildflowers, woven to a circlet of pearls, lay ready upon a nearby table. Morag twitched a fold of the skirt into place and smoothed away an imaginary wrinkle before stepping back with a melancholy sigh to survey the total effect.

" 'Tis the spit o' yer dear mither ye be, lassie. A pity it is ye've nae memory o' her. Such a fairy creature she were, all light and laughter. But 'tis proud she'd be this day, God rest her soul." Morag brushed a tear from her eye.

"None of that," Mary Kate told her. "I'll have only smiles on my wedding day. This marriage may not be entirely to my liking, but I mean to enjoy my wedding all the same."

"Aye, lassie, 'tis a happy day. Ye mun forgive an auld woman." She hugged Mary Kate again, then said she would see if Sir Adam and the others were ready to depart, adding that she would kindle a wee fire under Mistress Douglas, too. She was gone on the words, returning moments later with Duncan in tow.

He wore no mere plaid but his finest black velvet mantle over an emerald-green-and-black tuft-taffeta doublet and embroidered canions and netherstocks, and he sported a heavy gold chain across his chest in honor of the occasion. He did not wear a sword, however, for not even a Campbell or a MacGregor would dare profane a wedding celebration by starting a fracas. Smiling at his daughter, he took hold of her shoulders and kissed her soundly. Then he stepped back, the better to admire her.

"By my faith, daughter, you've the look of your mother all over again," he said in an unconscious echo of the housekeeper's words. He spoke with great tenderness and then was silent for a long moment. Recollecting himself with visible effort, he reached into a pocket cunningly concealed among the folds of his mantle and extracted a slim carved box, which he held out to her with uncharacteristic diffidence. "These were hers, lass. I've kept them by me for this day of days."

Taking the box, she opened it with trembling fingers. A long strand of shimmering, perfectly matched pearls lay revealed against a soft black velvet cushion. She drew in a deep breath but could find no words to express her emotion. She could not remember her mother, but gazing down at the pearls, she missed her. A girl's mother ought to be with her on her wedding day, she thought. That hers was not seemed suddenly most unfair.

Duncan gently took the pearls from her. "Here, lassie, let me put them on ye."

She held up her hair while he wrapped the string twice round her throat and fastened the gold clasp; then she turned.

"Oh, Father, I cannot . . . I don't—oh, thank you!"

He grinned at the disjointed speech. "Nay, lass, calm yourself. She wanted ye tae have them." He became serious again. "I will miss ye, daughter."

"I, too." Blinking back tears, she cast herself into his arms as love for home and everything familiar washed over her, underscored with fear of the unknown life ahead.

"There, there, lassie," Duncan growled huskily, holding her close. "Ye'll muss your dress gin ye greet so. It will be well. Ye'll see." He paused, holding her away to look anxiously into her eyes. "Ye're no still fashed wi' me, lass, are ye?"

She smiled. "No, sir, it will be well." She owed him that much, and his unmistakable relief touched her. He sighed deeply, clapped her on the shoulder, and called her a good lass.

"Well, this is a touching scene!" exclaimed Margaret from the threshold. She entered, yellow silk skirts arustle over her wide French farthingale, grinning at the pair of them. Then she winked at Morag, who stood forgotten near the bed. "I am certain my own father will send me off into wedded bliss with just such a boisterous farewell." When, with an audible sniff, Mary Kate dabbed her lacy handkerchief at a tear rolling down her cheek, Margaret cried, "What's this, then? Have you been crying, Mary Kate? Not that I wouldn't weep floods of tears if I had to marry Adam, but yours is surely a different case. Wipe your eyes, goose. 'Tis not the end but merely a new beginning. And if the thought of Adam saddens you," she added impishly, "just remember you are also getting a new sister. Me! There, that is much better. I knew I could make you laugh."

Indeed, Mary Kate was chuckling. "How ridiculous you are, Margaret. I shall be glad to have you for my sister."

"And a good thing, since you will be stuck with the kinship. But the parson awaits, not to mention my no doubt impatient brother, so pull on your gloves." She picked up the wreath and, under Morag's supervision, settled it atop Mary Kate's head. No pins could be used to fasten it, for to use them would be to bring bad luck. For the same reason, every garter, shoe-

string, hose-point, or petticoat lace on either the
bride's or groom's person would have to be loosened
before they entered the kirk.

Mary Kate worried about that last custom. There
would be fervent attempts to rob her of her garters,
possibly even before the wedding party left the kirk.
She had twisted extra silver and blue ribbons around
her sleeves in hopes that the rowdier lads would be
satisfied with the substitute, and so long as the word
had not yet spread that she and Douglas meant to
deprive their guests of a bedding, she thought she
would be safe enough. She had heard tales of brides
being stripped naked before the altar by enthusiastic
wedding guests, but surely Parson MacDole, a stern
and dour man, would not allow such goings-on in his
kirk.

She wondered what Douglas would think of the
highland ceremony. No doubt it would be different
from what he expected, for although the Reformed
Church of Scotland had been the official church of
the realm for twenty-seven years, the resistant highlanders held firmly by the traditions of the old faith
while paying no more than lip service to the new.
Still, she thought, if Margaret proved to be right and
her brother did intend to travel on the Sabbath, it
was a good sign that he would not be unduly distressed by any differences.

Her train of thought was interrupted when
Duncan gave her another hug. He went outside a few
moments later to assure himself that the boys who
were to prevent stray dogs from passing between
bride and groom—another harbinger of bad luck—
were ready to attend to their duties, and soon the
pipes began to skirl in the yard. It was time to leave.

Mary Kate hurried down the stairs, stepped into
her pattens and out into the garden. The din of the

pipes was nearly deafening, but the procession formed quickly. First went Duncan with his particular friends and honored guests, including Lord Strachan and his friends. They were followed by the pipers. Next came the young cupbearer with the silver bride cup, decked with blue ribbons and rosemary, followed by little girls strewing dried rose petals, myrtle, and more rosemary.

Mary Kate followed, escorted by four grinning lads who sported silver, blue, and gold bride laces tied with the ubiquitous rosemary about their sleeves. Behind her, led by Margaret, trailed all the unmarried maidens of the district, carrying bride cakes and garlands of gilded wheat, symbols of wealth and fertility.

Friends and neighbors who had not taken part in the procession awaited them at the kirk door, and soon Mary Kate found herself inside, kneeling beside Douglas, listening to the words that would make her his wife. When she stole a glance at him, it was a shock to find him gazing down at her with enough tenderness and warmth in his eyes to make her forget for a moment the emotional distance that she had attempted to erect between them. She bit her lip, unable to look away until a slight change in the parson's voice reminded her of his presence and the brief spell was broken. She faced forward, lifting her chin proudly, forcing herself to listen to the parson's words rather than dwell on the lingering, teasing memory of Douglas's expression.

An hour later, having promised honor, submission, and obedience to him until the Almighty in His wisdom saw fit to part them in death, and having listened to more than she wanted to hear from Parson MacDole regarding the wifely virtues of submission, obedience, and fruitfulness, Mary Kate stepped forth from the kirk a married lady. She was Lady Douglas

and wondered suddenly why she still felt like Mary
Kate MacPherson. All the preaching in the world
about wifely virtues would not change her, she decided, glancing up at Douglas, who grinned at her in
his usual impudent fashion. He would learn.

She had little time to think about such things, however, for after retiring briefly to repair the disorder of
their dress, the bride and groom were enthusiastically escorted by the wedding party in the traditional
walk around the kirk. To ensure good luck and good
fortune, it was necessary to keep the walls always
upon their right hand, not so easy a task as one might
have thought, since a good many of the gentlemen
had been celebrating the nuptial day since breakfast
and, in consequence, experienced more than a little
difficulty with their navigation

Mary Kate was escorted back to Speyside House by
the married gentlemen and accompanied by triumphantly skirling pipes, while Douglas, the ladies, and
all the unmarried men followed after. Altogether,
theirs was a merry company, and during the next two
hours it became merrier still. Just as much drinking
of good Scotch whiskey took place as the eating of
tasty victuals. The bride cakes were ceremoniously
crumbled over the bride's head, and the bridegroom
was toasted until by rights every gentleman present
—including the groom, who punctiliously returned
each toast with one of his own—ought to have collapsed under the tables in a drunken stupor.

The new Lady Douglas had lost all of her ribbons,
but the rest of her costume was still intact when
Douglas gave the prearranged signal for her to retire.
Since no one was expecting her to leave the festivities
so early, the exuberant dancing and general rowdi-
ness covered her exit. Only Margaret, who had also
been watching for Douglas's sign, saw her go. She,

too, slipped away, joining her new sister in Mary Kate's bedchamber.

"Godamercy!" Margaret exclaimed, shutting the door and leaning back against it. "What can Adam be thinking of? There will be a riot when he announces that you are leaving."

Mary Kate grinned, her head disappearing into folds of silver and lace as Morag, who had been awaiting her, pulled the dress off over her head. Shaking herself free, Mary Kate reached for her hairbrush. "Here, Margaret, be useful as well as decorative. You may brush the cake crumbs out of my hair." She sat on a stool and stretched out her legs, flexing her bare toes in front of the crackling fire. Margaret took the hairbrush and obediently began brushing the glowing red-gold curls. The maid Polly entered with mugs of ale and a platter of thick-sliced bread, cold lamb, and cheese.

"I mean what I say, Mary Kate." Margaret absently took a piece of cheese and nibbled at it while she brushed. "Those men below are nearly ape-drunk already, and they expect to take part in a proper bedding. I've heard them talking."

"Pass me some of that bread and meat, if you please. You trouble yourself without cause." Mary Kate bit into the slab of bread and meat and washed it down with a generous swallow of ale before adding, "Adam said he will attend to everything, and don't forget, a good many of those men below are his own, drunk or sober. They may not like his orders, but they will obey him."

Nodding, albeit doubtfully, Margaret observed that she wasn't certain she had the same blind faith in Douglas's ability to control his men as Mary Kate had. "But then," she added with a twinkle, "you have never seen him wrestled to the ground by a mere

stableboy. 'Tis true that Adam was but fifteen at the
time and the stableboy was three or four years older,
but nonetheless, there it is."

Laughing, Mary Kate bestirred herself and soon
changed into her traveling dress. The plain safeguard
and black jerkin that would protect her gown during
the journey and the dark-green-wool hooded cloak
she carried over her arm, seemed plainer than ever by
contrast to her rich bride clothes, and despite what
Douglas had said, she knew she would cause a sensation when she appeared thus attired before the rowdy
wedding party. Drawing a long breath, she turned
toward the door and the stairs beyond.

6

❧❧❧ ❦❦❦

*H*ow he managed it, she would never know, but Douglas had also changed from his bride clothes into more practical gear and awaited her now in the nearly empty hall below. His secretary, Johnny Graham, stood near the outer door, and a smaller, more wiry man stood alert near the door into the noisy front parlor. Mary Kate had seen the latter about the house only a few times, but she recognized him as Lucas Trotter, Douglas's personal servant. Both men appeared to be completely sober.

"Good lass," Douglas said. "The horses are out front. Are you ready to make a dash?"

Mary Kate cast a sudden, panic-stricken look at Morag and Margaret, behind her on the stairs. "Morag?" The old woman hastened down to her and gathered her into her arms. Mary Kate's eyes were swimming when she emerged from the hug. "My father! Where is he?"

"Outside," Douglas replied, his voice curt with impatience. When she looked at him entreatingly, his

expression softened. "He will ride with us, sweetheart, to the edge of his land. You can say a proper
farewell to him then. Johnny?"

Graham looked back over his shoulder through the
partially open doorway. "The men are mounted, sir.
Straight out."

Indignantly, Margaret swept down the stairs to
confront her brother. "Your behavior is barbaric,
Adam. You have no right whatever to steal poor
Mary Kate away from her own wedding feast like
this."

He grinned at her and gave her a quick hug.
"Good-bye, Roaring Meg, me lass. We'll see you in
Edinburgh wi' your namesake if not before."

"Adam, I was not named for a cannon!"

But he only laughed. "I've no time for this pliskie
nonsense, Margaret. Any day now, Jamie is going to
demand my presence at court, and I want to show
Tornary to Mary Kate and Mary Kate to Tornary
before that day. This feast could go on for a week or
more."

"But the bedding! I wanted to see a highland bedding."

"We will manage our own bedding ceremony,
thank you. All this toasting and jeering at the bedside
is a highland ritual I can well do without." Both
Mary Kate and Margaret blushed, and he tweaked
one of his sister's dark curls. "You are too bonny to be
compared to an ancient cannon, lass. Forgive me?"

"Aye." She laughed. "Again!"

A few moments later, Mary Kate was flung onto
her saddle and quickly surrounded by a number of
men on horseback, including Duncan and Lord
Strachan. The merrymakers, alerted finally to the imminent departure of bride and groom, were thus
firmly denied of their prey, but they subsided more

gracefully than either Mary Kate or Margaret had anticipated. There was still, after all, a great deal of food and drink, and the pipers were still going strong.

At last, with little ceremony and many farewells, both merry and ribald, Douglas, his lady, and their escort took their departure. They paused at the Mac-Pherson boundary long enough for Mary Kate to take fond leave of her father and for Duncan to offer her last bits of paternal advice, while Douglas held a brief conversation with Lord Strachan. Then they were off.

Their progress had been carefully prearranged, because as Margaret had foreseen, Douglas wished to make all speed. Thus the horses were put to as swift a pace as the rugged highland roads wending south through the Cairngorm Mountains would allow, and frequent changes were required. Though Mary Kate was indeed an excellent horsewoman, she feared such haste would overtax her endurance. Not only was the pace itself wearing, but the strain of the past fortnight had taken its toll. One chapter of her life had ended, and she felt as though she was riding with breakneck speed into the next. The present was no more to her than a crazy limbo betwixt the two.

Douglas had won yet another round of their conflict. Indeed, she had scarcely put up a struggle, for he had outmaneuvered her from the start, leaving her little choice but to submit to his will. In the future, she hoped she would give a better accounting of herself. The problem wasn't that she disliked him. She was not even certain, despite the many things she had said to the contrary, that she had ever actively disliked him. The fact was that she sensed in him a constant desire to assert his authority over her which stirred her highland blood to rebellion; however, determined though she was to guard her independence of spirit, she realized it would behoove her to tread lightly until such time as she might discover a course of action that had some chance of success.

After the first break in their journey, she paused before remounting to examine the symbol of her defeat, glowing warmly in a shaft of sunlight that lay across her hand. The ring was intricately designed to look as though several golden threads had been woven together to form a circlet.

"Do you like it, sweetheart?"

"Aye," she replied, suddenly shy in the midst of her all-male escort. To provide a female companion for her on such a rapid journey had not been thought possible.

"It suits you." He lifted her effortlessly back into the saddle. " 'Tis your own, too, lass. I chose it myself. There is a great, heavy gold thing, set with pearls, among the family pieces, but I thought it too large for your dainty hands. Besides," he added with a wry grin, "my mother is somewhat partial to it."

She grinned back. "I prefer to have my own, sir."

He nodded, his satisfaction clear, and they were soon off again, riding hard.

Darkness had fallen by the time they reached the manor house at Aberfeldy, where it had been arranged for them to spend the night, and Mary Kate was swaying in the saddle. Their host was away from home, but a stout housekeeper whisked them inside with promises of good food, reviving drink, and soft, dry beds. Lady Douglas wearily disclaimed any interest in food or drink and chose instead to retire immediately. Douglas, with a glance at her pale face and drooping eyelids, forbore to press her and ordered separate bedchambers. Mary Kate never gave a thought to the details of an ordinary wedding night but fell into a sound sleep the moment her head touched the pillow.

The journey to Stirling on the second day passed much like the first, though she ate a hearty breakfast and, once her initial stiffness wore off, seemed to manage the long hours in the saddle with greater ease. There was no pause at any kirk, though Douglas offered prayers for their safe journey before they started, and again, able through efficient planning to change horses frequently, they made good time, particularly since they had now left the rugged Cairngorms behind them.

Twice they avoided larger hamlets when they were out of the highlands, and Mary Kate knew without asking that Douglas had no wish to flaunt the fact that they were breaking the Sabbath. No one challenged them, however, and by nightfall she was exhausted again, barely managing to eat her supper before she fell asleep. Douglas carried her upstairs to her bed and, with a rueful grin, left her to the tender ministrations of a buxom chambermaid.

By morning of the third day, she was herself again and readily agreed to his decision, expressed over a generous matutinal repast, to finish their journey that same day. "It will mean traveling well into the night," he admitted, "but we'll have moonlight, and we should make Moffat before dark. We can hire outriders there."

She had been smiling to herself at the accuracy of Margaret's prediction, but his last words brought a bewildered frown to her face.

"Outriders?"

"Aye. We'll have lost a part of our escort by then, and although border raiders rarely attack private parties by daylight, the dark brings them out, and there'll be a fair border moon tonight to light their way as well as our own." He smiled at her dismay. "Don't fear, lassie. I'll see to it we're safe."

An hour later, Johnny Graham and more than half the men with them veered off at a fork in the road, bound for Edinburgh, where, Douglas informed his wife, Graham would do his best to delay a royal summons. That left Lucas Trotter and six others to travel with Douglas and Mary Kate.

They traveled rapidly again, stopping only to change horses and for brief refreshment as either became necessary. As Douglas had foretold, they reached the sprawling hamlet of Moffat before dark. He was known there and easily arranged for an escort of twenty armed men before suppertime, so they relaxed over their meal at the alehouse. Outside again, as he placed his hands on her waist, intending to toss her into her saddle, Douglas looked down at his bride.

"Tired, sweetheart?"

"I should be, should I not?"

"Aye."

"Well, 'tis odd, I suppose, but I'm not, not a bit."

"Good!" He laughed, his eyes twinkling wickedly, and the warmth of his gaze made her toes curl in her boots. When she blushed, he laughed again, lifting her at last to her horse.

Mary Kate settled herself firmly in the saddle, adjusted the hood of her thick cloak, and fixed her gaze upon a distant hilltop, determined to ignore the nerve-tingling tremors that had begun to stir deep within her.

Douglas swung into his own saddle and signaled his men to move on, but his amusement was nearly palpable. "It won't be long now, sweetling," he murmured, and there was, unmistakably, a deeper meaning to his words than the mere hint of journey's end.

He chuckled again when she made no response other than to lift her chin, but after a long moment when she still did not speak, he mused sadly, "Perhaps the journey will be longer than I thought, especially if my lady wife persists in this alarming silence. A long and dark and dreary journey for a poor, neglected husband. Long and dark and—"

Goaded, she snapped, "You said there will be a moon!"

"Aye, so I did," he agreed amiably, "but it won't simply spring up into the sky, you know. There is bound to be a period of darkness first. Lonely, silent darkness."

She glared at him and then fixed her eyes straight ahead again, determined to ignore him. But after a few moments of this treatment, he said coaxingly, "Am I such a beast, lady wife, that you will not speak to me?" When she remained mute, his voice sharpened. "Come, lass, look at me. This silence pleases me not. I promise no more teasing. Now, come. Speak to me."

This time she did turn, giving him a smile and a slanting look from under her lashes for his efforts. Deep inside, and well hidden, she savored a glow of triumph. He had nearly apologized. A small victory, perhaps, but a victory nonetheless.

"That is much better," he said, pleased. "Tell me more about yourself. We speak too often only of me, and I should like to hear more about when you were small." In this manner he encouraged her to talk, and she was soon comfortable again.

Their escort had split, some ahead, some behind. She could hear jingling equipage and, occasionally, low, murmuring voices. Progress was much slower now, horses first cantering, then slowing to a walk as darkness closed in around them. Douglas matched her tales with new ones of his own, and time passed quickly. It seemed no time at all, in fact, before they were riding between the huge gates that Margaret had described to her.

The moon had risen, but the road beyond was lined with trees, their dark branches intertwined overhead and nubbly with half-grown new leaves. Mary Kate peered ahead, anxious for her first clear glimpse of her new home. The trees parted at last, and she drew in a long, appreciative breath. Crowning the hill ahead, magnificently outlined by moonlight that edged stone towers and crenellated parapets with lustrous silver, stood Tornary Castle.

"Oh, Adam, it's huge."

"Only thirty rooms, sweetheart, and a good many of them naught but storage cells beneath the living spaces. 'Tis not so big for a castle. Do you like it?"

"It is beautiful. Why didn't you tell me?"

"I thought you knew," he answered simply. "I wondered why you didn't ask me to tell you about it."

And believed she didn't care, she thought. "I had no idea until Margaret told me."

"Well, no matter. You may see it all for yourself on the morrow. My father made it over to me nearly eight years ago. It is no fortress, but it will be a fair place to raise a family."

Soon they were passing into the torchlit stable yard. Soft light gleamed from nearly every window facing the yard, and men hurried to see to the horses and baggage. Mary Kate had brought only two leather satchels with her, leaving the rest of her things to follow by freight wagon.

Douglas gave precise instructions to the outriders and to his assorted minions, then turned with a meaningful smile to his bride. "We'll go in by the postern door. You may meet the household properly tomorrow, but tonight we have more important matters to occupy our time."

With a deep blush and a fervent if unspoken wish that he would lower his voice, Mary Kate allowed him to help her dismount. Seconds later she stifled a gasp when he swung her up into his arms but made no other protest as, with long, purposeful strides, he carried her into the castle and up a winding, torchlit stone staircase.

They emerged at last at one end of a wide stone gallery with a waist-high parapet that stretched the full length of the great hall below. Douglas's pace seemed to increase as he carried her along the gallery and through a small anteroom to the left, until he paused in front of a great carved oaken door.

"Welcome, wife." The door stood slightly ajar, and he kicked it wide, setting her on her feet just inside the room.

It was his bedchamber. Light from the hooded fireplace and a single candle in a bowl-shaped silver holder on the table near the bed cast a warm, golden glow over the arras-draped stone walls and the soft blue and yellow Persian carpet. The dominant feature of the room, however, against the wall opposite the fireplace, was the huge carved bed, its indigo velvet hangings looped back with thick, plaited golden cords. Matching curtains hung at the chamber's tall, arched twin windows, between which, upon the floor, against the wall, rested Mary Kate's two leather satchels. The servant who had brought them up so quickly was nowhere to be seen.

She blinked. Never in her life had she seen such a splendid room. The comfortable bedchambers at Speyside House and Critchfield Manor were austere by comparison.

Douglas gave her a gentle nudge. "Get you in, lass. I've no wish to spend the night lingering upon the threshold."

Still dazed, she took a few obedient steps forward.

Douglas lit more candles, then moved toward her, his eyes gleaming with intent. He reached out, pushing the hood of her cloak back from her face. "Ah, but you're a winsome wench," he murmured, "and I have waited so long." He drew her to him and lowered his lips toward hers.

Mary Kate tried to pull away, ducking her head and pushing ineffectively at his broad chest with two trembling, small hands, but he held her easily with one arm, putting his other hand under her chin, gently forcing her head up until he could claim his kiss. It was a long and probing one that sent rivers of flame rushing through her body from her head down to her toes, and long before it was over, she had melted toward him, turning limp and pliable in his arms.

When he released her at last, she stepped back, breathless, putting her hands to her face. He cocked his head, regarding her with amusement. "You cannot deny me now, lassie," he said softly. " 'Tis my right . . . this time."

"Aye, but . . ." She hesitated, then, her voice low, spoke the first words that came to mind. "But I am hungry."

"I, too." The gleam in his eyes deepened as he moved to take her in his arms again.

This time she eluded him. "I want food, Adam. My insides have shrunk away to nothing. Only listen for yourself."

For once he was completely taken aback. "But I've told them to put out the lights. I've sent Trotter and the other servants to bed."

"I want food," she insisted, knowing she was but stalling for time, yet wondering if he would yield to her wishes.

He gave a sigh of resignation. "I'll forage a bit then and see what I can find, but there are two great kitchens in this place so it may take a while." Then he grinned. "You may ready yourself for bed whilst I am away, sweetheart."

She nodded, her face pale, and as soon as the door had shut firmly behind him, she flung open her leather satchels. Hurrying for fear he would return too soon, she snatched off her clothes and threw her thin, cotton night rail over her head, twitching it impatiently into place and lacing the bodice with nervous fingers. She had to search through both satchels before she found her sheepskin mules, but with them on her feet and her hooded cloak wrapped closely around her for added warmth, her courage began to return.

Forcing the tumbled satchels shut again, she picked up the rest of her discarded clothing and laid it carefully over a back stool, then turned to survey the bedchamber more closely. She inspected the intricate tapestries, peeped daringly into a chest or two, and then moved to one of the tall, narrow, leaded windows to gaze out upon the moonlit night. She could see the moon's reflection upon the breeze-rippled waters of the Teviot at the bottom of the hill, and though the river seemed to run silently, rather than with a hearty rushing sound like the Spey, the scene reminded her of home, which at the moment seemed farther away than ever. She started when Douglas kicked at the door.

"Mary Kate, my hands are full!"

She ran to unlatch the door, and he came in grinning and set a jug of ale and a wooden platter piled high with sliced beef, bread, cheese, and fruit upon the low table near the fire.

"Fetch stools, lass. I've found us a feast."

Drawing up two low stools, she watched as he produced a pair of pewter mugs from a pocket of his jerkin and placed them on the table with the flourish of a magician. Then, flinging the jerkin to a nearby chair, he unfastened his doublet and, sending it after the jerkin, sat down opposite her in his shirtsleeves.

"Eat quickly, love. I've a strong appetite for things other than food, and I have not got a patient nature." Tactful for once, he ignored her blushes while he piled food on a trencher of bread for her and filled their mugs with ale. Then, drinking his own thirstily, he refilled it before turning to his food. Silence reigned while they ate.

Mary Kate munched slowly, observing her husband from under lowered eyelids. She found it difficult to digest the fact that she had actually been married to him for three whole days. He would have his way with her at last, and there was no way, barring divine interference, to stop him. With a tiny frown, she thought back once again to their first meeting.

Much had happened since that night. Mary of Scotland was dead, and as far as the Scottish people knew, her son James had done nothing to prevent her death. Knowing of her peril, and knowing, too, that for the Queen of England to try the Queen of Scotland for treason was both ludicrous and illegal, he had done little more than to issue a weak, formal protest after the fact. For him to insist now that he had not thought Elizabeth capable of putting a fellow monarch to death was foolishness. Only too clearly could Mary Kate remember the gravelly voice saying that it was impossible after the discovery of the Babington Plot that both Mary and Elizabeth should continue to live. If the men in Douglas's room that night had understood that much, surely James must have done so, too. Mary Kate wondered, not for the first time, if the king appreciated how avidly Douglas and others had worked to avert Queen Mary's death. Then, as her thoughts drifted idly, she found herself wondering how many other comely females had crossed the Douglas path while he was engaged in that intriguing business. Surely, she had not been the only one.

A low chuckle interrupted her reverie. "I'd give a penny for your thoughts, sweetheart, but I'll warrant I can save my copper."

"Why did you marry me?" she asked abruptly.

His answer was swift, filled with his usual bold impudence. "I doubt not 'twas because you are the most beautiful wench ever to dare deny me access to her charms. Have you finished?" His smile was sweet, but that unnerving gleam lurked in his eyes.

"Insufferable ape!" she snapped. "At least you married me before you tried again."

He stood up. "Temper, lassie, temper. You had too many protectors before, and I decided marriage was not so bad a penalty to pay for such a grand reward." Advancing, he pulled her to her feet, shaking his head in mock reproof. "I told you to uncase yourself. You've far too many clothes on."

She would have given much for the courage to resist him, but she did not dare. To claim her was his right. Standing rigid, she trembled when he opened her cloak and pushed it off her shoulders, letting it fall to the floor, but when he reached for the cotton lacing at her bodice, she stepped back involuntarily and stumbled over the heavy cloak and the low stool behind her. He caught her by both arms and pulled her close to him.

Her heart was beating tumultuously, and she shiv-

ered, scarcely knowing what to expect. Her knowledge of the sexual activities of married persons was
vague at best. She knew they sometimes slept together. She knew also that unwary females could be
ravished by brutal males. But no one had ever explained the details of such ravishment to her. She had
heard talk, of course, but always shaded with innu-
endo, and as a result, her feelings were a mixture of
fear, bewilderment, and an unfamiliar, coursing excitement.

Douglas's voice sounded gently against her ear.
"Easy, lass, I'll not hurt you. I know 'tis your first
time."

She didn't realize that she had been holding her
breath until it came out in a gusting sob, but there
was some small relief in knowing that he understood
her confusion.

He guided her toward the bed. "Come, lassie, trust
me. It will be well, you'll see." He steadied her beside
the huge bed and reached once more for the lacing.
Untying it with practiced fingers, he opened the bodice to reveal her heaving breasts, their smooth, milky
whiteness turned rosy by the candlelight. With
scarcely a pause, he hooked his thumbs under the soft
material at her shoulders and eased the night rail
from her body until, with a faint whisper, the garment slipped to her ankles.

His gaze moved appreciatively over her firm,
smooth body, and he let out a long breath. "Ah, but
you are bonny, lass. More bonny even than I'd imagined." He stroked her breast, smiling tenderly when
she trembled. "I'll teach you, lassie, so many things."
He leaned over the bed to pull back the blankets and
the fine linen sheet. "Climb you in, sweetheart. We
will begin your lessons as soon as I rid myself of these
clothes."

She obeyed, leaning back against silk-covered pillows, still tense but breathing less raggedly until he
began to remove his breeks. Then, turning away in
dismay, she screwed her eyes tight shut and remained
so, concentrating on the light scent of herbs wafting
from the heath padding beneath the feather bed, until
she felt his weight beside her. Hardly daring to
breathe at all, for she realized at once that there was
nothing now between his bare skin and hers, she
slowly, reluctantly opened her eyes when he commanded her to do so.

He had snuffed all but the one candle beside the
bed, and now he gathered her into his arms, holding
her quietly for some moments until her heart had
ceased to pound so thuddingly against her ribs. She
was grateful for his patience until she realized that
such patience no doubt came from vast experience.
Even then, she was glad that he knew more than she
did. She could trust him to initiate her, properly and
without awkwardness, into the mysteries of the marriage bed.

Raising himself onto one elbow, he smoothed her
hair gently away from her forehead, and she was astonished to discover how her body reacted to even
this light touch. She was intensely aware of his presence. He seemed bigger, more masculine, more powerful than ever. He stopped stroking her hair and
gently drew a single fingertip along her left cheek.
The color ebbed and flowed in her face, making it
appear first ghostly, then rosy, in the golden candlelight. He watched her closely, and Mary Kate looked
back at him, her eyes wide and wary.

"Relax, sweetheart," he murmured, and to her
amazement she felt her body relaxing, obeying his
command whether she wished it to do so or not.
Douglas's finger moved along the line of her jaw to

the point of her chin, then gently up to outline her
lips.

Suddenly, she wanted to kiss his finger, but she
resisted the impulse, fearing to break the spell that
she was under. His finger moved back to her chin and
then down the left side of her throat, lingering momentarily where her pulse throbbed. Ever so gently,
he lowered his head and began to kiss her.

At first his kisses were but flickering touches of
warmth upon her lips, but soon they became firmer,
more demanding, and she found herself responding
with a passion that astonished her. Her body had discovered a life of its own, ungoverned by her mind,
and every nerve ending shouted for more stimula-
tion. When, with his lips still in firm possession of
hers, Douglas began to push the sheet and blankets
away from her body, she moaned in brief protest, but
when his teasing finger brushed gently against the tip
of her breast, she gasped at the new sensations that
flashed through her. Her body began to strain toward
his touch, moving sensuously beneath his skillful
hands, and her moans became sobbing cries of pleasure. Hearing herself, she thought briefly that such
behavior must be improper, even wanton. What must
he think of her?

At that moment, he lifted his head, and he was
smiling, his eyes atwinkle in the candlelight. "This is
only the beginning, sweetheart," he said, "but I begin
to believe I have discovered how best to tame you."

She opened her mouth to protest, but the words
died in her throat when his hand moved lightly over
the soft mound of her stomach, then lower, pushing
the blankets further down, caressing her intimately,
possessively. Clearly, protest was useless. He was too
strong, too much in control of her body. She could do
nothing to stop him, so she watched his eyes, fasci-

nated, as Douglas's warm gaze followed the movements of his wandering hand.

The candlelight gave her skin an amber glow and glistened upon titian highlights in the tawny, silken triangle at the fork of her legs. His fingers skimmed over the silk.

She trembled again when she felt a single finger touch midway down the inside of her thigh, then slowly tease its way back up. The action was repeated along the other thigh, and then he began to trace the outer lips of the secret place itself. This firmer touch sent a fiery wave through her, awakening new feelings, introducing her to yet more incredible sensations. She was lost to it all. She had closed her eyes and was mentally submerged in the flood of her awakening sexuality. Her breathing was faster. Her body made more overt gestures of its own, urging him on, and Douglas saw the signs. She knew he did, for when she opened her eyes, he was smiling more broadly than before.

He began to speak in a low, caressing tone as he explained in detail what he meant to do next. His hand continued to move as he spoke, and since her body insisted upon responding to his lightest touch, Mary Kate found it difficult to attend to what he was saying, but she went still with shock when he took her hand and drew it toward himself, explaining that he would soon penetrate her body with his own. She tried to snatch her hand away, but he held it firmly.

"There is naught to fear, sweetling," he said quietly. " 'Tis only flesh."

"You will hurt me," she protested, eyes wider now than ever.

"Not very much, and only for a moment this one time, I promise. Afterward it will be pleasant."

"I daresay you know that for a fact," she replied tartly.

Douglas chuckled and, moments later, had rendered her helpless once more. Still, he did not rush things but continued to build her passions to fever pitch with his kisses and caresses, so that she scarcely realized his intent when he moved at last to possess her.

She cried out at the brief pain, but if what followed was not quite as pleasant as he had promised, there was enough in the wonder of it all to offset the discomfort. The second time he took her was better, and later, as she lay in his arms, drifting languorously into sleep, the thought crossed her mind that there were certain advantages to marriage, advantages of which she had not previously been aware.

7

⋙ *⋘*

*T*he following morning, Mary Kate awoke with a flood of memory from the night before, accompanied by a brief but sharp stab of shame and embarrassment. She was lying on her side, facing away from Douglas, and she couldn't decide whether she dared to turn toward him. His breathing came lightly, evenly, so she knew he still slept, but someone had opened the curtains. It would not be long before he awoke.

Even as she formed the thought, the rhythm of his breathing changed. He stirred. Then he was still. Too still. She knew he was awake. Very conscious of the fact that she was lying naked beside him, she knew also that she would have to turn over, that she could not bear not to see the expression in his eyes.

Accordingly, she moved slowly onto her back, slowly so that if she was mistaken and he still slept, she would not waken him. She turned her head to look at him and felt the warmth rush to her cheeks when her gaze met his twinkling eyes.

"Good morning, sweetheart," he said, grinning. "Did you sleep well?"

"Aye." The word was no more than a whisper.

His eyes were practically overflowing with amusement, but she refused to avoid his gaze, hoping thus to conceal any further discomfiture on her part. It occurred to her that what she really wanted to do was to dive under the covers, never to face him or anyone else again. But then he reached for her, his hand lightly brushing against the curve of her breast, sending tingles of pleasure through her body, and once she was in his arms, all thought of shame vanished and her previous embarrassment was forgotten as she submitted eagerly to his will.

The interlude was a brief one, for Douglas had no intention of spending the day in bed. Nevertheless, when they arose, Mary Kate's body was aglow with the warmth of spent passion and she gave no particular thought to her nudity as she moved to look for her clothes. A simple gown of gray wool with a narrow white lace ruff and matching lace at the cuffs had been pressed for her and lay now across the back of a tall armchair. She assumed that Lucas Trotter had seen to it and sent him a silent thank you.

They dressed quickly, and then Mary Kate followed her husband downstairs to the great hall, a vast and chilly chamber, to break their fast. As soon as they had done so, Douglas introduced her to the household servants. Their number amazed her, but her eyes rounded in further astonishment when he laughingly informed her that she had met only the upper servants.

"You'll come to know them all in time, lass," he said, still chuckling, "but come along now. I've got a wee surprise for you." Drawing her arm through his own, he led her out to the stable yard, where he shouted for Geordie Elliot.

A small, gray-haired man, bowlegged and weathered of face, emerged from the stables leading a sleek dappled mare, which stepped daintily, tossing her silver mane and tail. When he brought her to a standstill before them, Mary Kate turned to her husband, eyes shining.

"Oh, Adam, she is beautiful! What is she called?"

"Sesi," he replied, "though by the look of her, it ought to be Saucy. An appropriate bride gift, I believe."

"She's mine? Truly?"

"Aye, I thought she would stir a few fond memories of our courtship." He grinned, mocking her, and Mary Kate blushed. But she was too pleased with her gift to respond to his teasing with anything but pleasure. Sesi nuzzled her shoulder.

"Is she swift?" she asked Elliot.

"Aye, mistress. Good speed and a bonny temper." He eyed her small figure skeptically, adding on a note of doubt, "Master says ye've a good seat on a horse."

Douglas laughed. "She rides like thistledown on the wind, Geordie. Do you like her, lass?"

"Oh, Adam, how can you ask? May I ride her now?"

"Aye, I'll take you out myself when you've changed. But mind, lass," he added in a sterner tone, "you are not to leave the stable yard without a groom or go beyond the main gate without an armed escort. You mind that, too, Geordie."

The older man nodded in agreement.

"But, Adam, why not? I am not a child, and I have often ridden alone at home."

"This is not Speyside House, lass, nor yet Clan Chattan land, and since the queen's execution, the

borders are more dangerous than ever. The Scots are
bad enough, the English even worse, and wife stealing is a favorite practice for both, despite the fact that
it is a hanging offense. You will obey me in this, Mary
Kate, or you will soon wish that you had."

Fear that he might forbid her riding altogether was
all that kept her from arguing, for she believed that
he exaggerated the danger and was merely taking another opportunity to exert his authority over her. He
couldn't know much about life in the highlands, she
decided, if he thought there was never danger there.
She could take care of herself. But she stifled these
rebellious thoughts and nodded submissively, glad
when Douglas appeared to be satisfied.

They had their ride, escorted by twenty of his men,
and the district certainly seemed peaceful enough.
Mary Kate loved the rolling green, nearly treeless
hills with their vivid splashes of colorful wildflowers.
The people she saw were busy with planting, lamb-
ing, and other spring chores, making it difficult for
her to imagine any of them engaged in either battle
or foray. Surely, she told herself, her husband had
magnified the risks in order to frighten her into obedience.

There were more rides in the days that followed,
and each passed without incident, until even Douglas
could no longer deny the prevailing atmosphere of
peace. No news came to the castle of raiding parties
or other disturbances, for even the English were
quiet for the moment. Like the Scots, they had spring
planting to see to and sheep to be tended. The men
on both sides of the border were too much occupied
to indulge in other, more dangerous activities. Accordingly, the daily escorts were reduced in number
until finally, two weeks after their arrival, Douglas
offered to take his wife alone to old *Torr na Righe*,

pleasing her greatly because she had not yet explored
the village or the ruins of the castle above it and preferred to see both without an armed escort.

On the day chosen for their expedition, Douglas
ordered out the horse cart, a light two-wheeled vehi-
cle with a fur-covered seat and room behind for parcels and supplies. The cart was drawn by a sturdy
border horse, and they rattled along in fine style,
heading west across rolling, barren hills, down into
green and grassy dells, then up a more thickly for-
ested hill and down again into the narrow valley
formed by Borthwick Water as it wended its way to
join the White Esk.

"There is an ancient Roman fort where the waters
meet," Douglas told her once they had rattled across
a plank bridge and turned north onto the well-rutted
Roman road that followed the west bank of
Borthwick Water, "but we won't go so far as that
today. Would you like to take the reins for a while?"

She accepted them with delight, confiding that she
loved to drive. "My father built me a pony cart when
I was twelve. Morag was used to make up baskets of
food whenever anyone was ailing, and I delivered
them in my cart."

He let her drive until they reached the entranc-
ingly picturesque village that squatted upon a narrow, semicircular piece of ground between the
smoothly running water and the foot of the steep hillside rising from its western bank. The roadway, cobbled and narrow, was flanked on one hand by a low
stone parapet overlooking Borthwick Water and on
the other by several cottages, an alehouse, a smithy, a
carter's, and a number of shops, including a drapery
and chandlery.

Taking the reins from her, Douglas drew the horse
to a halt at the near end of the village in front of the

drapery, and once he had helped her descend to the cobbles, they walked to the top of the street and worked their way back toward the cart, visiting each shop in turn. Mary Kate purchased ribbons and a pair of lace mittens before they entered the drapery and she met Michael Scott, who astonished her with the news that he could order fabrics and other materials for her from as far away as London, Paris, or even Venice.

"We don't know how he manages it," Douglas confided when they returned to the cart, "and we don't ask. What with all the sumptuary laws and restrictions, 'tis my belief he traffics with English smugglers." He chuckled at her look of astonishment.

The ruins of *Torr na Righe* topped the hill above the village, and as they wandered up the narrow path to take a closer look, Douglas tried to draw a word picture for her of the once mighty though primitive fortress. Mary Kate, seeing little more than a pile of rubble, privately thought it looked more romantic from the road.

Their return journey was uneventful, and she hoped Douglas would lift his restrictions regarding her own excursions beyond the castle gates, but that hope vanished the following week when he announced that he had received orders at last to rejoin the king in Edinburgh.

"Jamie himself sent for me, or I'd bide here a while longer," he assured her. "I've no wish to leave." He was pulling on a pair of leather riding breeks as he spoke, and he missed her expression of disappointment.

Mary Kate was surprised by her own emotions. She didn't want him to go. Of course, she told herself, it was only that she was new to the castle and its people and might be lonely. Otherwise, she certainly wouldn't miss him.

Lucas Trotter handed him his rawhide boots, and he began to drag them on, saying, "I'll stay at my house in the Canongate, lass. Send word there if you have need of me."

"Take me with you." The words were out before she knew she was going to utter them, and he shot her an amused, speculative look from under his heavy brows.

"What's this? Never confess you will miss me." When she wrinkled her nose at him, he shook his head, that mocking gleam still lighting his eyes. "Not this time, lassie. I will have to make speed, and I have no knowledge yet of what's been happening whilst I've been away or what the king's plans are, or even if he means for me to remain any time in town. There's an earldom awaiting me if naught occurs to fling me out of royal favor, because Jamie wants powerful men whom he can trust here in the borders. How would you like to be a countess?"

"Wouldn't I still be Lady Douglas all the same?"

"Nay, that you would not. The Douglas earldom was forfeited by my ancestor, James, the ninth earl, better known as the Black Douglas. Our family was then the most powerful in Scotland, far more powerful than the crown in many ways and therefore too powerful for our own good. After the forfeiture, another branch, the Red Douglas, gained power, but their prestige is on the wane now, thanks to Morton."

Mary Kate nodded wisely. She knew that the treacherous James Douglas, fourth Earl of Morton and the last of several regents suffered by the young king, had been executed some years before for contriving the murder of the king's father, Lord Darnley. "But is not the Earl of Angus also a Douglas?"

she asked, remembering what little Margaret had told
her of the Douglas family history.

"Aye, sweet Archibald." Douglas grinned at her
look of puzzlement. "Ours is a complicated clan,
sweetheart. Angus is a Douglas, sure enough, but he
is also Morton's nephew, which is a strong point
against him. And although he contrived to retain
power for some time by making himself useful to Jamie in London," he added confidingly, "I fear that he
has recently fallen a wee bit out of favor."

"He was the king's emissary to Queen Elizabeth
before Queen Mary was murdered, was he not?"

"He was, and a rare muck he made of that business,
too. Jamie believes Angus ought first of all to have
been able to stop them from trying a Scottish queen
for treason against England, and secondly he thinks
Angus ought to have supplied him with better, speed-
ier information. Here, Trotter," he called over his
shoulder, "take this gear down to the yard."

Mary Kate bit her tongue, thankful for the brief
respite while his attention was diverted. Knowing as
she did that King James must have had all the information he required in October and that he had done
nothing about it, she thought it hard on Archibald
Douglas to be out of favor for such reasons. Although
she could not question the matter without risking
Douglas's asking a few embarrassing questions of his
own, she could certainly admit to confusion. "Since
Angus is an earl already, why cannot the king make
you the Earl of Douglas?"

" 'Tis a political matter," he said. "Jamie has no
particular reason to trust any but a very few amongst
his nobles, and right now he needs men he can trust
in positions of influence. Without his own standing
army to command, he cannot afford to grant anyone
sufficient power to challenge him in the field. His

liking for me is personal," he went on, "having naught to do with clan or politics. My lady mother is cousin to the Countess of Mar, that cold-hearted bitch who was Jamie's foster-mother, so we knew each other as children. He looked up to me because I was older and because I was kind to him, but though I have been fortunate enough to serve him in several ways before now, I doubt that our friendship is strong enough to tempt him to restore the Douglas title with all its attendant property and power. He would not wish to face the inevitable violent objections from other members of my own clan, for one thing. If he grants me an earldom, it would most likely be that of this county. Teviotdale is crown land now, although it used to be a small portion of the Black Douglas holdings, and, too, it is ideally situated for the purpose of increasing support for himself in the borders." He grinned. "Angus will be livid if I'm belted at all, because he's no wish to see our branch of the clan attain power again. 'Tis bad enough from his point of view that my father is a baron. He'd be apoplectic if Jamie granted me the Douglas earldom."

"But if Angus is out of favor—"

"Only for the moment. He's a canny one, is Angus, and he'll come about. I must get my business settled before he does." He flung his cloak over his shoulder with one hand and drew her close with the other. "I will miss you, lassie. I'll not be gone above a fortnight if I can help it, but mind you be a faithful wench." He kissed her soundly, thus neatly stifling her indignant protests.

When she could speak again, she lifted her brows and asked, "And what about you, sir? Will you be faithful to me?"

"Aye, Mary Kate," he replied with rueful amusement. "I'd be afraid to come home otherwise."

"Well, you may always return to your own hearth, I suppose," she muttered, her fingertips just touching his cloak.

He kissed her again, roughly, and moved toward the door. Before he reached it, however, he turned back with a frown. "One thing more, lass. You'll mind what I said before about not riding out alone. I will speak to Elliot, so you've only to tell him when you wish to ride and he'll provide an escort."

"Oh, Adam, in a whole fortnight there has not been so much as a lamb stolen. You said yourself that things are quiet."

He was implacable. "Mind me, Mary Kate. I'd not be pleased to hear you'd contradicted my orders." Since the idea that she could countermand an order of his giving had not entered her head, it took her a moment to adjust to the notion, and his eyes twinkled in response to the changing expressions on her face. "Nay, lassie," he said gently when she looked directly at him again, "you could not do it. Geordie knows better. And mind you play him no tricks, or I'll be forced to warm that pretty backside of yours when I return."

She glared at him then, but when he only returned look for look, she realized that the time was not right for battle. Sighing in resignation, she said, "Very well, sir, you have my word. But only whilst you are in Edinburgh."

Chuckling, he moved to hug her again. "Good enough. I know you've got better sense than to defy me when I'm here." With that, he kissed her again and was gone.

From a nearby window she watched him mount a big black gelding and take his place at the head of his men, and something acutely like pride stirred in her breast at seeing him so. Then he turned in his saddle and waved. How impudent, she thought, just to assume that she would be watching, but she watched until the last man had ridden out of sight.

Determined not to miss him, Mary Kate tried to keep busy. The rest of her belongings arrived two days later, accompanied by a groom leading Valiant and bearing messages from home. She read Duncan's scrawled note quickly, blinking away tears of homesickness, and then proceeded to bestow her things.

She had rooms of her own adjoining her husband's, and her first project was to put them in order. One was a bedchamber nearly as luxurious as his, and the other a small corner sitting room overlooking both the Teviot and the courtyard. She moved an armchair near the arched window looking onto the courtyard, placed her workbox beside it, and the sitting room quickly became a favorite retreat.

Several days were spent exploring the castle from cellars to turrets. She discovered that the second kitchen Douglas had mentioned, in the west tower, provided for the needs of the servants, while the first, in the basement beneath the primary rooms, provided for the family. Mary Kate looked into every garret bedchamber and examined each of the principal rooms carefully, finding more to admire with every step she took.

Standing at the top of the main staircase, with its flying arch, its paneled stone ceiling, and the wide stone steps that swept from the great hall up to the stone gallery, made her feel like a grand lady, while she found a childish delight in the festive murals depicting scenes from Scottish history that decked the outside timber gallery at the top of a wide, projecting, turnpike stair that led from the courtyard into the west wing.

Her inspection of the linen press and pantries

showed that Mrs. Jardine, Douglas's housekeeper, was adept at her duties, so Mary Kate gladly left the woman to her own devices, giving only cursory looks at menus and laundry lists when they were presented to her. She was not expected to deal with the household accounts, that being the business of Douglas's secretary when he was at home and his bailiff when he was not. And just as well, too, she told herself wryly, for although, thanks to Parson MacDole, she could read and write and do simple sums, long columns of numbers left her dizzy.

Learning from the housekeeper that Douglas took all his meals in the large and drafty hall, she decided to appropriate a room nearer the kitchens for use as a dining parlor similar to the one at Speyside House. The chamber she had in mind was currently used for storage purposes and was rather barren, but she enlisted Mrs. Jardine's aid and advice, and the two of them ransacked other little-used rooms for window hangings, carpets, and tapestries. Mary Kate ordered a small trestle table moved in. Two small, carved-back stools would provide seating, while a side table would be utilized as a dresser from which food could be served. Next, she began work on embroidered cushions to make the stools more comfortable, and when the room was completed, she expressed her satisfaction to the housekeeper.

"Aye, m'lady," replied that genial dame, " 'twas a fine notion, that. Ye'll ha' the morning sun, and the vittles will come warmer tae the table."

Occasionally she rode Sesi, but it irked her to be burdened with outriders, and though she wouldn't admit it even to herself, she missed her husband's companionship. Indeed, if the truth were told, she missed Douglas a good deal, especially at night. That she had responded so quickly and with such passionate abandon to his lovemaking still astounded her, but her early shyness and embarrassment had passed away altogether, and she had rapidly come to enjoy their sexual encounters as much as he had promised she would. That he was often as peremptory in other matters as she had expected him to be could not be denied, but she recognized his expertise in bed and reveled in it. Being able to sleep with her window open during his absence was no compensation at all.

The fortnight lengthened into three weeks, and still Douglas did not return. Likewise, he sent no message to explain the delay, so it was not long before Mary Kate's fertile imagination began to provide her with assorted visions of how he might be occupying his time, the least of which was that he might be involved in more secret meetings. The cushions for the dining room were long finished, and she had no desire to begin a new project. Her temper grew daily more uncertain as loneliness and boredom threatened to overwhelm her. She began to snap at the servants, and finally Mrs. Jardine, in a fit of compassion, suggested that she might like to add some of the MacPhersons' favorite recipes to the Douglas collection.

The notion appealed to her, for thanks to Morag she knew a good many MacPherson recipes by heart. Proceeding at once to the large pantry near the family kitchen, she soon found the great recipe book left by Lady Strachan for use by the castle's future generations. Mary Kate was amused to discover that mixed in with recipes for fruitcakes and white puddings were others for perfumes and restorative nostrums. Immediately following one for roast goose with herb stuffing was another marked "Particularly Fine Horse Liniment." Laughing, she turned to a blank page and reached for the quill and bottle of ink that

stood ready nearby. The book would provide prime
entertainment for another day.

Sometime later, while she painstakingly printed
out the recipe for Morag's lamb stew, she thought she
heard a cry from the kitchens. Laying her quill aside,
she listened carefully. The second cry was much
louder, nearly a scream. Her curiosity aroused, for
she was certain they had been cries of pain, she arose
from her chair and hurried to investigate.

As she approached the family kitchen, there were
further screams, agonized now, accompanied by the
sound of strident scolding. Pushing the door open,
she was greeted by the mixed aroma of curing hams
and roasting meats, and the sight of her cook, a stout
and querulous dame, standing near the enormous
canopied fireplace, gripping a young kitchenmaid by
the hair while she belabored the girl's back and shoulders with a yard-long wooden stirring spoon. A
crockery platter lay smashed upon the stone floor
with bits of meat and vegetables strewn among the
shards. Mary Kate took in the scene at one glance and
stepped forward unhesitatingly to interfere.

"Here, stop that at once!" she commanded.

The cook, visibly astonished to see her mistress in
the kitchens, dropped the wooden spoon with a clatter and released the sobbing maid. However, when
the girl cowered away from her and began with trembling fingers to clear the mess from the floor, Cook
quickly regained her composure. Drawing herself up
majestically, she folded plump hands across her
rounded stomach and declared, " 'Tisna your affair
tae mix wi', mistress. This whiskin' wagtail's ruint
your dinner and smashed a valuable platter besides. A
swingeing's nae more than what she deserves."

Angered by the impertinence, Mary Kate snapped,

"You forget yourself, dame. Hold your tongue." Stepping forward, she touched the weeping maid on the shoulder. "Come you now with me, lass. Your duties here are done for the day."

"What's this, then?" demanded the cook in high dudgeon, fists upon her ample hips. "The parlous callet's no done her work. There be more vegetables tae cut and yon pots tae scrub. She isna going nowhere!"

"By heaven's grace, do you dare to defy me?" Mary Kate's eyes flashed. "I will thank you to remember who is mistress here, Cook. There are other maids aplenty, or you may do the work yourself, but let me have no more of your insolence or the master shall be the next to hear of it."

"Aye, gin he returns," retorted the cook, uncowed. Tilting her head back and looking down her nose, she added with a contemptuous air, "Mayhap ye've a fancy tae comport yourself wi' laced mutton, which is nae concern o' mine, tae be sure, but by rights yon malkin should be standing barefoot at the kirk door and not running free in m' master's house." Pointedly turning her back upon her bewildered but nonetheless furious mistress, Cook shrieked for another maidservant to clear away the mess.

With a silent vow that Douglas would hear about the cook's behavior at the first opportunity, Mary Kate urged her sobbing charge through the great door, shut it firmly behind her, and turned the maid to face her. "There, there," she soothed when the sobs continued, "you must not allow her to upset you so. Especially in your condition," she added, taking in the girl's ballooning figure. "What is your name?"

Controlling her sobs with visible effort, the maid replied, "Susan Kennedy, gin it please ye, mistress."

"Kennedy," Mary Kate mused, frowning as she

mentally reviewed the menservants she had met. "I
remember no Kennedys, Susan. Does your husband
not work here, too?"

Susan regarded her feet. "I—I havna wed, mistress," she mumbled, her face suddenly scarlet.

"Not married? Then who—?" The imploring look
in the vivid blue eyes suddenly upraised to her own
robbed Mary Kate of the rest of her question as understanding swept over her in a wave of shock. She
drew a deep breath to steady her agitation and said
carefully through gritted teeth, "Never mind, Susan,
I can guess who the father of the child must be."

Mary Kate's cheeks were burning with rage and
mortification, and experiencing a sudden, strong urge
to move, she signed to the wary maid to follow and
led the way rapidly upstairs to her sitting room.
Scarcely giving Susan time to whisk her skirts
through the door, she slammed it and turned on her,
eyes blazing, only to check her wrath instantly at the
sight and sound of the maid's heaving breasts and
gasping sobs. Susan's lips were white, and she looked
as though she would swoon at any moment. Hurriedly, Mary Kate placed a strong arm about her
waist and supported her to the chair by the window.
"Sit here and calm yourself. I shan't murder you,
whatever I may look like."

Still breathing heavily, Susan subsided gratefully
into the chair but kept her eyes lowered. "Thank 'e,
mistress. I didna think tae come over sae weak."

"Not to be wondered at, I am sure. How old are
you?"

"G-going on for seventeen." She looked up then,
her eyes damp and dark with fear. "Please, ye'll no be
sending me home, mistress. There's many agrees wi'
Cook that I mun be punished by the kirk, and me

father would . . . he would . . ." She lapsed into hiccoughing whimpers.

Mary Kate was still struggling with the shock of her discovery, but she responded automatically to the note of anguish. "No one will send you away. I know well enough 'twas none of your doing. My husband is a difficult man to resist—impossible, no doubt, for one in your position. How long before your time?"

"A month, maybe two." Susan stared at her with wide eyes. "B-being from the highlands, as ye are, I didna think ye would understand, mistress."

"Well, I do, and you don't belong at any kirk door or in the kitchens with that horrid termagant. I think it will be best for you to care for my rooms instead. Would you like that?"

Susan gaped. "Aye, mistress." She blinked back new tears. "But the master—"

"A pox on the master. Dry your eyes and tell Mrs. Jardine that I have assigned you to new duties. She can tell the cook. Then you must rest. I doubt I will have more need of you today."

Susan rose heavily from the chair and managed an awkward curtsy, still eyeing her mistress warily. "I thank 'e kindly, mistress. Ye'll no be sorry. Please, dinna be angry wi' me. Had he been married then—"

"I know." Mary Kate sighed wearily, wondering if the mere fact of Douglas's marriage would have any effect upon such habits. "I am not angry, Susan. Not with you."

After the maid had gone, however, she snatched up a fur-covered cushion and flung it across the room. "Curse him! He deserves to be flayed!" Pacing back and forth, she kicked at furniture and ground her teeth. Was this sort of thing, she asked herself fiercely, not precisely what she had expected of him?

Did it not prove she had been right about the borderers' attitude toward women? Well, Douglas would
soon learn his error. She would teach him, at the very
least, to cultivate a proper respect for her anger.

Half an hour later, when a housemaid entered to
announce that her dinner was ready, she waved her
away, disclaiming all interest in food. Then she
thought about the cook's probable reaction to the
news that her ladyship wanted no dinner, and an unexpected chuckle bubbled to the surface as she realized how lucky it was for Susan Kennedy that she
was safely out of Cook's reach. Mary Kate's laughter
ceased abruptly, however, when the sound of shouting and hoofbeats from the stable yard penetrated to
her sitting room. Delight vying with wrath in her
breast, she jumped from her chair to look out the
window. The first person she beheld was Douglas
himself.

He flung himself from his horse and greeted those
members of the household who ran out to meet him.
His men were dismounting, laughing and shouting to
their friends, and she heard Douglas call out for food
and drink. When Geordie Elliot emerged from the
stable to take charge of the grooms, his master
clapped him on the shoulder. They spoke briefly before Douglas turned abruptly toward the postern
door.

Waiting no longer, Mary Kate flew to her mirror to
smooth her hair and straighten her gown. When the
sitting-room door was thrust open, she was seated,
demurely plying her needle.

Grinning, still booted and spurred, Douglas strode
swiftly across the floor. "Here, wife," he bellowed,
"what manner of greeting is this for a poor, tired
husband who has been long from his home fires?"

"Aye, too long," she replied steadily as he pulled her to her feet and enfolded her in a crushing hug.

Startled by her tone, he held her away again. "Art angry with me, lassie? I have been to Jedburgh and back on the king's business. Jamie craves a meeting with the border lords in early September. Aye, and you'll be a countess by then, or as near as makes no difference." She remained silent, and his next words were coaxing. "I've brought you a present, honey lass."

She did look up then, and he presented her with a dainty gold watch on a chain. Though it was a magnificent gift, she thanked him coolly, but when he had fastened its delicate chain around her neck, she could not resist picking the little watch up again off her breast and flicking open its elaborately filigreed case to examine the tiny hands and numerals. Looking back at Douglas, she found it difficult to remain angry with him. He was in high spirits, he was pleased with his gift, and he was home. However, the discovery of Susan Kennedy was too recent and too painful to be ignored. Her voice remained chilly. "I do thank you, sir. I have never had a watch before. I suppose I must congratulate you, too, upon a successful journey."

His eyes narrowed. "You *are* angry, Mary Kate. What is it?" When, after a long moment, she still had not replied, he said gently, "I am sorry, sweetheart. Have you been so lonely?"

Needing time to think before confronting him with his misdeed, she grasped at the straw. "You know I can read, sir. You might have written."

"Aye," he agreed, "I should have done. There just never seemed to be time, what with dancing attendance on Jamie one moment and flitting hither and yon the next. But I ought to have known you'd be lonely, cooped up here as you were. Geordie tells me you've scarcely ridden outside the gates at all."

"I do not like being followed everywhere I go by a host of armed guards."

"Well, I'll make it up to you then. Would you like to ride with me this afternoon?"

She nearly refused out of pique before an idea came to her, flashing into her mind so brilliantly as to be almost blinding. She knew at once how she could punish him, and the justice of it nearly made her smile. Instead, she looked up innocently through her lashes at him and said, "Aye, sir. I fear you must think you have returned to a shrew. Perhaps I do need a diversion. May we go into the village again? I-I need to purchase some embroidery silks," she invented swiftly.

His relief evident, Douglas agreed readily. "Valiant will be glad of the exercise. Geordie tells me he's been moping."

Her face fell. She had not considered Valiant; the stallion was too well trained by half for her purpose. She thought quickly. "Could we not take the horse cart, Adam, like we did before?"

Laughing, he admitted that sitting in the cart might be a relief after nearly two weeks in the saddle. "And is that all?"

"Oh yes . . . that is . . ."

"Well?"

"No escort?" Eyeing him beseechingly, she held her breath.

When Douglas threw back his head and laughed loud and long, Mary Kate regarded him with no little trepidation, fearing he had somehow managed to read her thoughts. But at last he said, "Oh, lassie, you *have* been cross. Not accustomed to having your movements curtailed, are you?" When she shook her head with a smile—had he but known it, one of profound relief—he said, "Ah, sweetheart, I know my absence must have been difficult for you, but Geordie says you have been very good, so today we'll do as you wish. But first I must eat. Come dine with me."

Mary Kate agreed at once, and when they went downstairs, she led the way to the new dining parlor, where places had already been set for their meal.

"What's this?" he demanded.

She explained, and he was as pleased as she had hoped he would be, saying that wives were undeniably useful creatures. He was spared an acid retort only by the prompt entrance of a maidservant with their dinner, which turned Mary Kate's thoughts once more, inevitably, to the cook. She decided the cittern-headed old trot would suppose her day had been turned upside down and inside out by now. Hiding a smile, she wished she could tell Douglas what she was thinking, for she knew the joke would tickle his ready sense of humor. But in order to tell him, she would have to betray her awareness of Susan Kennedy's condition, and she had no wish to do that just yet.

She realized, as she watched him devouring his food with gusto, that she was glad to have him home. He had done only what men did, after all. Perhaps, now that she thought about it, he had not done anything so dreadful. But no, she told herself, the incident was a clear example of the sort of thing she meant to put an end to, and when she thought of Susan again, resentment welled up within her. The seduction itself was perhaps a moot point, considering border tradition, Douglas's masculinity, and the fact that he had been unmarried at the time, but for him to flaunt the results of that seduction under her very eyes was unforgivable. She must and would punish him for that, and in a most satisfactory way, one that would see her revenged upon him in more ways than one.

8

Douglas was ready to leave as soon as he'd finished his meal, saying he didn't wish to chance being on the road after dark. He had sent word to the stables, so the cart was ready, and they were soon off. While he drove, he regaled her with gossip from Edinburgh, mentioning that he had seen his sister Margaret there and had paid his respects to Lady Aberfoyle.

"I even met his lordship. No one ever mentioned his existence before. I had thought your aunt must be a widow."

"Oh, no," she said, laughing, "but Uncle William is never much thought of, I fear. Even Father is surprised to see him when he accompanies Aunt on her visits. She rules the roast, I promise you."

"I don't doubt that. She scared me silly. Don't giggle. She's a tartar, a truly redoubtable old woman."

"Good God, sir, don't let Aunt hear you call her 'old.' 'Redoubtable' she would appreciate, but never 'old.' Did she like you?"

"I believe so." He grinned. "She scolded me fiercely for our hasty wedding. Said Duncan must have mismanaged everything in the worst way. But when I pointed out that a court wedding was out of the question at the moment, she pounced on what she calls Jamie's 'false mourning.' By the time she had finished reviling him, she was applauding my good judgment in having avoided his presence at our wedding."

Mary Kate chuckled. "My, you did get on well with her."

"Well, I think so." He told her more about his journey, and she noted quickly that he told her little of substance about what he had done, only bits and pieces about people he had seen, hardships he had endured, and anecdotes he had heard; so it was easy to let him ramble on, answering only when necessary, while she savored her own plans.

Some time later her attention was caught again when he mentioned his sister. "Margaret is to be married the end of next month, you know," he said. "The timing is excellent, since the meeting of the border lords takes place about ten days afterward. We'll go to Edinburgh well before the wedding, of course. I thought you might like to spend a month or two there."

"Oh, Adam," she exclaimed, "to think that I was disappointed at not being able to spend a month in the city with Aunt Aberfoyle! It will be much more fun with you. Shall we go to parties, and shall I meet the king?"

"Easy, lass." He grinned at her delight. "My plans are not yet settled. First you must meet my lady mother, and she will not wish to wait until Margaret's wedding day for that."

"Then your mother is well enough now to travel?"

"Aye. She is still too weak, Margaret says, to manage all the planning, but Margaret is now with my aunt and uncle from Braelairig and will be married from Ardcarach House. All my mother need do is to enjoy the company. But she wants to meet you at once."

"Then we must go to Strachan Court. When?"

"Well, today is Tuesday." He calculated swiftly. "How does a week from today suit you?"

"Perfectly." She was silent again, her mind on the promised visits. "I like Margaret," she said a few moments later.

"I, too."

"Do you think she will be happy with a man like Sir Patrick? Though she said he's border-bred, he sounds something of a weak old meacock to me."

"The devil he is!" he exclaimed. "Where the deuce did you get the damned-fool notion that Patrick is either weak or effeminate?"

"Well," she said, "Margaret told me that he is much older than she is and that he always lets her have her own way, so he must be a weaker man than most."

"Patrick Ferguson is only a year older than I am," Douglas declared indignantly. "We were at university together in Edinburgh. And as for 'weak,' I'd say he is mild of manner, perhaps, but he manages Margaret well enough."

"But if she always has her own way—"

"Nonsense. I have seen him bring her out of her altitudes with a quirk of his eyebrow. He is not temperamental, but he does know his own mind. I think you will like him."

"Oh." Privately she retained her doubts, thinking that Douglas was merely defending an old friend. Perhaps she would like Sir Patrick, but she couldn't imagine Margaret's exuberant spirits being quelled by any man's eyebrow.

Sight of the village ahead reminded her of the purpose of their outing. Soon Douglas would be brought to realize at last that his own wife was not to be so easily managed. He would learn that it behooved him neither to dictate to her nor to flaunt his cast-off women beneath her nose. Thoughts of Strachan Court and Edinburgh retreated, and she fairly quivered with the anticipation of sweet revenge.

They left the cart near the draper's again and wandered from shop to shop. Mary Kate purchased some hairpins and various other unnecessary items before they returned to visit with Michael Scott and his wife, Sybil, a buxom, fair-haired young woman with bright blue eyes and a dusting of freckles across her nose. Mary Kate, remembering her expressed need for embroidery silks, asked Sybil to help her make a selection.

"Since we are here," Douglas said, smiling, "why do you not have a look at some fabrics as well. You will be wanting a new gown for the wedding." He turned to Scott. "Have you something suitable for my lady?"

Michael Scott shook his head. "Not in the shop, sir, but there be a shipment coming, end o' the week." He smiled at Mary Kate. "What stirs your fancy, m'lady?"

She turned to her husband. "The wedding is to be very grand, is it not?"

"Aye, in the Abbey Kirk at Holyrood," he replied, "since Jamie himself has agreed to honor the occasion and since the Calvinists object to the use of the Chapel Royal."

Sybil Scott, who had been eyeing Mary Kate thoughtfully, said, "Green would suit ye doon tae the ground, m'lady. I expect our Michael could acquire some lovely Venetian silk."

Mary Kate glanced at Douglas. "Could we, sir? And perhaps cloth of silver for the bodice and over-skirt?"

He shook his head. "Not silver cloth—not at Holyrood. Dress restrictions are still enforced in the city, lass, and even an earl's wife does better these days not to appear in public in gold or silver cloth. A lot of the common folk will gather to see everyone emerge after the ceremony, and Jamie's got troubles enough without your adding to them."

"But I wore silver cloth for our wedding."

"In the highlands," he reminded her, "and it was your mother's gown, not a new one. To flaunt such stuff in Edinburgh where the Calvinists hold sway would be most unwise."

Her face fell. "What then? Must I wear wool to my chin?"

Sybil chuckled and began to wrap the silks they had selected in brown paper. " 'Twould be a shame tae case sae bonny a lady in wool, sir. Lace would be a better choice, I'm thinking. Top-o'-the-milk-cream color over that green silk would be right fetching. Wi' a lovely high ruff tae frame her bonny face. D'ye sew, m'lady?"

Mary Kate hesitated. "I suppose I sew well enough, but I have no hand for cutting or patterning," she admitted, accepting her parcel from the cheerful young woman.

"Never mind the pattern," Michael Scott put in with a smile. "Sybil has pictures of the new French and English fashions. You just choose what you will, and she can help wi' the rest if you like, or per-haps . . ." He glanced at Douglas. "What about El-speth Kennedy, sir? She was used to sew for your lady mother, and I'm told she likes to keep her hand in."

Mary Kate drew a quick breath at hearing the name Kennedy, but Douglas didn't notice. He was frowning thoughtfully.

" 'Tis a good notion," he said. "I've small opinion of Kennedy. He's a harsh man and uses his wife and daughters ill. But I like Elspeth, and she can use the gelt. We'll speak to her."

Lost in her own thoughts, Mary Kate heard no more of their conversation. No doubt, she decided, Elspeth Kennedy was Susan's mother, but how like Douglas to make such a decision without so much as consulting her wishes. It was no more than what one might expect.

Her resolve strengthened by the exchange, she readily agreed when Douglas said they must leave. They left the draper's with Michael Scott's assurance that he would send a message to the castle when the fabrics arrived. Mary Kate waited until Douglas had turned the cart toward home. Then, with a hasty shuffle through her packages, she flung up a hand in dismay.

"Oh, Adam, I've left a parcel. 'Tis the hairpins. I must have left them on the counter in the chandlery, for I remember setting them down to look at those queer rose-shaped candles. 'Tis a small brown packet. Will you be so very kind as to fetch it for me, please?"

He gave her a look of husbandly reproach, because the candlemaker's shop was at the far end of the village. It was not, however, far enough away to be worth the trouble of twice more turning the cart in the narrow roadway, so he obligingly handed her the reins and jumped down to do her bidding.

Mary Kate watched him go with smiling satisfaction, grateful for the nearly empty road. Except for an ancient crone walking with her market basket and a middle-aged shopkeeper taking his ease on his front stoop, there was no one in sight. She was certain Douglas would have sent a boy to run the errand had he but seen one.

He disappeared into the candlemaker's, and Mary Kate watched over her shoulder, nerves atingle, until he reappeared on the threshold with her parcel. Then she slapped the reins sharply and, as the startled horse began to lurch forward, shouted back at the top of her voice, "Enjoy your walk, Douglas, and give a thought to Susan when next you speak of Kennedys!" She caught a fleeting glimpse of astounded fury before her attention was demanded by her horse's rapidly increasing gait.

Filled with exhilaration by the success of her plan, she set a wicked pace, bouncing and jolting nearly all the way to the castle. The poor horse was blowing hard when she drove up the last hill and into the yard, his condition causing her to give brief thanks for the fact that Geordie Elliot was nowhere in sight. Flinging her reins to a skinny, red-headed, wide-eyed groom, she ordered him to have someone carry her parcels inside, then hurried up the spiral stairway to her sitting room, pausing only long enough to send a gillie to fetch Susan Kennedy. After all, she decided, her triumph ought to be shared, and who better to share it than Susan? Had she not suffered, too? For Douglas to have left the poor young woman to face his wife alone was but another example of his heedless arrogance.

When Susan presented herself some few moments later, Mary Kate was hugging herself with delight. "Oh, Susan, you'll never guess what I've gone and done!"

Susan looked rested and responded with a smile. "What then, mistress? Ye do look right pleased."

"I am." Mary Kate's eyes sparkled. "I have paid him back for the both of us. I left him to walk all the way home from Tornary village."

Susan gasped. "Ye've done what, mistress?"

"There, I knew I'd surprise you." She executed a skipping dance step. " 'Tis the perfect punishment, for he left me to walk home once, and the distance was nearly as far."

"Ye came away home wi'oot the master?" Susan's mouth fell open with shock when she finally took in the full meaning of her mistress's words.

"Aye, I did." Mary Kate hugged herself again with glee. "I will teach him to have a care for my wrath. We had the cart, and I just drove off and left him standing like a market cross in the roadway. Oh, the look on his face! I do wish you had seen him."

"But, m'lady—mistress, please listen—he will be fit to spit fire! Oh, mistress, 'tis small wonder he didn't catch ye up on the road." The maid shook her head, muttering, "He'll be ripe for murder, he will."

"But how should he have caught me, afoot as he was?" Mary Kate demanded, ignoring Susan's final comment for the simple reason that she had not heard it.

"Och, mistress, there be horses aplenty in the village, and he be the master. He could ha' taken any one o' them."

"I didn't think of that," Mary Kate admitted slowly. "I wonder why he didn't catch me, then."

Face to face with Susan's alarm, she began to recognize the enormity of what she had done. Once the idea for revenge had come to her, she had acted with her usual impulsiveness and without considering all the possible ramifications. She had known Douglas would be angry, but she had thought he would see humor and a certain ironic justice in what she had done. Now she wasn't at all sure of that. At least, she reassured herself, she hadn't lied to him. She had left a parcel in the shop, purposely, of course, but she had left it. And, although he had warned her against lying, he had never said anything about leaving him stranded. No sooner had that thought crossed her mind, however, than it was followed by the uncomfortable memory of what he *had* said about airing her grievances in public. She tried to convince herself that the village roadway hadn't been all that public, but . . .

"You think he will be really angry, don't you, Susan?" Triumph had evaporated. Her voice was small.

"Aye, mistress."

"What will he do?" She didn't wait for the answer she saw forming itself on Susan's lips. "Never mind. 'Tis enough that I have put him in a rage. He may decide not to let me go to Edinburgh for his sister's wedding next month, or he may punish me more severely." She swallowed hard. "He may even b-beat me."

Douglas had threatened her often enough, she remembered belatedly. Her face paled when she recalled not only his comments to Duncan about her petticoats but also the suggestive flick of his riding whip against his leg, the day he left her to walk home, when he had warned her not to put him to the trouble of fetching her.

Susan was nodding slowly. "Aye, he may be angry enough," she agreed. "But perhaps he will not."

"He will. Oh, I know he will!" Mary Kate tried to stifle rising panic in order to think clearly, but memory intruded, memory of the casual threat Douglas had made before leaving for Edinburgh when he had

warned her against attempting to countermand his
orders. His tone at the time had been light, but it
occurred to her now that she had not doubted his
sincerity. "He will if I am here. I must get away.
Quickly, Susan, run to the stables, or send a gillie—
you will be too slow. Order them to saddle Sesi at
once, and you'd better say I want a groom for just a
very short ride, or Elliot won't allow it. Quickly,
now, haste!"

Susan looked doubtful but dared not question her
mistress. She hurried out, and Mary Kate swiftly
changed to riding dress. When Susan reappeared moments later, her mistress had already begun to pack a
change of clothes into a straw basket, stuffing the articles in any which way in her haste. The maid helped
fasten the lid, and Mary Kate snatched up the basket.
Then, hurrying to the door, she spoke over her shoulder.

"He'll look for you, Susan. I shouted your name at
him."

Susan shook her head with a wry smile. "Nay, mistress, he'll think only of you once the lads below tell
him that ye've gone. He'd not harm me, any gate, out
o' fear o' doing an injury tae the bairn."

"Oh, I wish I were pregnant!" Mary Kate exclaimed with deep feeling. But she knew Susan was
right. He'd not bother with a maidservant once he
discovered his wife had fled the castle. He would be
hot on her trail. She had no time to lose. Spurred on
by the thought, she flew down the stairs to the yard,
where she was relieved to see the thin, red-headed
young groom leading Sesi and a bronze gelding from
the stables. Geordie Elliot was still nowhere to be
seen. The groom took the basket from her, regarding
it curiously as he strapped it securely to his saddle.

"Where be we headed, mistress?"

The query caught her by surprise. Where would she go? The most she could hope for was to find a haven until her husband's initial fury had burned itself out. The highlands beckoned, but she knew she couldn't reach Speyside House before Douglas caught her. Besides, Duncan had warned her not to run to him. Darkness would fall soon. She wouldn't heed that, but . . . She remembered Critchfield Manor, her aunt and uncle's house south of Edinburgh on the Jedburgh Road.

Mary Kate knew, for Douglas himself had told her, that she could ride directly east from Tornary to Jedburgh by following the road along the Teviot. Surely, from Jedburgh, it would be simple enough to ride north until she found the track leading to her uncle's house, and since Douglas would expect her to go directly north toward the highlands, she might thus elude him. But she could reveal none of these thoughts to the waiting groom.

Thinking quickly, she said in a vague tone, "Wildflowers, we'll ride just a short distance to gather wildflowers. What is your name, lad?"

"Gideon, mistress," he said as he helped her to mount.

"Well, Gideon, see if your horse is fast enough to catch me." With that, she dug her spurs into Sesi's flank and was away before the startled groom had gathered his wits to follow. Keeping the mare at a dangerous headlong gallop down the hill, Mary Kate did not slow until she had passed through the entry gates. Then she checked the mare only to look back and see that Gideon had followed, for she had no wish to make her journey without escort or change of clothing.

He was there, the basket banging against the gelding's flank as he urged his mount to the same fast

pace in an effort to overtake her. She did not allow
him to do so, however, until she had covered the two
miles to the ford where the river road crossed from
the north bank to the south. Noting then that the
road did not continue right along the riverbank but
led down into a grassy dale and then up a long hill,
she realized with a sinking feeling that it would be
some time before they would be out of sight of the
crossing.

"Mistress, wait!" Gideon shouted. When, impatiently, she slowed Sesi to a walk and let him draw
alongside, he said breathlessly, "This be more than a
short distance, m'lady. Do the master know where we
be a-going?"

Mary Kate resorted to a display of temper. "Of
course he knows, hodpoll. Come on, we must make
speed."

Greatly daring, he protested again. "We'll no get
far at this wicked pace, mistress."

In answer, Mary Kate spurred Sesi on again, forcing him to follow. She knew her sharp response had
probably done nothing to alleviate any fear Gideon
might have had of Douglas's wrath, but she knew,
too, that the lad would not desert her. Although he
must suspect by now that she was running away,
there was no way by which he could compel her to
return to the castle, and whatever happened, it would
go far worse for him later if he were to abandon her
now on the open road.

They had traveled a mile from the river crossing
and were approaching the crest of the hill at a brisk
trot when Mary Kate looked back over her shoulder
and uttered a cry of dismay. Even at the distance yet
between them, she had no difficulty recognizing either the huge chestnut stallion in full career behind
her or his lashing, spurring rider.

At her cry, Gideon had also glanced back, and now he shot her a look of troubled reproach, but she forced herself to ignore him and leaned into the mare's silver mane, urging her to a gallop. When next she looked back, she noted that the hapless groom had reined in at the side of the road and that Valiant, put to his most fiery pace, had already passed him and was steadily closing the distance. Appalled, she spurred desperately and used her whip, but Sesi was tired. It was no use. First the thunder of hoofbeats behind her became almost deafening. Then, just as she glimpsed the foam-flecked head of the stallion beside her, a large, leather-gloved hand shot out to seize the mare's bridle and the two horses were wrenched to a plunging halt.

Determined that he should mistake her fear for dignity, Mary Kate sat stiffly, looking straight ahead as she willed her trembling to cease and waited for Douglas to speak. When he said nothing, she dared a glance at his face, but what she saw was not encouraging, for his mouth was a hard slit and his eyes were ablaze with fury.

He spoke not one word, did not even look at her, but turned both horses and, his grip still tight on Sesi's bridle, guided her back down the road toward the waiting groom and the fast-approaching escort.

Pausing in front of the wretched Gideon, Douglas said crisply, "Go to Elliot directly upon our return, lad. He will wish to speak with you." Gideon nodded, his thin face pale, his eyes downcast.

Once Douglas had led Sesi past the other men, all of whom kept their expressions carefully blank and their eyes fixed upon the road ahead, he released the mare's bridle.

Squaring her shoulders, Mary Kate gathered her courage to speak. "Please, Adam . . ." She had to pause to clear her throat, for it felt as though she had swallowed all the dust of the road. "Please do not punish Gideon. None of this was his fault."

"I know whose fault it was," he answered curtly, still without looking at her. "Elliot may flay him with his tongue, but *Gideon* will not be flogged."

The emphasis in his statement sent icy fingers of fear racing up and down her spine, causing her muscles to contract sharply in anticipation of his intent. She squirmed uncomfortably on her saddle, and since she still found it hard to swallow, let alone to speak, the rest of the ride was accomplished in silence.

When they reached the stable yard, Douglas dismounted and lifted her from the mare's back. Her knees were weak enough to make her grateful when he retained his powerful grip on her arm; however, she had time to do no more than to note the gaping stares of the men in the yard before he propelled her relentlessly through the postern door, up the winding stair, along the gallery, and through the anteroom to her bedchamber. Flicking the latch, he kicked the door open and, thrusting her inside, slammed it shut again behind him.

"Now," he snapped, releasing her at last, "if there is an explanation for this idiocy, madam, I should like very much to hear it."

Her own temper roused by such rough treatment, she rounded on him. "How dare you! How dare you humiliate me in front of those men! And how dare you flaunt your . . . your . . ." She faltered, confused, because she couldn't think what to call Susan, whom she liked. "Your Susan Kennedys," she finished lamely.

"What affair of yours is Susan Kennedy?" he demanded.

"Oh, if that isn't just like you or any other man,"

she retorted scornfully. "Trying to make me wear the guilt for a sin you committed."

She would have gone on, but he interrupted, saying icily, "That will do, Mary Kate. We are discussing your conduct, not mine, and things that occurred before our marriage do not concern you in the least. I am still waiting for an explanation, if there is one, for your witless escapade today." Thumbs hooked in his wide belt, lips compressed, eyes narrowed, he glared down at her, clearly not willing to wait long.

She opened her mouth once or twice, but no words would come. Her flash of temper was over, leaving only fear of what he meant to do to her in its wake. His capabilities were still unknown to her, and while he towered above her, filling her mind with his size and his fury, thoughts tumbled over one another in her head without organization or logic—senseless, useless thoughts.

Douglas was impatient. "Have you naught to say in your own defense?"

She clenched her hands against her skirt, struggling for composure, for something sensible, even cutting, to say to him, holding back tears of frustration with a mighty effort.

"Well, madam?"

"I was so angry," she said at last, "and then so . . . so—" She broke off, not wishing to admit her fear to him. But when he still said nothing, she muttered, "I suppose I was a little frightened." When his only response was to frown more heavily, she added in a rush, "In truth, sir, I panicked, though I know I was foolish to do so." She stepped back. "Please, Adam—"

"God's blood," he swore. " 'Please, Adam,' will avail you naught. Did I not warn you? Did I not forbid you to indulge that highland temper of yours before the public eye? Did I not?"

She nodded, feeling small.

"In front of the whole village, madam! Aye," he insisted uncompromisingly when she looked up in protest. "Your insolent taunt brought every man, woman, and child within hearing out into the road. Had you but turned again, you might have appreciated your audience. They reveled in your daring." He was shouting at her now. "The tale will have spread through Teviotdale by now and will no doubt be entertaining all Edinburgh by morning!"

"Oh, no," she moaned wretchedly.

"Oh, yes!" he snapped, his voice still loud enough, she was sure, to be heard in the stable yard. " 'Tis a fine way for my wife to behave. I'd not be surprised if Jamie himself greets me with sympathy or—may heaven help you—with laughter. But you couldn't content yourself with that alone. Nay, you compounded your insolence by leaving the safety of this castle, attended only by a mindless, unarmed flunky, in direct defiance of my orders, to take a road leading into the wildest, most danger-ridden border country imaginable." He stood there, his feet planted wide, his thumbs still in his belt, leaning forward belligerently now and again as though to punctuate his words. His voice hardened ominously when he said, "Madam, your folly astounds me. Where in the name of Christ Almighty did you propose to spend the night?"

"I don't know where!" she retorted, her temper flashing anew in response to his relentless chiding. But when he took a step toward her, she recognized her error immediately, and hoping to mitigate his increasing wrath, she said quickly and with as much dignity as she could muster, "Adam, I'm sorry. I know what I did was foolish. I just didn't think."

She wished he wouldn't glower at her so fiercely,

for her leg bones felt as though they were turning to porridge. She wished, too, that she could maintain her spurious dignity, but the more certain she became that any attempt to defend her actions must prove futile, the more she felt a need to defend herself. "Truly, Adam," she said, speaking even more rapidly than before, "I wanted only to pay you back for leaving me alone so long, for not having had sufficient regard for my feelings to warn me about Susan before I discovered her for myself, and . . . and for making me walk home that time." She spread her hands. "I just didn't think, sir, about the rest."

Douglas sighed. "I know that, lass." His voice was quieter, more controlled, and she felt a brief surge of hope. "If that damned horse I took from the smithy hadn't gone lame, I'd have caught you on the road, but I snatched the first mount I saw, and when Hamilton, the smith, shouted at me, I paid him no heed. No doubt he tried to tell me the stupid nag had a loose shoe, for he threw one near the MacKenzie croft. They keep no horses, so I walked for half an hour before I found another, and a scrofulous nag it was. I had plenty of time to think, lass, and I thought about all those things. I ought to have told you about Susan, but I hadn't seen her and never gave her a thought. I couldn't send her away. She's carrying my bairn." He paused. "Had you been here when I got back, I might have bellowed at you or shaken you senseless for subjecting me to that scene in the village. I doubt I'd have done more."

He paused again, taking a deep breath as though to draw strength, his attitude one of reluctant determination. When he spoke again, his voice was stern. "Running away like you did was more than foolish, Mary Kate. Gideon was not armed, and nightfall was less than an hour away. 'Tis nearly dark now. You admit that you were frightened, and perhaps you had cause to be, but you'd have had greater cause had a raiding party found you before I did. You might have been killed. My orders are never given without reason, lass, and conditions being what they are in the borders just now, I cannot afford to tolerate your defiance. You need a sharp lesson for this day's work." He began to unfasten his belt.

Mary Kate backed away. "Wh-what are you going to do?"

"You know very well what I have to do," he retorted. "God knows I don't like it, but your own father would do the same. I know of no other way to be certain not only that you comprehend the gravity of your offense but that you will not dare to repeat it. Come here."

Mary Kate backed away another step, placing her hands protectively behind her and speaking quickly. "You are right, Adam, I didn't understand before. However, I do now, so—"

"Come here to me," he ordered inflexibly. "The sooner we begin, the sooner it will be done."

She shook her head stubbornly, though she knew there was no way to avoid what was coming. He was her husband, and here in his own home there was no higher authority to whom she might appeal. Had her own father been present, he could not have stopped him. Not, she thought bitterly, that Duncan would have tried. Douglas was right about that. Her father would say she was merely coming by her just deserts if only in that she ought to have guarded her temper and not let it carry her behavior beyond what Douglas would tolerate. But inevitable or not, she could not submit herself meekly to Douglas's discipline. She stayed where she was.

"Very well," he said grimly, starting toward her,

"but you will wish you had made this easier on yourself."

Mary Kate backed away hastily, putting out a hand in a brief defensive gesture only to jerk it back again when she came up sharply against the wall. There was nowhere else to go. Closing her eyes, she straightened and waited for Douglas's hand to descend like an avenging Fury upon her shoulder.

Standing there, she looked small, defenseless, and delicate, and as Douglas reached for her, he hesitated, for once uncertain both of himself and of his duty. No sound could be heard in the room except for their breathing, his even and controlled, hers ragged. A muscle twitched in his jaw when at last he squared his shoulders and grasped her left arm, pulling her toward him. Then, as he raised the heavy belt, an expression of distaste, even repugnance, flickered across his face. With a growl, he flung the belt aside.

Mary Kate opened her eyes with a sigh, but her relief was premature, for before she realized what he was doing, he had sat down on the nearest stool and she found herself draped helplessly across his knee, her skirts flung over her head, muffling the sound of the hard smacks that followed. He did not spare her, and the mortifying punishment seemed to go on forever, but at last he stopped, resting his big hand upon her bare bottom for a long moment. When she wriggled indignantly, instead of removing his hand, he began to stroke her gently but firmly enough to keep her where she was.

She stiffened, furious, swallowing her sobs and wishing she dared speak so that she might demand to know if he thought he would cool the flames or rub away the redness by stroking her, or if he was merely bent upon extracting the full measure of her punishment by continuing to humiliate her. But she knew she would not be able to talk without sobbing, and she would not give him the satisfaction of knowing he had hurt her, for she was determined to retain the last shreds of her dignity. When she squirmed again, he set her back upon her feet.

Yanking her skirts into place, she glared at him. Although the burning sensation in her bottom was rapidly receding, the humiliation she felt was worse than anything she had ever felt after one of Duncan's energetic thrashings, and she knew her cheeks must be as red as her bottom for they were certainly as hot. The awareness of what she must look like stirred her volatile temper yet again.

"You'll pay for this, Douglas," she muttered, unconsciously rubbing her backside. "I am a married lady, not a child, and though I have angered you by acting hastily and without thought, you might at least have made an attempt to understand that I have not been bred to the sort of blind submission you borderers expect from your wives."

Amusement had glinted deep in his eyes with her first sentence and the gesture that had accompanied it, but that amusement faded as she went on, and when she stopped to draw breath, his expression was unreadable. His tone was flat when he said, "You think that I have acted hastily, that I have treated you like a child?"

"Aye." Her glare challenged him to contradict her.

"Damn it, wench," he growled then, getting to his feet, "you don't know when to leave well enough alone."

She couldn't decide this time whether his anger was directed at her or at himself, but she had little time to consider the matter before he scooped her up into his arms and carried her to the bed, ignoring her sharp exclamation of dismay.

Silently Douglas laid her down and methodically stripped her of her clothing. Anger still glittered in his eyes, and when she moved to touch him, he stopped her, telling her curtly to lie still.

Wide-eyed, she obeyed him. By speaking to him as she had, she had meant only to show him that he had not cowed her completely, but there had been an exhilarating sense of power the moment she saw the fury leap again to his eyes, when she had realized how easily she could stir his temper. Just before he scooped her up it occurred to her to wonder if perhaps she had unleashed more anger than she could handle, and for a moment she feared that she would end up across his knee again, even that he might decide to use his belt, after all.

Removing his clothing, Douglas sat beside her, and his fingers began to trace patterns on her skin, teasing and stroking her breasts, her stomach, her inner thighs, even her most secret places, inflaming her whole body. In her relief, she yielded willingly to the glorious sensations he was creating within her, forgetting for the moment her outrage and the ache in her backside. She decided that somehow she had stirred his passions, and she began to look to the moments ahead with pleasurable anticipation, telling herself that if this was punishment, it possessed merits one had never before imagined. Several times she reached out to him, but each time he stopped her, and before long his lips and tongue began to explore where his fingers had gone before, until she was moaning, then crying out for release.

But Douglas refused to grant her that release. Instead, once he knew he had achieved his purpose, he took her, expeditiously and much too swiftly to satisfy her urgent needs. Then he dressed himself while she lay watching him with frustrated bewilderment in her eyes.

"That, madam," he said, looking grimly down at her, "is a punishment reserved only to adults. Is it more to your liking?" Without waiting for her reply, he left the room, shutting the door behind him.

Mary Kate stared at the closed door, her breasts heaving with pent-up passion rapidly turning to fury. "Knave," she muttered, dashing tears of humiliation from her eyes with the back of her hand, "How dare he use me so!" He had, she decided, proved himself once more to be a selfish, unfeeling monster who gave heed to no one save himself. To be sure, she had disobeyed him, but had she not had excellent cause to do so? Had it truly been so remarkable for her to be upset by the sight of his erstwhile mistress trotting about full-blown with his child?

That she had run from him instead of remaining to confront him with his perfidy was, she had to admit, somewhat lowering to her dignity, but had his subsequent behavior not proved that she had had good reason to try to protect herself? Forsooth, he was a villain, and she had been right to behave as she had. She would never speak to him again. He had used her abominably. She sat up, and pillows, cushions, and other loose articles began to fly about the room as she gave free rein to her temper.

At last, worn out, she got up and bolted her door and the door from the gallery into her sitting room. Then, pouring water from her ewer into the basin, she splashed her face in an attempt to calm her reeling emotions before curling up on the bed again under her blankets to consider and reject a number of plans for bringing Douglas to his knees. None appeared to be feasible.

Clearly he intended to show her that he was the

master at Tornary, and for the moment she could think of no good way to teach him the error of his ways. But somehow, she told herself, she would make him acknowledge her as a power with whom he must reckon. She was no feeble border wife, but a true highlander, and the sooner Douglas learned as much, the better it would be for both of them.

In a more orderly world, she reflected drowsily, women would be treated better as a matter of course. None would be subject first to her father's whims and then to her husband's, and even a border wife would have the right to say and do what she pleased in her own home without fear of punishment. She would be the equal of her man, not merely his chattel, and she would have no reason to submit to his demands against her will. She would have to answer only to her God, her king, and herself. It would be a perfect world; and gold, she told herself with a sigh, would no doubt grow on trees before such a world would ever come to be. Until that day, she knew she would have to keep her wits about her if she was to hold her own against the borderer. On that thought, she settled more firmly against her pillows and drifted into restless slumber.

9

⟫⟫⟫ ⟪⟪⟪

*W*hen Mary Kate awoke the following morning, sunlight was streaming through the windows, and at first she assumed that one of the maidservants had opened the curtains. Then she remembered bolting the doors and realized that her curtains had never been drawn the previous night. No one had come into her room. Her temper flared again. Clearly Douglas did not care enough about her welfare to come and see how she did. No doubt he was out and about, enjoying the fine spring morning. Not that she wanted to see him, of course, or would heed him if he demanded entrance. But he did not. The only person to tap at her door was a maidservant with her breakfast tray.

Mary Kate's first inclination was to refuse to let her in. She wanted to see no one. However, before she spoke the words that would have sent the maid away, she realized she was famished. Believing it advisable to keep up her strength, she admitted the girl and fell to her meal with good appetite. Then she dressed and went to the chair by the window in her sitting room to give deeper consideration to this business of marriage. Punishments suffered at her father's hand had rarely caused her much pain or brought more than a momentary afterthought, but her confrontation with Douglas had been another matter altogether. She needed time to think before she faced him again.

By midafternoon he still had made no attempt to speak with her. There was little activity in the yard below her window, nothing at all, in fact, to interfere with her reflections, and Mary Kate found her thoughts turning in an unexpected direction. Had she not promised faithfully in a highland kirk, before God and Parson MacDole, to submit to her husband and obey his commands. She had. But she had not kept her promises. Instead she had been a thoughtless, disobedient wife. Even a highland husband, one bred to respect a woman's opinions if not always her feelings, would have been sorely vexed by such behavior.

Before long, her anger gave way to contrition, her self-pity to self-reproach. She told herself that although she had been right to wish to teach Douglas to respect her and to treat her as his helpmate, she had carried the lesson too far. It was she who had been unfair, insensitive. She had fallen victim not to a brutal, uncaring husband, but to her own willfulness. She could not, in all fairness, blame the man for having lost his temper.

Suddenly it occurred to her that he might have left the castle. Perhaps he had even returned to Edinburgh, for he would not wish to take her to Strachan Court now, which was perhaps just as well in view of the fact that Lady Strachan would have little affection for the abandoned female who had made her son the laughingstock of all Scotland. No doubt, Douglas would also forbid her to attend Margaret's wedding.

Finally, sinking into the depths of self-condemnation, she told herself he had been right to punish her and should, in fact, have been more severe. As for what had followed, had she not taunted him, demanding to be punished as a woman and not as a child? Moreover, what gentleman, celibate for three weeks' time, would not wish to assuage his lust upon returning to his wife? Under such circumstances, she decided, his behavior had been perfectly natural.

With thoughts like these to encourage her, it was not long before she decided that it was she and not Douglas who must apologize. Therefore, when the maidservant came to see if she meant to take supper in her rooms, Mary Kate, with a burgeoning sense of her own nobility, asked her to inform Douglas that his lady would be grateful for a word with him. She then scurried about, tidying her rooms, and she was smoothing her hair before the Venetian glass in her bedchamber when the door opened ten minutes later. Disappointingly, it was only the maid.

Mary Kate managed a smile. "Did you relay my message to your master, Grisel?"

"Aye, mistress." The girl hesitated, eyeing her warily as though wondering which way her volatile temper would jump.

"Well?"

Grisel looked at the floor. "Forgive me, mistress, but master did say he's no minded tae coom tae ye the noo."

Mary Kate let the hairbrush fall to the floor and looked away, hating the pity she saw in the maid's eyes. So he would not see her, and he was more than likely still mad as a buck besides. In her present mood, the news was not unexpected, but it was a blow nonetheless. "Did . . . did he say . . ." She took a deep breath, collecting herself. To make a gift of her feelings to a servant would never do. "Did Sir Adam happen to mention when it will be convenient for him to see me?"

Grisel had clearly expected an outburst of temper, and she looked uncertain, giving Mary Kate to suspect that she was aware of much of what had transpired in that room the previous evening. Deciding the maid was frightened at finding herself in the thick of the storm, she did not press her for an answer, waiting patiently until Grisel swallowed carefully and said in a low, reluctant voice, "Master bids ye bide a wee here in your ain rooms till your guid health be full restored tae ye, mistress."

"I see. Thank you, Grisel." Her spirits lower than ever, Mary Kate watched the maid's hasty departure, then picked up her hairbrush and replaced it carefully on her dressing table. Dejectedly she wandered back into the sitting room. The storms of emotion had passed, leaving her drained and wilted, but she told herself that it would not do to sit moping until he chose to visit her. Her good health, indeed. No doubt he had put about some tale of illness, hoping to confound the servants. She wondered how long he meant to keep her locked up in her rooms. Not that she was really locked in, of course. She jumped up on the thought and ran to the door. It opened with its customary ease. She peeped out into the gallery. There was no one there.

Expelling a sigh of relief, she returned to her chair. So he expected her to maintain his pretense that she was ill, did he? Well, it might surprise him, but she would. Compared to what she had heard about other border husbands, Douglas had treated her mildly, and she no longer had any desire to punish him. She would await his pleasure.

Having arrived at this depressing conclusion, she hefted her workbasket onto the low table by her chair. At least she could occupy her time constructively. She opened the basket, intending to straighten its contents, but she had barely begun the task when she chanced to lay her hand upon the tapestry bell-pull she had been working at Speyside House. That morning seemed to be long past now, but she smiled and lifted the bellpull carefully from the basket. What could be more appropriate? She laid it aside and was engaged in sorting wools when Grisel returned.

"Please, mistress, d'ye be taking your supper in here? Ye didna say afore, ye ken."

"Most likely I shall, Grisel, but not until six o'clock and only something light. I've done little today to produce much of an appetite."

However, several hours later, when she arose to light some working candles to compensate for the fading daylight, she realized that she was very hungry. She was also bored with the needlework and with her solitude. So it was with a sense of relieved anticipation that, hearing the click of the latch as the sitting-room door opened, she looked up, expecting it to be Grisel with her supper.

Douglas stood upon the threshold.

"Adam!" The bellpull slipped to the floor unnoticed when Mary Kate scrambled to her feet.

"Aye, 'tis Adam himself." He grinned. "Have you done with your sulks then, lassie?"

"Oh!" Her eyes blazed involuntarily at the unexpected impudence, but at a quizzical lift of one of his eyebrows, she subsided.

The rapid change of expression made him grin

more broadly yet. "So Patrick Ferguson is not the only man blessed with powerful eyebrows," he said mockingly.

"Adam, you are—"

"Insufferable. Aye, you've told me. Is that why you sent for me earlier? To tell me so again?"

"You would not come when I sent for you." The eyebrow went up again and she regretted the petulance in her voice. "I didn't mean that like it sounded. I wanted to apologize."

"I thought so," he said, but there was none of the triumph she had expected to hear in his voice. He spoke gently. "I want no apology, lassie. That episode is finished and done, and if there is an apology to be made, it is I who should make it. Not for the skelping —you deserved that—but for what followed after. Though at first I was angry enough to make you wish you had never been born, you looked so small standing there that I was more gentle than I'd meant to be. Then you taunted me, and I lost my temper and punished you with something that ought never to be a punishment. Can you forgive me?"

"Oh, Adam, you are right." She looked up at him through a sudden mist. "There should be no apologies."

"Come here, sweetheart."

Needing no further invitation, she flung herself into his arms. Nestled there, she was aware of a mixture of deep relief and contentment, as well as another feeling, one that caused her every nerve to tingle and gave her a foolish desire to grin. Not wishing to consider this last emotion closely, she focused on the relief, wondering with dismay if she was coming to be like any simpering lowland female, just living and breathing for her man's approval. The notion stiffened her, and she disengaged herself with dignity, smoothing her skirts as she avoided his eye.

He tilted his head to one side, regarding her with amusement. "What now, lassie?"

"Nothing, sir, 'tis only that I am confused. You were so angry before, and now—"

"I don't stay angry, lass. Once I have my say, 'tis all over and done. Besides, I have missed your company, and I am famished. Shall we go down to supper?"

Later they sat companionably in a cozy parlor, he with his feet propped up before the crackling fire and she with a branch of candles on the table beside her, working determinedly on the tapestry bellpull. Douglas had teased her about it over supper, and she meant to finish with the thing for good. No mention had been made of Susan, and though Mary Kate wondered why she had not seen her, she hesitated to ask for fear that Douglas would misinterpret her curiosity. Instead she cast periodic, covert glances at him while she stitched. His eyes were closed and he seemed very relaxed. In fact, if one did not know better . . .

"Adam?"

"Aye?" he murmured.

"Are you asleep, sir?"

His feet dropped to the floor as he lazily stretched himself in his chair. "Nay, lass, I'm awake, but 'tis mighty warm in here. Do you really want to fuss with that thing, or will you have a game of chess with me?"

The needlework was set aside with a sigh. "I confess, I would much prefer to play chess. This thing will never be done."

Getting up to fetch the board, he spoke over his shoulder. "There can be no great hurry. I don't know what you will do with the thing when you finish."

"I can hang it on a wall. Why do you not install bells here like my father has at Speyside House?"

He shrugged. "Easy enough to shout. Besides, the house servants don't gather in the kitchens here. They're hither and yon all day, and the place is so big that it wouldn't be practical." Drawing up a highly polished parquetry table between them, he shook the chess pieces out of their velvet bag, then sat down and began to set out the black pieces on his own side of the inlaid board. Why don't you send that thing to Duncan for a New Year's gift?"

"That is a splendid idea, sir." She gathered the white pieces and laid them out, then moved her king's pawn.

Before responding to her opening, Douglas said quietly, "Suppose you tell me what's been preying upon your mind."

"My mind?"

"Aye. You have been sitting there staring at me since we came into this room. What is it?"

"I have not been staring."

"Well, as near as makes no difference. Now, out with it, lassie, lest you vex me again."

"Oh, very well." But she eyed him warily. "I was wondering whether to ask you what had become of Susan Kennedy."

"Easy enough to answer. I sent her home." He moved his king's pawn to meet hers.

"But what of her father? Not only does he terrify her but she fears he will force her to answer to the kirk for her sins."

"Steady, lass, I've not cast her off, and Kennedy knows that bairn she carries is mine. He'll not dare to touch her or to condemn her. For her to stay there indefinitely would not be safe, but Elspeth is ailing, and Susan's sister, Ellen, is away, so I sent Susan to tend her."

"Is Elspeth very ill? Ought we to do anything?"

"She'll do. I've a strong notion Kennedy's been knocking her about again. The man's a brute."

"In fact," Mary Kate retorted, eyes narrowing, "you do not approve of men who beat their wives."

His eyes twinkled appreciatively. "The cases are different, lassie. Elspeth has a blackened eye, and her face is cut. I also suspect she has a cracked rib or two."

"Oh." She thought that over for a moment while she brought out her queen's knight. "I suppose that is different." Her tone was doubtful, and he chuckled.

"Still feeling abused, sweetheart?" When she blushed, lowering her lashes and shaking her head, Douglas's expression grew serious again. "In truth, there is a great difference. A healthy smack or two on the backside does no harm and can do much good, but a man who would use his fists on a helpless woman is naught but a bully. I've no use for Kennedy or his ilk." He moved his queen across the board.

Mary Kate was silent, contemplating her next move. She made it and pushed a lock of hair out of her face, regarding him thoughtfully. "Adam, were you speaking the truth when you said that had I waited here for you, you would only have shaken me?"

A rueful gleam crept into his eyes. "I said that?" He removed his queen from potential danger.

"Aye." She cocked her head, waiting.

"Something tells me that you are determined to make me feel a brute, lassie, but it won't serve because you were warned. You deserved punishment and would have deserved it even had you not run away." He shot her a direct look from under his heavy brows. " 'Tis over and done now. Whether I would have punished you had the circumstances been different is naught but a moot point. Are you going to move that pawn?"

"Aye." She moved it, then added flatly and without looking at him, "You would have."

He grinned. " 'Tis likely."

Satisfied that she had not been wrong about him, she concentrated on the game. During the next hour they played in companionable silence broken only when one placed the other in check. Mary Kate had just begun to wonder if Douglas might be getting hungry again when the door flew open and Susan Kennedy burst into the room.

"Master, you must come at once! They've took Ellen!" She was panting, nearly spent, but her words were clear.

Douglas shoved the game table away and leapt to his feet. Two quick strides brought him to her side. "Steady, lass. Tell me the whole. Where is your father?"

"Home, sir, blaming me mother like usual. But she didna know about Ellen till now."

"What about Ellen?"

"She run off. Said she'd had all she could stomach o' me father and was for getting out. Ian Baird over tae the village wants tae wed wi' her, but me father said only gin he could pay, so they was running away tae Kelso tae be wed. 'Twas a raiding party, Ian said. He won free only 'cause the brigands thought they'd killed him. But they've took Ellen."

"Scots or English?" Douglas demanded.

"Ian thought Scot." Calmer now, Susan glanced doubtfully at Mary Kate, who smiled reassuringly before turning to Douglas.

"I want to help, Adam. What can be done?"

"You look after Susan, lass. I'll attend to the rest."

Susan protested. "I mun get back tae me mother, sir. I'd not ha' left her, but me father refused tae lift a wee finger. Said Ellen's taken her ain road and mun take the ruts as weel."

"Then I will go with you, Susan," Mary Kate declared.

"That you'll not," contradicted her husband flatly. "You are not to leave the castle, madam, nor you either, Susan lass. You are not fit to go back there tonight. I'll send someone to look after Elspeth." He glared at them. "You'll do as you're bid, the pair of you."

"Very well, sir." Mary Kate sighed. "Come along, Susan. I shall order hot possets sent up to my sitting room. I believe we will both be the better for one."

Douglas shouted orders that could be heard throughout the castle for men and horses, and was soon gone, leaving Mary Kate to minister to Susan. Once she had seated her comfortably with her feet up and the wine had come, she realized that the young woman was carefully avoiding meeting her gaze.

"Are you all right now, Susan?"

"Aye, mistress." Her eyes remained downcast. "Ye do too much fer me, m'lady. 'Tisna fittin'."

"Don't be tiresome, Susan. You are carrying Sir Adam's bairn. That makes you important to him, and so to me."

Susan looked up then. "But yesterday—" She hesitated, and suddenly Mary Kate realized what was troubling her. Susan, like every other servant in the castle, was aware that there had been trouble between Douglas and his wife. Unlike the others, however, Susan most likely believed she had been responsible.

Mary Kate shook her head. "What's done is done.

You must not blame yourself for aught that has happened. Did Sir Adam say anything to you?"

Susan nodded. "He sent for me straightaway after . . . weel, after he fetched you back." She paused, biting her lip, a reminiscent glitter in her eyes. "He were in an unco kippage, he were, but I told him about Cook, about how ye made her stop lambasting me and fetched me away." Susan relaxed, and a slow smile spread across her face. "Cook won't sauce ye again, mistress. I'll warrant she had a worse day than ye did yourself."

"Tell me."

"I told the master what she said about me and how she spoke tae ye, and when he'd got all I could tell him, he went down tae yon kitchen. Grisel was there, and she says he ordered Cook off home and said he'd hold back half her wages for her insolence. She's no tae coom back here the month."

Mary Kate was not impressed. Considering the state of Douglas's temper when he'd left her, she thought Cook had got off easily. She said as much to Susan.

"Och, but nay, mistress. Ye be overlooking *her* husband."

"Husband?" Somehow Cook hadn't seemed the sort to be encumbered with a husband.

"She be Hamilton's wife."

"Hamilton?" The only Hamilton she'd heard spoken of was the smith in Tornary village. "She is the smith's wife?"

"Aye, and a devil he be, wi' a temper tae mak a strong man flinch." Susan's eyes twinkled. " 'And 'tis said he were mighty cross, too, for after master collected the nag he'd left at yon MacKenzie croft and returned it himself tae the smithy, he told Hamilton why he'd sent Cook home wi' only half her wages. I'll warrant she's sorry the noo she spoke tae ye as she did."

Grinning at the probable understatement and unable to summon up an ounce of pity for the ill-natured cook, Mary Kate soon sent Susan off to bed, saying practically that there was nothing further to be done until Douglas brought them news of Ellen. Susan was exhausted and went willingly enough, but Mary Kate found it difficult to follow her own advice. Though she crawled into bed, her ears strained for sounds of Douglas's return, and she could not go to sleep. An hour later she got up, slipped her feet into her sheepskin mules, and crept into her husband's bedchamber. Only then, snuggled deep under his blankets with her head on his silken pillow, did she finally fall asleep.

Douglas barely disturbed her when he returned in the gray dawn light and got into bed beside her. Mary Kate sighed in her sleep and nestled close to him, letting him draw her into the shelter of his arm. She awoke hours later to bright sunshine and the tingling sensation of his finger caressing the tip of her breast through the thin cotton night rail. She stiffened.

"Good morning, wench."

"Oh, Adam." She smiled, her eyes glowing. "I'm glad you are back. Where is Ellen Kennedy? Is she safe?"

"Aye, safe enough." He buried his face in her hair, kissing her, nuzzling her throat, and finally taking possession of her mouth, while his hands played across her body, gently removing her nightdress, his caresses arousing her to a passion that matched his own. Much later, they lay back against the pillows, relaxed and fulfilled, her head on his shoulder, his arm holding her there lightly.

"Now, tell me," she demanded.

"We got her back, lass, thanks to Mrs. Jardine's Willie being a lad who could follow the track of a breeze through a forest, but she's in a bad way."

"Where is she? What happened?"

"She's here. I couldn't send her back the way she was. Willie took word of her safety to Elspeth."

"Well, what happened to her?"

Douglas shifted on the pillow so that he could look directly into her eyes. "They were men, and Ellen's a woman—a bonny wench, at that. Border brigands are not given to the use of courtly manners in their dealings with the fair sex, sweetheart. Ellen objected to their demands, so they forced her."

"You mean they ravished her?"

"Aye, and beat her nearly senseless when she fought them." He continued to look at her. "There were a number of them."

She stared back at him, horror dawning in her eyes. No wonder he'd not wanted to tell her. He had warned her, but she had never believed even border raiders capable of such brutality as he was describing now. "You were afraid that would happen to me," she said, subdued. "That's why you were so angry."

"Aye." He relaxed now that she understood.

Catching her breath with a shudder as she imagined herself in Ellen Kennedy's place, she snuggled closer to him and was silent for some moments before she added on a note of relief, "But you caught them, did you not? What will happen now?"

"We caught *some* of them," he said, smoothing wispy curls off her forehead. "There are more where that lot came from. As to what will happen, I've no idea. They were Scots, and we've sent them to Roxburgh Tolbooth to be held for the magistrate. Once I'm belted, I'll have more authority to act in such

matters, and I can tell you, I'd like to have hanged the
lot of them from the nearest tree. Most likely, though,
the worst that will happen is that they'll be flogged.
'Tis not as though Ellen were married or even
handfasted. Wife stealing is a hanging offense."

"I know. Will Ian Baird still want to marry her
now?" She knew that some men had strong feelings
against marriage with a woman who had been violently used by other men, as though they blamed the
woman herself for her misfortune. Mary Kate did not
know Ian Baird. It seemed that Douglas didn't either,
because he shrugged. "You are very causal about it,
sir," she said. "Have you no opinion in the matter? It
will be a question of first importance to Ellen."

"I'm sorry, lassie, if you think me uncaring. I am
not, but I cannot speak for another man. If he's a
Calvinist, he'll believe poor Ellen guilty of fornication and therefore unworthy to be his wife. It is possible, though, that it won't matter a whit to him since
she wasn't a virgin pure when they met."

Mary Kate sat bolt upright. "And just how do you
know that for a fact, sir?" she demanded, eyes flashing. His guilty grimace was all the response she
needed. "Have you worked your way through all the
Kennedy women, then? I'll warrant you began with
Elspeth!"

She knew she had gone too far when his dark eyes
narrowed and he reached for her with grim purpose.
But she eluded his grasp, skittering backward across
the great bed, snatching at her night rail on the way,
and covering herself with it as she hunkered back in
the furthermost corner.

Douglas, watching her, shook his head in wry
amusement. "I'll cry quits, lass. You should not have
said that, but I'll admit I provoked you. Now, come
away out of that corner."

She stayed where she was. "You did ask for it. And I've not met Elspeth Kennedy, after all. She may be as bonny as Susan and Ellen for all I know."

His lips twitched, but he managed a note of indignation. "She is not. She's as old as my mother, besides. Now, leave it lie before you do make me angry. You are to stop flinging my past in my face, lass."

She grinned at him. "I do not fling it, sir. It leaps. But I have learned one lesson. So long as such things remain safely in your past where they belong, I shall endeavor to restrain my temper."

10

❯❯❯ ❮❮❮

Mary Kate found Susan at her sister's bedside. Ellen Kennedy was pale, her face mottled with bruises, and she lay staring at the ceiling with glazed, unseeing eyes. Susan and the elderly woman who was the room's only other occupant got to their feet and bobbed curtsies.

"Mistress," Susan said, "this be Dame Beaton, the village herbalist. She ha' fetched herbs and medicines tae help Ellen."

The old dame cocked her head, showing a gap-toothed grin. "They be some as says I be t' village witch, m'lady." Her voice was high-pitched and cracked, but Mary Kate felt no fear of her and therefore decided she could not really be a witch.

"What can you do for Ellen, Dame Beaton?"

"There be little a body kin do, m'lady," said the dame. "I've gi'en 'er fennel and herbs fer 'er nerves, and sugar water tae cleanse 'er, but the best help'll be me pertickler powders. Puir lassie be bruised in spirit as much as in body, ye ken, and requires rest and

quiet. Me powders'll let 'er sleep wi'oot dreamin'.
Mayhap she'll be summat improved when she wak-
ens."

Mary Kate eyed the paper of powders skeptically.
"What powders are those, dame?" But the old woman
would not explain. Smiling mysteriously, she ordered
a posset brewed for Ellen and said she would show
Susan how to add the powders to it when it came.
Mary Kate told Susan to stay with her sister and not
to trouble herself over her other duties for the time
being, but Susan was concerned about her mother.

"Me father's bound tae be in an unco kippage," she
fretted. "I mun look tae me mother, mistress."

Mary Kate frowned. Susan would be of little use to
anyone if she were to spend all her time rushing from
castle to croft. Not only would such activity not be
good for her but Douglas wouldn't like it. He had
promised that he would see to Elspeth. She had an
inspiration.

"Look here," she said, "I am going to require a new
gown for Mistress Douglas's wedding, and Michael
Scott said Elspeth could make it up for me. It will be
more convenient for all of us, I believe, if she comes
to stay here whilst she works on it."

"Och, mistress, sae pleased she would be! But will
the master approve o' such a plan?"

Mary Kate shrugged with an impish grin. "He's
got naught to say about it," she declared. "If I wish to
have my sempstress near at hand, I shall have her. As
it happens," she confessed, still grinning, "it was his
idea to ask Elspeth to do the sewing, and I have only
been waiting for the fabrics to arrive. Michael Scott
said they won't be here till the end of the week, but I
know of no reason why Elspeth should not come to
the castle straightaway. She can help tend to Ellen,
after all."

"Oh, mistress, ye be sae kind. But who'll tend tae me father?"

"He ought to tend to himself," Mary Kate said tartly, "but if he objects to that, I expect he can take his meals with the men here. I will tell Mrs. Jardine to see to it."

And so it was arranged. Elspeth Kennedy arrived that very afternoon and was soon comfortably settled into the room next to Ellen's, and Mary Kate began to make plans for the trip to Strachan Court. However, the night before they were to leave, Johnny Graham arrived, bringing a message for Douglas, a royal order to present himself at Stirling Castle without delay. Jamie had need of him.

" 'Tis just as well, lass," he said, attempting to placate her. "Now you can be getting on with your gown. Nothing too daring, mind. Jamie mislikes feminine flamboyance." He grinned, and though she stuck out her tongue at him, she could not be angry. He was stuffing shirts into a satchel while Lucas Trotter attended to other preparations, and he would soon be gone. A courier had already been sent to Strachan Court with word of the change in their plans. "I'll not be away so long this time, lassie. A fortnight, maybe, but no longer. Then we'll go to the court for a good visit and on from there to town."

Less than an hour later, Mary Kate was once again watching her husband ride off with his men. This time, however, she had much to occupy her time and was not so desperately lonely without him. Her materials arrived as promised, and with the combined efforts of Elspeth Kennedy and Sybil Scott, a design was adapted to suit her. Elspeth seemed to have magical fingers for cutting and piecing, and both of her daughters were able assistants, for Ellen was soon up and about, mended in body if not in spirit. The work progressed quickly, and Mary Kate enjoyed it.

A full two weeks passed before Douglas returned, bringing her a message from the king. Jamie disliked having his favorite rush back and forth to Tornary Castle and had sent an invitation, commanding that Lady Douglas accompany her husband in future, in the hope that he might then be content to remain a while in town.

"I told him 'twould be several weeks before I return but that I'd bring you along. Have you missed me, lass?"

"Aye," she admitted, "but I have been busy, too." The gown was nearly finished, and she modeled it for him gaily.

The square-cut emerald silk bodice ended in a long busk-point below her waist, where fragile gossamer lace fell away in an inverted vee, revealing the lush folds of the emerald silk petticoat, brocaded in gold and belling out over a wide French farthingale. Green satin ribbon embroidered with tiny seed pearls and gold roses trimmed the neckline and banded the full-cut undersleeves just above their lace ruffles. The creamy lace oversleeves, not yet finished, would be faced with green silk, brocaded to match the underskirt and trimmed at the edges with narrow green ribbons woven through the delicate lace. Her ruff was likewise unfinished, for she was embroidering the lace herself in a swirling pattern of tiny golden roses. When it was finished, it would be wired to fan out stiffly in an arched framework behind her head. She planned to wear her rope of pearls and the tiny pendant watch Douglas had given her, while her favorite pomander would be suspended on its jeweled chain from the busk-point to hang some four inches above her hemline. She pirouetted for her husband, describing these artful details.

"I had planned to take the ruff lace with me to Strachan Court," she added. "Aunt Aberfoyle's sempstress will attach it for me in town. But there are still days of work to be done on the gown." She frowned. "I doubt you will wish to wait for it, sir, but perhaps it can be sent on after us."

"I want to leave tomorrow," Douglas admitted, "however, Johnny Graham came from Stirling with me. There is work for him to do here, but he will leave for the Canongate house in less than a fortnight. He can take it with him. Have you thought about what you will wear on your feet?"

"Shoes! Merciful heavens, I completely forgot. What shall I do, Adam?"

He laughed. "Never mind, lassie. You've green silk aplenty, have you not?" When she nodded, he said, "We shall draw a pattern of your dainty feet on brown paper and send it and the silk along with Johnny. He will see to the rest. You ought to wear more jewels than just your pearls and that trumpery watch, too. We will talk to my lady mother about that. You may wear whatever you like from the family collection, after all."

Mary Kate had learned much in the time she had spent at Tornary, and one thing that had been made clear to her was that border women wore their wealth—flaunted it, in fact—so that by merely looking at one, a person could tell what her status was, or, more bluntly, how wealthy her husband was. The lowliest border ruffian would not consider returning from a raid without some trinket for his lass, for to do so would be to admit failure. As the wife of a man of power, she knew she was expected to wear expensive trinkets and lots of them. No doubt, people who had already seen her without such stuff clinking about her person had regarded the lack with no little dismay.

Douglas had suggested on more than one occasion that she ought to put on something that sparkled a bit, but she had resisted decking herself out, not because she didn't have the wherewithal to do so—Duncan had given her her mother's jewelry, except for the wedding pearls, as soon as she had begun going to social affairs—but because she had been raised to consider such practices distasteful. In the highlands one did not flaunt one's wealth in that gaudy manner, nor would it have been wise to do so. Indeed, she did not think, considering the manners and morals of the borderers, that it could be particularly wise to do so here. But this was not the time to debate the matter, so she smiled at Douglas and turned the subject back to shoes.

As they made final preparations for their journey, Mary Kate began to think that he was leaving a great many things for Johnny Graham to attend to. Even in the stable yard the next morning, amidst the creak, jingle, and clank of harness, spurs, and swords, and the stamping and pawing of impatient hooves, Douglas thought of last-minute instructions; but Graham accepted them all with his usual cheerful aplomb. At last, Douglas swung into the saddle with an impudent grin at his wife, whose impatience was easily equal to that of the horses, and they were off.

They made quite a cavalcade at first, for since they would be going straight on to the capital from Strachan Court, there was a good deal of baggage tied in bundles and bandboxes to the sturdy ponies. But Douglas had no intention of matching his pace to theirs, so their escort was a large one. Ten armed men would ride ahead with their master and his lady, while twenty others accompanied the slowly moving baggage. Mary Kate never thought to protest this escort, Ellen's misadventures having sobered her, for the moment at least, to the reality of life in the borders.

Their journey was rapid and uneventful, through forests flecked with sunshine, up flower-dotted hills, and down into shady dells. The day was glorious, with sunny blue skies and a crisp light breeze, and when they arrived at Strachan Court more than three hours later, they were in excellent spirits.

The house, approached as it was by a tree-lined drive, came as a complete surprise to Mary Kate. Margaret's idle chatter had led her to expect a small but modern manor house, but as they rode into the cobbled forecourt with its surrounding green hedges and colorful herbaceous borders, she found herself gazing in awed amazement at a splendid baronial mansion.

To be sure, the house was modern, designed with intricate Gothic detail and constructed of brick and timber, but it was not small. Flanked by tall boxwood hedges, it stood two and a half stories above a raised cellar, its central pavilion extended on either side by symmetrical wings, each boasting two sets of oriel windows and a pair of outside end chimneys with corbeled caps. Five gables with carved finials punctuated the roofline, and broad steps sweeping from forecourt to entry were bounded by carved stone balustrades that curved at the top to continue across the entire front of the house.

At first glance the facade seemed to Mary Kate to be all glass, with windows everywhere. There were the four sets of oriels plus a great twelve-light window in the projecting entry bay. Indeed, even the spaces between projections seemed to be filled with windows, for except for the chimneys and the high brick foundation, which was nearly obscured by topiary yews amusingly shaped to resemble chess pieces, there was no open expanse of brickwork anywhere to be seen.

Aside from the amount of glass, the most outstanding feature of the house was its lovely woodwork, which Douglas pointed out to her, confiding that it was his father's pride. She was properly impressed, for the mullions, finials, and belt courses were all exquisitely carved. In addition, there were cartouches carved with heraldic devices beneath the central mullion of each upper oriel, as well as one bearing the Douglas arms located beneath the twelve-light window, above the magnificent entry.

Considering the number of windows, she was not surprised to learn that their approach had been noted immediately. Their horses made a great clatter on the cobblestones of the forecourt, but Mary Kate firmly believed that Lord Strachan's prompt appearance in the entryway was due to windows, not noise.

He waved cheerfully, calling out greetings as he hurried out and down the sweeping steps. "Send your men 'round to the stables, Adam," he shouted as he drew near. "My lads'll look after them. Good journey?"

"Aye." Douglas lifted Mary Kate from her saddle. "See to your skirts, lass, and take care the horse behind you don't trample you." He handed Sesi's reins up to a waiting henchman.

Within minutes, the forecourt was empty, and Lord Strachan could greet his daughter-in-law properly. He gathered her into an energetic hug while her husband looked on in indulgent amusement.

"She's even bonnier than I'd remembered, lad,"

Strachan said, laughing and holding her away again. "How do you like married life, my lady?"

She laughed back, her cheeks flushed. "I like it well enough, my lord."

"Then Adam must not beat you too often," he teased. But his twinkling expression sobered ludicrously when she looked quickly away and the becoming color in her cheeks deepened to a painful red. "Och, I've put my foot in it already," he groaned, shooting a reproachful look at his son.

Douglas grinned back at him and put his arm around Mary Kate, gathering her to him with a little shake. "You've done no such thing, sir. She is oversensitive. Compose yourself, lass."

Conscious, despite his smile, of a contrasting, firmer note in his voice, and aware, too, of the anxious look in his lordship's eyes, Mary Kate squared her shoulders and lifted her chin. "He speaks the truth, my lord," she said with a rueful smile. Then, recovering her poise, she turned to her husband with a saucy grin. "But he is an impudent knave all the same!"

Relieved, both men chuckled and started up the stone steps with her. "Where is my lady mother, sir?"

"In her sitting room, I believe. We'll go up to her now. She has a wee surprise for you." There was a note in his voice that Mary Kate could not interpret but that made Douglas look at him sharply as they passed under the arch of the magnificent frontispiece entrance and into the hall.

A great many servants hurried to and fro, all dressed in plain blue livery with Lord Strachan's crest stitched in silver on the men's shoulders and on the women's apron pockets. Strachan smiled at the bustle. "They've come to catch a glimpse of you, lass." He made a small gesture with his hand, and the hall cleared at once of all but those with legitimate business there. At that moment, a man emerged from a room to the right at the rear of the hall. He was grinning, and when he came nearer, Mary Kate realized that he was young, scarcely more than a boy.

"Ned!" Douglas strode forward to clasp him by the shoulders. "How are you, lad?"

"Well, sir, thank you, and in a pother to meet your lady."

"Then come along. Mary Kate, this is Ned Lumsden, a young cousin of mine. His father, Lord Berwick, sent him here a few years ago to serve as Father's page. You must be nearly ready to leave now, lad."

"Aye, sir." Light brown eyes twinkled as he bowed his curly dark head over Mary Kate's hand. " 'Tis pleased I am to make your acquaintance, my lady."

She smiled, liking what she saw of him. He was fashionably if simply attired and might someday be as tall as her husband, though presently the top of his head was only on a level with Douglas's eyes. But, though he looked to be about fifteen, she soon discovered that he was in fact rapidly approaching his seventeenth birthday. His slim body had already begun to fill out. His thighs in their dark, close-fitting trunk hose were well muscled, and his chest bade fair to be a broad one.

"Well, what do you think of the lad, Adam?" demanded Lord Strachan proudly.

"He's grown."

They chuckled, and his lordship went on, "Aye, that he has, well enough, and hasn't stopped yet, I'm thinking. But Berwick wants him back. Thinks he's ready to make his bow at court."

"And is he?" Douglas sent a sidelong glance at the

boy, who showed signs of increasing embarrassment
at being discussed in such a casual manner.

"Och, who knows? He's graceful enough with the
womenfolk, not that that will say aye or nay for him
in Jamie's court."

"Mind your tongue, sir," Douglas said, only half-
joking. "You'll be giving the wrong ideas to both of
them. There is chivalry enough at court."

"Mayhap, but it does not originate itself with the
king."

"Fair enough. When do you leave us, Ned?" Douglas turned back to the boy, showing no wish to indulge his father in this particular line of conversation.

"I am to go with you and the family to town, sir."

"Aye, so he will," interjected Strachan, visibly net-
tled by his son's demeanor, "but he's his duties to
attend to now. Get along with you, lad." Obediently,
the boy turned away, and his lordship added, "He's
been tending to my books."

"Books, my lord?" Mary Kate asked.

"Aye, lass. 'Tis a pastime of mine. I collect them.
Do you read? I'll show you." His enthusiasm was
squelched by his son who informed him, chuckling as
he did so, that although Mary Kate could read well
enough, this was not the time to show off his entire
collection. Taking his father by an elbow and putting
an arm around Mary Kate's shoulders, he guided
them both firmly toward the great open-string staircase in the left rear corner of the hall. Mary Kate's
eyes widened when the full impact of the staircase's
beauty struck her. Constructed entirely of oak
around an open well, the three-run stair was a magnificent example of modern craftsmanship. Between
its highly polished handrail and stringer, framed by
intricately carved and corbeled newel posts, it

boasted expertly crafted ornamental brackets. Mary Kate had never seen anything to equal it and said so.

"Thank you," Strachan replied. "We like it."

Douglas chuckled again, releasing his father's elbow as they began to ascend the stair. "He's as proud of it as he can be, lass. You have now assured your welcome. But just wait until you have a chance to look at some of the carved paneling in the parlor and the great hall."

They reached the top of the stair and emerged into the hall of the twelve-light window. Early-afternoon sunlight poured in, but Mary Kate had little time to look around before Douglas, guided by the sound of voices to their left, strode toward an open doorway and into his mother's sitting room.

Like the hall, it was well lit by afternoon sun that streamed through windows framed by hangings of beaten blue damask. The walls were paneled in oak and hung with cheerful landscapes and tapestries, while the furniture consisted of beautifully carved oak chairs and stools, decorated and made comfortable with gaily embroidered cushions. Against the wall opposite the window bay stood a magnificent almery. Smaller carved chests stood against the other walls, and a lovely carpet of deep blue and red covered a large portion of the highly polished oak floor.

Once inside the room, Douglas stopped short with a look of delighted surprise and exclaimed, "Megan!"

The younger of the two ladies seated in the window embrasure nodded, smiling. So, Mary Kate thought, this was his surprise. She had realized from the conversation downstairs that Douglas had not been surprised to see Ned, but her thoughts on the subject had gone no further. Now she began to understand the odd note in Lord Strachan's voice earlier.

Her husband remembered his manners. "Mother, how do you fare? You are looking well." He strode forward again, bent over the small, slender, dark-haired woman, and kissed first her hand and then her cheek. She smiled up at him tenderly.

"I am very well, indeed, my dear. Present to me your lovely bride." Her voice was low-pitched and full of gracious dignity. She smiled at Mary Kate, now only a few feet away, and despite lines of suffering etched at their corners, her eyes, as dark brown as her son's, twinkled warmly.

Douglas's grin was rueful. "Seeing Megan put all the words I'd prepared to speak straight out of my head." Mary Kate noted a gleam of mischievous laughter in the other young woman's eyes before Douglas's hand at her elbow recalled her to her duty. He drew her forward. "This is Mary Kate, my lady."

Mary Kate stepped forward and curtsied deeply, but Lady Strachan patted the low stool beside her. "Sit by me, my dear. I wish to become acquainted with you." When Mary Kate had obeyed, her hostess indicated her companion. "This is Adam's cousin, Megan, Lady Somerville. She spent a good deal of time with us as a child, and she and Adam are great friends. She is to go with us to town because her husband, Sir Reginald, has business that will keep him occupied at Somerville until shortly before the wedding. Megan is only a few years older than you are, so I know you will become good friends."

Lord Strachan made an impatient noise.

His lady smiled at him. "I know you are longing to return to your books, sir, but I charge you before you leave us to remember that Ned is to sup with us this evening. You must allow him time to dress."

"And so I shall, though I think it utter nonsense," replied his lordship with a wry grimace. "He ought to take his meals in the hall as he has always done and not be treated like one of the family until his formal duties here are finished."

She smiled, shaking her head. "He *is* one of the family, my lord, and he must have time to adjust to his new status. I should not like to see him carrying coals at court."

"He is hardly like to do that, madam, for a less servile brat I've never known, unless it be Adam here. Why, it has not been so long since I swinged Ned's backside for some impertinence or other, and well you know it."

"Aye, 'tis true enough," she said, laughing. "But, nevertheless, you agreed, my lord."

"So I did." His voice was gentler now, his eyes tender. "Only because you asked it of me, madam." He glanced at Douglas. "Coming along, lad?"

"Aye, if you will excuse me, Mother. I have my men to see to, and the baggage ponies will be along soon. 'Tis pleasant to see you again, Megan."

Lady Somerville raised laughing blue eyes to his and spoke at last. "If Aunt will allow it, I should like to accompany you, Adam. We observed your arrival from here, you know, and I confess that I have a wish to see that magnificent beast you were riding and to show you my latest acquisition, as well." Her voice was soft, with a lilt that made it sound like delicate music. At Lady Strachan's nod she arose, smoothing her skirts over her farthingale and giving Mary Kate an opportunity at last to get an unobstructed view of her.

Lady Somerville was as tall as Margaret, the top of her head nearly reaching Douglas's nose. Her fine golden hair was pulled smoothly away from her face and confined at the nape of her slender neck in an snood of gold net. Her face boasted smooth planes, a complexion of pale strawberries and cream, and high, well-defined cheekbones. Delicately arched brows and long, dark lashes set off large blue yes, and her nose was perfectly chiseled to match her perfect face. And as if that were not enough, Mary Kate noted grimly, Lady Somerville possessed a perfect figure as well.

She was slender, not built upon the magnificent lines of her cousin Margaret, but she had curves in all the right places and moved with a flowing feline grace that told Mary Kate she owed little of her figure to tight corsets. Her rose-damask bodice fitted her upper body like a second skin, emphasizing the soft curve of her breasts and her tiny waist. Her rose skirt and white lace petticoats, spread over a Spanish farthingale, made hushing sounds as she moved toward Douglas, and the sweet scent of French jasmine wafted gently from her person.

Mary Kate had surrendered her dark cloak and safeguard belowstairs, but in spite of their protection on the journey, she was well aware that her riding dress had suffered, and it was not one of her best gowns to begin with. Self-consciously she smoothed the rough material across her lap.

"Valiant will be pleased to make your acquaintance," Douglas said mockingly to his cousin, "and it will spare Mary Kate from your nonsense whilst she becomes acquainted with my lady mother." He offered his arm with exaggerated gallantry, and Mary Kate watched them go, feeling bereft. She remembered that Douglas had compared his earlier relationship with Megan Somerville to hers with Robin Mac-Leod—only not so innocent, he had said. She didn't know just yet what to make of Lady Somerville, but she did not believe for one moment that she and that young woman were destined to become friends. With a sigh, she turned her attention to Lady Strachan, forcing a smile to her lips.

II

⫸⫸⫸ ⫷⫷⫷

"*W*ell, my dear," Lady Strachan said cheerfully, "I am pleased and delighted to make your acquaintance at last. You have no idea how disappointed we were when Adam delayed your visit. My lord very nearly set off to fetch you himself and would have done so but for thinking Adam would mislike it." Her voice was soothing, and Mary Kate soon found herself engaged in comfortable conversation. "You must be wishing to refresh yourself," her ladyship said at last. "Did my son think to provide you with a maidservant?"

"No, my lady. He said there were servants aplenty here. Susan Kennedy, who usually does for me, was unable to make the journey." She felt her color rising, but Lady Strachan appeared not to notice.

"Kennedy? Not Elspeth's daughter!" When Mary Kate nodded, she said, "I remember Elspeth well. She married a brute of a fellow and had several children. Most of them died young. But what is this you say about Susan? I trust she is not ill."

"No, my lady, merely in a condition that makes it unsafe for her to travel," Mary Kate replied delicately.

"I see. But still Susan Kennedy."

Mary Kate blushed, nodding her head.

"Oh, dear. Does she even know who is the father?"

The flush grew deeper, and Mary Kate looked down at her hands, knotted tightly in her lap. "Susan is a good girl, my lady," she said evenly. "She had little choice in the matter."

There was silence, and she looked up to find Lady Strachan gazing at her placidly. "I believe I understand you, my dear." The older woman added candidly, "These are unpleasant incidents that we must endure. I trust you had better sense than to read Adam a curtain lecture."

"I read him no lectures, my lady, but I am ashamed to say my behavior was less than sensible."

"You may tell me all about it another time if you like," Lady Strachan said with a smile. "I should like us to become friends. But you must be longing to change your gown. Your baggage ought to have arrived by now." She rose to her feet, smoothing her russet skirts, and Mary Kate realized that she was only an inch or two taller than herself. She had expected to find her taller, as though so much dignity required height.

She liked Lady Strachan and felt comfortable with her, but she was grateful to her for not demanding more information about the unpleasantness with Douglas. She was not ready to discuss that episode with anyone yet and was dismayed that the subject had already been twice mentioned. She ought to have expected that, she realized, for Douglas's parents would always have an interest in the circumstances at Tornary.

They crossed the hall of the twelve-light window and passed into the great chamber. In days of old, and even now in some manor houses, this chamber would have housed the master's bed and would be the place where he dealt with business. At Strachan Court it was merely an oversized elegant parlor with carved wainscoting and a molded ceiling. Several marvelous carpets with floral patterns in shades of pale blue and gold decked the floor. Overlooking the forecourt were two window bays, into each of which had been built a low-backed settle. A huge hooded fireplace occupied the west wall, and once again excellent paintings hung on the walls.

Mary Kate followed Lady Strachan through one of the two doors in the north wall into a gallery, where a bank of windows on their right overlooked a charming inner courtyard. Bearing left, they crossed the gallery into another room, where a maidservant smoothing the coverlet on a huge carved bed turned at their entrance and bobbed a curtsy.

"Sarah, be so good as to tell Annie Jardine she is wanted," said her ladyship gently. The girl bobbed another curtsy, and when she had gone, Lady Strachan said, "You and Adam will have more privacy here than in the east wing. I have put him here and you in the next room. I ought to mention that Megan has the bedchamber off the window hall, whilst our own adjoins my sitting room. I should like nothing better," she added, smiling, "than to take you over the whole house, but I still tire easily and am supposed to rest before supper, so I shall leave you to your own devices for now. I think you will like Annie Jardine. She is your housekeeper's daughter, you know."

Mary Kate was pleased and expressed her gratitude, adding shyly, "I don't wish to keep you from your rest, my lady. I expect Adam will be along soon."

Lady Strachan laughed. "I don't know about that. Once he and Megan start remembering their childhood days, I am afraid it will be difficult to distract them."

Mary Kate's face fell, mirroring her thoughts, but Lady Strachan tactfully kept silent.

A moment later, alone, Mary Kate turned her attention to the bedchamber. Small trunks, roped bundles, and several boxes littered the floor, and she wondered where Lucas Trotter was and why he had not yet unpacked Douglas's things. She stepped over some of them to look more closely at the intricately carved bed with its beautifully embroidered green tester and hangings before remembering that Lady Strachan had said she was to have the adjoining bedchamber for her own use.

Curious, she walked through the connecting door to find a room of equal size to the other. Again the floor was cluttered with baggage, but there the similarity ended. The bed in this room was smaller, though the violet hangings were just as prettily embroidered, and the atmosphere was cozy rather than elegant. She crossed to the window. The room overlooked a charming hedge garden with a fountain playing in the center. Through an opening at the left end of the tall hedge she could see the white-pebbled drive that led from forecourt to stables. She wondered where her husband was. Surely he could not still be showing off Valiant to Lady Somerville.

On the thought came a peal of hastily stifled feminine laughter, and Lucas Trotter entered, accompanied by a young woman dressed in the blue full-length kirtle of the house servant. Her smooth light-brown hair was tied back with a ribbon, and her sleeves were rolled up. The fact that she was of some stature among the maidservants was indicated by her apron, which was of transparent cambric instead of the usual coarse linen.

Trotter noticed his mistress first but was undismayed. He smiled. "Mistress, I've brung ye Annie Jardine, and a rare handful she be, too. I doubt she'll be as useful tae ye as her brother Willie be tae the master, but my Lady Strachan says ye mun make do wi' her nanetheless."

The young woman laughed, her cheeks blooming. "That will be enough o' your nash-gab, Lucas Trotter. Run along wi' ye, else Sir Adam will find his bandboxes still on the carpet when he returns, and, certes, there'll be an unco tirrivee."

Reminded of his duties, the wiry manservant hurried into the other chamber, which soon echoed with the sounds of his industry.

Annie proved to be a successful product of her mother's teaching as Mary Kate was helped into a fresh gown and the boxes and bundles disappeared, their erstwhile contents settled comfortably in the trunks, chests, and large press cupboard provided for the purpose. Annie kept up a light chatter all the while, inquiring about the welfare of friends and relations at Tornary. She had already seen and spoken to her brother, but as she laughingly informed Mary Kate, Willie was a dour man, expert at tracking game but not inclined to gossip. Mary Kate liked the girl and willingly assuaged her curiosity, despite a nagging suspicion that neither her husband's mother nor Lady Somerville would approve of such open manners betwixt mistress and maid.

She did not see Douglas until he came upstairs to change for supper. She heard him first, laughing and shouting orders at Trotter while he dressed. She dismissed Annie, and a few moments later he entered.

"Greetings, lass. How do you like Strachan Court?"

"I cannot say, sir," she responded coolly, "for as yet I have seen but little of it."

He frowned. "Someone ought to have taken you 'round the place, sweetheart."

"And who should have done so, sir? Your father is with his books, and your mother still tires easily and must conserve her strength. Should I have requested a servant to escort me?"

"Nay, lass." He grimaced. "Say no more. I take your meaning well enough." He strode over to her and dropped to one knee, lifting the hem of her skirt to kiss it. "I am a vile beast to neglect my lady wife." He looked up at her. "That is what you truly would like to say to me, is it not?"

Unable to repress a smile at his un-Douglaslike posture, she shook her head. "Get up, sir. You should not kneel to me."

"I know," he agreed solemnly, "but I wanted to look into your bonny eyes, and 'twas the only way I could do so, downcast as they be." The sally succeeded in winning another smile. He had not actually apologized in so many words, of course, but it would do. Seated upon a stool at her feet, he told her of his afternoon. "Megan hasn't changed at all, though it must be five years since last I saw her. 'Twas when she married Somerville."

"Has she children?"

"Not a one, more's the pity, for I know Somerville dreams of lusty sons. He had one, and three daughters besides, by his first marriage, but the son was killed, hunting."

"Then Sir Reginald is older than your cousin?"

"Aye, closer to my father's age. In point of fact, one of his daughters is a year older than Megan. The other two are your age and younger. I wonder sometimes how she can be happy with him, so sweet and merry as she is. Sir Reginald is a strict, dour man who never laughs or jokes."

Mary Kate bit her tongue, deciding it would not be wise to comment that Lady Somerville seemed well enough to her, however grim her husband might be.

Douglas chatted amiably while they made their way down the stairs, through the entry hall, and along a short passageway to an anteroom with doors leading off it in every direction. One of these, set at an angle across the southeast corner, was flanked by chamfered pilasters supporting a broken pediment. A gillie stepped forward to open the door, and they entered the winter parlor to find the others already gathered there for supper.

The room was too large to be termed cozy, for it was fully twenty-five feet to a side, but it was cheerful. Candles gleamed from wall sconces all around the perimeter and from candelabra at either end of the laden, white-lined-draped trestle table. A fire roared in the great fireplace, and red velvet curtains graced the forecourt windows as well as their tall and narrow inglenook brethren. Once again the click of her heels was muted by carpet as, guided by Douglas's light touch at her elbow, she made her way to her place, pausing only to make her curtsy to Lady Strachan before she seated herself.

The ewerer approached with two assistants. While the first held the basin, he poured rose water over her hands, after which the second assistant handed her a verbena-scented linen cloth to dry them. Then they passed on to perform the same service for Douglas, and Mary Kate turned her attention to the table.

Square wooden trenchers marked each place. Most of the plate was pewter, though the great salt at his lordship's right hand and the spoons at each place were silver. Other beautiful silver pieces gleamed from the sideboards where they rested in anticipation of a feast-day. Huge platters of food already sat steaming upon the table, while others waited upon the dresser and sideboards to be served later. The carver, a leather case of knives attached to his girdle, stood poised behind Lord Strachan's chair. Once grace had been said, he stepped forward, swept away the small white cloth before his lordship, and with a grand flourish raised up the two long carving knives thus revealed. Using one to steady the joint, he sliced dexterously, removing the juicy slices to a platter as he worked.

Saucers of cameline and yellow sauce were set between alternate places for dipping the roasted meat, and Mary Kate either helped herself from dishes shared by her husband or was served by him. Musicians played softly from the window embrasure, and servants hovered throughout the meal, attempting to anticipate demands before they were made. Thus, when Mary Kate began daintily to lick her fingers before wiping them upon the napkin tied around her neck, one of the ewerer's minions sprang forward with a lave cloth. She smiled her thanks.

Another lad circulated with a basin into which the bones from various dishes were tossed. In the great hall with its rush-strewn floor, the custom still prevailed of tossing such bones and other bits to the floor, where they were pounced upon by the dogs almost before they landed. But here in the winter parlor, where the family took its meals, Lady Strachan had fixed upon the more civilized practice in order to spare her lovely carpets. Her new daughter approved.

Dish succeeded dish, saucers were replenished before they had been emptied, and French wines flowed freely, attended by the butler, who changed their glasses each time he poured. Although it was a light supper of only two courses, there was a wide selection of foods, and despite the number of attendants, conversation flourished.

Lady Somerville dominated the conversation, and it seemed to Mary Kate that she began every sentence with, "Adam, do you remember . . ." or perhaps, when she exerted herself to include Douglas's wife, "Have you ever told Mary Kate about the time you and I . . ." At first, Mary Kate attempted to take part in the discussion, but she was never allowed much more than an interested noise or two before the others plunged deeper into their reminiscences. Ned Lumsden did ask her at one point to tell them something about her own childhood, but she had scarcely begun to speak when her words reminded Lady Somerville of a humorous anecdote, which she at once began to relate to the others. Ned winked impudently from across the table, but although the gesture cheered her momentarily, Mary Kate made no further effort to join the general conversation.

Douglas became so engrossed in his cousin's tales that he absentmindedly stabbed at the stewed mutton with his dagger without looking, and narrowly missed slicing his wife's fingers as they dipped into the same dish. He did not hear her low cry as she snatched her hand away, but a sharp reproof from his father instantly reclaimed his notice, and he apologized profusely before returning his attention to his cousin.

Finally, the table was cleared of the second course,

the grease-stained surcloth was removed, and the ewerer and his helpers stepped forward again. While the butler prepared mugs of steaming spiced wine, other servants brought in the banquet, or sweet course, which consisted of plates of gingerbread, spiced fruits, and sugared delicacies, These were set upon the table along with a saucer of damson marmalade. Mary Kate refused the gingerbread but helped herself to a candied primrose from the sugar plate just as Lady Strachan announced her plan for a small gathering to take place at Strachan Court at the end of the following week, several days before the entire family would depart for Edinburgh.

"I have sent out invitations to a number of our friends," she said with her gentle smile. "No one from any great distance, of course, but there are a good number of people nearby who will wish to make your acquaintance, my dear. There will be feasting and dancing—disapproved of, I am certain, by our Calvinistic neighbors—but I know that music and dancing are beloved by the highlanders, and I want you young people to enjoy yourselves. You are to make one of the family that night, Ned," she added with a challenging sidelong glance at his lordship. " 'Twill be an excellent opportunity for you to accustom yourself to being a guest rather than a secretary."

"Thank you, my lady."

"Just see to it that you behave yourself, lad," growled his mentor, but Ned only grinned at him.

When they adjourned at last to the great chamber, Mary Kate was astonished to see her husband pick up a lute and begin to pluck away at it with the skill of a strolling troubadour. He made himself comfortable on a low stool near the roaring fire and called to Lady Somerville to name him a tune.

"Oh, Adam," she retorted, laughing, "you will be sorry you asked. You must know by now that my favorite is 'The Gaberlunzie man'—all ten verses of it!"

"Well, you must let me practice a while before I attempt so ambitious a song. What about you, lass?" He smiled at his wife.

"I didn't know you played."

"You know now," he said. "What would you like to hear?"

"I like ballads, or perhaps something sad. 'Bide Ye Yet,' or 'Here Awa'.' I also like 'The Gaberlunzie Man,'" she added, "though it is rather long."

"Good enough." He strummed idly for a moment or two, accustoming himself to the instrument, and then began to sing a love ballad, his voice a melodious bass. A few moments later, lost in the music, Mary Kate was startled when Annie Jardine appeared at her shoulder to ask if she needed anything. She sent for her embroidery. Lady Strachan was also occupied with her needlework, and his lordship soon bore young Lumsden off to the bookroom, while Megan displayed interest only in the music. Invited to join in the singing, she consented immediately, and 'The Gaberlunzie Man' was performed at last, as a duet.

Mary Kate found herself growing restless midway through the song. Somehow King James V's tale of the beggar who ran off with the landlady's daughter had lost its appeal, and when Megan sent a servant to fetch her music books, Mary Kate stifled a yawn.

"You must sing with us, Mary Kate," the older girl said sweetly. "I am certain I can find a part for you in several songs. I have three books of printed music for the lute, thanks to Uncle's penchant for collecting such things."

"I do not doubt it, Lady Somerville," replied Mary

Kate politely, "but I fear I have an indifferent voice. 'Twould be a pity to inflict it upon your pleasant harmony."

"Nonsense," said Megan, smiling. "Despite the efforts of the reformed kirk, everyone sings, and particularly, as my aunt said earlier, everyone in the highlands. One still has music for dinner, music for supper, music for weddings, and music for funerals. Tinkers sing as they mend their pots, milkmaids sing ballads, and even beggars have their special songs. When I think how my father moaned about the expense of my lessons—not just for singing and playing, of course, but for dancing, too—I simply cannot believe you do not sing perfectly well."

"Well, I do not wish to sing tonight," Mary Kate said flatly.

"She would prefer to tend to her stitching," said Douglas with a chuckle. "Otherwise it will be Christmas afore that lace ruff is done." He then proceeded, to Mary Kate's acute embarrassment, to relate the tale of the tapestry bellpull. Megan was still chuckling when her music arrived. Soon she and Douglas had their heads together over the pages, trying first one air and then the next, their singing interwoven with seemingly endless reminiscences. It seemed to Mary Kate that they spoke in a sort of code, as much in half-sentences and gestures as in proper English words, often thinking of the same thing at the same time and laughing, having no need to go into detail and never thinking to do so merely for her benefit.

Finally, stifling another yawn, she set her work aside and looked for Annie Jardine. The maidservants had set up game tables in the window embrasure at the far end of the room and some were engaged in quiet games of Irish and draughts, while others plied

their needles. Mary Kate signed to Annie, who arose
from her seat immediately and crossed the room.

"Aye, mistress?"

Mary Kate spoke in low tones so as not to interrupt
the others. "I wish to retire in a few moments, Annie,
and I shall want a hot bath if you can arrange for
one."

Annie didn't blink at the strange request but
bobbed her sprightly curtsy and set off to see to it.
There was a pause in the music, and Mary Kate
turned to her husband's mother, who was still working neat stitches into the linen stretched on her tam-
bour frame.

"My lady, will you think me churlish if I beg to be
excused? Or must I wait for prayers?" she added, uncertain as to the prevailing custom at Strachan Court.

Lady Strachan said serenely, "You may do as you
please, my dear, and I shall think nothing about it.
Our Ned reads a chapter of the Bible to the servants
each night, so that we are in compliance with the law,
but for the most part we still hold by the old traditions. Here in the borders, change comes slowly and
with great resistance. I, too, shall retire soon," she
added, "and Megan will attend me."

Mary Kate smiled. She had wondered if Lady Somerville would dare to outstay her hostess. Evidently,
she would not be given that opportunity. And it was
interesting, too, she thought, to learn that some matters were the same here as they were at home. She
knew that Douglas had done nothing to comply with
the General Assembly's recent decree regarding daily
prayer, but she had not thought about it before now
for the simple reason that when the news had reached
the highlands that every landowner must own a Bible
and a psalm book and must read daily from it in the

vulgar tongue for his household's edification, the notion had been laughed to scorn by the highlanders.

When she arose and bade the others good night, her husband shot her a quizzical glance but said nothing other than that he would be along soon.

"You need not hurry, sir," she replied calmly. "I am going to have a bath."

"A bath?" Megan was astonished. "You will catch your death, Mary Kate." Even Lady Strachan was surprised.

"Nonsense," Mary Kate said, enjoying the small sensation she had created. "A hot bath relaxes me before I sleep. There is no danger so long as the tub is well draped and I keep a fire going, and Annie will see to that."

Her husband, knowing that she indulged herself in a bath at least once every sennight, grinned at her. After observing to the others that at least she did not follow the financially ruinous example set by the late Queen Mary and bathe in wine, he demanded that his cousin return her attention to the music.

Later he entered his wife's bedchamber unannounced to find her wrapped in a voluminous nightrobe, seated upon a stool with her back to the fire while Annie brushed her hair. Mary Kate's cheeks glowed from the warmth, and her eyes lit at the sight of him. The canopy curtains had been removed, and two sturdy menservants were emptying her tub. Douglas waited only until they had departed before ordering Annie to bed.

Annie, having known him from childhood, looked calmly to her mistress for confirmation of the order.

"Aye, Annie, go to bed," Mary Kate said. "My hair is nearly dry now."

"Give me that hairbrush, Annie. I can do it."

She gave it to him with a smile and took her leave.

Douglas drew the brush gently through the silky red-gold curls, watching the firelight play upon the strands as they freed themselves from the bristles and floated back into place. Except for the rhythmic hushing of the brush strokes and the crackle of the fire, there was silence until at last he spoke.

"You were quiet tonight, lassie."

"Was I?"

"Aye." He set the brush down, placed gentle hands upon her shoulders, and turned her to face him. She looked up, her eyes clear, her cheeks still flushed. He drew her to her feet. "You smell wonderful, sweetheart, like lemon and spice."

"Carmelite water," she confided. "I made it myself and find it improves my bath. Was I uncivil, sir?"

"No, but you must learn to speak your piece, else Megan will do all the talking. That lass has her tongue hinged in the middle. Given half a chance it rattles like a clapdish."

Mary Kate chuckled. "You did not seem to mind, sir."

He did not deny the statement, but they were interrupted just then by Lucas Trotter, who inquired from the threshold between the two bedchambers whether his master had need of him.

"Get to bed, Trotter. My lass will tend my wants."

"Indeed, sir, and 'tis a fortunate man ye are, tae ha' such a bonny tirewoman."

Amused, Douglas shook a fist, and Trotter scooted out, his hands raised in mock defense. When the door had closed behind the brash little man, Douglas turned back to Mary Kate, grinning at her blushes.

"Come to bed, lassie. I've a wish to indulge my senses in the delights of Carmelite water."

"We should not leave this fire, sir," she demurred, "and I've not got my night rail on yet."

"Be damned to your Calvinist night rail," he grumbled. "You'll have no need of it this night. I'll tend the blasted fire, too, but I say to you as I said to that Jack-sauce Trotter, 'get you to bed!'"

Deciding it would be rash to tease him further, she padded obediently into the other bedchamber. A fire was burning on the hearth there, too, but it was smaller, casting little more than a warm glow. The only other light came from her chamber through the open doorway and from a candle stand near the great bed. The light from the doorway dimmed, then vanished, and Douglas entered, demanding to know why she was not in bed.

She lowered her eyelids demurely. "You told Trotter that I was to serve you in his place, sir."

Douglas chuckled, delighted. "So you shall, wench. Come here to me at once."

She moved toward him submissively. "I have never done this sort of thing before, so you must tell me what to do."

"I should hope so," he declared with mock severity. "You will begin by unlacing my doublet." As she proceeded, he assisted by giving detailed instructions, the likes of which Trotter had certainly never heard, and many of which made her blush or chuckle. But Mary Kate enjoyed herself, and by the time Douglas was ready to climb into bed, her robe had joined his clothes in a pile on the stool. He patted her appreciatively on her backside, telling her she was a good little serving wench who had earned her rest, but it was a good time later before he allowed her to sleep.

12

The next morning, after a breakfast of cold boiled beef, porridge, and ale, Douglas announced that it was time for Mary Kate's tour of the house. They began with the long gallery, an elegantly appointed chamber that stretched the entire rear width of the house and boasted fully glazed north and south walls overlooking the terrace, parterre, and hedge walls of the rear gardens as well as the peaceful inner court. Douglas drew Mary Kate's attention to the huge twin fireplaces that faced each other from the end walls, but she was more impressed by the gallery's linenfold wainscoting, the punched borders of which resembled elaborate stitchery, than she was with the exquisitely carved chimney pieces.

They paused to gaze at the garden view, then wandered to the east end, where a set of double doors opened into the bedchamber wing, consisting of four adjoining guest chambers, one pair facing the inner court and the second overlooking the herbary and the kitchen gardens. Next they came to a gloomy triangular hall that led to the rear stairs on one hand and to the front of the house on the other. Douglas pointed out his parents' and Margaret's rooms before they emerged into her ladyship's sitting room, having completed a circuit of the first floor.

"There are only servants' rooms upstairs," he said as he opened the door into the window hall. "We'll go on down—Good morning, Megan."

Lady Somerville turned at the top of the stair, and Mary Kate saw that she was dressed for riding. She did not look so rosy-cheeked this morning. In fact, she seemed pale, but Mary Kate thought her depressingly beautiful nonetheless.

Douglas explained that they had been looking over the house.

"How interesting," Megan said, her bored tone belying the polite phrase. " 'Tis such a glorious day, though, that I had hoped you might join me for a ride. Both of you," she added as an obvious afterthought.

"What about it, lass? We can finish this anytime."

Mary Kate would have liked to point out that they could also go riding anytime, but she only protested that she was unsuitably clad. Douglas brushed her words aside, telling her they would wait while she changed, and Megan agreed with an enigmatic smile that spurred Mary Kate to greater haste than might otherwise have been the case. When she returned a short time later, they were laughing and the roses were back in Megan's cheeks. Mary Kate bit her lip at their ease of manner, wondering if it truly had been five years and more since they were last together.

They soon reached the stable yard to find Sesi standing quietly and Valiant nervously beside a coal-black stallion, easily sixteen hands at the shoulder,

who snorted and pawed impatiently at the hard
ground. When the black heard his mistress's voice, he
responded with a twitch of his ears and a sound between a whinny and a chirp. Smiling broadly, Megan
stroked his cheek. He snorted again, tossed his proud
head, and pushed at her shoulder with his muzzle,
making her laugh.

"What a splendid animal!" Mary Kate could not
help her exclamation.

Megan smiled at her with unmistakable sincerity.
"Yes, he is," she agreed. "I call him Devil, of course,
though his behavior is never evil. He and Valiant are
rather a good match, are they not?"

It was true. Beside the two stallions, Sesi looked
like a pony, and Mary Kate felt the difference even
more once they were mounted. Douglas dismissed
the grooms, and the three riders had no sooner
cleared the stable yard than Megan issued a challenge
to race. The black plunged ahead with Valiant in hot
pursuit. Although Mary Kate urged Sesi to a gallop,
she was easily outdistanced and the other two were
soon lost to sight in the dense wood that loomed
ahead. Evidently they had already decided upon a
destination, but she did not know what it might be,
nor would the knowledge have helped her, since she
was unfamiliar with the wooded and hilly country-
side.

Unwilling to keep Sesi at a headlong pace over unknown terrain, she slowed her to a trot when she
entered the wood, and when the trail forked with still
no sign of Douglas or Megan, she drew rein. What,
she wondered, had possessed him? Surely he had not
left her behind on purpose. Or had he? The notion
occurred to her then that Megan might have issued
her challenge simply to see if Douglas *would* follow
her. Frustrated, bewildered, and angry, Mary Kate

turned back toward Strachan Court, riding slowly, not wishing to face the embarrassment of returning alone. No more than a moment passed, however, before she heard hoofbeats behind her.

Reining in again, she turned in the saddle, smiling so as not to let Megan see that she was angry. She was certain that Douglas would be shamefaced, apologetic; thus, she was astonished when he spoke sharply before Valiant had come to a complete stop.

"What's wrong? Why are you turning back?"

"You left me. I didn't know where to go."

"Don't be childish," he retorted. "We said we were riding up the ben path. If you were outdistanced, you had only to follow the uphill fork."

Stung by the injustice of his words, she replied hotly that, on the contrary, no one had seen fit to mention any destination to her, that the two of them had simply and quite rudely left her behind, and that, furthermore, if they wished to ride up the ben or anywhere else, they could do so without her company since that had so clearly been their intention from the outset.

She had barely warmed to her subject, however, before he interrupted, peremptorily commanding her to keep a civil tongue in her head. If there was even a hint of guilt scratching at the surface of his subconscious, it was not evident, and Mary Kate realized belatedly that she ought not to have criticized him in front of his cousin. His pride had been stung. As a consequence and with a fine disregard of his own for Megan's presence, Douglas proceeded to deliver a tongue-lashing that under ordinary circumstances might well have been expected to reduce his wife to tears, accusing her of discourtesy, selfishness, lack of generosity, and anything else he could think of.

Mary Kate heard him out in stony silence, biting

back blistering words of her own. She would have liked very much to answer him with a detailed and unflattering description of his own character, but she was well aware of Megan's interested attention, and she was not a fool. She knew exactly how he would deal with what he would interpret as bare-faced insolence from her. Therefore, she kept a guard on her tongue and forced herself to submit with outward meekness to his reprimand, while blinking away persistent tears of anger and frustration. She would not cry, no matter what he said. She would not give Lady Somerville that satisfaction.

But when he concluded by demanding that she improve her disposition at once and prepare to accompany them as planned, Mary Kate pleaded that she had lost her taste for a morning ride and would infinitely prefer to return to the house. To her surprise, Megan intervened before Douglas could expostulate.

"Do, for heaven's sake, let her go, Adam. Not everyone has such a passion for exercise as we do. Moreover, she looks pale. Perhaps she suffers from the headache." She smiled sweetly, causing Mary Kate to grit her teeth. "Shall we accompany you as far as the stables, my dear?"

"No, thank you," Mary Kate replied brusquely, knowing she sounded sullen but not knowing how to sound otherwise. "I shall do well enough by myself."

Douglas hesitated. He still looked angry, but now there was a shadow of doubt in his eyes as well, as though he realized that he ought not to ride off alone with his cousin. Mary Kate said nothing, hoping that this once he might give as much thought to her position as to his own. Unfortunately, her silence only irritated him, and with a near snarl, he glared at her and lifted his rein. "Go back then, if you wish to do so. But it would be best," he added, grim warning clear in his tone, "if you have done with these sulks before we return."

Tears clouded her vision, spilling over at last as she watched the pair of them disappear again into the small, dense wood. Once again, the honors had gone to Megan. Cursing herself for sheer stupidity, Mary Kate rode back to the stable yard, where an obliging and mercifully uncurious groom assisted her to dismount and took charge of Sesi.

Walking to the house, she would have gone straight to her own bedchamber had she not chanced to meet Lord Strachan in the great hall. The rushes on the floor there had been newly changed, and the scent of crushed herbs wafted into the air as she crossed the room. Servants were already setting up trestle tables for dinner and Strachan was in the midst of the bustle, conferring with his bailiff, but he dismissed the man and greeted Mary Kate with delight, declaring that since she was alone, she ought to come at once to see his books.

With a hope that her cheeks were not tearstained, she followed him to his sanctum, a spacious chamber with more of those magnificent windows overlooking the inner court. The other walls were lined with bookshelves piled with manuscripts and leather-covered tomes secured in place with fine gold chains. Side tables provided space for more manuscripts and more books.

In the center of the room stood a beautiful Italianate oak table with an elaborately carved underframing. An elegant, cushioned armchair had been pushed away from the near side of the table, and at their entrance, Ned Lumsden scrambled hastily to his feet from a back stool on the far side.

"She has come to see the books, lad," said Strachan, waving him back to his seat and pulling another armchair forward for Mary Kate. Before the next hour was done, she had learned a great deal more than she wished to know about illumination and the miracle of movable print. She had seen books on proper manners, history, and medicine, books of classical literature, and books in languages and even alphabets of which she had no knowledge. The information was all very interesting, to be sure, but she could not say that her interest matched her host's enthusiasm, so it was with unmixed relief that she greeted her husband's entrance a little more than an hour later.

Lord Strachan, in the process of selecting just one or two more excellent examples of something or other—she hadn't been attending carefully for some time—had not yet noted his son's presence, but Mary Kate looked at Douglas helplessly, and Ned grinned at him with undisguised impudence.

Casting a glance at the pile of books on the table beside his wife, Douglas raised an eyebrow and turned to his father. "Good day to you, my lord," he said, cutting unhesitatingly into what had been a running monologue. "I believe you are confusing my wife with your vast knowledge of your favorite subject."

Strachan turned quickly, pleased to see him but taken aback as well. He peered anxiously at his daughter-in-law. "I hope not," he said. "I know I tend to give my tongue free rein when I get to talking about my books."

"I have enjoyed your discourse, sir," Mary Kate assured him, smiling, "but perhaps we should stop now that Adam is here. I fear I shan't remember the half of what you have told me."

He looked disappointed but cheered considerably when Douglas mentioned that Mary Kate had still not seen all of the house and he wished to take her over the ground floor before dinner.

Cheerful again, Strachan suggested that they cross the inner court and begin with the garden hall.

The sun was high enough now so that half the courtyard was bathed in light, and the air was warm. The fish pond in the center was surrounded by a floral border and boasted a Cupid's fountain. Douglas reached into a hidden recess, and a fine, showery spray leaped up to surround the Cupid, splaying out over the pond below, causing golden carp to dart hither and yon for a moment until they became reaccustomed to the gentle splash.

From where Mary Kate stood, the sun's rays provided her with a rainbow arcing across the pond. " 'Tis lovely, sir."

"Aye." He looked at her searchingly, but she avoided his gaze, and they passed into the garden hall. Except for the long gallery above it, this room was easily the largest she had seen, certainly as large as the great hall and even more elegantly appointed. Once again, two opposing banks of windows gave one almost to feel that one was outside. But the most impressive feature of the room was the large hooded fireplace, where a gillie was busily laying a fire. Flanked by fluted pilasters and boasting an elegantly carved and decorated chimney piece, the fireplace dominated the western wall.

Douglas said briefly that the door to the right of the chimney led through a large, paneled parlor and two saloons to the great hall, while the housekeeper's parlor, pastry, bolting house, and kitchens lay beyond the garden hall's eastern door. Then, shooting the busy servant a look of unexplained annoyance, he guided Mary Kate outside onto the terrace.

They stood for a moment, drinking in the view of

the sun-ridden gardens below, where two middle-aged gardeners and a gardener's boy were industriously clipping hedges and pulling such minuscule weeds as had dared to disturb the perfection of the herbaceous borders. A pair of saucy jays screeched at each other unseen somewhere in the surrounding tall green hedges.

"Shall we walk a bit?"

She looked up at him, conscious of gathering tension, but then she nodded and let him tuck her hand in the crook of his arm. They went down the broad terrace steps and walked silently along the paths, away from the busy gardeners, until eventually they came to an arbor with a stone bench. Douglas pulled out his handkerchief and dusted the seat.

"Sit down, lass." When she had obeyed him, he said, "Do you feel better now?"

"Aye," she replied, her voice low, "unless you mean to shout at me again."

He sat beside her. "I didn't shout at you."

"You did. And in front of Lady Somerville, at that."

"Megan doesn't matter. She is family."

"Your family, not mine," she muttered, "and you didn't like it when I answered you in kind."

"I see." He digested her words for a moment while she wondered if she had vexed him again. "You are right," he said at last. "I should not have said what I said to you in Megan's presence. Forgive me?"

She stared at him, amazed. "Aye." She smiled. "I did not think you would apologize."

"Well, I've not finished with you yet, sweetheart, but I do know that a part of the fault this morning was mine. 'Twould be churlish not to admit it." He reached out to take her chin in his hand, making her look at him, and his expression grew more serious.

"But you were not very gracious to Megan, were you?" When she closed her eyes, he said, "Look at me, lass. That's better. Megan fears that you dislike her."

Perceptive of her, Mary Kate thought, but all she said was, "I doubt she loses much sleep for thinking about it."

Douglas frowned, dropping his hand from her chin.

Here it comes, she thought, watching him warily.

"Megan is my cousin and my friend," he said evenly. "I would like you to be friends with her. However, if for some reason you find that you cannot be, I will still expect you to be gracious. The good Lord knows she has tried her best to attach your friendship. Last night she went out of her way to encourage you to join us in the singing, but she met only with rebuff, and this morning your attitude toward her was barely civil. You will have to do better."

She sighed. "Very well, sir."

"I want you to apologize to her, lassie. I have already done so on your behalf, but you must say your own piece as well."

Mary Kate swallowed hard. She had not thought before of how he would interpret his cousin's behavior, but if he thought Lady Somerville was trying to be generous and hospitable, nothing she could say would alter his opinion. She would only come off second best in such a debate. The thought of apologizing galled her, but if Douglas wanted generosity, she would give him generosity. She stood up. "Where is she?"

He smiled, relieved. "That's my good lass. She went up to change her dress. We'll find her together, shall we?"

They found her in Lady Strachan's parlor with her

aunt and several maidservants, who were all industriously plying their needles. Mary Kate wished her
apology might be made more privately, but at the
same time, she was glad to have witnesses. She strode
briskly forward, holding out her hand.

"Lady Somerville, I have come to apologize. I was
uncivil to you this morning, and I would make
amends."

Lady Strachan looked surprised by Mary Kate's
words but not nearly so surprised as her niece looked.
Glancing at Douglas, however, Megan quickly recovered her countenance and took Mary Kate's hand,
giving it a warm squeeze. "There is no need for an
apology, my dear. I assure you, I did not regard the
incident in the least." Her words were accompanied
by a sugary smile that made Mary Kate long to smack
her, but she merely withdrew her hand, murmuring
that Lady Somerville was too kind.

Douglas was pleased with her for the moment, but
relations between the two young women continued
to be strained, and Mary Kate was constantly aware
of a taunt in Megan's attitude toward her. That very
evening, when the older girl challenged Douglas to a
game of cards and he accepted, the first game led to a
second and then to a third. Lady Strachan bade them
good night at last and retired, and soon afterward,
Mary Kate suggested that since the day had been long
and rather tiring, she, too, would like to go to bed.

Douglas waved her away. "I'll be along soon
enough, lass, as soon as I teach this wench that I am
still the master player."

Megan shot her a honeyed smile, and Mary Kate
hesitated, loathing the thought of leaving them alone
together, but then she decided that there was nothing
to be gained by remaining in the room simply to be
ignored by the two of them. As it was, Douglas

scarcely noticed that she had gone, and he still had
not arrived by the time she fell asleep in her own bed.

In the next few days their activities fell into a pattern. Strachan declared a holiday and bore his son
and Ned off hunting in the mornings, returning in
time for dinner, after which the afternoons were
spent playing at battledore and shuttlecock or watching Douglas and Ned play tennis.

Had it not been for Lady Somerville, Mary Kate
thought on more than one occasion, she would be
enjoying herself very much, for Lady Strachan was
kind, and his lordship was jolly and charming. But
Megan was making her life miserable. Mary Kate was
certain that she was doing her best to attract Douglas
to her bed; and, considering his past history, it
seemed almost inevitable that she would succeed if
indeed she had not already done so. As the date set
for Lady Strachan's party drew nearer, Mary Kate
found it more and more difficult to display a gracious
attitude toward the older girl.

Guests began to arrive on Saturday well before the
midday meal was served, and the dinner itself was a
veritable feast. Afterward, the family and guests
moved out onto the terrace for the sweets, which
were served with a variety of spicy drinks. As the
afternoon wore on, there were various games and
other pastimes to be enjoyed against a background of
unceasing, animated conversation until Lady
Strachan suggested that the ladies might like to retire
to enjoy a refreshing nap before the later festivities
began.

Mary Kate was delighted with the party. Most of
the guests had come purposely to make her acquaintance, and there were several handsome and unat-
tached young men who were quick to show their out-
spoken approval of the new Lady Douglas. Douglas,

too, had been charmingly attentive—probably, his
wife thought bitterly, because Lady Somerville had
been too busy renewing old friendships to flirt with
him. Mary Kate had also been flirting, however, and
when she agreed to Lady Strachan's suggestion, there
were a good many flattering groans of dismay.

Douglas laid a possessive hand upon her shoulder.
"You seem to have made a conquest or two, sweetheart."

"Aye, is it not wonderful?"

He grinned. "Just see to it that you behave yourself."

"And what of yourself, sir?" Despite his attentive-
ness, there was a certain amount of tartness in her
question.

But Douglas chuckled and, catching her close, gave
her a resounding kiss on the lips. When he let her go,
she was laughing and breathless. "The first dance is
mine, wife."

She curtsied and fled upstairs, knowing others
would follow. Since a late supper would be served at
eleven o'clock in the great chamber, the guests were
offered but a light repast in their bedchambers while
they changed, but by eight o'clock everyone had begun moving toward the long gallery.

The ladies were resplendent in bright colored silks
and velvets, the gentlemen hardly less so. For the
most part, feminine attire was informal, and only
older women who did not expect to take part in the
dancing wore farthingales. The younger ones wore
simpler gowns, allowing greater freedom of movement. Dancing was energetic exercise, not easily accomplished in stiff corsets and widely billowing
skirts.

Mary Kate wore a gown of dark red three-piled
velvet over gold lace petticoats. Her undersleeves

were of matching lace, and her low-cut bodice was trimmed with a falling lace collar and seed pearls. She wore no ruff, and her hair, though confined in a light, pearl-trimmed caul, was not elaborately coiffed. Her jewelry consisted of her delicate pendant watch, several gold chains, a necklace of pearls alternating with gold links, and a pearl-and-ruby ring.

Douglas had suggested more than once since their arrival that she ought to wear more baubles so as not to make him appear a pauper before his friends and relations, and as promised, he had presented her with several of the family pieces. But she continued to resist, saying that to deck herself out in such a way made her feel gaudy. That night, to please him, she wore an extra gold chain or two, the ruby ring, and even a pair of dangling golden earbobs; however, the moment she saw Lady Somerville, she began to wonder if she had worn enough.

Dressed in an exquisitely simple gown of shimmering lavender silk, Megan glittered with jewelry in the approved border tradition. Her smooth blond hair was confined in a lavishly ornamented clip; her hands and wrists gleamed with gold, silver, sapphires, amethysts, and pearls; and, some of her heavily jeweled chains and necklaces draped as low as her busk-point. If a man's affluence was judged by his wife's appearance, Mary Kate thought with a sigh, then truly Lady Somerville did her husband proud. She moved with the veritable clink of wealth.

The music began for the first dance, and Mary Kate pushed all thought of her rival firmly out of her mind. That night she meant to enjoy herself. Looking almost virginal with her glowing cheeks and sparkling eyes, she suffered no lack of partners, so although her husband disappeared into the crowd soon after that first dance, she paid little heed to his lack of attention.

It seemed no time at all before the musicians struck up for the galliard, the last dance before they would adjourn to the great chamber for supper. With a brief memory of the last time she had executed the fast-paced steps, with handsome Kenneth Gillespie at Critchfield, she happily accepted Ned Lumsden's invitation to be his partner; however, halfway through the dance, she caught sight of Douglas dancing enthusiastically with Lady Somerville. When the music stopped, she was near enough to see him give his cousin a great, laughing hug, and when Lady Somerville turned her face obligingly up to his, he planted a kiss squarely on her rosy lips.

Mary Kate stiffened automatically, then forced herself to relax when she noted several speculating glances cast first toward Douglas and then toward herself. Her husband, however, seemed completely unaware of the attention he had drawn as he went blithely into supper with his cousin on his arm.

Forcing a smile, Mary Kate turned to Ned. "Shall we go in?" The anxious look in his eyes when he agreed told her that he had seen everything, but he made no comment as they followed the others into the great chamber. They found places toward the end of one of the trestle tables, next to a gentleman who was clearly interested in no one other than his dinner partner.

Grateful to be spared the necessity of making polite conversation, Mary Kate nibbled her food without tasting it and expended the better part of her energy in an unsuccessful attempt to suppress her fury. She was aware of Ned's rapidly increasing nervousness as he cut meat for her that she did not touch and offered dishes that failed to tempt her, and she knew he hoped that she would do nothing to provoke the Douglas temper, but the longer she watched her husband and his cousin laughing and talking at the other end of the long table, the more she wanted to punish them both.

Her opportunity did not arrive until supper was done. But then, while servants swiftly cleared the remains and dismantled the huge tables, the guests moved toward the fireplace where spiced claret was being served. It was not a rowdy gathering while the steaming, ruby-colored liquid was ladled out first for one and then another, but a sufficient number of people were moving about to make it look purely accidental when Mary Kate, turning from the fire with her new-filled mug to find a smiling Lady Somerville directly in front of her, jerked her arm up as though it had been roughly jostled from behind and spewed hot spiced claret down the front of Megan's lavender silk gown.

Megan cried out in dismay, and a sudden hush fell. Several gloved hands flew to hide smiles, and one slightly inebriated gentleman failed to stifle his chuckle. The sound reached Douglas, and his dark eyes were narrow with suspicion when his gaze fell upon his wife.

Mary Kate presented an affecting portrait of horror and innocent contrition as she hastily offered to assist Lady Somerville in the changing of her gown, but it was Ned Lumsden who eased Douglas's suspicions and, incidentally, those of one or two others as well.

"My lady, pray forgive my clumsiness!" he exclaimed, striding forward from behind Mary Kate. "My great, oafish feet! Is there aught I can do to atone for ruining your beautiful gown? My handkerchief, perhaps?"

Megan disdained the offer, but Ned had succeeded

in turning Douglas's attention to himself. He with-
stood the forthcoming low-voiced lecture manfully,
thus allowing Mary Kate to make good her escape
under a pretense of proffering aid to the victim.

Stiffly, silently, Megan bore with her company until they reached the door to her bedchamber. Her
maid waited within, but the window hall was momentarily empty when she turned furiously on Mary
Kate. "That was no accident," she accused shrilly.
"You did that deliberately."

"Did I?" Mary Kate regarded her with sweet innocence.

"Aye, butter wouldn't melt in your mouth, would
it, madam?" Megan said, fuming. "But you had best
have a care. Should Adam learn that you did this to
me purposely, he would put you across his knee
again, quick as winking." And with that Parthian
shot she turned on her heel and disappeared into her
bedchamber, slamming the door shut behind her.

13

Mary Kate stared at the closed door for a full minute before she turned to walk back to the great chamber. Any thought of victory over Lady Somerville was gone, and in its stead was a void caused by the shock of the other young woman's final words. That Douglas's father and probably his mother had some awareness of her punishment was one thing, that he had confided the details to his cousin, quite another. But anger did not come. She almost wished it would, wished she had the strength born of anger to return to his side and tell him exactly what she thought of his betrayal. For betrayal it was. That incident had been a private matter between husband and wife. He had no business to discuss it with Lady Somerville.

As she walked dejectedly back into the great chamber, she realized that people were beginning to return to the long gallery, where the musicians had begun to tune up their instruments. The dancing would soon begin again. She glanced around, wondering where her husband was, and had just noted his presence in the midst of a small group of gentlemen near the far door when a cheery voice spoke beside her.

"All serene?"

Turning quickly, she found Ned grinning conspiratorially at her and managed to summon up a smile. "Lady Somerville is changing her gown. She did not desire my assistance."

"I'll warrant she did not. But she invited the trouble."

"Aye, perhaps."

"Adam suspects nothing," he assured her, "so you are perfectly safe unless you fear that she might tell him the truth and be believed."

Mary Kate shook her head with a wry smile. "To do so would be to force him to choose between us—choose knowingly, that is—and she is far too clever for that. She manipulates, but he does not see it because she does not wish him to see. But she will not bear tales to him." She paused, then added shrewdly, "I almost wish she would. He would think less of her then."

Ned took her hand and rested it upon his forearm as they began to follow the others back to the dancing. "You know, my lady," he said thoughtfully, "I have known Megan a good many years, and I think she is only having a game with you." When Mary Kate glared at him, he went on lamely, "Well, mayhap I know nothing at all, but I have always liked her before. I don't like this business, of course," he added hastily.

She smiled. "You need not concern yourself so with my troubles, Ned. Indeed, I have not even thanked you for coming to my rescue as you did. If you had not spoken up so quickly, Adam would soon have known the truth of the matter and I would be in the suds now for certain." She looked up at him. "Was he very angry with you?"

The young man shrugged. "Don't distress yourself unduly. He did no more than rebuke me for my supposed clumsiness, which made him feel better and didn't hurt me a bit. Now, if he had been *really* angry . . ." He grimaced with exaggerated fervor, and Mary Kate nodded sympathetically. She knew exactly what he meant.

A round dance was forming, and she accepted his invitation to join the fun, telling herself that she would do better to put her husband out of mind for a time. But some moments later, she caught Douglas's speculative gaze upon her just as Ned swung her so high that her feet left the floor amidst a riot of swirling gold petticoats. She laughed and was glad to note a moment later that her partner's eyes were twinkling merrily. When he whirled her up again, she felt as light as a feather in his strong grip and laughed even louder just to show Douglas what a good time she was having. But then she saw Lady Somerville approaching him, and her laughter died.

Megan had wasted no time. Elegant figured saffron damask had replaced the lavender gown, and from top to toe she now looked like old gold. Her underskirt was of deep brown with gold satin embroidery, matching that of the gown's full-cut undersleeves, while her plunging bodice exposed an alluring, very deep decolletage. Again she wore a vast amount of jewelry.

Douglas turned to greet her with a broad smile.

Mary Kate suddenly wanted to go to bed, to leave them to their fun. If Ned was right and Megan only playing games, then she would let her play without an audience. But the more she considered that course of action, the less she liked it, for it smacked of defeat.

Telling herself that there was no good purpose to be served by leaving the jade with a clear field in which to work her mischief, Mary Kate decided instead to take advantage of the many admirers she had acquired during the day. She would serve Sir Adam Douglas with a dish of his own sauce and see how he liked the taste of it. Accordingly, she threw herself into the dancing with more energy than ever.

Ned was soon sent about his business by another laughing cavalier, and as partner succeeded partner, Mary Kate kept a careful eye upon her husband. He had not danced with Megan for some time, but neither did he seem particularly interested in his wife. At one point, admittedly, he had taken a step or two in her direction, but Mary Kate had seen him coming and had quickly accepted an invitation from a handsome young man who swept her immediately into the dance that was forming at the time. She knew Megan had lodged no accusation against her, for there would have been immediate repercussions, but Douglas might still ask an awkward question or two. Or worse, she might lose her temper with him over his own behavior. It would be better, she decided, to avoid him altogether for a time.

He made no further attempt to approach her, although his eyes met hers upon more than one occasion. When he danced again with Megan later in the evening, after some of the guests had taken their leave, Mary Kate encountered a gleam of mischievous triumph in Megan's eyes. Turning pointedly away, she addressed a flirtatious remark to her own astonished partner, only to have him reply in kind. Recalled to her senses, she snubbed him firmly a moment later.

As the evening dragged on, she put more effort into appearing to enjoy herself, but her thoughts kept returning to Douglas and his cousin. Was she merely jealous, she wondered, and making too much of their relationship? To be sure, Douglas himself had shown little in the way of loverlike behavior toward Megan. His attitude was friendly, but thinking about his behavior objectively, Mary Kate had to admit she had detected nothing more than friendship. Moreover, though he had made no real effort to understand her dislike for Megan, he did seem honestly confused by it, and Douglas was not a fool. Was Ned right and her ladyship only having her own devious fun? But then, with deep humiliation, she remembered that gleam of triumph in Megan's eyes and the fact that the older girl knew about her punishment. How could Douglas have told her about that unless they were very intimate indeed with each other?

Mary Kate gritted her teeth, calling herself a fool and childish besides, reminding herself that it did no good to speculate about such matters. To hurl accusations at her husband as she had done over Susan Kennedy would likewise be of no use. She would have to be more careful, more subtle. If all else failed, she would simply ask him outright about his feelings for his cousin.

With these decisions made, she felt better and ready at last to face him. Since it seemed clear enough now that he believed the business with the wine to have been an accident, she decided she had nothing to fear on that score. Besides, she told herself, since she had stayed downstairs at all, there was little point in leaving him alone for Megan to do her worst.

She found him with a group of weary guests who had decided to sit out a dance or two to rest themselves. Several ladies were sitting on benches in a window embrasure, while most of the men leaned against the wall nearby. Douglas shot her a quizzical look, but the others greeted her cheerfully, and one lilting, musical voice rose above the others.

"Mary Kate," Megan said, "do come sit with us and rest your feet. I have just been telling everyone the most amusing tales about your husband."

Mary Kate tensed at the taunting note in her voice, but the others obligingly moved over on the bench to make room for her, and with so many watching, the invitation could not with any civility be refused. As soon as she had seated herself, Megan went on with a laughing tale about Douglas's prowess, or lack thereof, on the tennis court, followed immediately by more stories of his escapades as a child. Several others joined in these reminiscences, but Mary Kate's attention was fixed upon Megan, who made it sound as though she and Douglas had passed years in each other's continuous, intimate company.

Although Mary Kate knew such a thing to have been impossible, she felt the flames of her anger begin to burn again, and by the time the last tale had come to its humorous conclusion, she had forgotten her tactful intentions and wanted only to give free rein to her temper. But she could not speak in front of them all. She was forced to contain herself until the last guest had taken his departure, by which time she believed she had herself well in hand again.

Though Megan observed then with a sigh that it would be pleasant to relax for a time with a glass of wine to review the activities, physical exertion and lack of sleep had taken their toll and Douglas offered no objection when his wife suggested that they retire immediately instead. Lady Strachan, because of her health, had gone to bed soon after supper, but his lordship and Ned had lasted to the end. They both agreed with Mary Kate that the time had come for sleep, and no one else appeared to notice Megan's

frown of disappointment, but Mary Kate gained pleasure from it, shooting the older girl a mocking smile
as they left the room amidst a warm exchange of good
nights.

Lucas Trotter was waiting for Douglas, and Mary
Kate went to her own chamber, her mind working
rapidly. She was determined to speak to Douglas, but
she did not wish to antagonize him and hoped that
this time she could control her temper and remain
reasonable, calm, and controlled. She waited only until Annie and Trotter had been dismissed before approaching him.

He was standing near the hearth with its low-glow-
ing embers, draining a mug of mulled wine. His chin
was tilted up, and she could see the muscles work in
his throat as he swallowed the last few drops. He put
the mug down on the mantle shelf and, aware now of
her presence, turned to face her, stifling a yawn. He
looked tired, almost vulnerable. "Ready for bed,
sweetheart?"

"Aye." He held out a hand to her. "First I have
something to say to you, sir." Her voice was stiff with
determination.

His eyes narrowed, but he said calmly, "Do you
wish to speak here or may we go to bed first?"

She hesitated, experiencing a sudden sinking feeling that perhaps she had been mistaken, that perhaps
he was expecting a confession of some sort from her.

Fortunately, he answered himself. "Here, I think.
If I lie down, I shall probably fall asleep, which is
never a wise thing to do in the midst of a curtain
lecture." When her eyes flew wide, he chuckled, pulling up a pair of stools near the hearth. "Don't look so
amazed, sweetheart, You've been shooting dagger
looks from your pretty eyes these past two hours and

longer, making it only too obvious that I have done something to vex you. Whatever it is, tell me."

She sat down opposite him, trying to compose her thoughts. The fears were calmed again, but they had caught her off guard, disturbing her careful poise.

"Well, what is it, lassie?" There was an overtone of impatience now. He was tired. "Let's have it."

"You told her," she blurted, forgetting her decision to lead up to the subject gradually and with tact.

"I told what to whom?"

"Her! Your precious Lady Somerville." She looked away as she spoke, to stare grimly into the embers, and so did not see him stiffen at her tone. "You told her about . . ." She paused, swallowing hard. "About when you . . . when I . . . about what you did to me."

He understood at once and cursed fluently. "Is that what has been troubling you?"

She nodded, thinking that would do for a start.

"Megan's been flapping her tongue again, I see. I will have something to say to her about that, believe me." When she looked up at him accusingly, he admitted sharply, "Oh, I told her, but it was not as you think. You were in one of your sulks, and she asked me—in jest, mind you—if I was not sometimes tempted to smack you. I tried to laugh it off, but she asked point-blank if I ever had done so, and though I told her it was no concern of hers, she knew the answer by looking at me. I swear that's all, lass. We have not been discussing you behind your back."

She was far from satisfied, but the thought occurred to her that if she were to press the issue, he might well ask how Megan had come to mention her knowledge. Such a question would lead inevitably to a much more awkward discussion. Even now, if he were to take Megan to task for talking too much, the truth of the spilled claret would no doubt be divulged to him.

"Is that all, Mary Kate?"

"You kissed her!"

For a moment he looked puzzled. Then his brow cleared and he shot her a direct, unrepentant, even a challenging look. "Aye, you're right, I did. An innocent kiss in front of a roomful of friends. What about it?"

"You spend all your time with her."

"Women!" He snorted. "I do not spend all my time with her, and you know it. I don't know what has got into you, madam, but if you are angry because I danced often with her tonight, I'll tell you to your head that I did so only because you seemed determined to avoid me and I preferred dancing with my cousin to being accused of flirting with any of the local wenches. You are jealous without cause." He paused, glaring. "If anyone has reason, it is I, the way you were leading all those damned fellows about by the nose. And what about Ned Lumsden, eh? He was never far from your side that I could see."

He was building up a good healthy anger, and she stared at him, amazed. "You are jealous."

"Huh? Nonsense!" he snapped. "If I thought there were cause to be jealous, you'd have heard me say so long since." He controlled his temper with visible effort. "This discussion is pointless, Mary Kate. I am too tired to argue. If you would set aside your own foolish jealousies and your ridiculous highland prejudices long enough to make an effort to like Megan, I believe you would find the task not so difficult as you think."

She glared at him. "It is not mere jealousy that I feel, sir, and as for my prejudices, as you choose to call them, I have found little to prove they are not simple truths instead. Indeed, your failure to consider that there must be two versions to any tale does much to strengthen my opinion of border men. And if you are so tired," she added tartly, "perhaps I had better sleep in my own bed."

"Don't be absurd." He stood and pulled her to her feet. "You overreact, sweetheart, see demons where they don't exist. Now, cease your deaving, and come to bed."

She obeyed reluctantly, annoyed that he could still think her beliefs only foolish prattle and certain, too, that she was too keyed up to sleep. Nevertheless, she was exhausted and fell into deep slumber almost the moment her head touched the pillow.

The next morning, when she awoke with vague memories of wakefulness and disturbed dreams, she did not feel at all rested. Her eyelids were heavy with sleep, and she would have liked to remain right where she was, but she could not lie abed, for the family meant to attend service at the nearby village kirk.

Douglas made no attempt to cheer her, and she decided he must still be vexed with her. She was sure of it when some perverse spirit caused him to greet his cousin enthusiastically, complimenting her looks, her gown, her cheerfulness. If he mentioned anything to Megan about her flapping tongue, Mary Kate saw no sign of it.

She glowered at them both. So much for plain speaking. Obviously, she thought, her criticism had only spurred Douglas on to more outrageous behavior. That opinion was bolstered later by his actions on the way to the village. They waked in pairs along the dusty road, and with Mary Kate silent beside him, he had no qualms about carrying on a conversation over his shoulder with his cousins. Ned tried once or twice to draw Mary Kate into the discussion, but her responses were brief and unencouraging.

Douglas and Megan were in high spirits, their chatter punctuated with bursts of hilarity. When a courageous toad made a sudden appearance in the roadway and an equally sudden retreat back into the bordering scrub, they roared with laugher.

"Oh, Adam, do you remember when you put the toad under Mr. Browder's lecture notes at Tornary kirk?" Megan's lilting voice was full of merriment.

Douglas chuckled. "Aye. How the poor man jumped when he turned his page and the wee beastie flew out at him!"

"I remember, as well," put in his lordship wryly from up in front of them, "that someone else jumped a bit once we got back to the castle that day."

Douglas grimaced and cast a speaking glance over his shoulder at his cousin, making her laugh again, and although the two of them had to affect more sober demeanors when they reached the little stone kirk, they were still in excellent spirits when they took their places in the family pew. Lord Strachan entered first, followed by his lady. Then Megan gave smiling precedence to Mary Kate, allowing her to enter behind Lady Strachan, and Mary Kate found herself seated between her husband's mother and Lady Somerville before she recognized the latter's purpose. Douglas took his place next to Megan with Ned on his other side.

Several times during the service Mary Kate heard her husband and Megan whispering and thought angrily that Parson MacDole, back in the *clachan*, would have made short shrift of their lack of attention to the lesson. She well remembered more than one occasion when the dour man of the cloth had halted his sermon midsentence until some disturbance had been stifled. Once he had actually remonstrated with an errant soul right then and there, recalling him to the proprieties in no uncertain terms.

After a curious glance at Mr. Cory, the local parson, who also appeared to be a stern man, she sat quietly with her eyes properly downcast. Even the irritating whispers failed to arouse her enough to look up. But suddenly the minister's voice took on a new note, one more in keeping with her own feelings.

"Rose MacReady!" he bellowed. "Thou art condemned! Step forth and confront thy neighbors in thine infamy!"

Startled, Mary Kate looked up as a pretty young woman, barefoot and wearing sackcloth, was led up the aisle by the bailie and forced to climb the steps to a raised dais near the parson's lectern, to sit there upon a high stool. The young woman's cheeks burned scarlet with shame as she gazed steadfastly at her hands, clenched tightly in her lap.

"Our Lord," continued Cory in stentorian accents, "condemneth whoredom in deed or thought, Rose MacReady! Thou knockest at the gates of hell! Adultery, though it be committed only in thy mind, be yet a grievous sin. Repentest thou, Rose MacReady, before it is too late!"

The harangue continued, and it became clear that poor Rose MacReady, having been accused by her own husband of secretly lusting after another man, had been condemned without right or recourse to the cockstool, as highlanders called that seat of repentance for offenders against chastity. Mary Kate had never actually seen the stool put to use before, but she knew that poor Rose must sit there through at least one entire service, maybe even two or three, to suffer the agonizing humiliation of formal, public reprimand from the parson, after which she must confess her crime and repent of it before the entire congregation.

Mary Kate felt sorry for the girl, but the other witnesses did not seem to share her feelings. Several nodded in stern-faced agreement with Mr. Cory's searing words. Others hid smiles of derision behind lifted hands. One—a man with a bristly red beard—sat stiffly, staring straight ahead with no expression at all upon his face, and Mary Kate wondered if he was Mr. MacReady or even the "other man."

Her attention was diverted by a giggle, quickly stifled, from the young woman next to her. She glanced at Megan reprovingly, but the older girl paid her no heed. She was batting her lashes at Douglas and grinning mischievously, mocking Rose MacReady. Even Douglas appeared to be shocked by her behavior, but when he cast a speaking glance in the direction of his parents, his frown was more amused than angry. Megan subsided, but Mary Kate glared disgustedly at the pair of them.

When the long morning service was done, they walked out again into the open air. Instead of remaining with Lord and Lady Strachan as Ned did, Megan chose to attach herself to Douglas and Mary Kate while they moved from group to group of friends and neighbors. Every now and again she would rest a possessive hand upon Douglas's arm, playing the lady of the manor to the hilt and even going so far as to introduce Mary Kate to persons whom she had not yet met.

"This is Lady Douglas, you know. Sir Adam's wife." As though the explanation were necessary, Mary Kate thought angrily the third time it happened. Indeed, considering the older girl's proprietary air, perhaps it was necessary. She glanced at

Douglas, wondering how he would react to such outrageous behavior. He seemed only amused, however,
and not at all disturbed by Megan's antics.

By the time they returned to Strachan Court, Mary
Kate was seething. Lady Strachan had endured the
walk very well and readily agreed to her husband's
suggestion that they await the announcement of dinner on the terrace. She added that she would like to
have her tapestry-work in hand, in order that her fingers not remain idle, and Ned immediately offered to
fetch it from the winter parlor where she had left it.

Megan looked down at her skirts in dismay. "I cannot dine in all this dirt. The dust of the road has all
but changed the color of this gown."

Lady Strachan laughingly remarked that although
her own gown was in a like state she refused to bustle
about, throwing off one costume only to replace it
with another for dinner with the family. She would
shake out her skirts, but that was all. Megan insisted,
however, and started up the stairs.

Impulsively, Mary Kate announced that she, too,
would change her gown and, before any protest could
be made, hastened after Megan, catching up with her
at the top of the stairs in the window hall. "Lady
Somerville, one moment, if you please," she said in a
low, insistent voice. "I would speak with you."

Megan turned, her head cocked a little to one side,
her hands folded demurely at her waist. "What is it
now, Mary Kate?" She spoke impatiently, as to a re-
fractory child.

Mary Kate clenched her fists against her skirts, but
she was determined. "I can no longer tolerate your
behavior toward my husband. 'Tis unmannerly and
unsuitable." She kept her voice low and controlled,
since a servant might appear at any moment.

Megan's mouth quirked with amusement. "Do you

think so?" she said gently. "You know, my dear, you made that rather plain last night when you doused me with claret, but I must tell you, I took that little gesture as a challenge, a throwing down of the gauntlet, so to speak. I did not tell Adam, you know, though I might have done and I might well do so yet if you continue to annoy me. To hear such a tale will make him very angry, I promise you. I know him so much better than you do, you see, so if you mean to keep his goodwill, I fear you must exert yourself to keep mine as well."

The smugness was more than Mary Kate could bear. "How dare you speak so to me!" she snapped. "You are no lady, Megan Somerville. Indeed, you behave more like a wanton." She was speaking now without thought of what she was saying, and her voice grew louder as her temper rose.

Megan stared at her, that infuriating little smile playing about her lips until Mary Kate wanted to slap it off.

"Have you nothing to say?" she demanded. When Megan only continued her frustrating, smiling silence, she added sarcastically, "And you think yourself so clever. Well, I won't tolerate any more of this, and so I tell you. Today you dared to mock poor Rose MacReady, who only raised her eyes to another man, whilst you, my fine lady, would raise your skirts if any man so much as snapped his fingers to encourage you."

Megan gasped, and Mary Kate leaned forward, speaking with caustic animosity. "You seem shocked, madam, but I dare you to deny that you've been flaunting your wagtail wares in the hope of bedding my husband. Christ's blood, Megan Somerville, but you should think shame to yourself, for 'tis you that belonged this day upon yon cockstool, *saidhe* that you are!"

Megan went rigid with anger. "You go too far, madam," she declared icily. "I do not pretend to understand your barbarous Gaelic, but—"

"I understand it well enough!" snapped a grim voice from behind Mary Kate.

She whirled in shock to see Douglas nearing the top of the stairs with a wide-eyed Ned close upon his heels. Deafened by her own tirade, she had not heard their approach, but one look at her furious husband was enough. Mary Kate threw dignity to the wind, snatched up her skirts, and fled.

14

>>> <<<

*A*s she sped through the great chamber, Mary Kate heard Megan burst into tears behind her, and false though she knew such histrionics to be, she was grateful, knowing Douglas would pause to console his cousin and thus give her time to reach the privacy of her own bedchamber before he caught her. There could be no thought of avoiding an immediate confrontation, but his overwhelming fury had caused her to fear that he would bellow at her, or worse, right then and there, and she could not bear the thought that he might permit Megan and Ned to witness such a scene between them.

Her bedchamber was empty, and she continued across it to the half-open window, where she gazed with unseeing eyes at the fountain in the center of the hedged garden below. Birds called to one another, obliviously cheerful, but she did not hear them. While her mind raced, her ears strained for the sound of Douglas's footsteps. What could she say to him?

Cursing her impulsive tongue, she realized that she ought never to have allowed Megan to spark her temper. Indeed, she should have known better, feeling as she did, than to follow her upstairs. Then all thought was suspended. He was coming.

The snap of his quick, firm steps crackled through her mind as he neared her door. She did not turn but stood, waiting, holding her breath as he crossed the room, his footsteps muffled now by the carpet. Suddenly, his hands were upon her shoulders and he spun her roughly to face him. Mary Kate stumbled, but he caught her shoulders again, bruisingly. Then he was shaking her.

"Do not ever, ever let me hear such words from your mouth again!" he snapped, affected not one whit by the tears welling into her eyes. "By heaven, madam, I am ashamed of you, ashamed to find you capable of saying such insulting things to anyone, let alone to a relative of mine who wishes only to befriend you. There can be no excuse!" He stopped shaking her and glared, daring her to respond, but for once she was afraid to enrage him further, so she held her tongue. He continued harshly, "You will apologize for your insults, Mary Kate, and this time it will take more than a simple expression of your regret to satisfy me. Indeed, I won't be satisfied until you have begged Megan to forgive you and she has agreed to do so."

That was too much. She looked up disbelievingly, trying to steady her nerves. Her voice shook. "I will apologize, sir, if I must, for I ought not to have said what I did. But I will never beg that woman for anything. She provoked me to it. You do not know the things she has said or how she has taunted me. It is she—aye, and you as well, Adam Douglas—who ought to beg *my* forgiveness!"

His eyes narrowed dangerously when her voice began to rise, but he did not interrupt her. Now a short silence fell while he made a visible effort to regain control of his temper, and when he spoke, his voice was steady but contained a note she had long since learned to recognize. He meant to be obeyed.

"What anyone else has or has not said or done does not matter. What matters is that you have not behaved as Lady Douglas must behave." He paused but did not take his eyes from her face. "You threw that wine at Megan deliberately last night, did you not?"

Her breath caught in her throat, and she looked away, unable to meet his gaze.

"I thought so. That being the case," he went on coldly, "you may count yourself fortunate that I am not a more violent husband, for I am sorely tempted to school you here and now to better manners. Megan has suffered a great deal of unkindness from you. She does not fully comprehend your rudeness today because I did not trouble her with a translation, but she has been hurt and insulted. Since you are entirely at fault, you will humble yourself to her on your knees if necessary. I command it, madam."

With his last words he let his hands fall from her shoulders but stood looking down at her challengingly, daring her to rebel further against his authority.

Mary Kate said nothing, neither did she move. Her gaze was fixed upon the lowest fastening of his doublet, her damp lashes casting shadows upon her reddened cheeks. Her lips trembled, and her breath caught in quiet sobs. Except for the hushing whisper of the fountain outside and the disinterested chirping of the birds, there was no other sound.

Douglas sighed. "I will make your excuses to my lady mother, for you do not wish to appear at table.

You may use the time to compose yourself before approaching Megan. Do not be overlong about that, however," he added grimly. "My patience is not infinite, and your behavior has already gone beyond what I will tolerate. If you do not make your apologies quickly, the least that will happen is that you'll find yourself across my knee again, and this time I will not be so gentle." With that, he turned upon his heel and strode from the room.

Emotionally drained by her efforts to remain silent, Mary Kate stood where she was until the sound of his footsteps had faded into the distance. Then she sank down upon a stool near the window and brushed angry tears from her eyes with the back of her sleeve. She could still feel where his fingers had bitten into her shoulders, and there was an ache at the back of her throat from the harshness of his anger. But her thoughts did not linger upon these ills. He had ordered her to throw herself upon Megan's mercy, to abase herself to a woman she loathed.

How Megan would rejoice at her humiliation, she thought bitterly. An apology would have been difficult enough, God knew, but for Douglas to have demanded one of her would have been perfectly fair, for she had committed a grave offense by calling his cousin a bitch in heat to her face. Gaelic words, she mused, were always so much more graphic than their English counterparts. By calling Megan a *saidhe*, she had no doubt placed herself in *mortshainn* insofar as her husband's good opinion of her was concerned. She decided she had to do what she could to put things right, but to humble herself completely, as he had commanded, was out of the question. He might say she had not behaved as a Douglas must, but he himself must still think of her as a MacPherson or he would never have issued such a command. A Douglas humbled himself to no one.

The thought stirred some of her old spirit. Douglas had much to learn of MacPhersons, did he not? Did not the Clan Chattan motto warn against touching the cat without a glove? But the mental image of herself clawing at Douglas's hand consoled her but briefly, for she knew only too well that at this point, he would deal short shrift to rebellion of any kind. He had left her no alternative but to obey him.

She stood up, suddenly restless, anxious to have the hateful business over and done. Damn him, she thought, for ordering her to keep to her bedchamber, for forbidding her presence at the table. They were probably just now going in, smelling delicious smells, wondering where she was. No doubt he would provide her with a headache or some such thing as he had done at Tornary, but whatever the excuse, they would see right through it. Probably Megan was clinging to his arm at this very moment and would sit beside him, looking long-suffering and noble while he served her from the dishes they shared.

Mary Kate glanced out of the window, hearing the birds' chatter now. Sunlight sparkled invitingly on the gentle fountain spray, creating a host of dancing rainbows. The day was lovely. At least, out there it was lovely. A thought teased at her mind. He had not precisely ordered her to stay where she was. He had perhaps assumed that she would do so, once he had made it clear that she was not to inflict her presence upon the family at dinner. But he had not actually forbidden her to go outside.

Telling herself that she needed fresh air to relax her before her ordeal, she began searching for her safeguard, and less than a quarter hour later, she hurried from the house. Encountering no one on her

way to the stables, she was fortunate enough to find
the same dour groom who had helped her before.
Once again he showed not a trace of curiosity, sad-
dling the mare as ordered and accepting his dismissal
without comment. Mary Kate had no desire for company, believing that Annandale was too far north of
the border for her to be in any danger so long as she
remained on Lord Strachan's land.

Forcing all thought of the forthcoming interview
with Megan from her mind, she gave the mare her
head. Sesi was well pleased to have such freedom and
chose to stretch her legs upon a southbound track.
Mary Kate concentrated her attention upon the terrain. Hatless, letting the warm breeze blow her hair
and loving the caress of it across her face, she rode
until Sesi began to slow of her own accord. She had
no idea how great a distance they had covered, but
they had kept to the rough track, so she knew she
could easily find her way back.

They reached the crest of a low hill. Off in the
distance, perhaps half a mile or so, lay a thickly
wooded slake that looked as though it followed a river
or stream, and Mary Kate realized that she was
thirsty.

Ten minutes later she rode into the peaceful shade
of the wood. It was silent there, and soon she was able
to hear the babble of water coursing over stones. She
turned Sesi toward the sound. Sunlight played innocently through green branches, daubing lush and
fragile ferns with spatters of gold. Surely, she
thought, the silver glint just ahead was the same sunlight sparkling on water, for the sound of the splash-
ing brook came to her ears clearly now with a nearly
metallic jingle. She froze on the thought, her hand
jerking the rein with a suddenness that stopped the
mare in her tracks.

Sesi whinnied in nervous protest, but Mary Kate heard the sound again, not an odd note in the brook's song at all but the jingle of spurs and clink of harness. Before she could wheel the mare, however, the woods erupted with horsemen who quickly surrounded her, and a rough hand grabbed her bridle.

Sesi shied.

"Let her go at once!" Mary Kate cried.

"Nay, lass, she's like tae bolt, gin I do anything sae daft." He was broad-shouldered, thickset, and heavily bearded.

"You have no right! Release her!"

The man holding Sesi shook his head, his blue eyes sparkling with uncouth insolence. He grinned at the others. There were fifteen of them, she saw now, perhaps more. It was difficult to tell amidst the close-growing trees, but they were a motley lot, bearing arms ranging from calivers to broadswords, daggers, and dirks. They were not gentlemen, nor were they ordinary peasants or farmers. Their leader regarded her closely, his roving eyes drinking in every detail of her trappings and the rich gown beneath her safe-guard.

Embarrassed by his effrontery, she was nevertheless glad for once that she did not indulge in the border wife's practice of sporting every jewel she owned. She had even taken off her watch before she left, for it had a habit of bouncing uncomfortably when she rode. It lay now safely in the trinket box on her dressing table.

"What might a bonny wee lassock like yerself be a-doin' allanerly in a place such as this 'un, me lass?"

"That is no affair of yours," she retorted.

"Lass has spirit," the leader observed in an aside to his men. Then his voice hardened. "Answer me, lass."

"You have no right," she insisted. "I ride upon my husband's father's estate, and 'tis no business of yours whether I ride alone or otherwise."

Her words seemed somehow to arouse the whole group, to electrify the very air. The leader eyed her sharply. "Your husband's father?"

"Aye," she said, glad he seemed to know where he was. "I am in Lord Strachan's care, and I'll warrant that you do not wish to incur his displeasure."

The leader shook his head sorrowfully. "Och, but ye've gone and left his lordship's acres behind on yonder ben, lassie. 'Tis a greetin' shame, I grant ye, but I fear ye mun abide a wee wi' ourselves." He cast a sly wink at his men. "Methinks, lads, we've collected more than we thought tae find. 'Tis herself, I'm thinkin'. 'Tis Douglas's ain bonny lassie."

The note of triumph in his voice sent shivers racing up and down her spine. They were raiders. Why had she not realized it at once? Because, she told herself bitterly, she had foolishly thought herself too far north, of course. They must be Scots, though, not English. Even as the thought crossed her mind, the leader confirmed her worst fear.

"The Douglas owes us, lass. He's got five o' our ain lads locked up in Roxburgh Tolbooth, and we want them back afore yon assize court meets."

"But they forced themselves upon an innocent girl," Mary Kate protested without thinking, "and they nearly killed a man."

"Nearly?" exclaimed the leader. "Was he no dead, then? God's nails, but I thought certes he was wi' his Maker." His eyes gleamed wickedly. "But yon lass wasna sae innocent as ye might think, me lady. Eh, lads?" He leered, and the others chuckled appreciatively.

"She was nice, Uncle Rupe," declared a great hulk-

ing fellow near the leader. He seemed younger than
the others and spoke in a slow, careful voice. "I remember her."

"Do ye now, Wee Ranald? Well, that's a guid lad,"
replied the leader, grinning. "But just ye hush yer
gab now, afore ye frighten the bonny lady. Dinna
mind his gab, lass. He be gowkish, ye ken, just a wee
bit wowf."

The news that Wee Ranald was of unsound mind
was scarcely encouraging. Mary Kate had been
frightened from the moment the men had shown
themselves, but now her fear was painful, as though
every muscle in her body had tensed in an involun-
tary gesture of defense. Breathing was difficult, and
although her heart was pounding, it seemed to strain
to do so. Had these terrible men all had their way
with poor Ellen? Would her own fate be the same?
Oh, why had she not remained safely in her bedchamber?

The leader reached out to draw a rough finger
down her cheek, making her jump and bringing on a
fit of trembling. "Dinna fash yerself, lassie. We've nae
wish tae do ye harm. 'Twould be tae damage the
prize, gin ye take me meanin'."

"What do you want with me?" The words came in
a harsh whisper, for her voice had lost itself in her
throat.

"We aim tae mak' a wee trade, lass—yerself fer our
ain lads in Roxburgh. O' course, we'll ha' tae ask fer
boot as well, Douglas bein' gilded enow tae share wi'
them as is less fortunate than himself. But he willna
give a souse fer damaged goods. Now, be sae kind as
tae hand me yer rein, unless ye'd prefer a warm, comfortable place on me saddlebow."

Silently, she handed him her reins and allowed him
to lead the mare. The others fell in behind as they

forded the noisy little brook and traveled further south along the slake through the dense trees. They had left the track far behind when finally they emerged from the cover of the forest and began to make their way up a narrow, rocky glen. Mary Kate had no idea where they were or even if they were still traveling south, for the sun was hidden behind the surrounding hills.

She had already been gone much longer than she had intended, and the dismal thought occurred to her that Douglas would think she had run away again. She had meant to be back in her bedchamber before he would have cause to look for her, but that was impossible now. She shuddered to think what his most likely reaction would be when he found her gone. What, she wondered miserably, if he was so furious that he refused to order the bandits released? What if he declared the ransom demand too high to pay? Would these rough borderers still not risk damaging the goods then?

She stared at the burly man on the horse in front of her. How she would have liked earlier to have slapped the smirk from his evil face. And the rest of them—slobbering over her like rams at stud. That awful one they called Wee Ranald even looked like a ram, only not so intelligent. Thank God their leader could control them, she thought, though surely they must all realize that even if Douglas didn't want her back himself he would kill every one of them if they damaged what was his.

While these thoughts and others of their ilk were repeating themselves over and over in her mind, the party made its way through the rocky glen and came upon yet another thicket and then a small clearing. At the far end stood the sort of low, stone, thatched-roof hut known as a bourock.

Still grasping Sesi's rein, the leader swung down from his horse and held up his hands to lift Mary Kate down from her saddle. When his hands left her waist, one of them, as if by accident, caressed her breast. Angrily, she lifted her chin high and turned away from him, pretending to watch the others dismount. With a snort of amusement he shouted at Wee Ranald and another man to investigate the bourock to be sure it was "comfortable." Then he turned back to her and said, "Not that it will meet wi' yer ain high standard, lassie, but it will ha' tae do till the Douglas cooms tae claim ye." He squinted when she made no response.

She had not spoken since their initial exchange, but when several of the men behind them burst into laughter at some jest or other, startling her, a flicker of fear revealed itself in her hazel eyes.

"The lads willna harm ye, lass," the leader assured her again, cheerfully. "Like I said afore, whatever their instinct be fer lust, they ha' a mickle clear notion o' the Douglas temper and me own as weel. Ye'll serve me purpose best undamaged since Douglas is like tae demand yer safe return afore he'll set our ain lads free. We'll ha' our gelt first, o' course, but we can trust his word fer the rest."

Mary Kate pushed away the lingering fear that Douglas might not come for her. He had to come. Once she knew the reivers had her, he would find her. Disquietingly, another thought pressed itself upon her mind, that it might be better for her in the long run if they did harm her. Just a very little, of course —enough to mitigate Douglas's inevitable wrath. She did not think the fact that they had frightened her witless would weigh with him. In fact, he was more likely to regard that as the one positive note in the whole affair.

Drawing another long breath, she looked her chief captor squarely in the eye. "Does he know where I am?" Her voice was clear and steady, that of a lady of breeding, that of a Douglas or a MacPherson. Under the circumstances she was pardonably pleased with herself.

The bandit leader nodded toward the stone hut. "Get ye inside, lass. He kens the noo that we ha' ye, but he'll no be told where ye be till we fetch our ransom from him on the morrow."

She stared at him, aghast. "Not until morning?"

"We want him tae stew a wee while, so he'll do as he's bid."

"What if he will not?" To ask the question took nearly all the courage she had left, but she forced herself to make clear to him that such a possibility existed. "He will be angry with me for leaving as I did, for it is neither my usual custom to ride unescorted nor his to permit it."

The man looked her up and down in a way that made her feel exposed from head to toe, and his leering grin made her wish once more for the courage to slap him. "He will play, lass. Now, in ye go." He stood aside with mock gallantry, and she passed by him to enter the hut.

Inside, it was dry, but that was all that could be said to its advantage, for the dirt floor had not been swept for a long time, and there was no sign of recent habitation. A rickety table stood under the only window, which was no more than a hole in the wall where a few stones had been left out. The only other piece of furniture was a narrow but solid bench near the blackened fireplace. There was no hearth or hood, just a black space—no chimney, either—and Mary Kate, conscious of a distinct chill in the air, was glad they had not provided a fire for her comfort. The smoke would no doubt have asphyxiated her.

The bandit chief glanced around and crooked an eyebrow at the place before bellowing at Wee Ranald to bring the lass some warm blankets. He then produced a pair of leather thongs from his jerkin.

" 'Tis sorry I be fer this, lass," he said. " 'Tis a mortal shame tae hobble sae bonny a wench, but 'tis yer bonniness demands it. Twa o' me lads'll stay behind, and I canna trust 'em inside wi' ye on sae cold a night. Nor can I trust ye tae stay put on yer ain account."

She did not protest. The thought that he might otherwise leave the men alone with her in the hut without benefit of his protection, such as it was, was enough to stifle any notion of rebellion. That he intended to leave two of them behind was terrifying enough, even if they did remain outside.

Standing docilely beside the heavy bench while he bound her wrists behind her, she then sat down upon it while he tied her ankles and looped the end of the thong through a hole in the base of the bench, knotting it there so that she was anchored to the heavy piece. He had allowed only enough slack so that she could, when she grew cold or tired of sitting, lie down on the blankets that Wee Ranald dumped haphazardly on the floor by her feet.

A few moments later she heard the sound of retreating hoofbeats before silence wrapped the hut. The interior was gloomy. With the door open it had not been so bad, but with it closed the light from the tiny window was barely enough by which to see. The fact that she had not been gagged told her that the bandits had no fear of her being overheard if she called for help. Not to mention, she thought unhappily, that the two men outside would come in if they heard her.

She was soon stiff from sitting on the narrow bench, but she forced herself to stay there as long as possible, believing that somehow it would be worse on the floor, more humiliating if not more uncomfortable. She could retain some of her dignity while she sat, none lying down. Finally, however, even wriggling and shrugging could no longer loosen tired, aching muscles. She could bear her discomfort no longer and slid to the floor, welcoming the softness of the blankets beneath her.

By experimenting, she discovered that she could sit up but could not lean against the bench except sideways, and that position felt far from secure. Heavy as the piece was, it was also narrow and felt when she leaned against it as though it would fall over. Because of the way her feet were tied, she couldn't lean against the wall, either, unless she could drag the bench with her. She tried, but it was no use. The base merely dug into the dirt floor and stuck.

She could not sit for long, but she hunched up her knees by scooting on her backside and was able at least to lean over them. The stretch of her back muscles felt wonderful for the moment. But as time passed, slowly, the task of finding a comfortable position became more and more difficult.

She had no wish to dwell upon either her discomfort or her fears, but whenever she tried to think of anything else, she thought of Megan, safely back at Strachan Court, using her beautiful face, exquisite figure, and melodious—nay, purring—voice to beguile Douglas. Such thoughts as these only served to make her blood boil. And when she thought of Douglas, she saw him allowing, even encouraging Megan, basking in the warmth of her approval, savoring her wit, praising her intelligence, her generosity—panting, in fact, after the bitch. No, she decided, she could not think about that either. She wondered what time it was and decided it must be near suppertime, for she was starving. Supper? Remembering then that she had not even had her dinner, she wondered if they would feed her.

Their approach was heralded only by a ponderous footstep and the click of the latch, but the sounds were enough to alert Mary Kate sharply to their presence. The door swung open and a hulking figure filled the opening. Wee Ranald seemed to bend nearly double to enter the hut, followed by another man carrying a rough torch and a pair of candles.

"Uncle Rupe said ye wouldna be wantin' any supper, me lady, but we ha' brung ye some, any gate," Wee Ranald said in his sluggish voice. He carried a tin bowl and a manchet loaf, which he set down on the bench before bending to untie her hands.

"Ye munna loose her, lad," the other man said gruffly, regarding Mary Kate with hungry eyes, despite her rumpled appearance.

"Dinna be daft, Wat," pronounced Wee Ranald carefully. "She canna eat wi' her hands tied ahind 'er."

Shrugging, Wat lit his candles, then dropped the spark-dripping torch to the floor and stamped it out. He stuck the candles into their own melted wax on jags in the stone wall and then turned to gaze more closely upon Mary Kate.

Wee Ranald released her hands, then watched anxiously until she had rubbed feeling back into them before he handed her the tin bowl and the bread. The stuff in the bowl was a watery stew, but it tasted good enough when she scooped bits of meat from the broth with the bread. The man called Wat continued to

stare yearningly at her while she ate, making her skin
crawl, but she ignored him, and when she had finished, she glanced up speculatively at Wee Ranald.

"If you please," she said coolly, "I should like to go
outside for a few moments."

"I canna allow ye tae go ootside, me lady."

"But I must," she insisted pointedly. He started to
protest, but then Wat chuckled and Wee Ranald took
her meaning at last. Mary Kate could not be sure in
the dim light, but she thought the great hulking creature blushed. He said nothing more, however, merely
untying her feet and accompanying her wordlessly
outside. By the time they reached the woods nearest
the bourock, most of the numbness was gone from
her feet, and she turned to him, saying firmly, "I require privacy."

He hesitated, but then, taking in her small figure
next to his own huge one, he nodded.

She moved quickly away from him. Her business
was rather urgent, but it didn't take long, and she
suddenly realized she was free. Moving carefully, trying not to reveal her position, she began to weave her
way as quickly as she could away from him, away
from the clearing.

He called out to her to hurry, but she dared not
respond. A moment later he called again, his tone
more anxious. Then she heard him shout for Wat, and
she threw caution to the wind, wanting only to put as
much distance as possible between herself and the
two ruffians.

Unfortunately, it was dark and she had no idea
where she was or what direction would best serve her
purpose. She did know, however, that she was making too much noise, and when she heard Wat's gruff
voice behind her, she decided to go to ground and
hope for the best. Accordingly, she dived behind the

nearest tree and crawled into the dense shrubbery there, trying to ignore the twigs and branches that clawed at her back and skirts. Hearing another shout, closer than the last, she went still.

Footsteps crunched through the undergrowth, approaching nearer and nearer to her hiding place. She heard Wat cursing Wee Ranald for his stupidity in letting her out of his sight and promising, if they failed to find her, to tell his uncle what had transpired. Then suddenly, she saw a glow of light through the trees and realized that Wat had lit another torch. She tried to burrow further into the shrubbery, but it was no use. A moment later he loomed over her, grinning in satisfaction.

"Here she be, lad!" he barked triumphantly, adding in a harsher tone, "Coom out o' there, lass. I trow, we'll ha' tae see ye no do that again."

Mary Kate grimaced, but she could see no point in defying him, so she emerged slowly from the shrubbery. As she stood up and attempted to brush some of the twigs and leaves from her skirts, Wat grabbed her arm and thrust her roughly ahead of him, back toward the bourock. They met Wee Ranald in the clearing, and he followed them to the hut.

Wat shoved her inside, then jerked her around to face him, keeping a firm grip on her arm. "Ye should ha' known better than tae vex me, lass. Ye'll ha' tae mak' me happy again the noo."

Mary Kate stared at him in dismay, but Wee Ranald spoke up more quickly than usual. "Uncle Rupe said we was tae leave her be, Wat. Ye canna harm her, he said."

"Och, we'll no harm her, laddie, but she mun pay a sma' penance—just a wee kiss the noo, tae repay us fer the fright she gave us. Would ye no like tae kiss the bonnie wee lassie?"

Biting her lip, Mary Kate shook her head vehemently.

Wee Ranald hesitated.

"We wouldna hurt the lassie," Wat insisted, pressing this small advantage. "She owes us a mite fer our trouble."

"No!" Mary Kate cried, trying to pull free of his grip on her upper arm. "Let me go!" With her free hand, she dug her sharp nails into his knuckles where he held her arm.

He yelped, freeing her, but a quick blow from his other fist caught her on the side of the head and sent her spinning into a heap on the floor. Wat plunged after her. "By God's breath, ye'll gi'e us sport then, Rupe or nae Rupe. He isna here the noo, is he?" He grabbed the front of her gown, tearing it when he jerked her toward himself, only to howl again in pain when Wee Ranald buried both huge hands in his thick hair and yanked.

Mary Kate scrambled away as soon as Wat snatched his hands from her bodice to defend his own head.

Wee Ranald hauled the man to his feet, still by the hair. "Ye willna harm the lassie," he said stubbornly. "Uncle Rupe said the Douglas'll no want damaged goods. Now, gae ootside wi' ye." He pushed Wat toward the door, and Wat went whether he wished to do so or not. Rubbing his sore head, he shot a malevolent look back over his shoulder at Mary Kate.

When Wat had gone, Wee Ranald moved toward her purposefully, but she made no attempt to evade him and sat stoically while he tied her hands and feet again. "Ye shouldna ha' vexed him," he said heavily. "Certes, but he was in the right aboot that."

He snuffed the candles, and a moment later Mary Kate was alone again in the heavy, silent darkness. She let the tears come at last, but they did not flow for long. She scarcely had time enough to wonder what sort of spiders inhabited long-deserted bourocks before exhaustion caught up with her at last and she drifted into uneasy sleep.

When she awoke again it was still dark. Her eyes were sticky with sleep, and strands of hair stuck to her face. She tried unsuccessfully to blow one tickling wisp away from her nose. Her hands and feet were numb, but she decided the awful aching in her arms was what had wakened her. She was also cold, but the slightest movement hurt her, so she stayed where she was, on her side, trying to wiggle her fingers and toes. Eventually, they began to tingle, but that brought only more pain. She stopped, thinking she had heard a noise. There was nothing. Even the breeze was still.

She could see stars through the tiny window. There was a silver glow, too, that told her the moon was up, but scarcely any light penetrated to the interior of the hut. She no longer tried to push away the vision of her husband. The fear of his temper had faded, replaced by a longing so strong it seemed tactile. She didn't care any longer how angry he was with her; she just wanted him to find her.

She had been a stupid, jealous wife. Yes, jealous, she admitted now. How silly to keep pretending that her hostility toward Megan stemmed from anything more profound. Why had she not seen the truth before, she wondered, when she could recognize her true feelings so clearly now? She knew now that she had always cared much more about Douglas than she had wanted to admit, even to herself.

Not that it mattered any longer, she told herself bitterly, for even if he had loved her before—and there was no good reason to think that he had, despite the warmth of his smile and the gentle touch of his hands upon her body—he wouldn't love her now. He would be furious with her, again. But she deserved it this time, for he had been right. She ought to have listened to him for once and been more generous, more tolerant, even though Megan had been everything she had thought her to be and more. She realized dismally that since he would think she had run away rather than make her apology to Megan, he would most likely make good his promise to punish her again. Oh, why, she asked herself, had she ever left her bedchamber?

A sudden noise outside the bourock put an end to her musing, and she went perfectly still, hoping fervently that she was mistaken. But then, distinctly, came the sound of a pebble, loosened, rattling against other pebbles—a footstep. Her stomach tightened with fear, and she strained her ears, listening for the slightest sound. Even so, she barely heard the latch before the door swung slowly open, spilling moonlight across the floor. She held her breath when the light was blocked by a man's body. The door swung shut again. Then there came the stealthy scratch of flint against steel, and a candle flared into life, lighting Wat's leering face. Mary Kate screamed.

15

Wat flung himself upon her, smacking his open palm against her mouth. "Hush yer gab!" he hissed.

Mary Kate cried out again, but the sound was muffled beneath his hand.

"I told ye tae hush." He slapped her hard, making her ears ring, then got a firmer grip over her mouth, nearly suffocating her. The candle had fallen over when he lunged, and it guttered now, plunging them back into blackness. Mary Kate struggled, but there was little she could do to protect herself against him. He put his mouth against her ear. "I'll leave ye go, lass, but only gin ye cease yer screechin'. Mak' a sound and I'll throttle ye. D'ye tak' m' meaning'?"

She nodded, knowing he meant every word, and gulped in huge breaths of air when he released her. "Why are you here?" she whispered when she could speak. She knew the answer, but believing time to be her only ally, she hoped to get him talking.

"Ye ken weel why," he said briefly, reaching for

her bodice. She felt his fingers groping for the lacing. "Need light," he muttered. "Like tae see what I'm aboot."

"Please," Mary Kate said, as cold air touched her bare skin. "Don't do this."

He forced his hand through the opening he had made and pawed roughly at her breast. When she gasped with shock, he grunted, "Sae nesh ye be, lassie, but methinks we best be getting on wi' the business." He reached for the hem of her skirt, and she began to struggle again, twisting and turning in an effort to roll away from him, ignoring the pain that knifed through her arms with each movement she made.

Just as Wat forced her back and wrenched her skirt up, the door flew open and a huge figure erupted into the room accompanied by a flood of moonlight that lit the scene with an eerie, haunting glow.

Fairly snarling in his rage, Wee Ranald hurled himself at Wat, jerking him up, away from Mary Kate, and flinging him aside. *"Leave her be!"* he bellowed, advancing upon him again.

This time Wat was better prepared. As the young giant reached to haul him to his feet, the shadow of Wat's fist, delineated by a halo of gleaming moonlight, flashed up from the floor in a silver arc that ended with a resounding crack upon the point of Wee Ranald's chin, sending him crashing back against the corner behind the door. Striking his head against the stone wall with a sickening thud, the lad slid to the floor in an unnatural heap. Wat followed and heaved a kick into his ribs as a final gesture, but Wee Ranald made no sound, neither did he move.

Wat turned. "Nae reason the noo tae do wi'oot light," he observed cordially.

Mary Kate whimpered, trying to move away from

him, but the heavy bench gave her no room to ma-
neuver.

Paying no heed to her struggles, he searched the
floor for a moment before he found his candle and the
flint, but once he had them, the candle quickly flared
to life. He used it to rekindle the others, then stuck it
up beside them on another outcropping in the wall.
Too soon the soft glow of candlelight lit the hut.

Wee Ranald stirred, so Mary Kate knew he was not
dead, but he showed no sign of returning to consciousness soon enough to help her. Sick with terror,
she watched as Wat kicked the door shut again and
turned back toward her.

"We can bide our time the noo, lassie."

He moved slowly, steadily toward her, savoring
her fear. Then he was beside her, kneeling, pulling
her toward him, shoving his hand back inside her
bodice, all the while watching the changing expressions on her face.

She closed her eyes, trying to shut out the image of
his fiendish countenance as he leered down at her.

He snickered, then pinched her breast.

She cried out, her eyes flying open again.

"That's a guid lassie. Ye wouldna wish tae miss any
o' the frolicking, would ye?" He bent nearer, pushing
his face right against hers, growling, "Ye wouldna
give us a kiss afore, but I'll wager ye'll be fidging fain
tae do it the noo."

She pulled back, trying to press herself down into
the floor, but he held her, forcing his rough lips
against hers. Scrunching her eyes shut again, she
gagged, overwhelmed by the smell of his filthy body
combined with the taste of raw whiskey on his stale
breath. Struggling again, trying desperately to twist
her mouth away from his, she soon discovered that
her efforts only amused him. He was hurting her

now, bruising her lips, trying to force his tongue between her teeth, and she could hear him chuckling,
enjoying what he was doing, reveling in her terror.
The pain in her arms reached screaming pitch, but
she dared not open her mouth to let the scream escape.

The only warning she had of what came next was
the whisper of a footfall and a low snarl of rage before Wat's body suddenly went rigid and what had
begun as another chuckle ended in a liquid gurgle as
he was wrenched away from her. She found herself
looking up in stupefied disbelief at her husband.

Douglas wore breeks and boots and his heavy
leather jacket, and he was fully armed. Reading his
expression was difficult in the dim candlelight, but
though his attitude was one of tightly reined emotion, she could not think he looked overjoyed to see
her. He wiped his dirk on the dead man's shirt and
shoved it back into his boot top. It looked to her as
though a few drops of sweat must have run into his
eyes, for he dragged his sleeve impatiently across
them before he knelt beside her. Without a word, he
began to untie the thong at her ankles.

There was another sound, and a shadow loomed
behind him.

"Adam, look out!"

Douglas moved like a cat, turning, coming to his
feet, and unsheathing the slim Italian sword at his
side in one smooth, nearly effortless motion.

Wee Ranald lumbered groggily toward him from
the corner, a long dagger gripped tightly in his upraised hand.

Douglas waited for him, sizing him up, and Mary
Kate held her breath. The two men were nearly the
same height, but Wee Ranald easily outweighed
Douglas, and the way he shook his sore head slowly

from side to side made him look like a bear at a baiting, just waiting for his prey to be released. Douglas moved lightly on his feet, circling to get as much of the light as he could behind him, watching the other man with narrowed, hawklike eyes. Suddenly Wee Ranald lunged, but Douglas was ready. He parried the dagger thrust deftly, slid his own blade under, and then it was over. A look of pained astonishment crossed Wee Ranald's face as he crumpled, lifeless, to the floor.

Ned Lumsden, sword drawn, stood in the doorway. "The others are searching the woods," he said now. "I thought you might need some help."

Douglas nodded, sheathing his sword as Ned bent to examine Wee Ranald's body.

Mary Kate watched Ned. "Is he dead?" When the youth nodded, she turned toward her husband. "Oh, Adam, he tried to protect me from that awful man."

"Then better he should die quickly now than have to wait for the hangman," he muttered, kneeling again to deal with her bonds.

Another body blocked the door, and Mary Kate recognized Willie Jardine. His eyes grew large as he took in the scene, making her more conscious than ever of her loosened bodice.

"Be the mistress safe, master?"

"She'll do," Douglas replied curtly. "Fetch a couple of the others in here to deal with this vermin, lad, and see you keep your eyes skinned."

"Aye." Willie moved away, and Ned followed him.

Mary Kate could see that the darkness outside was melting away. Soon it would be daybreak. Circulation returned abruptly when the thong around her ankles was released, and she could not repress a gasp of agony.

Douglas glanced at her sharply, his expression mo-

mentarily reflecting her pain, but he made no comment, tossing the thong into a corner and moving
next to free her wrists. The pain resulting from this
simple act was tortuous, augmented as it was by severe cramps in her arms. Tears flooded her eyes when
she tried to move. Pressing his lips together, Douglas
rubbed her arms and hands briskly, determinedly ignoring the moans of protest she was unable to suppress. When his hooded gaze shifted briefly and
pointedly, she thought, to her open bodice, she made
a weak effort to cover herself, only to have him push
her hands away and yank the laces together so tightly
as to leave her gasping. He tied them with angry,
snapping movements.

"Can you stand?" His voice was harsh.

She tried but swayed, feeling nothing in her feet
but pins and needles.

Jaw clenched, he scooped her up into his arms just
as Willie returned, followed by two other men.

"Anything, lads?" Douglas demanded.

"Naught," replied Willie briefly.

"Nary hide nor horse," said one of the others,
clearly thinking a more detailed response was called
for. "Looks like this pair was the only ones left, master."

"Whistle up the others, then, Willie. We'll be off."
Douglas stooped, carrying her easily, and stepped
outside into the gray dawn twilight. One of the men
gave a piercing, shrieking whistle, and horsemen
emerged from the forest on all sides of the clearing.
There seemed to Mary Kate to be a great number of
them until they gathered together. Then she realized
they were Douglas's own men, no more than the
twenty who had ridden with them and with their
baggage.

She knew he was in a hurry, and there was corresponding urgency in her voice when she said, close to his ear, "Adam, I cannot ride back without first attending to a certain matter."

"Aye?" His tone was even, wiped clean of emotion.

She looked at him pleadingly, embarrassment tinging her cheeks with color, before he attended to her closely enough to comprehend her meaning. The touch of amusement in his eyes then gave her a sudden, though brief, sense of relief. Still carrying her, he stepped quickly into the woods behind the hut before setting her on her feet.

"Can you manage alone?"

"Aye," she replied firmly, determined to do so if it killed her. He turned his back, and although there was still a good deal of pain, she managed, feeling only relief when she limped back to his side. He made no attempt to pick her up again, nor did he hurry her. The moon still hung over the trees when they reentered the clearing, but its light had faded with approaching dawn. When a figure separated itself from the group of horsemen, she recognized Ned, leading his mount and Valiant toward them.

"Shall I help, sir?" He was looking at Mary Kate, worry written plainly on his usually cheerful face. "Perhaps you would allow me to hand her up to you once you've mounted."

"She'll do," Douglas replied abruptly. Ordering Valiant to stand, he lifted her onto the saddlebow. The great stallion trembled when her skirts whisked across his shoulder and flank, but otherwise he stood motionless. Because of her pain, she still had too little control of her limbs to attempt sitting astride, so she had to trust her balance while Douglas swung up behind her. When he put his arm around her to grasp the reins, she settled back gratefully against his chest, held there securely by his other arm.

"Where is Sesi?" she asked hesitantly.

"You didn't expect them to leave a valuable piece of horseflesh behind, did you?"

She fell silent with shock. The cursed reivers had stolen her beautiful little mare. The tears started again, spilled over, and rolled down her cheeks. "Oh, Adam, I'm so sorry."

"Not half so sorry as you will be when I've done with you," he said quietly. " 'Tis my sworn duty to protect you, lass, but 'tis a thing I cannot do when you persist in disobeying me. This is not the place or time to discuss the matter, however. We will talk later." He turned slightly, signaling his weary men, and they were off.

Mary Kate wanted to tell him that this time she hadn't disobeyed him, that she hadn't been running away, that she had intended to make her apology as he had ordered her to do. But she was certain he would not believe her, and she didn't know what else to say to him, so the long, slow ride back to Strachan Court was a silent one. One moment she wished he would speak, the next she was glad he did not.

She was certain that his anger back in the bourock had not all been directed at her, for she had seen pain in his eyes, and she knew he had been concerned about her safety. But that concern seemed only to have augmented the anger caused by his belief that she had run away again. Even if she could convince him that she had not done so, it would do no good, for she had gone alone when clearly she needed an escort. And of course, there was still the small matter of her apology to Megan.

Arriving at Strachan Court a short time after the dinner hour, they rode straight into the forecourt, and Mary Kate sighed as Douglas swung down and held out his hands to lift her to the ground. At least, she thought, all this painful business would soon be done, and maybe then they could move on to happier times, for she would certainly exert every effort not to tangle with Lady Somerville again.

She wondered if Douglas would lecture her first. She hoped he would not. His lectures tended to stir her volatile temper, and the last thing she wanted to do now was to fight with him. As he set her on her feet, she looked up at him, trying to gauge the extent of his displeasure with her. But he waited only to be sure that she could stand alone before releasing her and waving his men on to the stables. Ned went with the others, leading Valiant.

"Come along, lass." When she hesitated, suddenly incapable of walking meekly to her doom, he put a strong arm around her shoulders, implacably urging her past the topiary chessmen, up the broad steps to the entrance. He reached to open the door, but the handle eluded his grasp when Lord Strachan himself pulled the door wide.

"Welcome home, daughter!" he boomed. "Are ye safe, then?"

"Aye, sir. They did me no harm." She smiled uncertainly at him when he stepped aside to let them pass into the hall.

"I want a word with you, Adam," he said more quietly.

Douglas nodded, shepherding Mary Kate inexorably across the hall to the great stair. "As soon as I attend to one small, unpleasant duty, sir, I am yours to command."

Strachan said evenly, "I would speak with you now, my son."

Continuing up the stairs, his hand now grasping her upper arm, Douglas spoke curtly over his shoulder. "I have business with my wife that will not wait,

Father. When I have dealt with her as she deserves, I shall—"

"Adam." The single sharp word froze Douglas in midstride, and the coldly ominous tone in which it was uttered banished forever any thought Mary Kate had retained of Lord Strachan as no more than a kindly, bluff, occasionally blustery but harmless old gentleman. Douglas's grip tightened upon her arm, bruising her, but she was certain that he was unaware of what he was doing, certain, too, that the hand holding her trembled. Although his lordship had uttered but the one word and had not raised his voice, he had reminded them both in no uncertain terms that he was the master at Strachan Court.

Mary Kate glanced up at her husband.

Douglas's face was pale. He turned slowly on the stair to look down at his father.

"You forget yourself, sir," Strachan said in that same frigid tone. "Or have you grown so great with power that you now dare to defy your father in his own house?"

"No, my lord," Douglas said, subdued. "I crave your pardon. I will come at once." He looked down at his awestruck wife, gaining control over himself with visible difficulty. "Wait for me in your bedchamber, Mary Kate."

Strachan cut in smoothly before she could respond, "Her ladyship has been anxious about your safety, daughter. Go to her at once, if you please, and put her mind at ease. Adam will find you in her sitting room as quick as in your bedchamber."

Mary Kate glanced doubtfully at her husband.

His jaw was rigid with anger at having his direct order to her countermanded, but childhood training stood the test, and he held his tongue. He was her husband, and thus her lord and master, but in this house, he was first his father's son and, as such, owed him strict obedience. Slightly mollified by the fact that she was looking to him for confirmation of his father's command, Douglas nodded briefly.

Dropping a hasty curtsy to his lordship, who still waited at the bottom of the steps for his orders to be obeyed, she turned and fled gratefully up the stairs. As she neared the top, she heard Douglas begin to speak, his voice carrying easily up the stairwell—as easily, she realized now, as hers had carried down to him the day before.

"Father . . . my lord, forgive me. I was in a temper. I—"

"Your emotions are of no interest whatever to me, sir," Strachan interrupted, still speaking in that chilling tone. "I have much to say to you, but we will speak in my bookroom."

With that unencouraging statement ringing in her ears, Mary Kate reached the window hall, but before she had taken two steps toward the sitting room, she realized that she could not meet Lady Strachan and no doubt Lady Somerville, too, with her skirts crushed beneath her safeguard, her hair in a tangle, and her face undoubtedly filthy. So, hurrying to her bedchamber instead, she sent for Annie Jardine.

Annie was delighted to see her safe, and full of curiosity, as well, but she had thought to bring a manchet loaf, a wedge of soft cheese, and a mug of ale, so Mary Kate willingly obliged her with a brief tale while devouring the welcome food. When she had washed her face and hands and changed her gown, Annie would have continued the conversation while brushing her hair, but Mary Kate cut her short.

"I am safe home now," she said, "and I do not wish to speak further of the incident."

Annie took the mild reproof without offense and

fell silent. If she wondered where Douglas was now or how her mistress had come to be riding out alone of a Sunday and at the dinner hour, at that, she wisely kept such questions to herself.

For Mary Kate to see her domineering husband reduced to the status of a naughty schoolboy had been a unique experience, but she wondered now how the scene she had just witnessed, augmented by whatever was taking place this very moment in his lordship's bookroom, would affect Douglas's temper. She doubted it would be improved.

Lady Strachan was occupied with her endless needlework and Megan was reading to her from one of Lord Strachan's books when Mary Kate entered the sitting room a quarter-hour later. She curtsied to the older woman, avoiding Megan's curious gaze.

"Welcome home, my dear," Lady Strachan said with her quiet dignity. "We are grateful to have you safely restored to us."

"Thank you, my lady. I apologize if I gave you cause for distress."

"It would be odd indeed if you had not, Mary Kate," Megan interjected sweetly. "Whatever possessed you to run away like you did?"

"I did not run away," Mary Kate began hotly, promptly forgetting all the resolutions she had made regarding Douglas's cousin. "I only went for a ride to blow away my headache. I could scarcely help being abducted."

Megan looked only too ready to debate the matter, but Lady Strachan intervened smoothly. "I knew it must have been some such thing, my dear, though surely you know better than to ride out alone in these days of unrest, without a proper armed escort. However, I'll warrant my son has said all there is to say on that subject, so I shall not belabor it."

"Thank you," Mary Kate replied sincerely. Douglas had not mentioned that particular point yet, but she had no doubt that he would say a great deal about it soon enough.

"Do you take up your embroidery, my dear," suggested Lady Strachan. " 'Tis there upon the chest behind you. Stitching will make things feel normal again if you sit here quietly with us for a time. Megan does not like doing needlework, you know, but she has a beautiful voice for reading aloud, and I know you will enjoy Mr. Chaucer's tales, though there are many who disapprove of them. Continue, Megan dear."

Megan picked up her book and Mary Kate her workbasket, and except for the melodic cadence of the older girl's voice, there was no other sound until the door from the window hall opened and a gillie stepped into the room.

"If it please your ladyship," he said respectfully, bowing to Lady Strachan, "his lordship would speak wi' Lady Douglas in his bookroom."

Mary Kate tensed involuntarily at his words but laid her needlework aside and excused herself. Lady Strachan nodded, smiling encouragement, but her kindness didn't help, nor did Megan's feline smirk, fleeting though it was. Having seen Douglas's reaction to his father's displeasure, she could not wonder at the fact that her heart was pounding in her chest by the time she reached the bookroom. The door stood ajar.

"Come you in, child, and shut that door." Strachan was alone, and he did not appear to be angry. When she had closed the door, he bade her be seated and sat himself in a chair nearby. The room was full of light from the inner courtyard that glinted upon the delicate manuscript chains and the gold tooling of the

leatherbound tomes. There was a brief silence while
his lordship gazed searchingly at her, as though he
wondered how to begin, but at last he cleared his
throat with a great "harrumph" and said, "You have
no cause to fear me, lass."

She lifted her gaze from her lap, looked at him, and
smiled. "I do not fear you, my lord." It was true.
Now that she was face to face with him, she was no
longer afraid. The bone-chilling note she had heard
in his voice earlier was gone, and there was nothing
in his expression now but kindly compassion.

"I wanted to speak with you, Mary Kate, because
much though it mislikes me to have done so, I have
involved myself in your affairs. I have a need to explain my actions to you."

"What have you done, my lord?"

"I have forbidden him to beat you," he replied
bluntly.

Stunned by his words, she was silent, thinking it
would not become her to express her extreme gratitude for such timely intervention. It was as though he
read her mind.

"You have no cause to thank me, lassie."

"Have I not, sir?"

"No, for he is all the angrier at being frustrated.
One way or another you will suffer more for my interference than if I had left well enough alone, but I
did not consider your welfare."

"No?" She was puzzled now.

"My lady sets great store by you, lass," he explained, "and we leave for the capital in less than two
days' time. At best, even at the slow pace we shall
maintain, she will tire easily, and I do not want anything else to distress her in the meantime. Her contentment is of paramount importance to me."

"As it must be to us all, sir," Mary Kate assured

him. "Whatever happens next between Adam and me shall not be laid at your door."

"Bless you, lassie, but I fear you will have your work cut out to make your peace with him."

She smiled ruefully, agreeing with him.

"Tell me why you left," he said abruptly. When she opened her eyes in dismay, he added, "I will not usurp his authority further, but I do want to know what caused you to run away as you did from the safety of my house."

The rapid change of subject had caught her by surprise, but she made a heroic effort to cover her confusion. "I . . . I only went for a ride, my lord, and was taken unaware by the reivers."

"Cut me no whids, lass, else I will become angry. I want the short tale, if you please." His voice was gentle, but there was a stern note in it now, and her cheeks warmed in response.

She saw no point in persisting to refute the theory that she had been running away, but although she had no wish to reveal her jealousy or the pettier difficulties between herself and Megan, he would not be gainsaid. He encouraged her with a tact of which she had not known him capable, and little by little, falteringly, and not without a few tears, a good part of the tale was told.

When she had finished, he sat for a moment, elbows on the arms of his chair, silently regarding the tips of his fingers where they formed a tent before him. Then he looked up, and for a brief moment she was chilled by the icy glint in his eyes. It vanished when he caught her gaze upon him.

"You explain much," he said slowly. "I had seen some of the pliskie nonsense for myself, but I had no conception of its scope. Now that I do, I can promise you that you need distress yourself no longer." He stood up and moved to open the door for her. "I think it best that you return to your bedchamber for a time, lassie. It might appease my son somewhat to find you there should he return before supper is served. However," he added, giving her a direct look, "since you have already missed your dinner, you are to come down to sup whether he returns or no."

"Where has he gone?"

"I have no notion," Strachan replied with a twinkle. "He has been in a state of high emotion for some twenty-four hours now, and when I had done with him, he flung out of there in much the same resentful manner he was used to assume on such occasions when he was but a lad. In those days, depending upon what had transpired between us, he either took long walks through the woods, or wore some poor horse out, riding all out over the hills. Today I'll warrant it would be the horse." He grinned. "He has grown overlarge for skelping."

If he expected her to smile, he missed his mark. The portrait he had drawn of Douglas's probable state of mind overpowered any other thought she might have had, and she hoped her husband would choose to take a long ride, and particularly that he would remain away until after supper. Regardless of his father's instructions, she would not dare to defy him should he take it into his head to command that she keep to her bedchamber and miss the meal altogether, a command she knew him to be perfectly capable of issuing. And Strachan would not countermand such an order, for he had made it clear to her that he would usurp his son's authority no further. Therefore, it was with dismay rather than pleasure that she met Ned Lumsden on his way down the great stair. He stood aside to let her pass.

"Ned, has Sir Adam returned, then?"

"Nay, my lady. Not to my knowledge."

"You did not accompany him?" Somehow she had assumed without thinking about it that he had, merely because he had been with Douglas before.

Ned grinned. "Wouldn't I have liked to do that very thing," he said, "but Adam said this time was too dangerous and ordered me to remain behind. Threatened to flog me himself if I disobeyed him." He shrugged. "What would you? He was in a rare kippage, and I believed him. So here I am."

"But where did he go?"

Ned hesitated. "You must not trouble yourself about his safety, my lady, for he has his own men with him. He has ridden out to retrieve the ransom."

Mary Kate stared at him. Douglas had been so grim and uncommunicative at the bourock that she hadn't even thought to ask him about the ransom. It was enough that he had found her. But now it appeared that a ransom had been paid, and in an effort to retrieve it Douglas would take on the reivers with but twenty men at his back.

"Dear God in heaven." The color drained from her face, and Ned reached out a steadying hand, as though he feared she might swoon. He assured her hastily that each of Douglas's men was worth ten of the brigands and told her again not to worry. "Easy for you to say," she retorted, "but this is my fault. If I had stayed here, he'd have had no reason to pay them at all."

"Perhaps you are right," Ned agreed gently, "but it isn't only the ransom, you know. He made them certain promises."

Her hand flew to her mouth. "He didn't! Surely he never arranged for those dreadful men in Roxburgh to go free?" Douglas might have paid the money, but

she found it difficult to believe that he would agree to
their other demands.

Ned was grinning. "Perhaps I had better explain,"
he said. "After the business in the window hall yesterday, he came down to dinner, saying you were ill.
Megan had recovered her composure by then, so
there was no reason for my aunt or uncle to disbelieve him. His lordship even mentioned noticing that
you had been somewhat subdued in spirit on the
walk back from the kirk. They had gone on out to the
terrace immediately, you will remember, so they
heard nothing of what transpired betwixt—Well, in
any event, after dinner Adam took me aside and—"
He broke off again, coloring.

"Oh Ned!" she cried, immediately contrite. "I am
so sorry. He accused me of dousing Megan deliberately, and I didn't even try to deny it. I think he
suspected the truth all along."

"Aye," he agreed, pulling a face. "At the very least
of it, he retained some suspicions, and he was not
pleased that I had lied to protect you. But to pass over
that part as quickly as possible," he went on with a
wry smile, "he dozed on the terrace after dinner, and
when he awoke, Megan suggested a walk in the garden. Afterward she watched whilst we played tennis,
and no one realized you were missing from the house
until the ransom demand was delivered. Adam sent
word immediately that his men would be wanted directly after supper. Then he and Willie Jardine went
in search of your trail, so as to be ready to leave as
soon as the others had supped."

"He searched all night?"

"Aye, he thought the reivers would most likely
leave you somewhere whilst they collected the ransom, but he wouldn't take the chance of not finding
you—especially since he couldn't be certain that the

men wouldn't keep you with them—so he made arrangements with his lordship to meet the brigand chief at dawn in his place. As it happened, that was after you had been found," he added, "but his lordship could not know the search had been a success, so he agreed to their demands. The ransom he paid was a large one, so when he promised that they would be reunited with their compatriots before two days were out, they didn't think to study upon his words. They had refused to tell him where you were, but they did agree to release you. He promised upon the word of a Douglas, you see, and they knew to trust his pledge."

"But then Adam must mean to set them free!"

"Think, my lady."

"His lordship promised to reunite—oh!" She grinned at Ned as the meaning of the careful wording came to her. "Adam means to capture them all and reunite them in Roxburgh Tolbooth. But, how dangerous!"

"Not a bit. 'Tis meat and drink to him, my lady. Surely, you never thought yourself wedded to a carpet knight."

"Of course not, but I don't want him hurt, all the same. Especially since this was my fault."

"He's been searching for this band a long time," Ned said gently.

She nodded, acknowledging the truth of the statement, then forced a smile to her lips, knowing Ned well enough by now to be certain he would worry if he thought she did.

He returned her smile, visibly relaxing before he remembered that he had been on his way to inquire if his lordship had duties for him. Reminded, he took himself off in some haste.

Mary Kate continued up to her bedchamber, where she curled up like a kitten on her bed and soon fell asleep. She had been dozing for nearly two hours when she was disturbed by a timid scratching on the door to the gallery. Neither Douglas nor Annie would knock, so it was with a note of curiosity in her voice that she called out permission to enter.

The door opened slowly, and after a long pause, Megan stepped reluctantly inside. Her demeanor had changed a good deal since Mary Kate had answered Lord Strachan's summons to the bookroom sped along by her taunting smirk. Now, the young woman's usually flawless complexion was stained with blotches of color and her eyes were red from recent weeping. Her proud head was lowered, her chin trembled, and the look she cast Mary Kate was miserable, even beseeching.

16

➤➤➤ ⫷⫷⫷

"*M*ay I have speech with you, my lady?" Courtesy as well, Mary Kate thought, wondering what this was all about. Megan hadn't called her by title since her arrival.

"What do you want?" Her tone was sharp if not actually hostile. Barely glancing at Megan, she swung her legs over the side of the bed and sat up, smoothing her skirts, then reached up to tuck straggling ends of her hair back into her net.

Megan came farther into the room, shutting the door behind her. "I have come to make an apology to you." Her voice trembled, but she seemed otherwise in control of herself, and Mary Kate suddenly remembered Lord Strachan's promise. "I have behaved badly," Megan went on, "and I have come here because I must tell you how sorry I am."

"Very affecting, Lady Somerville," Mary Kate said scornfully. Not doubting for a moment that Megan had chosen her words as carefully as Douglas had chosen the words of his message to the reivers, Mary

Kate reveled in the other young woman's discomfort, wishing Douglas himself could see it. How the tables had turned, she thought. Megan couldn't possibly know that he had ordered his wife to make just such an apology to her, and now the shoe was on the other foot, exactly where it belonged.

Wanting nothing so much as to make her erstwhile adversary crawl, to humble her to her knees, Mary Kate went on in the same scathing tone, "Since I am quite certain that it was his lordship who demanded that you make this apology, I find it difficult to believe in its sincerity. No doubt he said things to you that you were sorry to hear, but I do not believe for a moment that you are truly sorry for your behavior to me."

"Mary Kate, please!" To her dismay, tears began streaming from Megan's eyes, and she stepped forward to sink down upon a low footstool before Mary Kate.

Mary Kate recoiled instantly. Although she had wanted to find Megan at her feet, to enjoy just such a display of humility, she now found it intensely distasteful. A woman so proud and beautiful as Douglas's cousin should not humble herself to anyone, any more than Douglas or his wife should.

Megan struggled to control her tears. "My uncle has commanded that I return at once to Somerville," she said wretchedly. "I am to be sent home to my husband in disgrace."

"Sent home?" Mary Kate was astonished. "What about Margaret's wedding?"

"Uncle said that that must lie with Sir Reginald to decide. But oh, Mary Kate, I know he will not permit me to go. He will be so angry, and he will say that since I have had my chance and mismanaged it, I deserve not to go. And he will be right." She brushed tears away with the back of her hand and slumped woefully on the footstool. "I have no one to blame for this wretched turn of events save myself."

Shamefaced and speaking haltingly, Megan described what had happened when she had been summoned to the bookroom not long after Mary Kate had left it. "I foolishly believed that somehow my uncle had heard of your rudeness to me yesterday and intended to make you apologize to me," she confessed reluctantly.

Instead, she had found her uncle in a flaming temper. He had accused her of insensitivity, rudeness, lack of hospitality, and—worst of all—of disgracing the proud names of Douglas and Somerville. He had ranted on and on for some time in that vein, and Megan assured Mary Kate that her ears were still ringing from the peal of his upbraiding, although the scene had taken place a good while before. She had spent the intervening time miserably, alone in her bedchamber, trying to decide what course might be the best one to pursue.

With a catch in her voice, she insisted that she had never expected her mischief to lead to such an end, that she had wanted only to see what sort of reaction her harmless flirtation with Douglas would evoke from Mary Kate, and she willingly admitted that she had allowed the business to go much too far. Now her uncle was adamant, and she could not appeal to Douglas for assistance. Even if he would agree to speak for her, she explained, his father would never listen to him.

"I am afraid of my husband," she admitted quietly. "My uncle promises to write him a letter, detailing my many unkindnesses to you. I—I am to take it to him when I return. Such a message . . ." She paused, gulping, visibly exerting control over rapidly rising emotion. "Such a message will enrage him beyond anything I have ever seen, I am sure of it, and his temper is formidable."

"You make it sound as though you fear for your very life," Mary Kate said suspiciously. "I doubt it can be as bad as that."

Megan managed a weak smile. "No, but it will be grievously uncomfortable, nevertheless." She threw Mary Kate a sapient glance. "Only consider how Adam would react if our positions were reversed."

Mary Kate fell silent. To imagine the Douglas fury were she ever to present him with such a message as Lord Strachan had promised to send with Megan was not difficult. His anger with her now would be as nothing compared to it, for the discord between herself and his cousin had been a matter easily kept within the family, a disagreement between two mere females, at that. Douglas had been angry when she had insulted Megan, but not angry enough to beat her. To be sure, he had been angrier, and still was, over her abduction by the reivers, but only because he thought she had come to grief through willful disobedience to his commands.

It was her safety that concerned him presently, just as it had been the day she had impulsively left the castle and ridden toward Jedburgh. That incident and her more recent difficulties would remain, for the most part, private matters between the two of them. If, on the other hand, she were to misbehave under someone else's roof and he were to learn of it from a third party, the matter would no longer be a private one.

Remembering how straitly he had warned her against making their affairs public, she could have no doubt that he would be enraged if such a situation ever arose, convinced that others would see in her actions a reflection of his inability to control her behavior. Bad enough, then, to have to face Douglas's wrath in such a case. But what about Sir Reginald, who had a reputation for being a harsher, more insensitive man to begin with? The thought of Megan's probable punishment made Mary Kate wince. Suddenly she no longer wanted vengeance of any sort.

"I am sorry for you," she said quietly.

"Please believe I never meant this foolishness to go so far, Mary Kate. You were right to say that it was my uncle's words that made me sorry, for until then I had been selfishly heedless of your pain. I amused myself at your expense, and besides being foolish, my behavior was wicked and thoughtless. I am truly sorry, both that I have hurt you and that I have caused this trouble between you and Adam. I think I must have been jealous," she added frankly, "and perhaps at times I did intend more than simple mischief. I am not proud of myself, but I never meant such dreadful things to happen to either of us. When Adam received that message from your captors . . . well, you cannot think how I felt."

She paused with a reminiscent grimace. "I promise you, the news made me physically ill, and at that moment, if I could have brought you back merely by confessing to him what I had been doing and suffering the consequences of his fury, I'd have done so and gladly. But then he brought you home safely, and everyone made such a fuss over you that I reacted childishly again when my uncle sent for you. I saw your fear when the message came for you, and I thought you were finally to be scolded for causing such an upset."

Mary Kate chuckled. "Oh dear, how little you know. To think that you can believe everyone made a fuss over me when Adam was, and is, truly livid with anger."

"But I saw him," Megan protested. "He was beside himself with fear when word came of your capture, and today he had his arm 'round your shoulders, helping you up the front steps."

Mary Kate stared, then shook her head in wry amusement. "Megan, he was not helping me. He was forcing me. The last thing I wanted to do just then was to go into the house with him. He thought—still thinks, in fact—that I ran away yesterday rather than obey his command to beg your forgiveness for calling you a bitch."

Megan's mouth opened. "Is that what that word means?"

"Aye, near enough." Mary Kate bit her lip, feeling warmth surge to her cheeks. "And I am sorry I said it. But Adam probably thinks being captured by brigands is nothing compared to what I truly deserve. He would like nothing better than to use me as you fear Sir Reginald will use you. But his lordship intervened." She grimaced. "He did so, mind you, not because he thought Adam's wrath unjustified but because he feared that Adam's beating me would distress Lady Strachan. In point of fact, I probably owe my escape directly to her. I'd not be surprised to learn that, knowing precisely what Adam would do in such a case, she begged his lordship to protect me. So much for fussing over me!"

"I didn't know." Megan shook her head. "I am so ashamed of myself, Mary Kate. My uncle is right. There can be no excuse for my behavior. I wish now that I had been kinder to you. We might have become friends."

"We can still be friends," Mary Kate said, smiling. "Perhaps, if I were to speak to his lordship—"

"Oh, if only you would! I confess I had hoped you would suggest such a course, for it is the only thing now that might weigh with him, but I could not ask, for I know I do not deserve your help. If you will try," she added huskily, "I will be forever grateful to you." She hesitated then, fiddling with a fold of her skirt. "He said I am to leave first thing in the morning, so perhaps you could speak with him after supper?"

Mary Kate nodded absently, for her mind was racing. She did not doubt that, in the long run, she could convince Lord Strachan to alter his decision, but she pondered the advisability of waiting until after supper to approach him. There was always the likelihood that Douglas would return and interfere, one way or another, and she wanted the matter over and settled before ever he heard about it. He would be displeased, to say the least, if Megan were sent home on her account to face Sir Reginald's wrath. On the other hand, perhaps it would alleviate some of his present displeasure with her if she were able to prevent that. On the thought she consulted her watch, flicking open the intricate gold case with her thumbnail.

"It lacks half an hour of supper," she said briskly, rising to her feet and shaking out her skirts. She moved to study her reflection in the Venetian looking glass on the wall by the press cupboard, speaking as she went. "Do you remain here, and I shall speak with him at once." Smoothing her hair, she turned. "Should Adam return in the meantime, pray tell him only that I am with his father."

Megan agreed with becoming gratitude, and Mary Kate sallied forth to confront his lordship in the bookroom. When she requested a private interview, he obligingly dismissed young Ned to change for supper, seated her in the big armchair, perched himself against the edge of the huge table, and gave her his undivided attention.

At first he refused to consider her request, giving it as his opinion that Megan had stepped beyond all bounds by applying to her for assistance in what he readily agreed was a pretty tangle. He declared flatly that although he might decline to exert his authority so far as to take a good stout rod to his niece's backside, he had no qualms whatever about sending her home to a husband who could be depended upon to exercise that authority to the fullest degree. When he added, smiling, that Mary Kate was displaying her own generosity of spirit by supporting Megan, she tried to disabuse him of that notion by insisting first that she believed the other young woman was being punished more harshly than the situation merited and, secondly, that her own motives were selfish ones.

Earlier, when she had described her difficulties to him, she had been honest without dwelling upon her own contributions to the problem. In describing the incidents preceding her departure from Strachan Court, she had said only that Douglas had given her a tongue-lashing for being uncivil to his cousin. Now, albeit reluctantly, she filled in more of the details, emphasizing the fact that she, too, had been much at fault. She even admitted having told Megan that she, rather than Rose MacReady, had belonged upon the repentance stool. That part did not anger Strachan, as she had feared it might. He even smiled a little. But he was no longer smiling when she finished describing precisely what had taken place in the window hall.

"Your coming to me this way speaks well for you, Mary Kate," he said then, "but I understand now why my son was so angry with you." He paused, and she waited anxiously, chewing her lower lip. "None of what you have told me excuses Megan's rudeness, nor Adam's, for all that. But where his was heedless, hers was willful, and nothing you have said alters that fact. That she, a Douglas born, could so forget her duty . . ." He shook his head grimly. "Common courtesy, if nothing else, is expected of her at all times, and I am not inclined to forgive her easily."

"She knows you are displeased with her, my lord, and she is sorry for what she has done, so can you not reconsider your decision to send her home? Sir Reginald will be furious with her. She is certain that he will not allow her to attend the wedding, which will disappoint Margaret as much as it will disappoint Megan. Her absence will also distress her ladyship," she added shrewdly, "and there is still Adam to be considered. You yourself said that I shall have difficulty making my peace with him, but my task will be doubly difficult if he believes that Megan is being sent home in disgrace on my account. And that is what he will believe. She has apologized to me, after all, and I find that I am able freely to forgive her. I should like her to be my friend."

He stood upright and walked to the window, where he remained some minutes, lost in thought. Mary Kate kept silent. When he turned, his expression was stern, and she held her breath.

"I care not one whit for Sir Reginald's fury," he stated firmly and unencouragingly. "The lass deserves his fury. And her disappointment at being made to miss the wedding is likewise of no concern to me. As for Adam, I'm tempted to have another talk with him that he would enjoy even less than our last one. However," he added with an eye to the changing expressions on her face, "I confess to you that I had not thought about what his reaction to Megan's departure might mean to you. If he were simply going to miss her company, I'd say 'God rot him,' for he deserves to miss her. But I'd not want him to blame you for aught of my doing, lass, and I agree now that he may well do so. Moreover," he went on thoughtfully, "it would mean much to me and to my lady as well if you and yon prickling lass should form a friendship, much more than it would mean to know that Megan was back at Somerville sporting a striped backside." He grinned at her, raising her spirits considerably.

"Then she is to stay?"

"Aye, for the present. But you are to tell her for me that the future rests with herself. Her husband has every right to know how she comports herself when she is away from his sight, and I will certainly have something to say to him on that subject when next we meet. You may explain to her that the wording of that conversation will depend entirely upon my opinion of her behavior betwixt now and then."

"I will tell her, sir, at once. I promised to return to her before supper." Smiling, she rose and began moving toward the door, looking back only to say, "Thank you, my lord."

"Aye, you're welcome, but lassie—"

She turned. "Aye?"

"Don't feel too smug about your success with me," he warned. "You've still an unpleasant time of it ahead of you, and methinks not all of it is unmerited."

She grimaced. "I doubt I shall have any opportunity to forget that, sir, but with Megan to stand my friend, I believe it will not be so bad as it might have been."

"Aye, 'tis true," he agreed. "Get along with you

now. You've little enough time before supper, and you tell that lass for me," he added firmly, "that she is to present herself at the table. I'll brook no sulks."

Mary Kate agreed and a few moments later was excitedly reporting the success of her mission. Megan's relief was profound, but it flagged when she learned that her uncle still meant to speak to Sir Reginald.

"Don't distress yourself unduly," Mary Kate recommended. "Such a discussion cannot take place for more than a fortnight, so we have plenty of time in which to change his mind." When Megan looked doubtful, she laughed at her. "Bustle about now. You must wash your face, for 'tis time we were alow. I am like to starve if I don't eat soon."

"Oh, no, I cannot. I must look a fright, Mary Kate, and I feel utterly nauseous after all my upset. I cannot face them all like this. You must make my excuses for me."

Sighing, for she had hoped it would not be necessary, Mary Kate relayed his lordship's command, whereupon Megan offered no further protest and proceeded at once to do what she could to repair her ravaged complexion. Her eyes were still red and puffy, but the tearstains were gone when she meekly followed Mary Kate to the winter parlor. She seemed to have regained most of her composure by the time they joined the others, but sitting through the meal was clearly an ordeal for her, and she did no more than pick at her food. Neither her aunt nor Ned commented upon her appearance, but the air was pregnant with the young man's curiosity, if not with Lady Strachan's.

Mary Kate had expected to hear sounds of her husband's return long before she and Megan descended the great stair to supper, and when he had still not

put in an appearance by the time they adjourned to
the great chamber for the evening, she did not know
whether to be concerned or relieved. By bedtime,
however, she was undeniably worried, and by their
expressions, so too were the others.

Lord Strachan and Ned, contrary to their usual
custom, had chosen to remain with the ladies, for by
now everyone knew that Douglas and his men had
ridden in pursuit of the brigands. Mary Kate found
after an hour of listening to small talk and to Megan's
aimless plucking of the lute's strings, that she could
no longer keep her eyes open and reluctantly went to
bed. She left the door to Douglas's bedchamber ajar,
certain that she would thus hear his return, and
promptly fell asleep.

The next morning when she awoke, the door was
shut. A few minutes later, as she lay in bed wondering if she dared look to see if he were really home,
Annie Jardine entered from the gallery, carrying a
ewer of hot water. She set it upon the wash stand and
moved to open the curtains.

"Annie," said Mary Kate anxiously, "did you shut
the door to Sir Adam's room, or did someone else?"

Oddly, the maid seemed to brace herself. She did
not turn from the window. "Nay, mistress. Sir Adam
shut it himself sae as not tae disturb ye."

"Then he is home." Mary Kate sighed. "And Sesi?"

Annie turned slowly. "Safe in her stable, mistress.
And your jewels be in m'lord's lockbox in the bookroom."

"My jewels?"

"Aye, didna ye know? They was part o' the ransom."

She hadn't known, but the information made sense.
If she hadn't been in such a hurry when she left
Strachan Court, she would have put her watch away

properly in her jewel case. Then, when she looked for
it later, she would have known. But since she wore so
little jewelry at a time and had heedlessly tossed the
watch into the open trinket box on her dressing table,
she had had no idea until now that the jewels were
gone. However, it didn't matter since they were back
now and her beloved Sesi was safe in her stable.

She sighed again. Now perhaps she would be able
to clear the air with Douglas, to tell him what she had
learned about her feelings, alone in the bourock. Perhaps she would even discover whether the little signs
she had seen from time to time indicated a possibility
that he returned some of those feelings.

"Are the men all safe, Annie? Was anyone hurt?"

"All safe enough, mistress," Annie said with a carefully casual air, "and they got the reivers, every last
one o' them. Our Willie says most of 'em are wi' their
Maker, but four are on their way tae join their feck-
less comrades in Roxburgh Tolbooth, just as master
promised. And as tae injuries," she added more reluctantly, "I might as well tell ye that he did suffer a
sword cut tae his left arm, but Trotter tended it and
said 'tis naught. One o' the others had a nasty slice
taken out o' his leg, but that, too, will mend in time,
barring infec—" She broke off with her mouth hanging open when Mary Kate scrambled out of bed.

Not having comprehended at once what Annie had
said, she was white now with the realization that
Douglas had been wounded. She spoke hastily. "Get
my things, Annie, and quickly. What is the hour?"

"It lacks a guid while to dinner, mistress. There be
nae need for haste. My lady expected ye would sleep
late and said I wasna tae disturb ye earlier." She
spoke hesitantly, as though she would say more but
knew not whether she should.

"I must see Sir Adam," Mary Kate insisted. "Even

if he is still sleeping, I must see for myself that he is well."

"He isna here, m'lady." Annie spoke as though the words were dragged from her mouth against her will.

"Not here? Don't be absurd, Annie. What do you mean?"

"Please, mistress, he went wi' the others tae Roxburgh and said he will ride straight on tae Edinburgh from there. He were here only the few hours tae sleep whilst Trotter got his gear 'n' all together."

Mary Kate stared at her maidservant. "Did he leave a message for me?"

Annie had watched her warily while she broke the unwelcome news, but now she looked away helplessly. "Nay, m'lady, none that I ken. He may ha' said something tae the mistress or tae m'lady Somerville."

But Mary Kate knew he had not done so. Though he might have made some vague, polite statement to his mother, that would be all. He had gone away without a word to her.

Despite his father's orders to leave her be, she had expected him to scold her at the very least, if only to relieve his temper after all the worry and distress she had caused him to suffer; however, it was clear now that he would not speak to her at all, that she would not even see him for some days to come. As a punishment that would be far worse, for it meant that they would travel to Edinburgh without his escort. What would people think of such behavior? She brushed a strand of hair off her face and, becoming aware of Annie's apprehension, took herself firmly in hand. The situation was dreadful, but it was none of Annie's doing.

"Fetch my clothes, Annie," she said gently, "and do not, I beg of you, look so wretched. Being the bearer of unwelcome tidings is not easy, but one no longer kills the messenger."

"Nay, m'lady," Annie said, looking alarmed at the very thought. "I didna mean tae fash ye. Certes, young master meant naught by sae rapid a departure. 'Tis nobbut that he didna trust the others tae bring yon reivers safe tae Roxburgh wi'oot him. He wants tae see them end where they canna mak' more mischief."

"That will do," Mary Kate said more sharply than she had intended. She was sorry for her tone but consoled herself with the thought that it was not proper to allow Annie to discuss such things with her. The maid was a servant, after all, not a friend. An hour later, however, she was wishing she could snub Megan so easily.

On the whole, dinner was not as difficult an ordeal as she had anticipated it would be. Lord Strachan commented on the successful capture of the reivers, of course, and his lady expressed gratitude that the success had been achieved without loss of life or limb amongst their own. But the subject of Douglas's abrupt departure was scrupulously avoided. He might just as well have been snug in his bed, Mary Kate thought, as halfway to Roxburgh. She sensed a sympathy for her difficulties among the others; however, no overt attempt was made to discuss them with her until after dinner when Megan drew her inexorably into the warm inner courtyard.

"You look dreadful," Megan said when they had seated themselves on the stone bench. "Did you quarrel with Adam again before he left?"

Her frankness accomplished what tact would never have done. "I wish I had," Mary Kate said dismally. "I didn't even see him. He didn't even say good-bye."

Her eyes welled with tears, but Megan wisely expressed no sympathy.

"How uncivil of him," she said briskly, "but he said nothing to me, either, you know. Or to anyone else, except no doubt for my aunt. I suppose he was in too great a rush to be bothered with common courtesy."

"But what will people think when he arrives in Edinburgh without us? They will know at once that something is wrong."

Megan chuckled then with unfeigned mirth. "Don't be a goosecap, Mary Kate. You didn't imagine that Adam would plod tamely along with his mother's cavalcade, did you? You, of all people, must know how he travels. He might have made an effort, of course, but it wouldn't have been long before some errand or other occurred to him that necessitated his leaving us behind long before we reached the city. No one who knows him will think it the least odd when he arrives before us."

Mary Kate acknowledged the truth of these words and began to feel better. Nevertheless, it was a relief four days later, after a long, tiresome, and uncomfortable journey, to discover that Megan was absolutely right. No one seemed to think it at all strange that Douglas had preceded the rest of his family to the city. Mary Kate had been particularly concerned about her initial reception at his house in the Canongate; however, when at last they approached the tall, imposing house standing in its own grounds, she barely had time to catch her breath after it had been identified for her by the others before the front doors were flung wide and a familiar figure appeared on the threshold.

"Welcome, welcome, everyone!" Margaret cried as she ran down the steps to the circular drive to greet them, waving with one hand while she held up her voluminous skirts with the other.

Mary Kate forgot all her troubles in the delight of seeing her new sister again, and Margaret hustled them all inside for refreshment, saying that Douglas, not knowing exactly when to expect their arrival, was with the king and had asked her to play hostess in his absence.

"I am to introduce you to the housekeeper and help you choose a personal maidservant," she informed Mary Kate, who explained that the latter duty was unnecessary, since Annie Jardine had requested and been granted permission to serve her.

Lord and Lady Strachan departed for Ardcarach House half an hour later, taking Ned and Megan with them, and Mary Kate, alone with Margaret, found herself subjected to a searching stare. She tried to meet it but failed and turned away, biting her lip.

"I knew it." Margaret sighed. "Something is wrong. Adam has been either gruff or silent ever since he arrived, and now you look just wretched. He blamed his rude behavior on that stupid sword cut, but I didn't believe him then, and seeing you now, I believe it less than ever. You may come along with me upstairs to your bedchamber, my lass, for you are going to tell Aunt Margaret all about it." She paused only long enough to make good her promise to introduce Mrs. Comfort, the housekeeper, before bustling her protesting charge up the stairs.

Mary Kate held a hurried mental conference with her conscience, assuring it that she would tell Margaret no more than was necessary, but she might as well have spared herself the effort. Inside her bedchamber, Mistress Douglas unhesitatingly dismissed Annie, then pulled two armchairs up to the cheerful fire and demanded to be told the whole.

Mary Kate, attempting to evade the question, was quickly brought to remember that although she had, in her married state, somehow come to think of the unmarried Margaret as being younger than herself, such was not, in fact, the case. Indeed, Mistress Douglas was of an age with Lady Somerville and possessed besides all the authority of superior size. She would brook no nonsense, and although Mary Kate was never certain afterward how it had been accomplished, Margaret soon coaxed the whole sorry tale out of her.

The details were tangled, of course, necessitating that Margaret ask many questions, but she managed nonetheless to put herself in possession of nearly all the facts of Mary Kate's recent history. She shook her head over Susan Kennedy, laughed at Mary Kate's revenge, and seemed unsurprised by Douglas's retaliation. She expressed proper indignation at Megan's behavior, sisterly disgust at Douglas's blindness, distress over his demand for an apology, and horror at Mary Kate's capture by the reivers. In fact, she exemplified the perfect audience, and Mary Kate warmed to her quickly, explaining details she would later scold herself for divulging. One such detail was her description of the frozen expression on Douglas's face during his confrontation with Lord Strachan.

Margaret grimaced. "I have seen that look," she said. "Indeed, I have felt it upon my own face more than once. When my father's temper is aroused, his voice can freeze the sun. 'Tis a thoroughly discomforting experience."

"I believe you," Mary Kate said with simple sincerity. "But now you know everything. Adam set off with his men to capture the brigands, then delivered them to Roxburgh and came straight on to Edinburgh. I thought everyone would know by the manner of his arrival that something was wrong."

"Well, they won't," Margaret said flatly. "I warrant no one will think twice about it unless you go about with a long face. Everyone knows how my mother travels and how Adam abominates a turtle's pace. But something must be done to right things between you, else there will be talk soon enough. And with my wedding day fast approaching, if they are going to talk about Douglases, I want them to talk about the beautiful bride, not about her doltish brother and his moping wife."

Mary Kate summoned up a wan smile. "But what can I do? He is too angry to speak to me."

"Let me think," said Margaret. "I have seen this reaction before, you know. Adam generally has a sunny temperament, but when he gets angry, he needs to fire up into a good red blaze till his temper burns itself out, or else it tends to smolder deep down where no one can see it, which is not at all a good thing. 'Twould be best if he were to roar at you the first moment you and he are alone together."

When Mary Kate bit her lip at the vision this suggestion produced in her mind, Margaret shook her head. "I said it would be best. I didn't say he will do such a thing. He will not. Too much time has passed for that. He will be chilly and very polite instead. Therefore, if you want to clear the air, you have merely to enrage him once more and be willing to take the consequences. Then we can all be comfortable again."

17

❧❧❧ ❧❧❧

Margaret sat back in her chair with an air of thorough satisfaction, while Mary Kate stared at her in dismay. "You must be mad, Margaret," she said finally. "The last thing I want to do is to vex him further. I want to make my peace with him, to explain everything to him."

"By all means," Margaret agreed amiably. "If you think you can turn the trick by discussing this muddle with him, go right ahead." She paused, and her eyes began to twinkle. "My own experience has shown that he does not tend to be particularly reasonable when one of these moods sets in, but perhaps you will be more successful than I ever was."

The statement was not an encouraging one, and Mary Kate remembered it later when she sat at one end of the long, linen-draped dining table, with her husband, resplendent in gold velvet and dark blue silk, at the other. He had returned late in the afternoon, some time after Margaret's departure, and had sent a message to her bedchamber, informing her that he would present her to the king that evening.

The news was exciting, and she would have liked to ask him a number of questions about what to expect upon such an occasion, but the servant who brought the message added the information that Douglas would be unavailable until supper. When they met at the table, his manner was aloof and uninviting. Though he asked politely about her journey, gazed searchingly at her from time to time, and even complimented her upon the deep green velvet gown she wore over golden petticoats and a wide Spanish farthingale, he snubbed a solicitous inquiry about his wound, and his tone when he did so was barely civil.

Mary Kate was thrown into confusion both by her excitement at the prospect of meeting the young king and by her desire to clear the air with her husband. But with the servants in constant attendance, there was no opportunity for private speech, nor did she attempt to create one, for his lack of encouragement deterred her.

When they reached Holyrood Palace, Douglas guided her to a reception room full of chattering people. Musicians played from a gallery, but no one danced. Instead, the courtiers and ladies stared at newcomers and discussed their neighbors. Many eyes turned toward Mary Kate as her husband led her toward James VI. Self-consciously she held her head higher, knowing that she could not be faulted on her appearance and feeling proud to be seen with Douglas, whose demeanor showed no indication of his displeasure with her. Smiling, he nodded to a friend here and an acquaintance there, not pausing in his progress up the room, however, until they stood directly in front of James.

Mary Kate sank at once into a deep curtsy, green velvet and gold skirts billowing. The noise around her faded, and her husband's voice sounded clearly over her head.

"May I have permission to present my lady wife, Sire?" His voice held a trace of amusement, but Mary Kate dared not glance up to see his expression. She must await his majesty's pleasure. It was as well that she did not look up, since James was indulging himself in close scrutiny of those of her assets that were most easily viewed in her present position.

"Christ's blood, sir," he exclaimed at last, "a pox on thee for denying us this pleasure afore now. Were it to our royal taste, Douglas, we'd clap thee in heavy irons for such lack of generosity. Instead, I believe I shall write a poem to her most obvious charms."

"Have mercy, Sire," Douglas said, laughing, and with no discernible apology in his voice. "I feared to bring her to your majesty's notice before I had her safely wedded lest she succumb to the well-known Stewart charm."

"Rise, Lady Douglas," the king said wryly, "and join our conversation ere his impertinence treads too heavily upon our royal sensibilities. He'd make a poor offering to our jailers at the Tolbooth."

"Thank you, Sire." She arose, looking fully at him now, her clear gaze meeting one just as direct.

She had heard much about this young man who held the reins of Scotland so tenaciously. He had recently celebrated the twenty-second anniversary of his birth, and he looked much as she had expected him to look, though perhaps a shade taller. She had heard he was short, even squat, when in fact he was of medium stature. Of course, the Stewarts were noted for their great height, so perhaps he was short by comparison to others of his clan, but his shoulders were broad enough to meet any standard.

She had also heard it said that he was deformed, which was nonsense. His legs in their silken trunk hose were slightly bent, and one foot appeared to be turned slightly outward, but there was no great deformity. Of course, the worst that was said was that he was no Stewart at all, or Stuart, since he used his father, Lord Darnley's, English spelling of the name.

Mary Kate gazed at the face in front of her and promptly dismissed such tales as fabrication. She had seen more than one portrait of his parents, and there before her were Darnley's sad, hooded eyes and thick light brown hair, as well as Queen Mary's tiny mouth and long nose. As she watched, the mouth turned down and tucked in at the corners.

"Do we meet with thy approval, Lady Douglas?"

Flushing, she caught her breath and spoke hastily. "I beg your pardon, Sire. 'Tis only that I have never met a king before. Pray forgive me for gawking like a peasant girl." She glanced helplessly at Douglas, but although his expression was warmer than she had expected to find it, he made no move to assist her.

James chose to be generous, chuckling when he followed the direction of her gaze. " 'Tis no use looking to that scoundrel for aid, for he is no chivalrous knight. He has greater aspirations than mere knighthood. He looks to join the rogues of our land who call themselves 'noble.' "

Douglas grinned at him. "Sire, cease your jesting. My lady wife is unacquainted with Your Majesty's sense of humor. He knows right well, madam," he added, turning his smile upon her, "that I am the king's man through and through and have no wish to join with any others, whatever they choose to call themselves."

"So you say," James replied, his voice tinged with cynicism, "but we have learned, *Douglas*, to trust few who wear the badges of nobility."

Douglas dropped to one knee, and his voice was gruff with sincerity. "My Lord King, believe me your trusted servant, come what may. I have sworn fealty, Sire, and time will prove my oath trustworthy, Douglas or no."

"Oh, get up, damn you," James said irritably. "Christ's sandals, Adam, have done!"

Obediently Douglas got to his feet, but he showed no sign now of his earlier amusement. His expression was so serious that it seemed to make James uncomfortable.

He glanced first at Mary Kate and then back at her husband. "Damn you, Douglas," he said softly. "Very well, then. You shall judge whether we trust you." He turned away and lifted his hand in an imperious signal to Lord Hamilton, a small and slender man who approached with quick, short steps and listened intently while James whispered in his ear. Mary Kate had met Hamilton and knew him to be one of the most powerful members of the court. She watched now as he listened to James's whispers. He glanced at Douglas and grinned, then nodded and stepped away from the king, clapping his hands loudly.

"Silence in the room!" he bellowed in a voice that seemed entirely too big and deep for him. "Silence for His Majesty."

The king turned to face the now silent, curious gathering and, with a graceful gesture of his hand toward the stunned Douglas, began to speak. "Much of the power of the state," he said, his voice carrying easily and with no apparent effort to the far corners of the vast chamber, "lies in the wisdom and eminence of its counsel. In particular, the throne of this realm is elevated and strengthened when there are many loyal men of noble status. Therefore, in our wish to enhance the order of the Kingdom of Scotland, to secure the safety of its borders, to add to that number of loyal nobles by whose counsels we are directed, and for our support in times of adversity, we do intend to invest Sir Adam Douglas of Tornary with the county of Teviot, to him and to his heirs of his name for all time henceforward. The ceremony shall take place here at our palace of Holyrood on the first Sunday of September so that he may take his proper place at the meeting of our lords of the borders two days thereafter." James stepped back, grinning his triumph while the people around them cheered. "Art satisfied, my lord?"

The question was nearly drowned out by the other noise, but Douglas heard it and dropped again to one knee, taking James's hand and pressing it to his lips. "Indeed, my liege, I am more than satisfied. I am deeply honored."

Mary Kate heard the exchange, noted the quaver in her husband's voice, and knew he was much moved. She smiled down at him, but then, as James drew him to his feet, the full significance of what had just transpired struck her. Sir Adam Douglas had been a powerful man before because of his friendship with the king. But Adam Douglas, Earl of Teviot, would be a greater power in his own right. How disappointing that his parents should have missed such a moment, she thought.

But they had not. Even as the thought crossed her mind, Margaret approached, laughing, her parents close behind. With everything happening so quickly, Mary Kate simply had not seen them in the crowd.

"Shall you demand now that I curtsy whenever we

chance to meet, my lady countess?" Margaret demanded.

Mary Kate's senses whirled. For the first time she recognized her own change of status. Countess. She, Mary Katharine MacPherson Douglas, would soon be the Countess of Teviot. My lady Teviot. She tried the sound of it in her imagination and let it echo through her mind. Whatever she had said to the contrary in the past, the sound was nice. Very nice. Lady Teviot, Lady Teviot—

"Lady Douglas!" Jolted from her thoughts, she realized that His Majesty was repeating himself. Confused, she dropped a curtsy, nearly overbalancing herself in her haste.

"Forgive me, Sire, I was not attending." She heard Margaret chuckle behind her, and James's voice when he responded also contained a note of amusement.

"Arise, madam. We merely asked how you will like to be Countess of Teviot. Art proud of thy husband, lass?"

"Aye," she replied, glancing at Douglas, who was presently deep in conversation with Lord Hamilton. "I shall like being a countess, too, Sire, very much."

The other guests had moved in upon them, laughing, talking, and offering congratulations, when suddenly Mary Kate's attention was diverted by a hand laid familiarly upon her shoulder. Turning, she found herself face to face with Kenneth Gillespie, whose handsome face she was certain she remembered only because she had been dancing with him at the very moment she had first laid eyes upon Douglas.

"Well met, sir," she said.

"Greetings, my lady." He grinned down at her. "I should congratulate your husband upon his good fortune as the others do, I suppose, but I confess to having a decided preference for your company."

"I am honored, sir."

"Nay, madam," he replied. " 'Tis I who am honored, and I would be the more so should you accept my invitation to dance." Indeed, the musicians had struck up again, and James had evidently given permission for the dancing to begin, for a circle of dancers was forming for a Spanish pavane. Mary Kate hesitated, not knowing whether it would be seemly to accept Gillespie's invitation. The decision was made for her.

"Go along with thy cavalier, Lady Douglas," James said. He stood behind her and had evidently overheard Gillespie speaking to her. "Don't trouble about thy husband. There are arrangements to be made and the revenues to discuss. If my lord Hamilton will but come to bear witness?" Hamilton, still standing beside Douglas, agreed, and the three men left Mary Kate to enjoy the merrymaking.

She danced with Gillespie and found him as charming as she remembered. If his gaze was occasionally a shade too intimate for her taste, she attributed that to the difference in manners at court, where she had heard that men indulged in vulgar behavior and women allowed liberties otherwise unheard of in polite company. Certainly she would not allow liberties herself, and she had seen nothing else to account for such tales, but if the tales were told, she knew there must be a grain of truth somewhere, and Gillespie's attentions were marked. She did not spend all her time with him, of course, but allowed Margaret and her parents to introduce her to their friends, including, at long last, Sir Patrick Ferguson.

He was taller than Margaret and solidly built with broad, strong-looking shoulders, solid, muscular thighs, and a trim waist beneath his light-blue-and-white satin doublet and lavender trunk hose. Tight blond curls were cropped close around his ears, his blond beard was short and pointed, and even his eyebrows were pale blond above ocean-blue eyes that twinkled like sunlight on water. The planes of his face were smoothly chiseled, and when he smiled the lines at the corners of his mouth and eyes deepened into the weathered creases characteristic of an outdoorsman. She knew from Margaret's chatter that he loved farming and all manner of sport, but he seemed equally at home here in Holyrood Palace.

"I am pleased to make your acquaintance at last, Sir Patrick," she told him, smiling, "though I have heard so much about you that I already feel as if I know you well."

Margaret grinned at his look of dismay. "Pay her no heed, sir. I told her only good things, so she scarcely knows you at all."

Sir Patrick laughed, delighted, and said to Mary Kate, "She is in the right of it, you know, my lady. I have many faults."

"I believe we all have faults, sir," she replied, "but I like what I have heard, and I like what I see."

Not at all taken aback by her frankness, he returned her smile and asked if she would care to dance. She danced a good deal that night, enjoying several dances with Ned Lumsden, who acquitted himself well, and one more with Kenneth Gillespie. The latter seemed to assume that they were old friends, but he did not infringe overmuch, and her pleasure in the evening would have been undimmed had it not been for the behavior of her husband.

When Douglas returned, he did not seek her out as she expected him to do but joined a group of his friends instead. In fact, Mary Kate was unaware of his return until she saw him lead a beautiful young redhead into the dance. It had not occurred to her until that moment to wonder how he would conduct himself in public now that he was married. With shock, she soon realized that his behavior was exactly what it had been at Critchfield Manor. He laughed and flirted and played the gallant, leading first one, then another adoring damsel onto the floor. It seemed to his wife that a veritable bevy of dazzling beauties clamored for his attention. Clearly his injured arm no longer troubled him, but he did not once ask her to dance. Watching him, her eyes soon began to glitter with suppressed anger, and she threw herself into the merrymaking with frenetic energy. What she really wanted to do, she told herself, fuming, was to comb his hair with a joint stool. Lacking one, she would serve him as he served her instead.

By the end of the evening she was exhausted. She was able to say nothing of consequence to him on the way home because of the chairmen, but she was determined to have it out with him the moment they were safely inside their own house, where they could be private.

When they reached the Canongate, Douglas dismissed the chairmen and followed her into the house. She turned to face him in the hall, saying coldly, "Adam, I would speak with you."

His mouth tightened at her tone, and he glanced at the gillie who was closing the door behind them. "Now?"

She nodded, her face set with determination.

"Very well, come into the parlor. Fetch me ale, lad."

The gillie hurried off to do his bidding, and Mary Kate pulled off her cloak, tossing it onto a nearby chair in a heap. She promised herself she would remain calm if it killed her, for she had no wish to arouse his temper, but she had to let him know she would not tolerate such treatment from him again. And she had to make an effort, too, to clear the air between them. She waited until the gillie had returned and departed again.

Douglas quaffed his ale and set down the mug on a side table. "Well?"

She swallowed. Once again, the opportunity had come and she didn't know how to begin. Perhaps, she mused, it would be better not to make any hasty accusations, not until his displeasure with her had abated. "I . . . I wanted to tell you that I have made up my quarrel with Megan," she said finally.

"I know. I spoke with my father tonight."

Her breath caught in her throat, and she shot him a searching look. What if Lord Strachan had made good his threat to tell his son what he thought of his behavior? "Wh-what did he say to you?"

"Naught of any particular import." His eyes glinted enigmatically. "He merely gave me the impression that you have at long last learned to get on with Megan. I assumed that she had accepted your apologies."

Mary Kate nodded, breathing more easily. She had been foolish, she thought, to fear that Lord Strachan would say anything critical of his son on such a night as this had been. But she could tell by the searching expression in Douglas's eyes that she had stirred his suspicions, and she didn't want him to know about the things she had told his father. Therefore, she decided she would be wiser not to expound upon her new relationship with Megan. In fact, it would perhaps be safer to change the subject altogether. "Did he tell you I was not running away when those dreadful men caught me?"

"No," he replied evenly, "and if you have convinced him of that, it is more than you will accomplish with me."

"But I wasn't, Adam, I swear it. I wanted only to get out of my bedchamber into the fresh air. I gave Sesi her head and paid no heed to the direction she took. The time passed more quickly than I realized."

"Don't lie to me," he warned her. "Remember that Willie Jardine reads track better than other people read books. We know exactly how far south you were when they caught you, madam, so it will do you no good to profess your innocence to me now."

She opened her mouth to protest but realized immediately that to do so would be useless. She must have been farther from Strachan Court than she had realized. Bracing herself, she asked steadily, "Adam, do you still intend to punish me?"

"It would be pointless to do so at this late date, don't you think?" he replied with a sigh, adding, "It would be wise, however, for you to give careful attention to your conduct whilst we are here in Edinburgh."

She frowned. This conversation was hardly clearing the air. Perhaps it would prove necessary, after all, to heed Margaret's advice and make him angry. Reluctantly gathering her courage, she forced herself to look up at him boldly. "And what of your own conduct, sir? I did not think well of it tonight."

His initial expression indicated genuine surprise, but she could not be certain, for his eyes narrowed quickly. "You did not appear to be concerned at the time, madam," he retorted, "and you will soon find that at court a man is not expected to dance attendance upon his own wife."

"And what of wives, Adam? Don't they demand similar freedoms?"

"My wife will conduct herself in a proper manner," he replied shortly. "Now, if this conversation is
finished, I suggest we go to bed."

He had kept a rein on his temper, but his expression was forbidding, and Mary Kate's courage failed
her. If she could have made herself believe that to
goad him further would eventually put them back on
a comfortable footing with each other, she might
have dared to do so, but at the moment there was too
much distance between them to be certain what the
result of such pressure would be. Anticipating his re-
actions was proving to be difficult. Margaret was
right. He was unreasonable in his present mood, and
unpredictable besides.

She slept in her own bed that night, and the next
morning Douglas informed her that they would attend Sunday services with the king. It seemed to her
that the entire day was spent at devotions, except
what time was passed in quiet, very dull conversation
with courtiers who would rather have been engaged
in merrier occupations. That night she slept alone
again, awakening late Monday morning to learn that
Douglas had gone hunting with James. Sighing with
frustration, she arose and dressed, then decided to
break her fast downstairs before asking the housekeeper to show her over her new home.

Mrs. Comfort, wearing her courtesy like a polished
shell, was pleasant but different in every way from
the amiable Mrs. Jardine. Mary Kate could not feel as
easy with her as she could with Annie's mother and
was not at all tempted to confide in her. They had
seen the vast, colorful gardens at the rear of the
house, all the primary rooms, the linen press, the gallery, and the chief pantry before Mrs. Comfort
turned toward the kitchens. Mary Kate was wondering how she could politely decline to continue with-

out offending the woman when, turning a corner, she came smack up against Ellen Kennedy. She exclaimed, and the pale young woman dropped a hasty curtsy.

Ellen was much improved since Mary Kate had last seen her, but her complexion was still colorless and her light-blue eyes were dull. "I hope ye willna be vexed, mistress," she said, looking up. Her voice was soft, not unlike Susan's, but it too lacked animation.

"Of course I am not vexed, but what are you doing here in Edinburgh?" When the girl hesitated, Mary Kate realized that she was uncomfortable in the housekeeper's presence. "Here, Ellen, you must come with me. You will excuse us, Mrs. Comfort. Ellen surely has news of Tornary, and I confess to a longing for word from home. I will see the kitchens another day."

"As you wish, my lady," the housekeeper said graciously.

Mary Kate quickly took Ellen into the parlor and insisted that she be seated. The girl obeyed without comment and folded her hands placidly in her lap.

"Now, Ellen, first of all, how are you, and how do your mother and Susan fare?"

"As well as might be, mistress," she answered. "Susan hadna yet birthed her bairn when I left, and I still be taking Dame Beaton's powders now and anon when I canna sleep, but we're all of us as well as might be, thank ye kindly."

"But why are you here?"

" 'Twas thought I might be useful gin any odd thing need doing wi' yer dress for the wedding. Mr. Graham suggested it, said I might prove useful." She spoke in a monotone, and it was as though she repeated a lesson.

Mary Kate regarded her closely. "I am grateful, Ellen," she said quietly, "but I thought you would be preparing for a wedding of your own by now."

Color suffused the girl's cheeks, and her hands clutched at each other in her lap. She took a deep breath, letting it out slowly. "He didna want me." Despite her efforts, the words came in a whisper.

"Oh, Ellen, how dreadful for you! But surely Ian Baird doesn't blame you for what happened."

"As to that, I canna say, but there was talk—a deal o' talk," she added bitterly. "I never saw Ian, mistress. He sent the message wi' his brother that we'd best not see each other again."

Mary Kate could imagine the sort of talk there had been. She herself, knowing of Douglas's association with Ellen and then hearing the brigand's comments, had begun to form an unflattering opinion of the girl's character. But now, face-to-face with her again, all such thoughts dissolved in a wave of compassion.

"I am truly sorry," she said, "but perhaps 'tis for the best. If he could give you up so easily, he cannot be much of a man. I am very glad that you are here."

"Thank ye, mistress. Happen ye've the right of it."

"I have," Mary Kate said firmly, adding, "They caught those reivers, you know."

"I heard, mistress. The master told me. He saw the last o' them hanged at Roxburgh. Somehow he prevailed upon yon magistrate tae believe that the first lot had conspired wi' the second tae steal yer ladyship. That mun ha' been a frightful experience fer ye, mistress."

"It was," Mary Kate agreed. "I don't mind telling you, they frightened me witless, but fortunately, Sir Adam found me before they could do more. What they did to you was worse."

"Aye. 'Tis glad I am that they be gone."

They talked a while longer before the housekeeper

interrupted them to announce that Mistress Douglas and Lady Somerville had come to call and Ellen excused herself.

The three friends were soon comfortably occupied with an exchange of tales about the previous evening's activities. Megan had retired early with a sick headache and had missed the king's announcement; however, Margaret had described it to her later in detail. It appeared that they had had other conversation as well, for Margaret accepted the friendship between her cousin and Mary Kate without question, despite the fact that, in all her confidings the day before, Mary Kate had said nothing that might betray Megan's present difficulties with her uncle. They had also apparently discussed Mary Kate's marital problem.

"Megan disagrees with me," Margaret announced suddenly. "She doesn't believe you ought to enrage Adam at all. She thinks you ought to be extra good and loving instead." She wrinkled her nose, plainly expressing her low opinion of such a notion.

Megan smiled at her. "'Tis a better plan than yours, for heaven's sake. But perhaps it would help more if I were to speak to him."

Something deep within Mary Kate rebelled at the thought of Megan pleading her case to Douglas. "Please don't," she begged. "That would only make matters worse."

"I promise I wouldn't do that. He is not an inflexible man, you know. He simply has too many things to think about just now. To know that you helped me would please him."

"I know you wouldn't mean to cause trouble, but only consider for a moment." Mary Kate pushed a straggling curl away from her left eye and attempted to put her feelings into words that would make sense.

"If you discuss the matter with him, how can you tell him about his father's anger without telling him what caused it?"

"But my own actions caused it. And Adam's. Oh." Megan stopped short with a grimace. "Adam will want to know how his father found out about all that, won't he? I don't suppose he would believe that one of the servants told him or that my uncle deduced the whole from any voluntary confession of mine. Adam knows me too well to believe that I would willingly submit myself to my uncle's displeasure."

"Of course, he would not believe such things. Nor would he believe that his father had had some sort of a prophetic dream. Moreover, no matter how carefully we wrapped it up, he would still suspect that we have been discussing his behavior amongst ourselves, and I know he would dislike that."

"Oh, Mary Kate, he must know we talk about him," Margaret protested. "He would have to be a witless coof not to know it."

"Perhaps he does know," Mary Kate agreed quietly, "but I'll warrant he thinks any such conversation must be complimentary. Only consider Sir Patrick's reaction. He wasn't surprised to learn that you had said nice things about him. He even admitted to having faults. But I'll wager my best jeweled cap he'd not have been so pleased to hear that you had already described those faults to me."

"But I haven't!"

"Of course not, nor would you do so. I wouldn't discuss Adam with anyone else either, but Megan was there when everything happened, and you badgered the bits and details out of me yesterday. Besides, I need help from someone who knows him. I don't like him to be angry with me."

"Well, I told you what to do," Margaret said, "and I

still don't see that it would hurt all that much for
Megan to speak to him. After all, he's angry partly
because of your behavior toward her. When he real-
izes that the two of you have become friends, he
ought to relent a little at least."

Her suggestion sounded almost plausible. After all,
Lord Strachan did not seem to have made clear the
fact that she and Megan were truly friends now, only
that they were no longer enemies, which was not at
all the same thing. And she had told Douglas only
that an apology had been made. She knew that there
was something amiss with Margaret's logic, but she
could not for the moment think what it was.

"It won't hurt for him to realize that we are
friends," Megan said slowly, "but he will see that
much for himself. And I don't think he is truly angry
because of any particular action of hers toward me.
The transgression strikes closer to himself than that."
She paused, collecting her thoughts, then went on
musingly, "I think he was angry first because she hit
him with some truths about his own behavior. Add to
that the fact that she disobeyed him, frightened him
senseless by being captured by brigands, then dared
to be present when my uncle scolded him like an un-
ruly schoolboy, and I think she has the right of it. I
must not become involved."

Silence greeted this assessment of the situation, and
all three young women turned for a moment to their
own thoughts. Margaret spoke first. "Megan's argu-
ment makes sense, Mary Kate, but that doesn't alter
what I told you yesterday. The longer you allow this
situation to smolder, the worse it will be when it—
that is, when Adam ignites." She paused, and a gleam
lit her eye. "Of course, if you go on behaving like you
did last night, it won't be long before you discover,

will you or nill you, that you have followed my advice to the letter."

"Whatever are you talking about, Margaret?" She had said nothing to them about her conversation with Douglas the previous night. Even Megan looked puzzled.

"Jealousy, my dear." Margaret waved a hand airily. "You don't think my brother will sit patiently by whilst you indulge yourself with a host of flirts like Ned Lumsden or Kenneth Gillespie, do you? Particularly Mr. Gillespie."

"What nonsense is this?" Mary Kate was stunned. "If Adam even noticed who my partners were, which I take leave to doubt, how would he dare to take exception to any one of them?" she asked hotly. "Especially in view of his own behavior!"

"Don't be daft, Mary Kate," Margaret said flatly. "What he does himself has never entered into the matter. What you do is all that counts with him, and it always will be."

Silenced, Mary Kate knew she was right. Douglas expected his wife's behavior to be above reproach. Had he not said so again only the night before? And his expectations would no doubt be even higher now that an earldom was in the offing. But, by the same token, he clearly intended to continue doing just as he pleased. She glanced at the other two, now arguing between themselves. They meant well, but in this instance she would have to depend upon her own wits, for no matter how much she wanted to make her peace with Douglas, he still had to learn that he could not dictate her behavior. Not unless he agreed to set a standard or two for himself.

18

>>> <<<

*H*aving made the decision to handle the situation herself, Mary Kate had not the least notion of how to begin. Margaret's plan of making Douglas angry seemed self-defeating, and Megan's plan meant she must meekly submit to his every whim. She needed time to think, and to get that time, she decided to avoid any immediate confrontation. She would be as distant and polite as he was himself, giving him no further cause to complain of her behavior, at least not until she was ready to meet his demands with a few demands of her own. For once, she would not be impulsive. She would think everything through carefully before she acted.

Therefore, two days later, when he announced that he wished to give a supper party the following week, she agreed without a blink so that he would not suspect the panic rising beneath her surface composure. Never before had she arranged anything beyond a gathering or two in her father's house, yet Douglas expected her to arrange one fit to be graced by the

king's presence. Determined not to disappoint him,
she hastily sent a messenger to Ardcarach House to
request the immediate assistance of Lady Somerville
and Mistress Douglas.

Margaret came alone, saying that Megan was indis-
posed but would be up and about in no time, since
her affliction did not seem to be a serious one. She
laughed when Mary Kate explained her problem, and
said, "If that isn't just like Adam! I suppose you
ought to be grateful that he gave you a few days'
notice. He might just as easily have sent a message at
noon to say that Jamie would arrive to sup at five."

Mary Kate was unnerved at the thought.
"Godamercy, I don't even know how to prepare for
next week!"

"That should not be difficult," Margaret said. "Is
Johnny Graham anywhere near at hand?"

"Why, I don't know," Mary Kate admitted. "He
has scarcely ever been around before, so I never gave
him a thought."

"Well, give him one now, because very likely he is
the solution to your predicament."

A gillie was dispatched at once to discover Mr.
Graham's whereabouts, and that young man entered
the parlor in person five minutes later. Mary Kate
had no sooner put the question to him than her worries were over.

"I shall see to everything, my lady," he said. "You
need trouble your head about it no longer. I shall
present all my lists to you for your approval, of
course, including the guest list and the menu, but
beyond that you may trust everything to my judgment."

Mary Kate thanked him, conscious of a wish that
all her troubles might be resolved so easily, and in the
days that followed, Johnny Graham and Mrs. Com-

fort organized all the details of her supper party with experienced ease. She had only to approve the results of their industry and to choose what she would wear.

Graham left a tentative menu for her perusal the very next morning, and she had just decided to give it her enthusiastic approval when the parlor door was thrown open with more flourish than usual.

"Lady Aberfoyle, mistress!" The gillie's announcement barely preceded the entrance of a quick, little, gray-haired woman in a rustling, lace-trimmed, puce-silk dress cut high to a wide ruff and long to her lace-covered wrists. Her full skirt billowed over pink petticoats and an immense French farthingale, and the layered-leather heels of her mules clicked a tattoo beneath it as she crossed the hardwood floor toward Mary Kate, who scrambled to her feet with more haste than grace.

"Aunt, wherever did you spring from? Adam told me you were out of town."

"*Sir* Adam, my dear, not 'Adam' when you speak of him to me," Lady Aberfoyle reproved briskly. "You might have said 'my husband' or perhaps simply 'Douglas,' but never only 'Adam.' "

Mary Kate smiled fondly. "I beg your pardon, Aunt."

"That is not necessary, my dear. 'Tis merely that polite society demands certain conventions of us all, and there are those amongst us who continue to insist upon observing the proprieties despite the unhappy tendency at Holyrood to ignore them. How do you fare, child? Are you in an interesting state of health as yet?" Her ladyship ignored the fiery blushes caused by her question and seated herself with little heed for her voluminous skirts, her bright blue eyes fixed steadily upon her niece as she waited for her reply.

Mary Kate fought down her blushes. "We have not been married very long, Aunt Aberfoyle."

"Long enough. And 'tis best to begin the business as quickly as may be. In point of fact, getting married in such a scrambling fashion might give some folk pause to think—"

"Aunt! Surely, you never—"

"Of course I did not, but I had to make mention of it, did I not? Now I can put the long-noses in their places with a clear conscience. Are you going to offer me refreshment?"

Repressing an urge to be flippant, Mary Kate quickly begged her pardon again and sent for ale and biscuits. During the next half hour, on her best behavior, she managed to hold her own against her aunt's fond inquisition, issued a personal invitation to the forthcoming supper party, and even remembered to ask after her uncle.

After Lady Aberfoyle had departed, Mary Kate found Johnny Graham behind a huge, battered, old desk in the room he called his office. Having formally approved his menu, she told him that her aunt had accepted their invitation.

"Thank you, my lady," he responded cheerfully. "Perhaps, you will just cast your eye over the guest list now, to see that no one has been forgotten."

She agreed and discovered only one name that caused her any dismay. "Sir Reginald Somerville? Surely, he has not yet arrived in Edinburgh?"

"No, my lady, but Sir Adam expects him any day now, so his name must be included."

"Of course." But she was thinking frantically that he was arriving too soon. The days had flown by since their arrival in town, and she had no idea yet what Lord Strachan meant to say to Megan's husband. That afternoon she discussed the matter with her two confidants, who had come to bear her company while she finished the embroidery for her ruff for the wedding.

The roses were back in Megan's cheeks, and she appeared to be completely well again. She nodded when Mary Kate warned her that Somerville was expected to attend their supper party.

"I had a message from him this morning," she said with a little sigh. "He thinks I have imposed upon my uncle's hospitality long enough and gave instructions to open Somerville House at once. I shall remove there tomorrow."

"My father has said nothing about what he means to do," Margaret put in, answering Mary Kate's unspoken question. "I have not the least notion what he will say to Sir Reginald."

"Nor do I," said Megan.

"Well, I think you ought to ask him," Mary Kate said practically.

The other two stared at her in blank dismay.

"You're raving," Margaret said. "You don't know my father very well yet or you would know better than to suggest such a course of action."

"I couldn't possibly ask him," Megan said, adding with an odd little smile, "I don't believe matters will be so bad as I had feared, though."

The others gazed at her expectantly, but she would say no more. Lord Strachan, too, kept his own counsel, so that by the evening of the Douglas supper party, the young ladies were no wiser than they had been before.

That evening came all too soon, and shortly before five o'clock, Mary Kate descended the main stair to the front hall with her husband. Douglas looked sleek and elegant in a beige velvet doublet and hose slashed with emerald silk. A tawny, shanks-trimmed cloak

was thrown back from his shoulders; the hilt of his
dress sword, worn at his left side, was decked with
jewels; and he wore a gold-and-emerald disk on a
heavy gold chain around his neck.

He was in a good mood, and Mary Kate, her right
hand resting lightly upon his forearm, felt more at
ease with him than she had felt since her arrival in
Edinburgh. His arm was warm beneath her fingertips, and she could not resist giving it a gentle
squeeze. When she looked up from under her thick
lashes to find him smiling down at her, she felt a
stirring in her body that made her wish she had the
nerve to ask him to take her back upstairs. Not that
he would, of course, she reflected. Not with the king
expected at any moment. But perhaps later, after everyone had gone . . . perhaps then he might be re-
ceptive to enjoying some conversation with her.

Having discovered beforehand what he meant to
wear, she had chosen a purled velvet gown of lustrous dark gold that emphasized the golden highlights in her hair. The dress was adorned with a collar of magnificent emeralds, and she wore matching
bracelets upon her wrists. Her cap was likewise decorated with emeralds. Perhaps, she mused, it was still
not so much jewelry as he would have liked her to
wear, but she need not worry too much about that,
for his eyes had lighted at the sight of her and she
knew she looked magnificent.

The hall was still empty, so she excused herself to
oversee preparations in the dining room. The white
cloth had been laid upon the long table, and two pan-
tlers were busily laying out square trenchers of fine
pewter, silver-handled knives, and silver spoons. No
guest in the Douglas house would have to supply his
own utensils.

The smell of roasting meats wafted to her from the

kitchens when another servant entered with two huge platters of cold delicacies for the first course. He set them on the sideboard, and Mary Kate was tempted to help herself to a marchpane ball or a slice of Italian soft cheese, but she decided against it, knowing Douglas must be wondering what was keeping her.

She returned to the hall just as the first guests were announced. The king arrived not long afterward, and the party was soon in full sway. At half-past six o'clock they adjourned to the dining room, where ale, French wines, and good Scotch whiskey flowed abundantly from the first course onward, and the gathering became correspondingly more jovial as the time passed.

By the time the fish course was served, the party was a merry one indeed. A pottage of haddock served with sweet almond butter was followed by plates of red herring, salted eel, broiled chines of salmon, baked turbot, and lamprey fritters. The food throughout was plain and plentiful, just as King James liked it, but there were sauces aplenty for those who required them, and Mary Kate, meeting her husband's warm gaze, knew every dish was well prepared. Johnny Graham, Mrs. Comfort, and their helpers had done an excellent job, she decided. She must remember to thank them all.

Once the gathering had adjourned to the large ground-floor withdrawing room, where the butler and his minions were ladling out spiced ale and mulled wine to those who cared for such drinks, Mary Kate felt that at last she could relax and enjoy herself. Almost at once, Ned approached, bringing her a mug of mulled claret.

"Your first Edinburgh supper party appears to be a success, my lady."

"Thank you, sir," she replied demurely. "How do you find life at court?"

He grinned at her. "Amusing. There is something happening every minute. But I confess, there are moments when I miss the peace and quiet of his lordship's bookroom."

"You are jesting."

"I promise, I am not. 'Tis the damnedest thing— begging your pardon."

"Unnecessary." She cocked her head curiously. "Do not tell me that you would prefer to return to Strachan Court."

Laughing, he shook his head. "Perhaps not."

"Good evening, Lady Douglas." Kenneth Gillespie nodded briefly to Ned, then continued as though the younger man weren't there at all, "Do we dance tonight, my lady?"

"I do not know, sir. The musicians will begin playing again shortly, but as to dancing, that must depend as always upon the king's pleasure."

"Of course." He glanced haughtily at Ned. "Leave us, lad. I wish to be private with her ladyship."

Abashed by this high-handed treatment from an older and more experienced courtier, Ned made a hasty bow and departed.

Mary Kate was amused, but she did not hesitate to scold Gillespie. "That was not kind of you, sir. He has been a good friend to me."

"Not as good a friend as I should like to be, I hope." His voice was husky, and he reached to take her hand in his. "I would prefer more privacy than this, you know. You are always my delight, dear lady, but tonight you sparkle like golden treasure. Your eyes are more brilliant than the gems at your throat and wrists, and your lips remind me of prize rubies. Age-old phrases, mayhap, and I trust you will forgive my inability to turn an original one, but these are well-worn only because they are so damnably apt. And your hair . . . let me see if I can do better with your hair. Not spun sugar or gold, but—"

"Hush, sir," Mary Kate interrupted quickly, pulling her hand free and shooting a quick, sidelong glance to either side to see who might be near enough to overhear him. "You must not say such things to me. I am a married lady."

"Nonsense, my dear. Married ladies need to hear such things just as much as unmarried ladies do. Mayhap even more so. I'll warrant your husband, fool that he is, does not whisper pretty things in your lovely ear."

"Sir Adam is not a fool," she declared hotly.

"Then, he does say such things to you?"

She hesitated too long and read derision in his eyes.

"Exactly. I have observed his neglect of you, you know. He is unquestionably a fool." He paused again, letting his words sink in, then added softly, persuasively, "I have heard that this house boasts a lovely garden. Mayhap you would be kind enough to show it to me."

" 'Tis too dark out now," she protested, flustered.

"There is a moon."

"I dare not, sir. 'Twould be too much remarked upon."

"Let them remark. 'Tis nothing out of the way, and surely Douglas does not deserve to keep you entirely to himself."

"Why, what can you mean by such talk, sir?"

"Look yonder, lassie." He gestured to where Douglas stood in laughing conversation with the king and several others. Mary Kate had expected her husband to approach her when everyone rose from the table. Instead, there he was, standing with a lovely young

woman whose name she could not presently call to
mind. The young woman's hand rested possessively
upon his forearm, and he appeared to be entirely re-
sponsive to her smiling eyes. He even gave her hand
an affectionate pat a moment later as he looked down
into her face to speak to her. James made a comment,
and everyone in the group laughed.

Mary Kate's eyes flashed. "Perhaps the air is too
close in here, after all, sir. A brief turn about the
garden will provide a welcome change."

"As you say, mistress. The fresh air will aid our
digestion more than this wine will." He took her mug
from her and handed it to a passing gillie, then
tucked her hand into the crook of his arm, and they
walked thus companionably through a small anteroom to a pair of tall French doors, and out into the
garden.

As he had predicted, a moon just past its prime cast
a gentle, eerie light upon shrubbery and trees. The
night was still except for an occasional cricket's trill
or the murmur of a bird. No breeze disturbed the
leaves. Music and laughter drifted from the house,
but with the doors closed, the sound had a distant,
muted quality. The garden was unoccupied.

Exceptionally conscious of Gillespie's nearness,
Mary Kate felt a twinge of guilt as the impropriety of
her defiant gesture was rapidly borne in upon her.
Reluctant now, she allowed him to proceed, but
when he turned off the main path, she halted.

"We must go back, sir."

"In a moment," he murmured. "Let us walk a little
farther first." His hand closed over hers, and he
urged her on a few more steps. They were out of
sight of the house now.

Feeling desperate, Mary Kate dug her heels into

the dirt path, forcing him to stop. "Please, sir, I ought not to have come out here with you."

"Do you not trust me, Mary Kate?"

Well, of course she did not trust him, she thought, behaving as he was, but somehow it seemed both foolish and discourteous to tell him so after she had agreed to come out with him. "My husband will be vexed, sir."

Too late did she recall Margaret's warning. Mary Kate knew that it would not weigh with Douglas that his own behavior had prompted her acceptance of Gillespie's invitation. He would be concerned only with her conduct, nothing more. Bitterly, and likewise belatedly, did she remember her resolve to do nothing whatever to give him further cause for complaint.

"We must return." She spoke urgently but quietly, feeling a sudden, unexplainable need to whisper.

He, too, spoke in an undertone, turning to face her. "If you insist, my lady, although I doubt there be cause for alarm. Mayhap," he added more gruffly, "you would favor me with just one kiss before we go inside?"

She fought down angry blushes, more conscious than ever of her vulnerable position. Gillespie had every advantage should he choose to force his attentions upon her. "I will not, sir," she said, striving to keep fear from her voice. "You must not ask such a thing of me."

He placed his hands upon her shoulders. "I cannot help myself." His voice throbbed with restrained passion, and she knew she had made a dreadful mistake by coming out with him. He began to draw her closer, his strength outmatching hers when she resisted, and she could not bring herself to oppose him more vehemently lest the noise of a struggle invite discovery. His grip was relentless. In order to avoid the impending pressure of his lips against her own, she turned her face away and then went perfectly still, her eyes growing big with shock at the sight of her husband standing at the intersection of the two paths.

Douglas stood there, his feet planted wide, his arms folded across his broad chest, grimly watching them. "I must ask you to unhand my wife, sir," he said. His voice was tight as though he exerted every effort to keep from bellowing, and his eyes glittered dangerously in the moonlight, bringing Mary Kate a swift, clear memory of his reaction the afternoon he had found her alone in her father's garden with Robin MacLeod. How, she wondered, could she have forgotten that moment until now?

Gillespie's hands fell away from her shoulders, and as he took a hasty step backward, his right hand shot for his dress sword, only to arrest itself midmotion when Douglas shook his head and said regretfully, "Do not draw your weapon, sir. I've no wish to spit you here in my garden with His Majesty but a hundred feet away." He stepped aside and gestured toward the main path. "I should take it favorably, however, if you would return to the house and grant me a moment alone with my wife."

His basilisk gaze shifted to Mary Kate and she shivered with a sudden chill. She sensed rather than heard Gillespie's quickly indrawn breath.

"Her ladyship will not want me to abandon her to your tender mercies, Douglas," he said grimly. "I believe we should all return together."

"Christ's wounds, man," Douglas snapped, "don't be a fool! If we return together, 'twill call attention to the matter, which is precisely what I wish to avoid."

Gillespie hesitated, glancing uncertainly at Mary Kate. His right hand still hovered near his sword.

"Please go, sir," she begged.

He shrugged. "Very well, my lady, since you ask it of me, but the outcome of a match between us might not be as he predicts, you know. I am accounted an excellent swordsman." He glowered at Douglas.

"For the love of God, Gillespie, have done with these airs of false nobility and go. She is my wife. I won't murder her."

Mary Kate was not so certain of that and watched Gillespie's departure with misgiving. But whether she desired to be or not, a moment later she was alone with her husband.

"What in the name of Christ do you mean, coming out here with that fellow?" he demanded before Gillespie was out of sight.

She gathered herself to meet his wrath with as much dignity as she could muster. "I made a mistake, sir."

"You're damned right you made a mistake," he retorted. "Gillespie is naught but a hanger-on, a man who trades on his father's position with the king. Indeed, were it not for his father, he would not so much as cross my threshold, for he's a scoundrel with a reputation from here to John O'Groats, and you have no business to be private with him anywhere, madam, let alone in your own garden with Jamie himself nearby."

He had the right of it. She knew he was right, that his reaction this time was not the result of mere borderer's possessiveness. Nevertheless, she had to try to make him understand her reasons.

"I said I made a mistake, sir. I was angry because you were flirting, so I accepted his invitation, but I know right well that I must not make your behavior an excuse for my own. I shall avoid his company in future." She held out her hand to him. "Please, Adam, I know it was wrong and I shan't do it again, so can you not forgive me?"

Though he ignored her hand, the wind had gone out of the sails of his anger. His mouth opened only to shut again. Then his eyes narrowed. "You were kissing him."

"No, I swear it. You saw!"

"Aye, I saw you," he agreed grimly. In two strides he was upon her, his hands gripping her shoulders. "I saw that he had his arms around you, and I saw that you weren't putting up much of a fight. But if it's kissing you want, madam, you will have to make do with mine, for I do not share my possessions."

With that his lips came down hard upon hers. Then his arms went around her, crushing her against him until she could scarcely breathe. She struggled briefly, but he only held her closer, and his kiss became more searching, less bruising, as his tongue probed for passage between her teeth. In nearly automatic defiance of his will, she resisted him only to suffer the hard grip of his fist in her hair. He yanked, jolting her head back, and her mouth opened involuntarily.

Mary Kate tried to tell herself that it was humiliating to be treated in such a barbarous manner, that she longed for the courage to bite him. But her knees were weak, and the feelings coursing through her would not be denied. It had been too long since she had felt his hands on her, and her body yearned for his touch. Though she feared to swoon from lack of air, something deep within her longed for him to go on doing what he was doing. She began to respond with increasing passion.

He released her.

She staggered when her knees threatened to give way but regained control of herself quickly, motivated by the searching look in his eye as he gazed down at her. She reached out to him.

"Adam?"

He relaxed then, but his tone when he spoke was grim. "Don't try to cozen me, lass, for I am still displeased with you. Over this matter and over others as well." Before he could continue, a door crashed open in the distance and the garden was suddenly filled with shouts and laughter. Douglas turned with a growl of frustration when familiar voices called out, demanding to know their whereabouts. "Come along," he muttered. "We'll finish this conversation later."

Not knowing whether to be thankful for the respite or sorry, Mary Kate went with him to meet the others, hoping her face would not betray the turmoil within her breast. A moment later, separated from Douglas by the merry searchers, she found a grinning Margaret at her side.

"Did we rescue you?"

"Not entirely." Mary Kate sighed. She had a feeling that it would have been better for her had Douglas been able to say all he wanted to say before they were interrupted. As they made their way back to the house, she scarcely lent half an ear to Margaret's earnest explanation that she had seen Mary Kate and Gillespie leave, followed by Douglas a moment later, and had feared the eruption of a difficult scene. She apologized for not coming outside sooner, but Mary Kate merely nodded, her attention still occupied with her own thoughts. Margaret's next words caught her notice, however.

"Sir Reginald Somerville," she said, "arrived but a few moments ago. He is talking to my father now."

Mary Kate had assumed from his absence that Sir Reginald had not yet arrived in the city, but as they entered the house, Margaret explained that he had only been delayed by a previous engagement. A moment later she nodded toward a large, portly gentleman with close-cropped gray hair and a neatly trimmed beard who was talking to Megan.

Mary Kate watched curiously. For a moment, the conversation between the two seemed to be perfectly ordinary, he speaking, she listening. Then Megan nodded hesitantly in response to something he said, causing him to frown heavily. He spoke further, and a moment later Megan's gaze fell away from his and color suffused her cheeks.

Mary Kate's glance met Margaret's. "That doesn't look to be going very well."

Margaret shook her head, then smiled widely at the same time a cheerful voice spoke from behind Mary Kate.

"You've become devilish elusive, mistress." Sir Patrick Ferguson stepped up to join them, and Margaret grinned at him saucily.

"Did you miss me, sir?"

"Aye, wench. And I find it deuced inconvenient to have to search you out in a crowd like this. Take a turn of the room with me now. I would have speech with you."

She indicated Megan and her husband. "We have been watching them. I fear he looks none too pleased with her."

"Mayhap he is not," Sir Patrick agreed, "but 'tis none of our affair, mistress. Come away now."

Margaret wrinkled her nose at him. "It may not be my affair, sir, but Megan is my cousin, and I cannot wish to see her in difficulty. Just pause a moment," she pleaded hopefully, "till we determine which way the wind blows with Sir Reginald."

Sir Patrick said nothing, but the very faintest trace of annoyance creased his brow.

Margaret looked away from him with a shrug. "Oh, very well, sir, if you will insist."

Pointedly, he offered his arm, and Mary Kate could not suppress a chuckle at her memory of Margaret's airy insistence that Sir Patrick always let her have her own way. It was clear that Douglas had described him more accurately. Margaret, hearing the chuckle, tossed her a grin as she went off on Sir Patrick's arm, and Mary Kate's attention was soon claimed by another guest.

A few moments later she realized that Sir Reginald had joined the group surrounding the king. Douglas and Lord Strachan were there, too, laughing and clapping each other on the back. Megan was nowhere to be seen. Condemning all men for a set of heartless villains, Mary Kate set out in search of her and soon found her in the little sitting room upstairs, blotting her eyes at the Venetian glass over the fireplace.

Megan turned with a watery smile. "I hope you do not mind."

"Of course not. Was it so dreadful?"

Megan shook her head. "No, I am thankful to say it was not." Her smile was more natural now. "Do not regard these foolish tears. They are no more than a reaction to having the matter over and done at last. He was displeased, of course, that my conduct was less than perfect, but my uncle has actually told him little about what happened."

"Sir Reginald certainly doesn't seem angry now," Mary Kate told her. "When last I saw him, he was laughing."

Megan's eyes twinkled. "I am not surprised to hear

you say so. You see, he might have been angrier with me but for the fact that I was able to tell him that I am shortly to bear his child."

"Megan! Why didn't you tell us?" She remembered the older girl's various indispositions, but there had been no pattern to them, and she had always been told that a lady with child might expect to be ill only in the mornings.

The older girl chuckled. "I was not perfectly certain myself until several days ago, and I thought it best to ensure that he would hear the news from no one else first. I knew how he would react, you see, both to my uncle's information and to mine, and I thought my best recourse would be to hold my news in reserve until he had begun to scold. I believe I gauged the matter admirably well."

"I'll warrant you did." Mary Kate smiled, firmly suppressing all thought of her own troubles in the light of such delightful tidings.

But Megan looked at her searchingly. "You appeared to be brooding when you came in. Is anything amiss?"

"Naught to speak of," she prevaricated. "I am tired, I suppose." She did not know whether to be glad or not when Megan accepted her at her word, but there was nothing to be done, and she could only be pleased that her friend was her normal self again when they went downstairs.

Gillespie had departed, but it was not long before Mary Kate realized that a good many of her guests were aware that something had occurred in the garden. Even James glanced at her oddly more than once. She wondered if he, too, had seen her leave with Gillespie. That thought brought others upon its ʼ ɘls until she was mentally scourging herself for her ᵗidity in allowing Gillespie to take her outside at all. When everyone except the last few male guests had departed, she took herself wearily up to bed. Douglas, she knew, would stay below until the last man had gone, so perhaps she might contrive to be asleep before he came upstairs. He would not wake her then, surely.

Annie was waiting for her, and once her dress was off, Mary Kate sat down at the dressing table in her night rail and let the maid take the pins from her hair. As Annie began to draw the brush through her thick tresses, she closed her eyes, relaxing to the familiar, relaxing rhythm. She did not hear the door open.

"Leave us, Annie."

The hard note in Douglas's voice stopped even Annie's courage. Laying the brush gently upon the table, she left without a word.

Mary Kate's eyes had flown open at the sound of his stern command, and it took all her strength of purpose now to remain where she was when he advanced upon her. She wanted to escape but knew it would be impossible, so she gathered her dignity and turned to face him. One glance was enough to tell her that his temper had not been improved by the delay.

Douglas leaned over her menacingly enough to make her toes curl in their fleecy slippers. "You are not so much as to speak to Gillespie again. Do you understand me, lass?"

"Aye, sir," she replied, striving to keep her voice level. "I have already apologized. I know not what else to say to you."

"How could you be so feebleminded in the first place?" he demanded tightly. "Surely, you must be able to judge a man of his stamp by now, so I cannot think what demon possessed you. Why, half the company must have seen you go out with him, madam! Would you cuckold me in my own house?"

The tight rein bridling her emotions snapped at these harsh words, and her temper flared up to match his own. She jumped to her feet, pushing past him, startling him with the magnitude of her fury. "How could I, you ask?" She whirled to face him again, arms akimbo. "I will tell you, sir, that the one true thing you say is that I ought to recognize a man of Gillespie's stamp. Am I not married to such a man myself? Did you not seek to seduce me at our first meeting? And furthermore, did you not flirt openly right here in our own house, this very night, with that chitty-faced wagtail who clung like a limpet to your arm? Why, you fawned over her like a . . . like a—"

Her words broke off with a sharp cry when he slapped her. The blow was not a hard one, but it stung, and her hand flew to her cheek.

"That will do!" he snapped. " 'Tis time and more, madam, that you learned to keep a civil tongue in your head." He went on, growling at her first, then shouting, fanning himself into a tirade that grew more fiery with each new accusation he flung at her, as though every word provided fresh kindling for the blaze.

Her mind absorbed but few of the harsh words he lashed at her, though she read the gist of them well enough. Once again, his behavior was unimportant, her own central. But when he added that he was disgusted with her, that he could not think how he had been so foolish as to marry her in the first place, the words cut through her like knives. Her face went white, and a flood of hot tears spilled silently from her eyes and down her cheeks.

His anger collapsed at once. "Mary Kate, I didn't

mean that. None of it! I swear I did not. That was temper speaking, lassie, and jealousy. You must believe me. I was angry and didn't think about what I was saying. Forgive me!" His voice cracked on the last words. "Oh, sweetheart, you must forgive me." He held out his arms, and with a choking sob, she flew into them, her knees nearly giving way completely as his strong arms closed tightly around her.

"Oh, Adam, I am sorry, too. I knew I was wrong the moment I went outside with him. Only I was angry, too. But you are right. That was no excuse." She looked up at him, blinking away her tears. "Has everyone gone?"

"Aye, lassie," he answered gently, stroking her silky hair. "I sent them away. Come to bed now. 'Tis time we learned to be friends again, I think."

Willingly did she go with him, and willingly did she respond when, naked beside her, he began to arouse her as only he knew how to do. She gloried in the feeling of his hands on her body again, and in the sense of power she experienced when he reacted to her lightest caress. And when his lips sought pleasure where his hands had gone before, she threw her inhibitions to the winds and followed where he led, delighting him with her ardor and enthusiasm. It became a game—a laughing, teasing game—to do to him whatever he did to her, until passion overwhelmed them both, sending them soaring together to a fervent climax, after which they collapsed to the pillows again, satiated and fulfilled.

Smiling contentedly, Douglas drew Mary Kate close, and she nestled there, her head resting in the hollow of his shoulder, her body limp beside his. He moved only once, silently, to kiss her, and moments later, when his breathing changed to the slower, more measured rhythm of sleep, she smiled, well isfied with the way their evening had ended. He still had expressed none of his feelings about her abduction or the business with Megan at Strachan Court, but his burst of temper had eased the tension between them at last, and she had no wish to discuss the other matters further if such discussion could be avoided.

19

⋙ ⋘

*T*he days that followed were filled with Margaret's wedding festivities, culminating the night before the wedding itself with the groom's feast at Ferguson House. When Douglas announced after supper that it was time for the footwash, Mary Kate expected a ritual similar to that of the highlanders, where bride and groom washed each other's feet. However, it quickly became obvious that lowland tradition was somewhat different when with great pomp and ceremony a huge washtub was borne sloshing into the great hall, accompanied by servants bearing towels and soap.

The tub was set carefully upon the floor in front of the groom while Douglas, in a prepared and amusingly pompous speech, begged that Sir Patrick would permit his friends to show their great respect for him by washing his feet. Laughing, Ferguson agreed, but no sooner were his bare toes plunged into the water, than the true nature of the exercise became clear. Strong masculine hands clamped down upon hi shoulders and arms, and from behind a number of backs there suddenly appeared coarse bristle brushes and buckets of grease mixed with soot.

Sir Patrick's legs were soon smeared with the horrid stuff and then scrubbed clean with the brushes, but no sooner was the task completed than the results were declared unacceptable, and the whole procedure was begun again. The men were energetic and so boisterous that the ladies began to fear for Sir Patrick's very safety. At last, however, he emerged, well-soaked from top to toe, but laughing as loudly as any of his friends.

The following morning, Mary Kate and Megan attended Margaret while she prepared for the bridal ceremony. Once her glossy, unbound curls had been parted to fall in two loose plaits framing her glowing face, the lovely biscuit-colored gown of Florentine silk was slipped carefully over her head amidst expressions of excited approval from her attendants. Boasting sleeves of exquisite Morisco work and a high pleasance ruff, the gown was cunningly designed with as few ties as possible, so that Margaret could adhere to tradition without being in danger, as were so many other brides, of losing her dress.

At last the wedding party wended its way to the Abbey Kirk at Holyrood amidst much pomp and ceremony, but no skirling pipes, for as Mary Kate had discovered to her astonishment, music in the streets was forbidden in Edinburgh. A huge crowd had gathered in the street outside the kirk, but the people laughingly made way for the bridal party.

Inside the kirk, the pews were filled to overflowing with friends and relatives of both bride and groom, since the pews alone did not provide sufficient space for all the guests, many had brought their own stools to place in the aisles and at the rear of the kirk.

Mary Kate was fascinated by the differences between highland and lowland traditions. Edinburgh celebrations were said to be at once rowdier and more formal than their counterparts in the north, and she quickly saw the truth of that statement.

Ordinarily, and but for the king's wishes, Mary Kate knew Margaret would have been married in her parents' home. There would be no walk around the kirk today and no formal bedding ceremony tonight. However, some things would be the same, including the loosening of the knots and the business of the bride's garters. Gold and silver ribbons had therefore been threaded through the Morisco work of Margaret's sleeves, and when the marriage had been solemnized and the minister's exhortations exhausted, those ribbons were stripped away before the new Lady Ferguson emerged from the Abbey Kirk.

The aftermath was just such a frenzy of merriment as the Calvinists most deplored, Mary Kate thought, chuckling. Margaret was finally forced to remove her real garters on the kirk steps so that they might be divided among those still clamoring for favors from the bride; however, thanks to the strength of her masculine bodyguard, the bride accomplished her return journey through the streets of Edinburgh without incident and entered the feast hall at Ardcarach House to the strains of lively music. Sir Patrick and his friends came next, followed by the general company —the women in pairs and the men by seniority—till upwards of four hundred people filled the huge hall.

The bridal couple took their places at the head of the board, surrounded by their closest friends and family, including, of course, the king. The rest of the guests were accommodated for the most part at nearby tables, although some sat on beams of timber resting upon stones near the walls and had to make do as best they could. No one seemed to mind these accommodations, however, and each guest was soon served with a horn spoon and a cog of broth, followed by a hotch-potch, then meat, fowl, and fish courses, and finally the bride's pie.

When the feasting was done, the servants began to remove the tables from the center of the room and the bagpipes changed their tune to warm up for a reel. James, sitting next to the bride, declined to dance but grinned and nodded when Douglas whispered in his ear, and Sir Patrick was quick to catch the signal. Jumping to his feet, he grabbed his wife by the hand and, encouraged by cheers and laughter, guided her to the cleared area for the first dance. The others stood to watch, thus giving the servants opportunity to clear away the rest of the debris. Then the rest of the bridal party took to the floor, and the dancing began in earnest.

Some hours later, a simple repast consisting only of cheese and bannocks, whiskey, and ale, was served by gillies from a side table. Then the musicians struck up again, and the younger guests resumed dancing, while their elders sought out areas of more quietude, and the company began to thin. A short time later, there was a sudden surge of motion at one end of the room as Sir Patrick and his lady scrambled toward the door, but the others were ready for them.

Servants armed with old shoes stood along the way to belabor the bridegroom, and neither Margaret nor Sir Patrick reached the awaiting coach unscathed. Several of the younger men called for horses to accompany the pair through the streets to Ferguson House. The escort would not be allowed to enter but would no doubt continue their merrymaking in the streets outside the bridal windows until forcibly removed by the watch. Since there was to be no formal bedding ceremony, none of the women followed. Margaret's own maidservants had already removed to Ferguson House and would attend her there.

As Mary Kate returned to the feast hall with the others, thoughts of the future drifted through her mind. Everything of late had been building toward this day, and she had taken no pause to look beyond it. The activities of the past week had kept her too busy to think much about her own affairs.

Though her relationship with Douglas ran more smoothly now, she knew it still remained fragile. Perhaps, she thought, with Margaret's wedding over and done, they would have time together in the week ahead, before his investiture ceremony and the subsequent meeting of the border lords, to begin sorting out their differences. She hoped so, for Megan would return immediately to Somerville and Margaret and Sir Patrick would soon depart for Craigdarroch, leaving her without allies.

She had no time to consider the matter, however, because the first person she saw when she reentered the feast hall was Kenneth Gillespie, who was bearing down upon her with a look of purpose in his eyes. Although he had been present at several of the earlier wedding festivities, she had successfully managed to avoid his company since the scene in the garden. Now there appeared to be no acceptable way to escape him.

"I bid you good-day, my lady," he said, "and trust I find you in pleasant spirits."

"Pleasant enough, sir," she replied calmly, though she could not help a quick, darting glance around the room to see if their meeting was being observed. Douglas was not in sight, and no one else appeared to be paying them any heed. She turned back to find Gillespie smiling at her. "Does something amuse you, sir?"

"Perhaps it does," he responded cryptically. "Come away from this rabble for a moment or two, and I shall explain just what it is that makes me smile."

"I must not, sir. Surely, you realize that our disappearance into the garden the other night was observed by more than one. My husband would be displeased now, were he even to see us conversing."

"Then he shall not see us. Come along, my dear, to another chamber where we may be private."

"Mr. Gillespie, you must not ask that of me. Indeed, I do not desire to be private with you and have never meant for you to think otherwise."

His brow creased in a quizzical frown. "Is that so, my lady? I had believed you to have a care, nay, even a tendresse, for me. Mayhap I mistook the matter. Indeed, I must have done so." His gaze met hers searchingly, and she nodded, not knowing any other way to answer him and wanting only to bring this dangerous conversation to an end. The expression in his eyes hardened. "I see. Nevertheless, I believe I must insist upon a private conversation between us two."

"Sir, you cannot. You must be crazed."

"Your husband's life may well depend upon my goodwill, madam, so mayhap you will reconsider your refusal."

Mary Kate's mouth twisted in scorn. Though he seemed sincere, his assertion must be naught but a clumsy attempt to frighten her into complying with his wishes. "I do not believe you, sir." She watched him closely, but her words brought not the slightest change to his expression.

"Believe me," he said grimly.

"How can Sir Adam's life possibly be in danger here?"

"He has committed treason."

Four words, she thought. Four simple words, yet they smacked upon her senses like a cold, wet sheet snapping in the wind. Then disbelief surged through her, flooding out every other thought, washing away the horrible fears that had threatened to freeze her very processes of logical thought. Not Adam. Anything else, perhaps, she might believe of him, but not this, not treason against king or country.

She shook her head. "You lie, sir. 'Tis a charge that can never be brought against my husband. King James has no supporter more loyal than he."

Gillespie glanced around now, clearly fearful that her sudden pallor and agitation might be observed. "I have proof, my lady. I do not make this charge lightly, I assure you. But we cannot discuss it here. Come with me to another room."

"I cannot," she insisted. "Our departure together would be remarked upon, which would occasion further unpleasantness. I shall meet you in Lady Ardcarach's sitting room. 'Tis on the first floor, to the right of the stairs."

She could not deny him now, for even if he lied, his lies must go no further, lest others should choose to believe them. However, she was unable to follow him directly because several guests intercepted her, desiring to comment upon the wedding. It was a struggle to keep her worries concealed while she laughed and chatted, but she managed to do so, although it was quite twenty minutes later before she slipped into the little room at the top of the stairs and shut the door behind her.

Gillespie turned from the window. "At last. I had

thought you intended to ignore me, madam, which would have been most foolish of you."

"I had more difficulty getting away than I thought I would have, sir. Now, explain this nonsense, if you please."

" 'Tis simple enough. My father informed me this morning that Sir William MacGaurie has been arrested for treason."

She regarded him blankly for a moment before she remembered Douglas's companion at Critchfield Manor. But then a spate of memory followed—the signal that had summoned Douglas from her side, the agitation displayed by Johnny Graham at his delay, not to mention the bits of conversation she had overheard. Her cheeks drained of color.

"So you do remember him," Gillespie said softly. "I was not certain that you would. Did you know that they held a secret meeting that night at Critchfield?" Once again her expression gave her away, and he favored her with a grim smile. "You never cease to astonish me, my dear. I wonder what else you know. Perhaps you will not be surprised to hear the charge against Sir William—that he plotted before our queen's execution both to overthrow King James by returning Mary to the Scottish throne and likewise to assassinate Elizabeth. Mary would then have claimed the English throne as well. Your fool of a husband was involved in that whole plot from start to failure."

"No, that cannot be." The words were no more than a rough whisper. Her knees threatened to betray her, and she sank limply onto a nearby stool.

" 'Tis perfectly true, my dear," Gillespie insisted, moving nearer to look down upon her. "Your precious Douglas was in the scheme up to his eyebrows, so if the truth comes out, you will shortly be a widow, with your own future subject to the king's whim." He paused, his eyes bright with malicious intent. Then he added pointedly, "I have kept silent, so Jamie knows nothing *yet* of your husband's involvement with MacGaurie and the others."

"What do you intend to do, sir?" Her voice was still weak.

"Why, not a thing, my dear." When she looked up quickly, hope springing to her eyes, he smiled, adding gently, "Not if you are kind to me."

Mary Kate could have no doubt as to his meaning. Initial shock and fear were soon overcome by helpless frustration, followed immediately by outrage and fury. Throughout this spate of emotions, she struggled to contain her temper. She needed to think. Despite Douglas's comments and other negative things she had heard about Gillespie, she had never expected to find him capable of such despicable tactics as these. How dared he put her in such a position? For that matter, she asked herself angrily, how dared Douglas? She was past the point now of belief or disbelief. She knew well that, true or not, this tale could not reach the king's ears.

Briefly, she considered the possibility of sending Gillespie to the devil and telling Douglas the whole, trusting him to make all right and tight with James. But the notion was quickly rejected. If Gillespie's tale were true, Douglas's head would be forfeit. And even if it were not, the precious earldom would slip from his grasp. He might well be ruined.

She remembered the gravelly voice at Critchfield: *It is impossible now that both Mary and Elizabeth shall continue to live.* The words took on new meaning now if the men in that room had been plotting to assassinate Elizabeth. And she remembered, too, her feeling at the time that the conversation was but a continuation of an earlier discussion.

Remembering next that Douglas had told her that Archibald Douglas, Earl of Angus, would like nothing better than to make as much mischief as possible with regard to the earldom soon put her in mind of the long-standing tension between the red and black Douglas factions. Douglas wanted his title. And he had told her that James believed Angus ought to have supplied him with better intelligence from England. Why had Angus not done so?

Was it possible that Douglas had joined MacGaurie and the others with good intentions, meaning to do all that could be done for Mary, and then had withheld vital information from the king for no reason other than to undermine Angus's influence? That possibility fit the facts as she knew them very well, better than any other, and it would certainly explain why James continually insisted that he had not known how great Mary's danger was, not, in any case, early enough to prevent her execution.

She hoped she was wrong about what she was thinking, but even if she was, she could well imagine the twists and turns Gillespie's rumors would take once they began their tortuous wandering through the Scottish populace. The key words would be *plot* and *Mary*, and from there, depending upon the loyalty of the speaker, the tale could take various routes, none of which would do Douglas's reputation any good.

Since he was close to James, the king could be linked to almost any accusation made against him, except, of course, to the overthrow of his own government. But Elizabeth would not hesitate to believe that James had conspired to assassinate her, and that would put paid to James's passionate desire to occupy the English throne after her death. And although Mary Kate had never before had cause to doubt her husband's loyalty to the king, she had likewise never discovered any reason to believe James more loyal to his friends than any other monarch might be.

One way or another, the king had made very little fuss about his mother's fate, so he could scarcely be expected to support a friend accused of plotting against him or against Elizabeth. Mary Kate realized that it was not even beyond the realm of possibility that once the rumors began someone might hint that Douglas and James had conspired together to murder Mary. Since the king's popularity was tenuous at best, James could not afford so much as a whisper, no matter how false, that he had plotted against his mother.

Not that Gillespie need hope that matters would go so far, of course, she told herself, still thinking rapidly. It would be enough to insinuate that James had had prior knowledge of the English intent to execute Scotland's queen, for it would be but a simple step beyond that for the Scottish people to assume that he had knowingly allowed, if not actively supported, her death. Mary Kate recognized at once that the easiest way for the king to disassociate himself from all such rumors would be for him to disassociate himself from Douglas the moment Douglas was accused of complicity in any plot whatsoever.

Appalled at the course of her rapid, if somewhat confused thoughts, she looked up to find Gillespie's steady gaze still upon her. She looked away again, but she knew it was no use. She would have to submit.

"How can I trust you to do what you say if I comply with your demands, sir?" she muttered at last.

"You have my word that the information I have will go no farther so long as you keep your part of our bargain," he said.

She repressed a shudder. "But there were others at

Critchfield, not to mention Sir William himself. Won't they speak? The king's men have ways to make them, you know."

"No other will dare to speak up lest he incriminate himself, and I doubt that Sir William will betray any of his friends. He is a man of both courage and honor." He paused with a slight smile. "Should word of Douglas's involvement reach the king's ears, my lady, you may of course consider our pact dissolved."

She nodded vaguely. "What . . . what will our 'pact' entail, exactly?" She could not look at him, but she detected a note of amusement in his voice when he answered her.

"I think you know, Mary Kate." He reached out his hand and drew her to her feet, but when he attempted to pull her nearer, she resisted.

"You cannot mean here and now, sir!"

"No," he agreed regretfully, still holding her hand.

"Then where? When?" She could scarcely speak the words.

He did not reply immediately, and she looked up to see why not. His features had hardened, and when he finally spoke, the amusement that had colored his tone earlier was gone.

"I had truly never meant to use my knowledge as a weapon," he said harshly. "I had thought to make a gift of it to you. For whether you think it or not, lassie mine, you did encourage my attentions, both before you met your husband and since. I believed you cared for me. Therefore, I think you must agree that you are only reaping the consequences of your thoughtless trifling. It would be best if you accept your penance gracefully. I am not fond of tragedy scenes." His eyes gleamed maliciously. "I shall call at your house tomorrow."

"My house?" Such a possibility had not occurred to her.

"More convenient than for you to visit my lodgings in Prince's Street, I assure you," he responded blandly.

"You cannot!" Only his tightened grip on her arms kept her upright as she cried out in breathless outbursts, "What of my husband, the servants? 'Tis impossible, sir. You are mad!"

"Do not fear my coming whilst Douglas is at home, lassie mine. He would be damnably in the way. As for the servants, I am certain you can manage to get rid of them."

"He will kill you for this," she muttered wrathfully. "Christ's blood, sir, but I would like to kill you myself!"

"No doubt, though I am distressed to hear such violent language upon your pretty lips, my dear. I had not thought it would be necessary to take such precautions, but be certain that I shall arrange matters to my own benefit. My premature demise must not seem desirable either to you or to your quick-tempered husband. I see that now. So, unless you are prepared to send me to my Maker this very moment, I should advise most earnestly against such a course."

"Then you do mean to tell someone else."

"No, I shall simply arrange for the information to reach James in the event of my sudden death."

"I see."

"I hoped that you would," he murmured dulcetly.

She glared at him, but there was nothing else she could do. She could not murder him on the spot, as he must know very well, but his smug expression made her wish that she carried a dirk inside her bodice so she could surprise him. She did not have a weapon, however, so she exerted herself to maintain her dignity and hoped he would never know how frustrated or how frightened she was. "Very well, sir," she said at last, "you have made your position clear. I shall look to see you on the morrow."

His grip, which had relaxed, tightened again when she moved to disengage her hand from his. "First a taste of future delights, lass." And, though she struggled to avoid them, his lips found hers, bruising them against her teeth when she clamped her mouth shut against him. He released her, smiling. "You are sweet as honey, lassie mine. I look forward to a long and intimate acquaintance."

With those words he was gone, leaving her to scrub the back of her hand fiercely across her lips in a futile attempt to erase the lingering feeling of his mouth against hers. Tears sprang to her eyes at the memory of what had passed between them, and she racked her brain, trying to think of a way to stop him. She could think of nothing suitable, so she found a mirror and repaired her face, then went slowly back downstairs.

The fact that she found Douglas in a good mood made matters doubly difficult, and several times before the festivities ended, she was tempted to tell him everything. But each time the opportunity slipped away, and once they had returned to the privacy of their own home, she finally admitted to herself that she simply could not bring herself to tell him anything about the matter at all.

He was being kind and thoughtful, and there was no indication that he even knew she had spoken with Gillespie. Perhaps if she had told him at once . . . but to tell him now would only stir his temper, and he would no doubt blame her for the whole affair. He would deny Gillespie's accusations, which would force her to confront him with the information she had gained by her eavesdropping, and that she still had not the courage to do. Such a confession, she was certain, would make him despise her, and God alone knew where the business would end then.

As they went upstairs to bed that night, she mentioned hesitantly that she was exhausted and looking forward to a good night's sleep. Douglas grinned and observed that since Trotter and Annie had both been given a free evening in honor of the wedding he had hoped that she would valet him again. But it had been a long day for everyone, and he did not press her.

Thankful for his easy mood, she hurried to her own bedchamber, changed quickly, then returned to him, knowing that if she insisted upon sleeping in her own bed, he would demand explanations that she was unwilling to provide. On the other hand, she was not at all sure that she could lie in his arms without confessing the whole to him. But then, as she watched him pulling back the bedclothes, it occurred to her that if she were to tell him about Gillespie now, he would be furious simply because she had agreed to meet the man, Gillespie's threats notwithstanding. Indeed, the more she thought about her problem, the larger it seemed to grow.

She climbed unhappily into bed and Douglas quickly followed. As she had expected, he drew her into the curve of his arm, but he had accepted her hint and made no overtures. He did not even speak except to wish her a gentle good night, and she lay there stiffly, trying desperately to relax so that he might not guess that anything was amiss. At last, his even breathing told her that he had fallen into restful slumber, but she slept fitfully herself and by morning was in a worse state than ever.

Douglas, waking and stretching languorously, turned to look at her, his gaze sharpening as it took in her chalky complexion and the purple circles beneath

her eyes. "Are you feeling well, lass? You look as pale
as the ashes on yonder hearth."

Forcing a smile, she pushed herself higher on her
pillows. "I believe the past week's activity is catching
up with me at last," she replied carefully. "I am
rather tired."

Sitting upright, he laid a cool hand upon her brow.
"You have no fever," he said, "but it would not come
amiss, I think, if you were to stay in bed today and
rest."

The notion was an appealing one, but Gillespie
would not be turned away by any supposed illness.
No doubt, if she were to claim ill health, he would
make just the sort of frightful scene she hoped to
avoid.

"Perhaps I shall rest an hour or so," she said, "but I
must get up later, you know. Your sister and Sir Patrick will be making some of their bride visits today.
We cannot turn them away." She waited, suddenly
hopeful. Gillespie had said he would come only if
Douglas were away. God willing, he would stay at
home today to greet his sister and her new husband.

"They will have to visit me with Jamie, then, for I
am off within the hour," he replied, swinging his feet
to the floor and little realizing how much his words
unsettled her. " 'Tis the Sabbath, of course, so he dare
not hunt, but he wants company all the same. I am to
meet him at the Abbey Kirk and spend the day with
him. He invited you to come along, lass, but one of us
should be here to greet the bridal pair this afternoon,
and I do believe you ought to rest." He strode to the
door then and shouted for Trotter.

The Sabbath! She had forgotten what day it was.
Of course she must attend at least the morning ser-
mons. Far better, too, to go before she sinned than
after. But not with Adam. And certainly not with the

king. She would never survive a day in their company without somehow giving herself away. And to avoid Gillespie would be to anger him, thereby making him more dangerous than ever. Better to get the matter over and done.

"Perhaps you are right, sir," she said with forced calm. "I shall rest now and go to the wee kirk 'round the corner later. Annie or Ellen will attend me there."

"There are no pews in that kirk, lass, so take a gillie as well to carry your stool," he said, turning back toward the bed. "The maids don't like to do it, and I shall rest more content if I know you've got a man with you."

Mary Kate choked, earning herself a pair of swift clouts on the back. If only he knew, she thought, catching her breath with difficulty and assuring him that she was fine, that she had only swallowed the wrong way.

Trotter entered then, diverting him, and she saw Douglas on his way a scant half hour later with vast relief. The moment she knew he had left the house, she scrambled out of bed and sent for Annie to help her dress, hoping Gillespie had not anticipated Douglas's early departure and wishing devoutly that she had cultivated the Calvinist habit of staying in chapel all day long. She could not do so today, however, without occasioning comment.

20

The door opened, but it was Ellen Kennedy, not Annie, who appeared. Ellen looked cheerful this morning. "Annie disna feel sae pert the day, mistress. Shall I attend ye in her place?"

"Thank you," Mary Kate replied. "I want to dress for service at the kirk. The marbled silk gown will do. I hope Annie's illness is not serious."

"Nay, mistress." Ellen bustled about, collecting the things necessary to prepare her mistress for kirk, but she paused briefly, allowing herself a chuckle. "The servants was given a wee barrel o' whiskey tae celebrate Mistress Douglas's wedding, and I fear yon impudent Trotter encouraged Annie tae inebriate herself. She isna feeling sae lively the day, but 'tis naught tae mak' a song aboot."

Mary Kate smiled, but such was her mood that she could only wonder if Trotter had taken advantage of Annie's weakness. She did not speak her thoughts aloud, of course, for it was none of her affair, and

Ellen would think the less of her for indulging in idle curiosity.

" 'Tisna my place tae speak, mistress," the maid went on softly, "but ye look a wee bit hobbledy yourself. Would ye no like tae stay abed the morning and attend yon sermon when ye've had your dinner and all?"

"No, Ellen, though I thank you for your concern. I passed an indifferent night, but I doubt I would sleep now, either."

"Mayhap ain o' me powders from Dame Beaton would aid ye, mistress. I ha' yet more packets, for I havna required but a few o' them here in Edinburgh. Ain powder, mixed wi' a cappie o' wine or ale, would send ye right off gin ye will or will ye no."

Mary Kate thanked her but refused, insisting that she had to get chapel out of the way so as to be at home if Margaret and Sir Patrick chose to begin their bride calls that afternoon.

Sometime later, sitting beside Ellen with the gillie who had carried their stools standing against the rear wall of the crowded little kirk, Mary Kate tried to compose her thoughts long enough to attend to the lengthy sermon. She experienced little success, however, and could only be grateful when it ended. Hoping God would forgive her her preoccupation, she wended her way reluctantly home again, but Gillespie had still not shown his face when she sat down to her solitary dinner.

She was soon finished and knew that the servants would appreciate her small appetite, since most of them had Sunday afternoons from dinner onward free to attend services. With that thought came realization that that must be exactly what Gillespie was waiting for. Of course, she told herself reassuringly, she would not be entirely alone even then, for Annie was upstairs in bed and Ellen, having attended service with her, had said nothing about going out again. And, too, there was always at least one manservant on duty in the front hall.

Indeed, less than half an hour later, the young gillie who had attended her that morning showed Gillespie into the cozy little parlor off the hall. "The mon says he were expected, mistress," the lad said doubtfully.

Mary Kate arose from her chair, hoping she looked more poised than she felt. "How kind of you to call, sir," she said, adding to the gillie, "You may go now, Tammie."

The lad gave her an odd look, and knowing her voice had not been steady, she began to fear that she would not be able to go through with the dreadful business.

" 'Tis to be hoped he don't think aught's amiss, my dear," Gillespie drawled, approaching nearer as soon as the door shut behind Tammie. "I have looked forward to our little interlude, you know, and would much dislike its being interrupted."

She eluded his grasp. "You must be patient, sir. There are few servants nearby at the moment, as I am sure you know, but the house is certainly not deserted."

"Then get rid of the rest of them," he said calmly.

"And just how would you propose that I do that?"

"That, lassie mine, is your own affair."

Somehow, here in her own house, face to face with him, she felt less fear than she had thought she would feel, and her mind began to work more smoothly yet when she realized once and for all that she could not submit herself to him no matter what the consequences might be. From that thought was born the next, that she must contrive to outwit him. But how? Thoughts tumbled furiously over one another as they sped through her mind, one after another, only to be rejected.

He would not merely go away if she told him to do so. Of that she was certain. Nor would he believe the onset of a sudden indisposition or any other excuse she might contrive. If only she could send for someone, for Megan, Margaret, or her Aunt Aberfoyle. A mental vision of a confrontation between the redoubtable old lady and Gillespie forced her to hide a smile. She knew that Sir Patrick and Margaret were the most likely persons to call, but decided Gillespie had probably considered that possibility. In any case, they were not here now.

"Come here, Mary Kate." His voice was gruff with suppressed passion, and there seemed to be no way of delaying him much longer. "Come here, I say." He held out a hand, and somehow, as though under a spell, she began to walk toward him.

The door opened just then, and Mary Kate whirled, startled by the sudden, unexpected interruption. "Forgive me, mistress," Ellen said in her quiet way, curtsying, "but yon gowk, Tammie, forgot tae ask ye gin the gentleman will wish tae ha' a cappie or a dram. D'ye wish for aught, sir?"

Gillespie expressed immediate denial, but a sudden, wonderful thought shattered its way into Mary Kate's busy mind, and she spoke quickly, forcing a light laugh.

"Nonsense, sir. Of course you must take a cog with me. Whatever would my husband say were I to turn a guest thirsty from his house? Ellen, Mr. Gillespie will have a cog of Dame Beaton's delicious punch, and I shall take a small glass of sherry wine." She stared hard at the young woman, but Ellen's expression did not alter by so much as the twitch of a hair.

"At once, mistress."

"It will do you no good to delay the inevitable, lassie mine," Gillespie said the instant the door had shut. Coming up behind her, he pulled her close, slid his hands possessively over her bodice, and began to caress her firm breasts.

Longing to slap him, Mary Kate said grimly, "Please, sir, you will disarrange my gown, and the maidservant will return right speedily."

"A pox on the maidservant!" he said curtly. But he released her. "This is not well done of you, dearling. You but delay matters, and if we dally, your husband will be upon us. You cannot wish for that to happen any more than I do."

"No, sir, but if you will recall, I wished for none of this. And Ellen would have thought it odd had I offered you no refreshment. Allow me time to compose myself, I pray you."

"Very well." He sighed. "We shall take a cup together, but do not think to dawdle overlong. My patience is but thin stuff at best."

Ellen returned a moment later, bearing a pewter mug and a wineglass on a silver tray. She served her mistress first, then presented the mug to Gillespie, watching with undisguised interest while he took a first, cautious sip.

"Excellent," he pronounced. "What's in this brew, lass?"

"I dinna ken, sir," Ellen replied truthfully. " 'Tis Dame Beaton's ain concoction o' herbs and spices mixed wi' whiskey. She will be pleased tae learn it meets wi' your approval."

"You may go now, Ellen," Mary Kate said swiftly, lest Gillespie demand information about Dame Beaton.

He hardly waited for the latch to click behind the maidservant before he tossed off the rest of his drink and moved purposefully toward Mary Kate. "If you want that wine, lassie mine, you had best drink it down quickly. Do we stay here or go upstairs?"

She would have liked to delay longer, but she didn't dare try to take him upstairs. "Here," she said finally, wondering how long it would be before the powders would take effect. That they might not work at all also occurred to her. Just because they allowed Ellen to sleep was no guarantee that they would in any way affect a strapping young man like Gillespie.

When he took the wineglass from her hand and set it on a nearby table and then turned back to take her in his arms, she did not resist, believing instinctively that the powders would work better if she did not agitate him. Nevertheless, it was all she could do to submit to his caresses. His lips crushed down possessively upon her own, while his right hand swooped to untie her laces, then crept inside her bodice and beneath her lace-edged shift to caress her naked breast.

Mary Kate shuddered, clenching her fists in order to keep from clawing at him with her long fingernails. His tongue began to probe for entrance between her teeth, and just when she was certain she could bear no more, the door opened again behind her.

"Och, mistress!" The young gillie stared, mouth agape. "Forgive me, mistress. I—I . . ." Tammie continued to stand rooted upon the threshold, goggling.

Gillespie straightened quickly, his eyes narrowing in annoyance. He barely had time to recognize the lad, however, before the powders took their toll. Since his hand was still inside Mary Kate's bodice and his other arm still encircled her waist, he nearly took her down with him when he collapsed. The disquieting sound of tearing cloth reached her ears but

went unheeded while she fought to recover her balance if not her poise. The gillie's unexpected appearance had caught her completely off her guard.

Color flooded her cheeks as she struggled to pull
the front of her gown into place, and she could think
of nothing to say except that Gillespie had been taken
ill. "Fetch Ellen Kennedy," she added desperately.
"She will know what to do."

Tammie fled and soon returned with Ellen, who
took in the situation at a glance and knelt down, pretending to examine Gillespie.

" 'Tisna bad, mistress. He ha' naught but fainted.
Gin the lad here will help us put him on yon window
bench, the poor mon will soon be up and aboot
again."

Tammie helped willingly, but when he had been
dismissed from the room, Ellen turned a worried look
upon her mistress.

"What did the lad see, mistress? He were in an
unco tirrivee when he coom tae fetch me."

Mary Kate grimaced. "He saw that viper hugging
me. He may also have seen that his hand was where it
had no business to be, for he came in just before the
stupid man finally collapsed. I am so glad that you
understood me, Ellen, and were able to help. I am
afraid I've flung myself into the suds again."

"Aye, mistress, I doot ye not. Tammie came in tae
mak' certain ye were safe—all anerly wi' such a mon
as that one, as ye were, and m'self not liking the look
in his eyes. 'Tis tae be hoped the lad disna run
straight off tae the master wi' sich a tale as he mun be
burning tae tell."

"Godamercy!" Mary Kate exclaimed. "He must
not. Run after him, Ellen, and fetch him back at
once."

But although Ellen made haste, she had to report

that Tammie was gone. "What will we do now, mistress?"

"I do not know," Mary Kate said miserably. "How long will that doltish coof be unconscious?"

"I canna say," Ellen confessed. "I emptied three full packets into his cappie. I only hope tae the guid Lord I havna killed the mon."

"Well, I hope you have," Mary Kate retorted, "because I cannot think for my life how I shall explain this muddle to the master. I suppose we must simply leave the stupid man where he lies, and I shall be forced—God help me—to tell Sir Adam the whole sorry tale. But oh, Ellen, how angry he will be!"

Ellen could not deny the truth of those words. "Master might force ye tae mak' penance afore the kirk, mistress, for sich a thing. Tae stand accused o' lust . . ." Her voice faltered. She could say no more.

Mary Kate stared at her, her vivid imagination presenting her with a clear picture of Rose MacReady on the stool of repentance. She had heard, too, that in Edinburgh such matters were dealt with much more sternly than elsewhere. Women accused of lust or fornication could be bared to their waists and scourged through the streets of the city. All the color had drained from her face before good sense came to her rescue.

"He won't," she said tightly. "To do so would be to make this business a public affair, which he would abominate above all else. But what he will do to me himself," she added with a grimace, "does not bear thinking about."

The two young women looked helplessly at each other until the tense moment was shattered by a sudden, thunderous pounding upon the front door.

"Oh, no!" Mary Kate cried. "He cannot be here so soon."

" 'Tisna the master," Ellen replied practically. "He wouldna knock on his ain door. 'Tis more likely Mistress Margaret and Sir Patrick come tae call."

"Well, they must not see Gillespie. Quickly, Ellen, help me move him."

Spurred on by repeated pounding on the door, they seized Gillespie by the shoulders, dumped him unceremoniously off the window seat, then dragged him any way they could into a small adjoining antechamber, where they shut the door upon him. He hadn't so much as stirred.

Mary Kate hurriedly relaced her bodice, noting that it had been ripped between two of the eyelets. The rip was not serious, however, and she tucked the ragged edges under, saying, "Hurry, Ellen. No one else is here to answer the door."

Smoothing her apron, Ellen ran into the hall, pausing at the door long enough to sweep loose strands of her blond hair under her cap before admitting the visitors. Laughing merrily and demanding to know why they had been kept standing upon the stoop, Margaret and her new husband entered, accompanied by Ned Lumsden, whom they had met on the pavement below.

Mary Kate stared at the three of them, feeling as though she had had a narrow escape in more ways than one. The others went on laughing and chatting, and she made mechanical responses, unable to keep her thoughts off the possible corpse lying in the antechamber as she listened to her guests with one ear while keeping the other cocked for sounds of her husband's return. Certain as she was that the gillie had gone to fetch him, she did not have to tax her vivid imagination to suppose what sort of tale the lad would tell him or what his reaction would be.

"Mary Kate, what is it?" Margaret's voice broke

through her thoughts, and she looked up to find all three of her visitors staring at her with open curiosity.

"What is what?" she replied vaguely.

"Ned has spoken to you three times and you have not answered him once. And you never explained, now that I come to think about it, why it took Ellen so long to answer the door. Something is amiss. I know it is. Where is Adam?"

"At Holyrood, I suppose." It was too much to hope that the king had sent him on a mission into England or to some more distant land.

"Well," Margaret said indignantly, "I think it is shameful that he is not here to greet us when he must have known we would be paying our bride visits today."

"Do not trouble your head unnecessarily," Mary Kate said wretchedly. "He will be home soon enough." She strove to keep her voice steady, but thinking of Douglas just then sent shivers shooting up her spine. When he heard that she had been making love to Gillespie, he would be enraged again, and just when things had been going well between them at last. If she escaped this time with a whole skin, it would be marvelous indeed, and it would be even more marvelous if he did not send her home to Tornary in disgrace. Then Gillespie would tell his awful tale of treason, and since she wouldn't even be in Edinburgh to plead for the king's mercy, Douglas would be hanged, drawn, and quartered.

"Mary Kate!" Though Mary Kate had not been aware of movement, Margaret was kneeling now in front of her.

Mary Kate shook herself. "Forgive me. I am not myself today."

"No, that you are not," Margaret agreed. "Have you quarreled with Adam again?"

"Not yet," Mary Kate replied without thinking.

"Not yet!" Margaret grabbed her by the shoulders none too gently and gave her a shake. "Mary Kate, collect your wits at once and tell me what has happened. At once, do you hear me? There is no use prevaricating, either, for I shall not rest until I know exactly what has happened. If you want Patrick and Ned to leave, I will send them away, but you will tell me. Come now, at once. I mean what I say."

Mary Kate knew that much very well. She looked first at one anxious face and then at another, wishing she knew what was best to do. It occurred to her then that with Douglas no doubt on his way at that very moment, they would all know the whole sorry business soon enough anyway. She shrugged, then said simply, "Kenneth Gillespie is behind that door yonder."

In disbelief, her three guests stared at her, then turned as one to look at the antechamber door and back at her again, before all three in a chorus demanded immediate explanation.

She described the matter as clearly as she could without betraying Douglas completely, and when she had finished, Margaret and Ned both exclaimed their dismay, while Sir Patrick remained silent, thinking.

After a long moment, he smiled at Mary Kate. "It appears to me," he said mildly, "that the most immediate problem is the disposal of Gillespie, regardless of whether he is dead or alive. That business will be a good deal simpler if he is alive, of course, so perhaps, young Lumsden, you will ascertain his present condition for us."

Ned complied with alacrity, soon returning with

the information that, although Gillespie was still unconscious, he was breathing normally.

"Then I have a plan," Sir Patrick said. He appeared to Mary Kate to be more amused than dismayed. "It would be best, I think, if we were to remove the primary cause of Adam's annoyance before his return, since it can serve no good purpose for him to kill Gillespie. Such an act would cause a scandal, and Jamie dislikes scandal."

"But what about when Gillespie talks?" Mary Kate cried. "For I doubt that anything will stop him now. And I must tell you, sir, though I cannot explain the difficulty fully, that there is a certain amount of truth in what he will say. Adam's life will be in danger."

Sir Patrick became serious again, though he still did not seem overly concerned. "I know your husband like I know myself, my lady. Not only have we lived near each other all our lives, but I was at university with him, and I promise you by my faith as a borderer that whatever Gillespie knows, the telling will not endanger Adam's life. I think you have been spun a fairy tale, but even if you have not, you will find your husband well able to take care of himself once he knows what the danger is against which he must guard himself. I counsel you to tell him all that Gillespie has told you. Do not leave out a single word, no matter how unpleasant the telling may be for you. I know it will be difficult, for I agree that he will be in a thundering temper when he arrives. But if you care for him, niggle not with your pride or your conscience. You must make him listen to you."

If she cared? No one could know how much. But how, she wondered, could she make Adam listen? The doing sounded simple enough when Sir Patrick commanded it, but she knew it would not be simple at all.

Margaret understood her difficulty. "Good sir," she said, smiling wryly at her husband, "pray tell us all just how Mary Kate is to make my brother listen to her. Since he has already suspected an improper relationship between her and that dreadful Gillespie person, he will be in a perfect frame of mind to believe every word his impetuous gillie chooses to prattle to him. I tell you here and now that there will be a wretched, long time passing before Mary Kate is able to make Adam do anything but shout at her, or worse. She must needs see him bound and gagged if she would *make* him listen!"

"Be that as it may," Sir Patrick replied firmly, watching Mary Kate, "it is her duty to prepare him for what trouble lies ahead, and so she must. I do not know how you will manage it, my lady, but truly, you must." He turned then to his wife. "Stay with her, lass. Ned and I will return as quickly as we may. Perhaps, if we can get back before Adam does—"

"He can then have the pleasure of pitching us all out into the street before he deals with poor Mary Kate," Margaret interjected with an ironic laugh.

"Mistress!" Ellen called from the front hall, sending a chill of anticipation racing down Mary Kate's spine. The maid appeared upon the threshold, twisting her hands and glancing in anxious dismay at the open antechamber door, where Gillespie's leather-shod feet were clearly visible. "Mistress, 'tis your aunt's coach! Her manservant be a-coming up yon steps the noo. Whatever will we do?"

Sir Patrick murmured irrepressibly, "A pity we cannot ask her to lend her coach to us to transport Gillespie's carcass." Then, when a knock at the door goaded both men to hasty action, he added reassuringly over his shoulder, "We'll take him out the back way, my lady. Have no fear. Just attend to your visitor. Little though you may think it now, she may well prove to be a blessing in disguise."

Mary Kate thought both his levity and this last odd notion of his completely irrelevant to the matter at hand, but she dared say nothing to delay him. Instead, trying desperately to compose herself, she told Ellen to admit Lady Aberfoyle at once. How, she wondered as she moved swiftly to take her seat again, had Gillespie ever thought he could have his way with her in a house as busy as a village square on market day?

Looking down quickly, she saw that the tear in her bodice was noticeable again and tucked the ragged edges under, tightening the lacing with a hope that her sharp-eyed aunt would fail to notice the damage.

Sounds of bumping and thumping in the antechamber had barely died away into the distance when her ladyship entered briskly with her usual silken rustle and clicking heels.

"Good morrow, good morrow, my dear ones. What a pleasure to see you, Lady Ferguson, but where is that handsome new husband of yours?" Presenting her cheek to each of them, she allowed them to kiss her as they rose to make their curtsies, then seated herself with a swirl of her huge farthingale. Her sharp, birdlike gaze settled closely upon Margaret as she waited with parted lips for that young lady's reply.

Margaret smiled sweetly. "It is pleasant to see you, my lady. We scarcely had an opportunity to exchange words with you yesterday. I regret that Sir Patrick was unexpectedly called away, but he did not believe his business would occupy him overlong. My brother will also return soon, I believe."

"I did not think we should enjoy the pleasure of your company today, Aunt," Mary Kate put in

quickly, knowing that if she were not diverted, Lady
Aberfoyle was perfectly capable of demanding to
know the precise details of any business that could
occupy Sir Patrick on the Sabbath.

The old lady nodded at Margaret. "I came hoping
to see the bride, of course. I knew they would not
choose to include a dreary old woman in their first
bride visits, but they were certain to call here, so not
being so high in the instep as to take offense where
none is intended, I came here to await their arrival
with you. 'Tis my pleasant good fortune to find Margaret here with you now."

"My dear lady," Margaret exclaimed, laughing,
"had we but known you wished it, we would certainly have included you and Lord Aberfoyle in our
visits. Sir Patrick and I are very fond of you both."

Mary Kate thought her aunt blushed, but the old
lady recovered rapidly, snapping out her next words.
"Pish tush, let us have none of your butter sauce,
miss. I know your cozening ways well enough. And
why, may I ask," she added tartly, turning a gimlet
eye upon her niece, "am I always kept waiting
for refreshment in this seemingly well-appointed
house?"

Mary Kate smiled at the familiar reproof and called
through the open doorway to Ellen, still on guard in
the front hall, to fetch Lady Aberfoyle a cup of her
favorite spiced ale. Ellen bobbed a curtsy and left,
coming back into the room a short time later, just as
sounds from the antechamber heralded the imminent
reappearance of Sir Patrick and Ned. Mary Kate was
astounded by the speed with which they had dispatched their errand, for they had been gone less
than a quarter hour. They entered as Ellen was about
to take away the tray.

"Good afternoon, Lady Aberfoyle," Sir Patrick

said cheerfully, adding, "Hold there, Ellen lass. If that's ale you're serving, Ned and I would be right glad of a cappie."

Ellen bobbed and turned away, only to stop short again when the sound of the front door crashing back on its hinges froze everyone in place.

Douglas strode in rapidly, his face flushed with fury. He cast a swift glance around the room. "Begone, all of you," he ordered harshly. "I would be private with my wife."

"Your imminent ascension to the peerage," Lady Aberfoyle declared in chillingly haughty accents, "has adversely affected your manners, young man. Or is it perhaps your common practice to eject your guests so rudely?"

Her chair faced away from the entry, so Douglas had not seen her immediately, and her frigid tone brought him whirling to face her. He bowed curtly. "I beg your pardon, madam, if I seem wanting in grace. I assure you that were the matter not an urgent one I should never behave so to family or to guest. I trust you will forgive me."

"Don't be tiresome," she replied frigidly. "I have only this moment received refreshment, and I have no intention of allowing you or anyone else to throw me out of this house until I have drunk my ale, unless, of course, you intend to do so yourself, sir, bodily." She glared at him, daring him to reply. "No? Then it will do you no harm to contain your soul in patience and your temper in pretense of calm until I take my leave. No good ever came of losing control over one's emotions."

When Douglas straightened, his jaw tightening ominously, she added sternly, "Sit down, sir, and let Ellen fetch you something to mellow your spleen. Then, when our visit has come to its natural conclu-

sion, we shall depart with our dignity intact and you
may say all that you wish to say to your wife. That, in
case you have forgotten your manners altogether, is
how such matters are conducted by civilized persons
in this modern age of reason."

The color drained from his cheeks as she spoke,
and when she had finished, he brusquely begged her
pardon for his incivility before turning away toward
the front window in undisguised embarrassment and
frustration.

Margaret and Ned stared at Lady Aberfoyle in
awe, but Mary Kate noted that although he had
turned away from the rest of them, Sir Patrick's
shoulders showed a suspicious tendency to quake
with suppressed laughter. Realizing that her aunt had
momentarily stemmed the tide of Douglas's fury, she
set her thoughts to racing.

"Will ye tak' a dram then, master?"

Ellen's question, spoken timidly, planted the seed
of an idea in her mistress's quick thoughts. Glancing
at Douglas, who seemed not to have heard the maid's
question, Mary Kate gathered her courage.

"Bring Sir Adam a mug of that excellent punch we
had earlier, Ellen," she ordered, her voice shaking despite all she did to control it. "That will be just the
thing to quench his thirst and calm his mind."

Ellen's eyes grew round with horrified dismay, but
now that the decision was made, Mary Kate nodded
firmly.

"Quickly! He does not wish to be kept waiting."

She dared not look at any of the others, but she
knew from someone's sharply indrawn breath that
her intent was understood in at least one quarter.
The others avoided looking at her, too, although in
Sir Patrick's case this was clearly not due to shock.
Though he had turned toward her again, he still had

to fight to keep his merriment under control, and he showed signs now of being in dire straits.

For a long moment no one moved; then, with a shrug and a sigh, Douglas turned from the window, drew up a chair, and sat down, stretching his long legs out before him.

Lady Aberfoyle instantly engaged him in small talk, soon dragging the others into the conversation whether they wished to participate or not.

When Ellen returned with the drinks, she served her master first. Her hands were trembling and her face was chalk white, but Mary Kate noted thankfully that Douglas was too preoccupied with his own concerns to notice, and the maidservant escaped as quickly as she could to serve the other men their ale.

Douglas took the first sip from his cup. He noticed nothing out of the ordinary and swilled the drink down thirstily, as though by such an action he hoped to hurry Lady Aberfoyle.

The old lady would not be rushed, however, and the whole scene took on an oddly dreamlike quality for Mary Kate. She replied when spoken to directly but watched her husband's growing impatience with rising alarm. Time stretched out, and what was actually less than five minutes or so seemed nothing less than an eternity. But finally, just as suddenly as Gillespie had succumbed, so did Douglas. His eyes glazed over, and he slumped in his chair, his head lolling sideways.

Lady Aberfoyle snorted. "Swine-drunk! As bad as an Englishman. I ought to have known. No wonder his manners were so disgusting."

Mary Kate didn't deny the accusation but watched anxiously as Sir Patrick hurried to her husband's side.

After a hasty examination, he grinned up at her.

"He'll do, lassie. Just taken a wee drap over the mark, I expect, as her ladyship suggested."

"This is no occasion for mirth, Sir Patrick," scolded Lady Aberfoyle. "You men. All the same or worse." She got to her feet and twitched her wide skirts into place, nodding regally to Mary Kate. "I will take my leave now, my dear. The good Lord knows you are safe enough whilst he remains in that disgusting condition, and the head he will have when he awakens ought certainly to make him more tractable then." She turned imperiously to Ned. "You may see me to my coach, Mr. Lumsden."

Then she was gone, leaving the other three to stare at one another, their countenances expressing a myriad of emotions, ranging from horror and surprise to unrestrained amusement.

"She stayed to protect me from Adam," Mary Kate said in hushed astonishment. "Who would ever have thought it?" She directed her gaze at Sir Patrick. "What did you do with Mr. Gillespie, sir?"

"Rolled him in the dust, stripped him of his purse and jewelry, and turned him over to the watch for a vagrant," that gentleman replied, chuckling. "The watchman thought much the same of him as your aunt thought of Adam, so he will no doubt leave him in solitude to sleep it off before he is questioned. Then I fear it may take the good Gillespie some time to establish his identity, though I trust he will manage to do so before they flog him out of the city at the cart's tail."

Mary Kate's eyes twinkled in response to his unholy amusement, but before she could make a comment, Margaret interrupted them.

"Never mind that now," she said. "Mary Kate, how did you dare to do such a thing to Adam? I could scarce believe my ears when I heard you order that punch. You will be amazingly fortunate now to get out of this affair with your head tight upon your shoulders, let alone with a whole skin. Ellen, too!"

With a grimace, Mary Kate admitted that her sister-in-law most likely had the right of it. "But Sir Patrick said that I must make Adam listen to me," she said reasonably, "and you yourself admitted that I should have to tie and gag him in order to achieve such an end. I could think of nothing else to do."

Margaret stared at her with her mouth wide open, but Sir Patrick's laughter spilled over at last, and tears of merriment were streaming down his cheeks by the time Ned returned.

21

First his eyelids flickered.
Then a muscle on the left side of his jaw twitched, as
though he became aware of the gag before he exerted
himself to open his eyes. Or perhaps he exerted himself because of it.

Mary Kate had pulled a back stool up close to the
bed and sat now, hands clasped upon her knees,
hunched forward so as not to miss the least hint that
he was waking. And he was. With the first twitch of
his eyelid, she had stopped breathing. Planning for
this moment had been one thing; living it was quite
another. Douglas opened his eyes.

She had been prepared for anger, or thought she
had. But for a moment he was bewildered rather than
angry. He frowned. Then his gaze encountered hers,
and his expression hardened. He moved to sit up and
became aware for the first time of the ropes that
bound him to the bedposts, whereupon his expression altered ludicrously from annoyance to astonishment and disbelief. He did, in fact, turn his head first

to one side and then to the other, as though his vision must confirm what his other senses had told him. Then, sharply, he looked back at her, and despite the breath she had been holding, she took in more air in a sudden gasp at the blazing fury in his eyes. He struggled at the bonds, and she knew brief terror at the thought that he might break free. But the knots held.

She gathered her courage to speak. "It would be best, sir, if you do not struggle. The bonds are tight, and you might do yourself an injury." The sound of her voice was unfamiliar, as though she listened to someone else, someone whose heart was not thudding loudly enough to be heard in London and whose toes were not rattling in her shoes, someone who was altogether poised and indifferent to consequences. Nonetheless, the very fact that she could speak at all calmed her. She sat straighter and squared her shoulders. "Adam, I have much to say, and this was the only way I could be certain you would listen to me."

He managed to grimace in spite of the gag, but the fury in his eyes abated somewhat.

Mary Kate collected her thoughts. She knew her voice would work properly now, though she dared not meet his gaze except for brief seconds from time to time. She twisted the ring he had given her on their wedding day.

"I know you are furious with me, sir, and I cannot blame you, but I cannot bear to have all this misunderstanding, even deceit, between us any longer. If you despise me for the things I am about to relate to you, then so be it, but I hope you may find it in your heart to forgive me instead—if not at once, which may well be too much to ask, then at least someday." She paused, darting a glance at him.

Though his expression was still forbidding, she saw that she had succeeded in capturing his attention.

Breathing more steadily now, she said carefully, "You have taken umbrage at what you choose to call my flirtation with Kenneth Gillespie—" When he growled beneath the gag, she studied the reflection of the sunlight on her ring, glad he could not speak, and went on, steadily insistent, "You must believe me, sir, when I tell you that I never sought to flirt with him. I know I behaved badly at Critchfield, but that was through innocence and high spirits, nothing more. And I had eyes and thought only for you afterward, never for him. He chose to take advantage, however, of our small acquaintance, to presume upon past meetings." She forced herself to look directly into his eyes. "I give you my solemn word, Adam, that there never has been and never can be more than that between him and me. I pray you will believe me." Her voice dropped to a whisper with these last words, but she did not look away, and he did not growl again.

Emboldened by his silence, she allowed herself to study his countenance for some clue to his feelings, deciding briefly that the new expression in his eyes would have been encouraging had she not come to the most difficult part of the whole business. It would be nice, she thought, if she could simply stop at this point and beg his pardon for having annoyed him, but the matter was not so simple as that. He would demand explanations, and she would be back where she had begun, with him bellowing at her or worse. Better, she decided reluctantly, to get the whole business over and done at once.

"I know you will find it difficult to believe that I have not encouraged him, and I know it has looked as though I have done nothing to *dis*courage him."

The anger that flickered in his eyes then made her swallow hard and drop her gaze, wishing the next thing she had to say were easier.

"I—I must tell you, t-too, that he said himself that he thought I had a t-tendresse for him. He said he thought so even before you married me. But if he truly thought that, sir, it was by fault of my innocence, never by design." She paused again, then muttered, "I know you must wonder why I did not come to you and tell you that he had become a nuisance, and I should like nothing better than to be able to say that that was entirely his fault. Indeed, the temptation is great to lay all the blame for this madness at his door, especially since he is not here to defend himself. But that would be neither a fair nor a true statement. And if I did somehow encourage him to believe that I was attracted to him, then the gravest fault is mine. In any case, when he demanded today's meeting, I was unable to rebuff him, not because I did not want to do so, but because he threatened to lay information against you if I was unkind to him, information that I was unable, for reasons of my own, entirely to disbelieve."

She had looked away again, but a sharp movement from the bed caught her attention, and she looked up to find him quizzing her with his eyes. She bit her lower lip. "I scarcely know how to continue, Adam. What I did was inexcusable, and I had hoped you need never know of it, but since you are truly in danger now, I must tell you everything. Last winter at Critchfield, I overheard part of your conversation with Sir William MacGaurie and the others. Johnny Graham's odd behavior and your response to it aroused my curiosity, you see, so I followed you back to your bedchamber purposely to discover what was going on. I . . . I listened at the door." She did not dare to look at him now but studied her fingertips instead. "I would never have done such a despicable thing had I not had too much mulled wine to drink, and if I had never heard what I heard then, perhaps I would not have reacted as I did when Mr. Gillespie accused you. However unwisely, I would no doubt have sent him rapidly about his business. But I knew you had worked with the others on Queen Mary's behalf. He called it a conspiracy. He said you and the others meant to overthrow the king and return Queen Mary to the throne. He even said there was a plot to assassinate Elizabeth. In any event, I knew his accusation alone would be dangerous to you, and some of what I had overheard myself led me to believe that some part at least of what he said might be true."

She still could not bring herself to look at him. "There is more," she said quietly. "Yesterday at Margaret's wedding party, he told me of Sir William's arrest, and he threatened me, told me that if I refused to grant him certain favors he would go straightaway to King James with his accusations, but that if I behaved as he wished me to do, he would forget what he knew. He said he would call upon me here today. I-I thought I was prepared to do as he demanded."

The silence was unbearable. She had to look at him. But looking did her no good at all, for his expression was entirely unreadable, as though he had drawn a curtain over his feelings.

She went on wretchedly, "Not until he was actually here in the house did I realize I simply could not go through with it. I made up my mind then to tell you the whole, although I confess I had not planned to tell you so soon as this or in this particular manner. Having decided to tell you at all, however, I realized that, one way or another, I had to thwart him until I could think of how to dispose of him."

At a choked sound from beneath the gag, she looked up to see a glint of amusement in her husband's eyes. At this auspicious sign she sighed with deep relief. "Perhaps, sir, if I were to remove your gag, you would be more comfortable."

He nodded vigorously.

She leaned forward, reaching for the knot at the back of his head, but paused before loosening it. "I shall not untie you yet, Adam—not until I have told you the rest—so pray do not ask that of me. And I warn you now that if you lose your temper, I shall replace the gag."

He frowned heavily, causing her to draw her hands back from the knot.

"Perhaps I ought first to finish what I wish to say, sir, since I doubt you will be able to cage your tongue once the gag has gone. First of all, I assure you that Mr. Gillespie was unsuccessful in his attempt to have his will with me. The details of his visit are therefore unimportant. I can relate them to you later if you insist. It is far more important now that I tell you how sorry I am for having had to place you in this undignified position. My aunt believes you were swine-drunk and will no doubt make some sharp comments the next time she sees you, but I truly thought this the only way to make you hear me out. Had I attempted to explain the matter in any other fashion, you would have lost your temper long before I had finished, and we should have had a dreadful quarrel, presuming of course that you had allowed me to speak at all. At least this way I shall have had ample opportunity to present my defense, meager though it is. There is none at all, of course, for listening in upon your private conversation, but now that things have come to such a pass, I know that I must tell you everything so that you will be able to defend yourself when that horrid man takes his tale to the king." She looked at him again and sighed. "I shall

remove the gag now, sir, and you may say what you
like to me." So saying, and with fingers that trembled
only a little, she unfastened the gag.

Douglas worked his mouth for a moment. Marks at
its corners showed that the cloth had been tied uncomfortably tight.

"Loose my bonds as well, lassie." His voice was
low and surprisingly gentle.

She looked at him miserably, but she had known
the moment must come sooner or later. Slowly, she
unfastened first one knot, then another, and another.
He sat up, rubbing numbness from his wrists, and
untied his left leg by himself while she struggled
with the ropes securing the right one. Then he
swung his feet to the floor.

She stepped back two paces.

"Come here, Mary Kate."

She stood still, facing him, with no wish to go
closer. "Adam, I know you must be fearfully angry
with me, but—"

"Come here, lass." The tone of his voice did not
alter but remained low-pitched and calm despite the
glint of unmistakable amusement that had crept into
his eyes.

Mary Kate didn't see the glint, however, and her
feet were leaden as she moved to obey him. A moment later she stood directly in front of him, her eyes
downcast.

"Am I to understand that you agreed to submit to
Gillespie's unconscionable demands in order to protect me from Jamie's wrath?" he asked, still in that
gentle tone.

She nodded. "Aye, but I did not submit to him,
sir."

"So you said, more than once. I should be interested to know how it came about that you were able

to avoid doing so. How exactly did you . . . uh . . . dispose of him? I believe those were your words."

"Aye." She glanced at him uncertainly, but there was nothing in his demeanor now to indicate the state of his temper. "I . . . that is, we stripped him of his purse and handed him over to the watch for a drunken vagrant."

"We?"

"Well, to speak truly, Sir Patrick and Ned did so," she confessed, still watching him closely.

"Do they know about this madness, then?" There was a new, sharper note in his voice.

"No, sir," she replied hastily, anxious to calm him again. "Not about all of it. Only that Mr. Gillespie was annoying me and that I did not wish . . ." She hesitated.

"Did not wish to bring the situation to my attention?" he suggested helpfully.

She nodded, explaining the rest in a rush: Ellen's assistance, Gillespie's collapse just as Tammie surprised them, the gillie's flight, the hurried concealment of Gillespie when Sir Patrick's knock sounded at the door, and her own continual fears. Then she paused before mentioning that she assumed that Tammie must have carried his tale to Holyrood.

"Aye, he did that, which is why I came home in such a rage, of course. Had it not been for your aunt's presence—"

"And Ellen's sleeping potion," she interjected ruefully, admitting the worst.

"Is *that* what it was?"

"Aye, in your punch. It sent you off straightaway, just as it had Mr. Gillespie earlier on."

"I see." He regarded her steadily. "You have been busy, have you not, madam?"

She bit her lip but did not answer, waiting uncomfortably for whatever would come next.

He stood up, looking down at her sternly. "I do not approve of listening at doors."

"No, sir." The words came in a whisper.

"However, you seem to feel even more strongly about that fault than I do. I should have been much more displeased had you confided the information you overheard to anyone else."

"I would never have done that," she muttered.

"No," he agreed gravely, "I do not believe that you would have, although that does not minimize your fault. Moreover, I do not approve of wives who conspire with others to deceive their husbands."

"No, sir, but truly I did not intend to deceive you."

"Then why did you not tell me about this pliskie nonsense with Gillespie before now?"

Wretchedly she spread her hands. "I could not tell you what I had done at Critchfield. I have been told all my life that such behavior was contemptible, even criminal. I feared the knowledge of what I had done would make you despise me. Indeed, I could bring myself to tell you today only because I . . . because Sir Patrick said—though, truly, he does not know the whole tale—that you would have to know everything I knew in order to be prepared to deal competently with the king's wrath."

"Jamie will not be angry, sweetheart." He spoke more gently than she had ever heard him speak before.

Puzzled, she looked up, searching his face for explanation. "But you were working with Sir William to free Queen Mary. I heard you. And Sir William was arrested for conspiring to assassinate Queen Elizabeth in an attempt to restore Mary to the throne of Scotland and to put her on the throne of England as well. Mr. Gillespie said James would consider such a conspiracy no less than treason."

"So he would, had that truly been my cause. But you ought to have known better, lassie. I am, first and last, the king's own man. His trust in me is not ill-founded and never will be, for my loyalty is to him and has never been to any other."

"But you did try to free Queen Mary," she protested. "You knew she was to be executed, and you said you would do what you could to save her."

"We knew the English intended to try her for treason," he said patiently. "Even if we could have been sure that the result of such an undertaking was preordained, Jamie could scarcely have raised an army only to protest an English trial."

"But the trial cannot have been legal," Mary Kate said, striving to keep her voice as calm as his. "A sovereign of Scotland surely cannot be tried for treason against England. Only a subject of Elizabeth's—"

"That is naught but a quibble," Douglas said. "However accurate your logic may be, Elizabeth is queen and had the power to do what she did, and if she was willing to take such a risk—for risk it was to set such a precedent—then there was naught to be done to stop her. You ought to have listened longer," he went on wryly. "We did arrange to send Jamie word of the trial, and there was a concerted effort to save her life. But everything was done secretly, diplomatically, and with the king's full knowledge. If MacGaurie conspired further to assassinate Elizabeth or to put Mary on the throne of England, even to return her to the Scottish throne in Jamie's place, it was not done with my help or within my hearing, for he knew full well that my association with him and the others was arranged at Jamie's command. The king had agreed to no more than a diplomatic effort to persuade the English to free Mary, and he wished me to keep him informed of activities performed on her behalf, but my specific task was to do what I could for Mary without antagonizing Elizabeth. That was the main reason for not making Mary's potential predicament known to the Scottish people before Christmas. There would have been an outcry, perhaps even more than that, and Elizabeth might have been seriously annoyed."

"But Mary might have lived," Mary Kate said stubbornly.

Douglas sighed. "Sweetheart, Jamie had no reason to believe that her life was truly threatened. So long as he believed that Elizabeth would hesitate to take the life of another monarch for fear of setting that precedent I mentioned earlier, Jamie dared not antagonize her unduly. That is why he was vexed with Angus. Angus was in London and ought to have been cannier about what was going forward there. It was he who kept insisting that Jamie need not fear an execution, who kept telling him Elizabeth would never do so daft a thing. Jamie *was* surprised by the execution. He'd never had cause to believe Elizabeth would go so far."

"You believed she would," Mary Kate said, knowing she risked angering him again but needing to have every point explained. "I heard someone say that it was impossible that both Elizabeth and Mary should continue to live. If that did not mean you were going to do away with Elizabeth, then surely it meant that Mary was meant to die. The king must have understood that much, too, if you repeated those words to him. Did you?"

"I did." Douglas paused a moment, clearly ordering his thoughts. Then, with a rueful smile, he said, "Even more than Jamie wanted the crown of Scotland does he want the crown of England, lassie. Had Mary agreed to leave well enough alone—that is, to have left him in full reign over Scotland and to withdraw the claim she made years ago to England—he might well have worked harder to free her. That much I cannot deny. But she insisted upon ruling, if not in his place then at his side. He hardly knew her, lass. He saw her only as a rival for Scotland and as an obstacle to getting England. He would have protected her if he could, but he truly did not want her free."

"I knew it," Mary Kate breathed.

"Aye, well, that last bit is for your ears alone, lassie. You are not to repeat what I've said to you today. If I did not trust you to keep your tongue well caged behind your teeth, I'd not have told you so much. But I do trust you, just as Jamie trusts me and as I would have you trust me, too. Indeed, I ought to be angry with you for doubting me," he added, placing a finger beneath her chin and making her look up at him. "I am his man and I serve only him, Mary Kate, so you see, Gillespie has his information a mite distorted. He may yet manage to stir up a wee mare's nest, and he will certainly have to be dealt with, but I am safe enough from his threats, I promise you."

He was so close, and she had trembled at his touch, but he did not seem angry now. Still, the atmosphere was fragile, and she believed that one wrong word would shatter his calm like a piece of Venetian glass. So it was that she did not speak, and the silence lengthened until he broke it himself.

"Is that the only reason you did not confide in me?"

She shook her head.

"Well, then?"

"I was afraid," she said simply. "We seemed to be building a better understanding between us, and I

feared to upset it. You had been so distant before.
First so angry, then so distantly polite, and then after
that night in our garden when you found me alone
with him . . . well, I feared to make you angry
again. When I ran away at Strachan—"

"Ran away? I thought 'twas a mere taking of the
air," he said mockingly.

She shrugged. "You will never believe that, however, nor will any of the others. Indeed, I am no
longer perfectly certain that I believe it myself. I did
think at the time that that was all I was doing, but I
wish to put it all behind us now. If we can do that
only by having it that I ran away, then so be it. Your
father said I was too far south not to be running from
something, and I suppose he could be in the right of
it, even if I didn't realize it then. After all, he understood about Megan when you did not."

"What about Megan?" he asked more sharply.

"That she truly was attempting to stir coals between us," Mary Kate said. "She admitted it, and
your father made her apologize to me. He was going
to send her home, but I spoke to him and he changed
his mind. I had not meant to tell you about that," she
added ruefully. "The words just came of their own
accord." With a small sigh, she lifted her chin and
gazed directly into his eyes. There was a look in them
that she could not decipher.

After an uncomfortably long silence, he said, "So
you wish to put all that has happened behind us, do
you?"

She nodded, watching him warily.

"And how do you propose to accomplish that aim,
madam? Am I merely to suppress my displeasure
with you now that you have confessed your sins?"

Biting her lower lip, Mary Kate felt warmth rise to

her cheeks. She would be foolish indeed, she thought, to expect such a thing of him.

He was waiting for a response.

"No, sir," she said finally, reluctantly. "I would not suppose that." When he still did not speak but waited, watching her, she added, "I don't know what I expected you to do, exactly. I suppose I thought you would be angrier about all this. Perhaps, unconsciously, I was following Margaret's advice. She said I ought to give you an opportunity to lose your temper and then, once I had suffered the consequences, things would get back to normal again. I did think, after your anger that night in the garden—" She broke off, swallowing hard. "But this is much worse, of course."

"Indeed it is. So Margaret knows all, does she?"

Mary Kate chewed her lip again.

"Did my so-helpful little sister suggest what those consequences might be?"

"No, but I certainly never meant to follow her advice, either. Circumstances ordered matters otherwise, and then today I was afraid you might . . . well, that you would—" She broke off again, unable to put that thought into words.

"That it would mean another skelping?"

She nodded, not looking at him.

"You deserve one," he said slowly, as though he were mulling over a suggestion. "You have behaved disgracefully, have you not? Let me see . . ." He ticked the points off on his fingers. "First you ran away from my father's house, causing me a great deal of distress, embarrassment, and inconvenience. Then you insisted upon playing fast and loose with a bounder whose intentions were clearly dishonorable from the outset. You admit to having listened at doors, a habit that, though I should not myself define it as contemptible, is certainly not admirable. Next you engaged yourself in highly improper, not to mention dangerous, dealings with your would-be seducer. Then you drugged me, causing me to make a fool of myself in the presence of Lady Aberfoyle, a woman whose good opinion I value. Following upon that, you had me carried ignominiously to my own bedchamber to be bound hand and foot to my own bed by two friends who you insist have not heard a complete explanation of your reasons for wishing to do such a thing to your lord and master and yet who agreed to help you do it. Indeed, the worst of this may well be that you have kept a great deal of pertinent information from me but have involved those same two gentlemen, who have no business to be involved." He shook his head. "Not a pretty list, madam. But then, perhaps allowances ought to be made, since you never wished to marry me in the first place."

Shocked by the sudden, unexpected turn of his accusations, Mary Kate cried out sharply, "No, Adam! You mustn't make allowances for that. Please, sir, you must not!" Tears sparkled in her eyes, and she blinked them back, regarding him anxiously through the mist. "Truly, I had rather you would beat me than believe me unhappy in our marriage."

"So you are not displeased now that you will be a borderer's countess, lass?" He spoke quietly, but there was an underlying note in his voice that was difficult for her to interpret. Rather than being a mere statement of fact, his words sounded much more like a challenge and also as though her reply was of grave importance to him. To make such an interpretation was, she told herself, probably to make too much of what was no doubt an imagined inflection. Nonetheless, she gave careful thought to her answer.

"It is not being your countess that pleases me, Adam," she said at last. "It is being your wife. Most of the prejudices I labored under when you first expressed a desire to wed with me were as foolish as you said they were. Meeting Margaret, Megan, and your mother certainly proved to me that the women of the borders are neither as meek or as submissive as I had expected to find them."

A smile lit his eyes. "Nay, lassie, the women of the Douglas family, at least, are rarely meek or mild of spirit. But it was not primarily the women who concerned you, I believe. 'Twas the men, was it not?"

"Aye, but most of those concerns disappeared once I had discovered for myself that there are as many different types of men in the borders as there are in the highlands."

"Still you did not think you were valued as you deserved to be," he said quietly.

Mary Kate regarded him steadily. "I think my certainty that a border husband would treat me as his chattel got mixed up with my jealousies, sir, till I knew not whether I was on my head or on my heels. Once I recognized the jealousy, I began to sort out my true feelings. Though you are, in truth, an arrogant knave," she added daringly, "I have, since recognizing those feelings, known only happiness and contentment except insofar as I have managed to displease you. I fear, however, that whatever affection you may once have felt for me must have dissolved altogether by now."

"It has not." His voice was gruff and his hands, suddenly gripping her shoulders, were unsteady. "Dare this arrogant knave take your words to mean

that you—" He broke off when, for once, his natural
assurance abandoned him.

"That I love you, Adam?" she finished softly. "Aye,
sir, I do with all my heart. I wanted to tell you so
after you found me in the bourock that morning, but
at first you were too angry and then you went away.
And once we were here in the city, the time never
seemed right for the telling. I was afraid that even to
mention what I had discovered about my feelings
would mean that I would have to explain the rest of
the tangle to you."

Her eyes sparkled with unshed tears, but she
would have said more had she not lost her breath
when he crushed her against his chest in a vigorous
hug. Silence reigned for a moment, though she could
hear his heart pounding. Then, finding it difficult to
breathe, she tried to free herself.

The pressure of his arms lessened when he realized
her plight, but he did not release her. Instead, his lips
brushed against her curls, and his voice came again in
a low murmur. "Naughty wench. I ought perhaps to
have paid more heed to the accusations you made
against Megan, but what a muddle you have made of
all else."

She inhaled gratefully but spoke her next words
warily, next to his chest. "Art still angry, sir?"

"I ought to be," he declared in a firmer tone. "Lord
knows, I ought to blister your pretty backside for all
this insanity. "No man—or woman either—would
blame me if I did so."

"No, sir."

"No one," he repeated. "Most sensible persons
would recommend such a course."

"Would they, sir?"

"Aye," he replied flatly. "I am convinced 'tis true."

"But you follow your own course, do you not?" Mary Kate suggested demurely.

"Do I?"

"Aye, sir, I have many times observed that to be so. A true border knight does not allow himself to be influenced by the opinions of others."

"Does he not?"

"No, sir." She gazed up at him limpidly.

He chuckled. "Do you seek to bewitch me, lassie, with your lovely golden eyes? You cannot do it. You deserve to be punished."

She held her breath, watching him anxiously.

He chuckled again, and his arm tightened briefly before he tilted her chin up and answered the unspoken question in her eyes. "There will be no skelping this time, sweetheart."

She breathed more easily, but he had not finished.

"I have a better plan." He grinned, reaching to unlace her bodice. "You are so bonny, lassie. I like it when your eyes grow wide and your lips part. I can just see the tip of your wee tongue between your teeth." He slid the gown off her shoulders and began, lightly, to caress her breasts.

She trembled at his touch, but she made no move to resist him. Indeed, she had no wish to resist him.

His left hand moved to release the tie at her waist. "Let me think now," he mused softly. "I think one wee bairn a year for the next twenty years ought to keep you safe at home and well out of mischief, do not you?"

"Adam!" she gasped, as much in response to the feelings aroused by his busy hands as to his words.

"By God, lass," he muttered hoarsely as the ribbons parted and her gown fell to a heap on the floor, "I hope we have learned enough about each other now so that all the nonsense can take its proper place behind us. I love you more than I love life itself, and I can tell you that this state of affairs here and now is more to my liking." He lifted her gently onto the bed.

As he climbed in beside her and took her into his arms, Mary Kate gazed up at him lovingly, savoring the magic words he had just spoken. He loved her. He had said so, had put his feelings into words at last. Until that moment, she hadn't realized how much she had longed to hear such an admission upon his lips. Her kisses became more passionate as his teasing hands inflamed her body. If he desired to punish her in such a manner as this today, she reflected happily, he might do so as often as he liked and with her good-will. Indeed, she would encourage him with every highland woman's wile at her command.

FREE FROM DELL

with purchase plus postage and handling

Congratulations! You have just purchased one or more
titles featured in Dell's Romance 1990 Promotion. Our goal
is to provide you with quality reading and entertainment, so
we are pleased to extend to you a limited offer to receive a
selected Dell romance title(s) *free* (plus $1.00 postage and
handling per title) for each romance title purchased. Please
read and follow all instructions carefully to avoid delays in
your order.

1) Fill in your name and address on the coupon printed below. No facsimiles or
   copies of the coupon allowed.

2) The Dell Romance books are the only books featured in Dell's Romance
   1990 Promotion. Any other Dell titles are not eligible for this offer.

3) Enclose your original cash register receipt with the price of the book(s)
   circled plus $1.00 **per book** for postage and handling, payable in check or
   money order to: Dell Romance 1990 Offer. Please do not send cash in
   the mail.
   Canadian customers: Enclose your original cash register receipt with the
   price of the book(s) circled plus $1.00 **per book** for postage and handling in
   U.S. funds.

4) This offer is only in effect until March 29, 1991. Free Dell Romance requests
   postmarked after March 22, 1991 will not be honored, but your check for
   postage and handling will be returned.

5) Please allow 6-8 weeks for processing. Void where taxed or prohibited.

Mail to: Dell Romance 1990 Offer
P.O. Box 2088
Young America, MN 55399-2088

NAME_____

ADDRESS_____

CITY_____STATE_____ZIP_____

BOOKS PURCHASED AT_____

AGE_____   (Continued)

Book(s) purchased:_____

_____

_____

I understand I may choose one free book for each Dell Romance book purchased (plus applicable postage and handling). Please send me the following:

(Write the number of copies of each title selected next to that title.)

☐ **MY ENEMY, MY LOVE**
Elaine Coffman
From an award-winning author comes this compelling historical novel that pits a spirited beauty against a hard-nosed gunslinger hired to forcibly bring her home to her father. But the gunslinger finds himself unable to resist his captive.

☐ **AVENGING ANGEL**
Lori Copeland
Jilted by her thieving fiancé, a woman rides west seeking revenge, only to wind up in the arms of her enemy's brother.

☐ **A WOMAN'S ESTATE**
Roberta Gellis
An American woman in the early 1800s finds herself ensnared in a web of family intrigue and dangerous passions when her English nobleman husband passes away.

☐ **THE RAVEN AND THE ROSE**
Virginia Henley
A fast-paced, sexy novel of the 15th century that tells a tale of royal intrigue, spirited love, and reckless abandon.

☐ **THE WINDFLOWER**
Laura London
She longed for a pirate's kisses. . . even though she was kidnapped in error and forced to sail the seas on his pirate ship, forever a prisoner of her own reckless desire.

☐ **TO LOVE AN EAGLE**
Joanne Redd
Winner of the 1987 *Romantic Times* Reviewer's Choice Award for Best Western Romance by a New Author.

☐ **SAVAGE HEAT**
Nan Ryan
The spoiled young daughter of a U.S. Army General is kidnapped by a Sioux chieftain out of revenge and is at first terrified, then infuriated, and finally hopelessly aroused by him.

☐ **BLIND CHANCE**
Meryl Sawyer
Every woman wants to be a star, but what happens when the one nude scene she'd performed in front of the cameras haunts her, turning her into an underground sex symbol?

☐ **DIAMOND FIRE**
Helen Mittermeyer
A gorgeous and stubborn young woman must choose between protecting the dangerous secrets of her past or trusting and loving a mysterious millionaire who has secrets of his own.

☐ **LOVERS AND LIARS**
Brenda Joyce
She loved him for love's sake, he seduced her for the sake of sweet revenge. This is a story set in Hollywood, where there are two types of people—lovers and liars.

☐ **MY WICKED ENCHANTRESS**
Meagan McKinney
Set in 18th-century Louisiana, this is the tempestous and sensuous story of an impoverished Scottish heiress and the handsome American plantation owner who saves her life, then uses her in a dangerous game of revenge.

☐ **EVERY TIME I LOVE YOU**
Heather Graham
A bestselling romance of a rebel Colonist and a beautiful Tory loyalist who reincarnate their fiery affair 200 years later through the lives of two lovers.

Dell

TOTAL NUMBER OF FREE BOOKS SELECTED _____ X $1.00
= $_____ (Amount Enclosed)

Dell has other great books in print by these authors. If you enjoy them, check your local book outlets for other titles.